Cheri
it's
Marlene

Love
at FIRST
FLIGHT

one round trip that would
change everything

MARIE FORCE

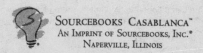

SOURCEBOOKS CASABLANCA™
AN IMPRINT OF SOURCEBOOKS, INC.®
NAPERVILLE, ILLINOIS

Published by Sourcebooks Casablanca, an imprint of Sourcebooks, Inc.
P.O. Box 4410, Naperville, Illinois 60567–4410
(630) 961–3900
FAX: (630) 961–2168
www.sourcebooks.com

Library of Congress Cataloging-in-Publication Data

Force, Marie Sullivan.
  Love at First Flight / Marie Force.
    p. cm.
  1.   Man-woman relationships—Fiction. 2.   Fiances—Fiction.
3. Fiancees—Fiction. 4. Hairdressing—Fiction. 5. Attorneys—Fiction.
6. Florida—Fiction. I. Title.
  PS3606.O7S26 2009
  813'.6—dc22
                        2008051870

Printed and bound in the United States of America
                QW 10 9 8 7 6 5 4 3 2 1

To everyone who loved my books when they were held together by binder clips, who refused to allow me to give up, and who shared every hill and valley of the roller coaster ride right along with me... You know who you are. This one's for you.

Chapter 1

THE BOSS HAD PICKED A HELL OF A TIME TO GET CHATTY.

A bead of sweat rolled down Michael's back. As Baltimore City State's Attorney Tom Houlihan pelted him with a rapid-fire series of pre-trial questions over the phone, the departure time for Michael's flight to Florida crept closer. He needed an exit strategy, and he needed it now.

Travelers swarmed through the gate area while Michael struggled to stay focused on the call despite the chaos around him. Tugging on his burgundy silk tie, he released the top button of his shirt and watched a line form to board the flight.

"And Rachelle?" Tom asked.

"I saw her last night," Michael said. "She's antsy, but hanging in there." He flipped through some other notes on his laptop, hoping to anticipate Tom's next question.

"How antsy?"

"Well, she's a teenager stuck in protective custody. You've got daughters, so you can probably imagine."

An exotic scent filled Michael's senses, drawing his attention away from the call. He glanced at the seat next to him where a young woman with silky dark hair and an olive-toned complexion watched with dismay as a gate attendant slipped a "Delayed" sign over the flight number.

"Michael?" Tom said.

Michael tore his eyes off the woman. "I'm sorry. What did you say?"

"I asked if there was anything else you needed from me."

"We should be set until jury selection. I'll want your input then. George prepped the last of the witnesses today. We've covered all the bases, so try not to worry."

"Yeah, right," Tom said with a wry chuckle.

"I'll check in first thing on Monday."

"Enjoy the party. Hopefully, it's the only time you'll be engaged."

Michael laughed, relieved that Tom seemed satisfied—for now. "That's the goal. I appreciate the time off. Have a good weekend." He ended the call and caught the tail end of the gate attendant's announcement. "What did she say?" he asked the woman next to him.

She glanced over with a distressed expression on her stunning face. "Ninety-minute delay."

A jolt of desire surprised Michael. He was on his way to visit his fiancée and to attend their engagement party, so what was with the unexpected reaction to a pretty stranger? Pretty wasn't the right word. Strikingly beautiful was more like it. Since they now had ninety minutes to kill, he decided to indulge the curiosity. "Where're you heading in Jax?"

"Jacksonville Beach."

He noticed her eyes were fixed on the gate attendant who slid the updated departure time into a slot on the board.

"My boyfriend's working there for a year. How about you?" She glanced over at him with soft brown eyes that drew him right in.

He couldn't remember the last time anything other than the upcoming trial had captured his attention so completely. "Amelia Island. My fiancée lives there with her parents."

"So you're doing the long-distance thing, too, huh?"

"Yeah, and it sucks. How long have you been doing it?"

"Almost seven months," she said with a sigh. "Five more to go."

"Six months down and eight to go for us. We're getting married in April."

"Well, at least we both know it won't last forever. I don't know how people do it indefinitely. That would make me even crazier than I am now."

"For real."

"What do you do?" she asked.

"I'm a prosecutor for the Baltimore City state's attorney."

Her eyes widened. "Wow, that's so cool."

"More like overwhelming—especially lately. What about you?"

"Nothing quite so exciting. I'm a hair stylist."

"That sounds like more fun than putting people in jail."

Her smile engaged her entire face, and his heart skipped an erratic beat.

"It is until someone hates their haircut, but fortunately that doesn't happen to me very often."

"What do you do when it does?"

"If they're truly upset, we offer them a freebie next time, but usually they come back telling us they got all kinds of compliments on their new look."

Hoping to keep her talking, he ran his hand through his mop of wavy brown hair. "I could use your services right about now."

"You should stop by the salon sometime."

"Where do you work?"

"Panache in the Inner Harbor."

"I wish I had time for a haircut. I'm going to trial in just over a week."

"Can you tell me about it?" She turned in her chair and pulled her legs up under her.

"It's the Benedetti brothers," he confided in a low tone, thrilled to have her full attention.

She gasped. "Oh my God!"

Gang members Marco and Steven Benedetti were accused of gunning down three teenaged boys in the city.

"My co-worker's cousin was one of the kids they killed. Timmy Sargant."

"We're going to get them."

"I hope so," she said softly. "I really do."

"Attention in the gate area. Announcing the arrival of Flight 980 from Providence with continuing service to Jacksonville. For those of you waiting for the Jacksonville flight, we'll begin boarding as soon as the thunderstorms clear out of the Jacksonville area."

"I wish I was going to Providence," he said.

"Why's that?"

"I'm from there. My family lives in Newport."

"How'd you end up down here?"

"I went to Georgetown Law and met my fiancée, so I ended up staying here. Then her parents moved to Florida, and here we are living apart. How'd you meet your boyfriend?"

"We went to high school together. We've been together ten years, since junior year."

"So then you're... twenty-seven? You look older than that."

"You're not supposed to say that to a woman," she said, laughing at his sudden embarrassment.

"What I meant is that you look much too sophisticated dressed all in black to be only twenty-seven. Is that better?"

"Nice save," she said with a grin. "We wear black in the salon—it's the uniform."

"I'm Michael Maguire, by the way, and I'm thirty-two."

Smiling, she reached out to shake his hand, and an odd current traveled through him at the feel of her soft hand in his. He had to remind himself that he was supposed to let go.

"Juliana Gregorio. Nice to meet you, Michael Maguire, thirty-two."

"So how come you aren't married to that boyfriend of ten years yet?" he asked with a teasing grin, not sure why the answer suddenly mattered so much to him.

"We just haven't gotten around to it, I guess. I've been asking myself that question more often in the months since Jeremy's been gone."

"You'll get around to it."

"We'll see." She nibbled on her thumbnail. "For some reason, I feel like there's a lot riding on this weekend."

"Why do you suppose that is?"

"I don't know. Everything was going along pretty well for months, but he's been kind of remote on the phone the last few weeks. I can't figure out what's up."

"I'm sure it'll be fine when you see him. Paige's

parents are having an engagement party for us this weekend, which is the number one reason why I'd rather be heading north instead of south."

"You're not excited about the party?"

"I'm dreading it. It's so stupid when you consider all the same people will be at the wedding less than a year from now."

"That's true."

"It's a waste of time and money—two things her parents have way too much of."

Juliana smiled, and Michael found himself riveted by her every expression. Her face flushed under the heat of his scrutiny, and she looked away. He wondered if she thought he was one of those weird strangers women were taught to fend off in self-defense classes. She'd probably run for her life if he acted on the urge to lean in closer for a better whiff of the earthy, spicy scent that was driving him mad.

Reminding himself he was a grown man and not a hormonal teenager, he made an effort to keep the staring—and the sniffing—to a minimum and the conversation light. By the time the gate attendant announced their flight, he felt like he had known Juliana for years rather than an hour. Since the plane wasn't full, they chose seats together.

Her cell phone rang just as she took it out to turn it off. "Hi, Dona. I can't talk. I'm on the plane, and I have to shut my phone off soon."

While pretending not to hang on her every word, Michael watched her stiffen with tension.

"You promised me! You said you'd handle it!" Another pause. "I'll call Vincent." She ended the call and dialed another number. "Vin, you gotta help me out. Can you take dinner over and check on Ma tonight? Dona totally bailed on me." Pause. "Vincent, *I'm on an airplane.* You've got to do it." She lowered her voice. "Please."

Something about that softly uttered word tugged at Michael's already over-involved heart, making him wish he could fix all her problems. *What the hell is that all about?*

"Thanks, Vin. I really appreciate it. I'll talk to you Sunday." She shut the phone off, returned it to her purse, and stared out the airplane window.

For a long moment, Michael debated whether he should say anything. "Are you all right?" he finally asked.

"Yes. Sorry."

"Don't be."

"It's just my family. They drive me nuts. My mother, she needs… She has problems."

"That's tough. I'm sorry."

"I'm sorry I have to deal with it every day of my life."

"Do you have brothers and sisters?"

"Two of each, but they're much older than me and mostly useless. How about you?"

"I'm the baby, too. I have three older sisters."

"I'll bet they doted on you," Juliana said, seeming relieved by the shift in conversation away from her troubles.

He grinned. "Oh, yeah, nonstop torture. They were forever dressing me up as their living doll. Don't tell anyone that. It'll kill my image." Noticing how she clutched the armrest as the plane hurtled down the runway and lifted into the sky, he wanted to offer her a hand to hold but didn't.

"Are you close to your sisters?" she asked once

they were airborne and she'd released the death grip on the armrest.

"Yeah, all of them. They're married with scads of kids who're the most adorable kids in the world, of course."

She smiled. "Do you see them very often?"

"I get up there every now and then, but it's harder since Paige moved to Florida. Whenever I have a free weekend, I end up down there."

"Is your family coming to the party this weekend?"

"They couldn't get away for it, but that's fine with me. My folks and hers don't have much in common."

"You must be excited about the wedding at least."

He thought about that for a minute. "I'd be more excited if it hadn't turned into such a circus. I've already heard enough about it to last me forever, and I've got eight months to go."

"Big to-do, huh?"

"The biggest of to-dos, which is not at all what I wanted. But she's their only child, so I gave in."

"It must've been hard for you to get away so close to the trial."

"We've been working weekends for months now, so my boss wasn't thrilled, believe me. But he's a good friend of the Admiral's. That's Paige's dad."

Juliana raised an eyebrow. "You call him 'the Admiral'?"

"*Everyone* calls him 'the Admiral.' He retired as superintendent of the Naval Academy last year."

The stewardess came to take their drink order.

"Can I buy you a drink?" he asked.

"Why not?" She ordered a gin and tonic, and he asked for a beer.

He paid for the drinks and saluted her with his can. "Cheers. Here's to a good weekend."

"I'll drink to that."

"Ladies and gentlemen, as we make our final approach into Jacksonville, we thank you again for choosing Southwest Airlines. Enjoy the weekend."

Juliana looked up, surprised by how fast two hours had passed as she chatted with Michael. The thought of seeing Jeremy in a few minutes filled her with nervous energy and excitement.

"Are you ready?" Michael asked.

He had the bluest eyes she'd ever seen and a sexy smile that made her tingle all over when he directed it at her. "As ready as I'll ever be."

"I'm sure you'll have a great time. Keep in mind that all guys suck on the phone. Paige is forever complaining that I never have anything to say."

Juliana appreciated his attempt to bolster her confidence.

"How about you? Ready to put on your best party face?"

"I don't have much of a party face."

"You've got five minutes to get one."

"When do you go back?" he asked.

"Seven on Sunday evening."

"Me, too!"

"We can compare notes," she said, oddly relieved to know she would see him again.

"I'll look forward to it."

They gathered their bags and walked up the Jetway and through the terminal together. When she spotted Jeremy waiting for her, she looked over to say good-bye to Michael, who had made eye contact with his fiancée, a waiflike blonde with porcelain features and big blue eyes. She looked like she would break if hugged too hard and wasn't at all what Juliana had pictured for him.

"I'll see you Sunday," she said to Michael.

"Have a good one," he said, walking toward Paige as she went to Jeremy.

"Who's that guy?" Jeremy asked when she reached up to hug him. He was eight inches taller than her and still built like the football player he had been in high school.

"Just someone I sat next to on the plane. How are you?" She looked him over for clues to what was troubling him lately, but he looked the same as he always did. He kept his curly blond hair cut short now that he was older, but when she met him it had been six inches high and unruly—a lot like he had been then.

"Fine," he said, leaning down to kiss her.

She turned away from the scent of stale beer on his breath. "Have you been drinking, Jer?"

"Just a few beers with the guys after work," he said with a shrug. "Your flight was late, so I had time to kill."

Judging by the glassy look in his eyes, Juliana could tell that he'd had more than a few and was disappointed he had done that on the night she was coming to visit.

Holding hands, they walked by Michael as he hugged Paige.

He glanced at Juliana, and the dismayed expression on his face made her sad for him.

Chapter 2

"WHERE ARE WE GOING?" JULIANA ASKED AS SHE DROVE Jeremy's Toyota SUV south from the airport and followed his directions past the exit for Jacksonville Beach where he lived in a small rented house with two of his co-workers from Baltimore. She usually stayed with him there when she came to visit.

"I have a surprise for you," he said with a charming smile.

A rush of emotion reminded her of how much she loved him. "Really? Tell me!"

"No, you'll have to wait." He reached for her hand. "It's good to see you, babe."

"Is it?"

He looked over at her. "Of course it is. Why would you ask that?"

"You haven't seemed all that happy to hear from me lately."

"It's been so crazy here. There's a lot of pressure to meet the next deadline, and the install isn't going well. We've had one setback after another. Everyone wants to get it done and get out of here."

"Is that all it is?"

"What's with you, Jule?" he asked, exasperated. "Where's all this coming from?"

She focused on the road, annoyed that she'd had to do the driving. "Never mind. Let's just have a good weekend." These days, they were under so much pressure to make the most of the brief time they had together.

He let go of her hand to change the radio station.

They drove in silence for a while until he directed her to turn into the Sawgrass Marriott Resort at Ponte Vedra Beach.

"What are we doing here?" The lush landscaping and manicured golf course were beautifully lit. A sign on the lawn pronounced the course to be the "Home of the PGA Players Championship."

"I got a bonus last week and decided to splurge."

She let out a squeal of excitement. "For real?"

Smiling, he glanced over at her. "Does that mean you approve?"

"Definitely."

They checked in and were shown to a luxurious oceanfront room with a king-sized bed.

She nibbled on her thumbnail while he tipped the bellman. "This is going to cost a fortune, Jer," she said when they were alone.

"Don't sweat it, babe." He pulled open the sliding door and stepped onto the balcony. "Come on out."

The surf pounded in the darkness as she joined him.

He brought her closer to him and leaned in to kiss her.

They'd been lovers for so many years that he was home to her, no matter where they were. He ran his tongue along her bottom lip, and she wrapped her arms around him, wanting him desperately. She just wished he didn't taste like stale beer and smell like cigarette smoke.

"I love you, Jule: I've missed you so much."

"Me, too," she whispered as his cell phone rang.

"Ignore it," he said against her lips. When the phone rang again, Jeremy pulled away from her to turn it off. "Sorry about that."

"What if it's work?"

"They're going to have to live without me tonight. I've got better things to do."

"Do you mind if I take a quick shower?"

"As long as it's quick, I'll allow it."

She left him with one last kiss and took her bag into the bathroom. After she showered, she stood in front of the mirror brushing her long dark hair until it fell in soft, shiny waves down her back. The ivory silk nightgown she bought just for this weekend with Jeremy made for a striking contrast with her olive complexion. As she brushed her hair one last time, Juliana suddenly thought of Michael and the strange look on his face when he greeted his fiancée at the airport. She wondered how his weekend was going so far.

Emerging from the bathroom, her heart raced with anticipation and desire. She couldn't wait to make love with Jeremy after so many weeks apart. But when she saw him sprawled out on the bed fast asleep, the disappointment hit like a fist to the belly. He'd had enough beer to knock him out for the night, and she knew from experience that there was no point in trying to rouse him.

Juliana ventured onto the patio and curled up on one of the lounge chairs to listen to the pounding surf. Filled with frustration, she hoped Michael's evening had gone better than hers.

The bright sunlight streaming into the room woke her early the next morning. Stretching out the stiffness from a night in a strange bed, she glanced over at Jeremy.

Before this interminable separation, they had lived together for four years. People often asked her why they hadn't gotten married, especially after they marked their tenth anniversary together. The only answer Juliana could ever give was that he hadn't asked her. More than one friend recommended an ultimatum, but Juliana had never seen the need for threats. What they had was special, and it always had been.

Jeremy transferred into her high school at the beginning of their junior year, and tugged her out from behind the dark clouds of life with a needy, alcoholic mother to life with him in the sunshine. With his quick wit and talent on the football field, he fit in right away with kids who had been indifferent to Juliana for years. Before she knew it, she'd been elevated from obscurity to half of a couple whose names were mentioned together so often that JeremyandJuliana took on the same easy cadence as peanut butter and jelly.

After graduation, she pursued a career in cosmetology while he studied electrical engineering at Johns Hopkins. When all the couples they knew in high school either moved into marriage and families in the suburbs or broke up during college, they continued on with just an occasional discussion about marriage. Until he had been transferred to Florida for this endless year, they hadn't spent a night apart in four years. And even though they had never actually taken the vows, Juliana considered them married in all the ways that mattered most.

They had also discovered there was a lot more to making love than what they'd done as fumbling teenagers overwhelmed by a love they were too young to fully understand and hormones they were powerless against. Back then Jeremy lived with a single mother who worked second shift as a nurse, so they took full advantage of the ample opportunity to work on getting it right.

Juliana ran a finger down his chest, and he gathered her closer. She kissed his shoulder and snuggled up to him.

When he finally opened one blue eye, he winced at the bright light and seemed to realize all at once that he was still dressed in yesterday's clothes. "Oh my God," he groaned. "I totally conked out on you."

"Yep."

"I'm sorry, babe. Are you pissed?"

"No."

He ran his hand up and down her silk-covered back. "Disappointed?" he asked with a cajoling smile.

"A little."

Nuzzling her neck, he said, "Let me hit the bathroom, and then I'll make it up to you."

Having shed his clothes in the bathroom, he came back a minute later, slid into bed, and reached for her. "I'm sorry I fell asleep." He brushed the hair back from her face. "All I thought about this week was being with you."

"I know. Me, too."

"I'm sorry I blew it," he said, capturing her mouth in a long, slow kiss flavored by toothpaste.

"I forgive you," she said, already breathless. "I've missed being able to touch you."

He tugged at the sheet to uncover her and cast an appreciative glance at the ivory nightgown. "Wow, look at you."

Juliana buried her face in his soft chest hair. She remembered that chest before the light dusting of golden blond hair took up residence.

He tilted her chin up and brought his lips down on hers.

His kiss was among the most familiar things in her life—the way his tongue sought out hers to tease and entice until she was drowning in him. He hooked his thumbs under the nightgown's spaghetti straps to ease them down and filled his hands with her breasts. "So, so beautiful."

Juliana wrapped her arms around him, trying to move him to where she wanted him most.

"Mmm, not yet," he whispered.

"Jer… I want you."

He teased her until her nipples were hard and pulsing. "Don't you miss this, babe? Don't you miss being able to do this any time we want?"

"Yes," she sighed. "I miss it so much."

He sucked hard on her nipple, and Juliana cried out.

"Mmm, so hot. So sexy." He kissed his way to her belly and beyond. With his hands on her knees, he urged her to spread her legs and settled between them.

Juliana quivered with desire.

Trailing a finger through her dampness, he avoided the spot that throbbed for him.

"*Jeremy…*"

"What?" he asked in a teasing tone.

"Come on!"

"Are you in a rush?"

She moaned.

He replied by pushing two fingers into her.

Gasping, she raised her hips to take him deeper as her climax began to build.

He dipped his head and added his tongue. After all the years they'd spent together, he knew just how to please her.

Her legs falling open in surrender to his skillful tongue and fingers, the orgasm ripped through her with shattering speed.

"I love that," he whispered, shifting over her. "I love the way you let go."

Her body was still pulsating when he buried himself in her. "Only for you." She wrapped her arms around him and brought him in for a kiss.

As their eyes met, she was filled with contentment. Looking up to find him there, where he had been for so long, was like coming home. But she saw sadness mixed with the desire and love in his eyes. The sadness was new. Before she could process the discovery, he began to move faster.

"Come with me, Jule," he whispered in her ear. "Come with me."

Juliana closed her eyes and soared.

"I'm starving," he muttered against her chest a few minutes later. He gave her a quick kiss and rolled over to get up. "Join me in the shower?"

She stretched and took in the glorious sight of him prowling naked around the big room. "In a minute."

"Don't be long."

Juliana heard the shower go on just as Jeremy's cell phone rang. Wondering why he had bothered to turn it back on and who would be calling him so early on a Saturday, she reached for the phone on the bedside table. "Hello?"

Silence.

"Hello?" Juliana said again.

When there was still no answer, she closed the phone to check the caller ID.

"Jule! Come on."

Juliana walked into the bathroom. "Jer?"

His hair full of shampoo, he pulled the curtain aside. "What?"

"Who's Sherrie?"

Chapter 3

PAIGE POUNCED THE MOMENT SHE AND MICHAEL WERE in her champagne-colored Mercedes coupe.

"*Whoa!*"

She wrapped herself around him as best she could in the tiny car. "Kiss me, Michael."

Michael glanced at the people getting into the car next to them. "Not here."

"One kiss?" she pouted.

That pout rendered him defenseless, and she knew it. He leaned in to kiss her and was hit by a surge of lust. The only area of their relationship that never gave them any trouble was their ability to fire each other up with just a touch, a look, or in this case, a kiss. When her eager tongue wound around his, he groaned and tore himself away. "Hold on, honey."

Her hand landed in his lap. "If you insist," she said with a saucy smile.

He grabbed her hand just as it reached its destination. "Paige! Stop!"

She flopped back into her seat. "What's your *problem*, Michael? We haven't seen each other in a month, for Christ's sake."

"And whose fault is that?"

She started the car and backed out of the parking space with only the briefest of glances behind her. "I've been busy planning *your* wedding. I can't just come up there any old time you want me to. Besides, the last time I was there you were so busy with work I hardly saw you."

"If you hadn't moved down here, we wouldn't be having this discussion, now would we?"

Fuming, Paige handed a five-dollar bill to the parking attendant. "Here we go," she muttered.

Her two-carat diamond engagement ring sparkled under the lights of the tollbooth. As it occurred to Michael yet again that he would be paying for that ring for the next three years, he couldn't help but wonder if the marriage would last that long. The thought startled him. When exactly had he begun to have all these doubts?

They drove north on Interstate 95 in silence.

After a while he reached for her hand and was relieved to feel her fingers tighten around his. *That blew over faster than usual.* He truly loved Paige. She could be so sweet and generous, but just as often she could be a spoiled brat. He was seeing more and more of that side of her as they planned their wedding. Unfortunately, his family had seen just enough of it to give them serious reservations about his plans to marry her.

Resting his head back, he realized how exhausted he was. The trial preparations were kicking his ass, and the idea of spending the weekend with the Admiral, Mrs. Simpson, and two hundred of their closest friends sucked what little energy he had right out of him. What he really needed this weekend was sleep.

Paige took the exit for A1A on the way to Amelia Island where she lived with her parents in a six-thousand-square-foot home so sprawling they'd installed an intercom system so they could find each other. Raised with three sisters in a six-room ranch house, Michael thought the Simpson's home was obscene. Nearly everything about their lifestyle offended him, but since he and Paige would be living far away from her parents after they were married, he didn't care how they chose to live.

"I'm sorry," Paige said softly. "I don't want to fight this weekend."

He kissed her hand. "Neither do I, but I'm really fried, hon. The trial has me by the balls."

"How's it going?"

That she bothered to ask told him she was trying. "It's getting close. I've got to write my opening at some point this weekend."

"Not while you're here! We've got so much to do. We're picking invitations and registering tomorrow before the party. Then there's brunch on Sunday. You can't work!"

Michael took a deep breath. He never should have agreed to this weekend, but it was too late now. "I'll fit it in."

After a thirty-minute ride, they arrived at the two-story taupe monstrosity surrounded by lush land-scaping with artful lighting hidden among the palm trees, crepe myrtles, and flowering hibiscus bushes. The autumn evening air was thick with humidity and cricket music. Michael steeled himself for his audience with the Admiral, who'd pulled some strings to get Michael the job with the Baltimore City state's attorney and never missed an opportunity to remind Michael he owed him one.

They were waiting in the spacious great room when Michael and Paige came in through an elaborately tiled foyer the size of his parents' entire house.

"Hello, Michael," Eleanor Simpson said, brushing a polite kiss over his cheek. As always, she looked as if she just stepped out of the beauty parlor. The thought reminded Michael of Juliana.

"Mrs. Simpson, Admiral." He extended a hand to the imposing older man. When Admiral Simpson shook your hand, your hand knew it.

"Good to see you, Michael," the Admiral said. "The flight was late, of course."

"Bad weather," Michael muttered.

"Can I get you something to eat?" Eleanor asked.

"No, thank you. I'm good." He was so tired that the thought of eating made him sick.

"A drink then." The Admiral walked over to the bar to fix Michael a scotch on the rocks even though he preferred a beer, and the Admiral knew it.

"Thank you, sir," Michael said as he accepted the drink. He had known the Admiral for four years and had never once addressed him as anything other than Admiral or sir. Sometimes both.

"How's the trial shaping up?" the Admiral asked.

"Everything's going well."

"You look tired," Eleanor said.

"He's beat," Paige said, pouring a glass of white wine.

The Admiral continued like they hadn't spoken, which, in Michael's experience, was nothing new. "Got yourself an ace in the hole with that little girl. Bet you're keeping a close eye on her."

"Yes, she's in protective custody."

"They'd sure love to get their hands on her. No, you can't afford to lose her."

"We're not going to." Michael gritted his teeth against the urge to scream. *Does he honestly think I need to hear that right now?*

"Daddy, don't bother him about the trial. He needs a break."

"You brought your tuxedo?" Eleanor asked.

"Yes, ma'am."

"Well, Joseph, let's give these young people some time alone." She ushered her startled husband from the room. "We'll see you in the morning."

"Goodnight," Paige and Michael said together.

"Well, that was totally unexpected." Michael had been anticipating no less than an hour of small talk with the Simpsons, with at least half of it devoted to a grilling about the trial.

"She could tell you didn't want to talk about the trial, and he wasn't going to let it go."

"Have I mentioned I love your mother?"

Paige laughed. "She has her moments." Glancing over at him, her cheeks flooded with color. "Can I kiss you *now?*" she asked in a small voice that tugged at his heart.

"I wish you would." He put his untouched drink on the glass coffee table and reached for her.

The kiss was as hot and lush as the Florida night. For four years she had bewitched him with her unique blend of innocence and sensuality. She gave him all she had in every kiss, and after the long weeks apart she was even more open and giving than usual.

"Let's go upstairs," she whispered, flicking her tongue over his ear.

He hated having sex in her parents' house, but they'd done it before and would no doubt do it again. Taking her hand, he followed her up the stairs to the guest suite over the garage, comforted by the fact that her parents' room was almost a football field away from them.

She locked the door and pulled her top over her head. Her breasts were surprisingly full on her slight frame, and her nipples puckered in the air-conditioned room.

As he watched her strip down to a thong, Michael shed his suit coat and pulled off his tie. A tussle in the sheets with her would take him from exhausted straight to downright depleted.

Unbuttoning his shirt, she buried her fingers in his chest hair and swirled her tongue over his nipple.

Unable to resist her, he ran his hands down her back and cupped her bare bottom.

Lifting her against his erection, he drew a moan from her. "I love you so much, Michael."

He had the wherewithal to grab a condom from his bag before he carried her to the big bed with the lace canopy.

Urging him down beneath her, she said, "Let me." She rained kisses over his face and chest. "You're so tired. Let me love you."

He sucked in a sharp deep breath when her white-blond hair brushed his belly.

She unbuckled his belt and slid his pants and boxers down to the floor and then kissed her way back to where he wanted her most.

He groaned when she stroked him first with her hand and then with her mouth. Gasping, he reached for her.

"Not so fast." She took him deep into her mouth, all the while stroking him with her hand.

He groaned. "Paige, *please…*"

"Mmm, I've missed you so much," she sighed.

"You're going to finish me off before we get to the good stuff."

In a low sexy voice, she said, "Are you saying this isn't good stuff?"

"No," he panted. "Definitely not saying that."

Laughing, she took him to the edge of insanity before she rolled on the condom and straddled him. Enveloping him in her heat, she arched her back to ride him with abandon.

When he felt her clutching him from within, he gripped her hips to meet her at the top, pulling her down to muffle her shriek with a kiss.

She fell on top of him like a rag doll, and Michael wrapped his arms around her, steeped in the scent of roses that would always remind him of her.

"That scream of yours is going to get us busted one of these days."

She snickered. "You can make me scream legally before too much longer."

"Eight months," he said with a sigh.

She kissed his jaw, his chin, and lingered at his lips.

"Paige?"

"Hmm?" she said as she ran her tongue along his lower lip.

"Marry me now. Let's not wait eight months."

Startled, she stared at him as if he had lost his mind.

"Let's just get married. We can go to Vegas or to a J.P. I don't care. I just want us to be married. Now." The urgency in his voice surprised even him, but if the strong reaction he'd had to Juliana was any indication, he needed to do something about this state of limbo he and Paige had been living in for far too long.

"Michael, it's all set. The wedding's all planned. You can't just throw this at me now."

"Then come home with me. I need you with me."

"But *I* need to be with my mother before the wedding, and all my friends are here."

Michael eased her off him so he could sit up. "Can I ask you something?"

"Of course."

"What are you more excited about? The wedding or our marriage?"

"What the hell does that mean?" she asked, turning away from him.

"Look at me." He took hold of her arm. "Marry me. Right now. No bells, no whistles. Just you and me."

Her eyes flooded with tears. "You're not being fair. I've dreamed about this day my whole life. You'd really deny me this?"

"Then come back to Maryland with me until the wedding. I can't do this long-distance thing any more, Paige. I just can't."

Her expression softened as she brushed the hair back from his face. "You're so tired. Why don't you get some sleep? You'll feel better in the morning." She discreetly rid him of the condom and went into the bathroom to flush it. When she came back, she pulled the covers up around him and reached for her clothes. Once she was dressed, she leaned over to leave him with a lingering kiss. "I love you, Michael. I can't wait to marry you."

After she left the room, he realized she hadn't answered his question.

Chapter 4

JEREMY FROZE AND THE WATER BEAT DOWN ON HIM. Blinking furiously as the shampoo slid into his eyes, he ducked back under the shower.

Juliana needed only that one frozen moment to confirm that she had stumbled upon what—or rather *who*—had been distracting him lately. A wave of nausea choked her as she walked out of the bathroom to find some clothes.

Knotting a towel around his waist, he came out a moment later still dripping. "It's not what you think."

She pushed past him, slammed the bathroom door, and locked it. After she scrubbed all traces of him from her body in the shower, she got dressed, her hands shaking as she fought the urge to scream.

Dressed and waiting for her when she came out, Jeremy crossed the room to her. "Let me explain."

She couldn't even look at him.

"It's nothing. She's just a friend."

"You're lying," she said in a small voice. "I saw it on your face."

He took hold of her hand. "Let's take a walk."

She pulled her hand free of his grip. "Don't touch me."

"Juliana, please. Take a walk with me. Let me explain."

Since she didn't know what else to do, she slid on flip-flops to follow him outside. Accompanied by the roar of the pounding surf, they walked down a long boardwalk to the beach. Juliana continued to fight the need to shriek. This could *not* be happening. *Not Jeremy. Not my Jeremy. He wouldn't do this. Would he?*

He walked along the water's edge with his head down. Finally, he looked over at her. "You know I love you, babe. I love you more than anything. I always have."

Juliana didn't trust herself not to scream, so she said nothing.

"I've missed you so much since I've been here. It's like my whole world is out of sync because I don't have you with me. I had no idea how essential you are to me until you weren't there every day."

"So you decided to replace me?"

"Oh God, *replace* you? There's no replacing you. You're *everything*." He paused, looking pained. "But that's kind of the problem."

She stopped walking. "What are you talking about?"

"I want us to get married when I get home."

"*What?* After all these years you can't just blurt that out when there's clearly something else going on."

He took her hands and gazed into her eyes. "I love you. You're my family, Jule. I want to marry you and have babies with you. I want the forever we were always meant to have."

Her breath caught on a sob. *How long have I waited to hear that?* "So what's the catch? If you want all that with me, who's this Sherrie person?"

He sighed. "She's just this girl who hangs out with us. She's nothing."

"Then why is she calling you when you're with me?"

His handsome face clouded with annoyance. "That's a very good question."

Juliana pulled her hands free and walked away.

He caught up to her. "Jule? I meant it. I'm not prepared to ask you properly this weekend, but I want to. Soon."

"Can I ask *you* something?"

"Sure."

"If your 'nothing' friend Sherrie hadn't called this morning, would we be having this discussion about marriage and babies and forever right now?"

He looked stricken.

"I don't buy it, Jer. Where's this been? You've had the chance to say all this for years, but you never did. My friends have been telling me forever that I needed to give you an ultimatum, but I never saw the need. Now I'm wondering if I've been a total fool."

"In ten years there's been no one but you. You know I haven't so much as looked at another woman."

"Until now?"

"That's all I've done, Jule, is look."

For some reason she believed him, but suddenly she felt cold all over. "You want to do more than look, don't you?" she asked, her voice so soft it was almost lost in the roar of the ocean.

A tortured look crossed his face. "*God,* how can I say this?"

"Just say it! I can't stand this!"

"I've never been with anyone else. Since I was seventeen, there's only ever been you. I remember so vividly the day I met you. I took one look at you, and I was a goner. We should be married by now, Jule. I know that. It's just sometimes I wonder what it would be like to, you know—"

Her heart shattered into pieces. "To be with someone else."

His eyes glistened with tears. "I love you. In my whole life I'll never love anyone but you."

"But I'm not enough for you," she said, choking on a sob. *Had anything ever hurt this much?*

"That's not true! How can you say that after the way we just made love? It's not about you being enough for me."

She wiped the tears from her face. "Then what?"

"I'm afraid if I don't get some shit out of my system now I won't be faithful when we're married."

If he had punched her in the stomach he couldn't have hurt her more. Her knees buckled, and she dropped to the sand as sobs overtook her. He couldn't be saying these things. This was *not* happening.

He knelt down next to her and took her in his arms.

She didn't have the strength to push him away.

"Jule." He kissed her forehead and then her cheek. "Please. Don't do this. I'm sorry. I never meant to hurt you."

"*What did you think would happen?* That I'd just say, 'Have at it, Jer? Sow your wild oats, and give me a call when you're done?'"

"Don't you ever wonder how it would be with someone else?"

"*No!*" She pushed him away. "No! No! *No!*"

He seemed taken aback by her vehemence.

"You've *always* been enough for me. It would never occur to me to wonder about other men."

"Never?"

"Never."

He buried his face in his hands. "Fuck." His hands muffled his voice.

"You said it."

"Look, let's just forget all this, *please?* I'm a stupid ass. That girl means nothing to me. I swear to God."

"I can't just forget this, Jeremy!" She knew she sounded hysterical but didn't care. "How can I live with knowing you want to be with someone else?"

"Because I'm telling you I won't do anything about it."

"So I'm supposed to go home and wonder what you're up to down here? I don't think so."

"I thought you trusted me!"

"I didn't know I couldn't!"

"This is so fucked up! I've been faithful to you forever! I admit to having thoughts—and that's all they were— *thoughts*—about someone else, and you act like I've been fucking my way through Florida or something!"

She whimpered.

He sighed and put his arms around her. "I'm sorry, babe. I'm so sorry. This whole situation sucks. None of this would've happened if I hadn't taken this goddamned job down here. If I'd known it would cause all this trouble for us I wouldn't have done it. The extra money's not worth it."

She rested against him because she didn't know what else to do. He had been her world, her life, for so long that the idea of living without him was unimaginable. But how could she live with what he had said? Would she always wonder if he was thinking of someone else? Would he come to resent her because they met too soon? Did he *already* resent her for that?

"Hey," he said after a long period of silence. "Why don't we get something to eat? You'll feel better when you eat."

She got up to go with him, but she knew nothing would make her feel better.

Chapter 5

THE IVORY-FROST LENOX GRAVY BOAT FINALLY DID IT for Michael. After two hours of listening to Paige and her mother go on and on about eight-hundred-thread-count Egyptian cotton sheets and Tommy Hilfiger towels, the delicate china gravy boat didn't stand a chance with him.

"Excuse me," he said. Before Paige or her mother could utter a word, he got up and walked away. He rode the nearest escalator down to the first floor of Dillard's. Wandering into the mall, he let his thoughts drift to the opening argument that had been running around in his mind during the endless morning.

Ladies and gentlemen of the jury, we have before us what's commonly known as an open and shut case. An eyewitness will testify that she saw the defendants shoot the three victims. We'll introduce ballistics evidence that ties the gun registered to Marco Benedetti to slugs recovered from the victims. We can prove that both defendants fired a gun that fateful evening. You'll hear testimony from friends of the victims who heard them arguing with the defendants earlier in the day. So you're probably asking yourselves: if this case is such a slam-dunk, what're we doing here? (Insert dramatic pause.) We're here because the Constitution of the United States gives everyone—even two cold-blooded killers—a day in court. Your job is to make sure they spend the rest of their days in prison.

I've got to write that down! Spotting a pharmacy across the mall's main thoroughfare, he walked over to buy a notebook and pen. He had almost managed to get the whole thing on paper when Paige stormed up to where he sat on a bench next to a fountain.

"Michael! What are you doing?"

"Hang on a second."

"I will *not* hang on a second! Why did you leave like that? What's wrong with you? Don't you care about the things we'll have in our home?"

"Um, no, not really," he said without looking up.

With a furious sweep of her hand she knocked the pad off his lap.

Leaning over to retrieve it from the floor, Michael wanted to reach up and throttle her. *God, she could be such a bitch sometimes!* "Cut it out, Paige."

"You cut it out!" Her raised voice attracted curious stares. "What the hell is with you this weekend?"

"I'll tell you what's *with* me. I have a huge trial starting next week. I told you this wasn't a good weekend for me to be here, but you and your parents planned this party without even asking me."

"You know it was the only weekend we could get the club."

"Oh, well, if that's the case, who cares if it's a bad weekend for the groom?"

"I don't know why you're being so unreasonable. It's like you don't even care about our wedding."

"I don't. I tried to tell you that last night, but you didn't want to hear it. What I *care* about is the marriage, but I'm starting to seriously wonder if I even want that."

She recoiled as if he had hit her. "*Michael.*"

Her mother joined them. "Everything all right?"

With her hand resting over her heart, Paige stared at her fiancé in stunned silence.

"Everything's fine," Michael said. "Are we done here?"

"Yes," Paige said softly. "We're done."

"Okay, then," Eleanor said. "Let's go home for lunch. I have the books from the stationery store at the house, so you can pick the invitations this afternoon." She rattled on without realizing the happy couple wasn't listening.

Michael struggled with his bow tie in front of the mirror in the guest bathroom. He never had figured out how to tie a bow tie properly, which was something every other man in Paige's life was probably born knowing how to do. He hadn't had much need for that skill before he met her.

Taking another stab at the tie, he thought back to the first time he ever saw her, across the room at a gathering of third-year law students at the dean's house. She had come with her father, the dean's friend, and Michael could still remember the lavender cashmere sweater and matching wool skirt she wore to the late-afternoon cocktail party.

The Admiral had been in full dress uniform, and he somehow managed to command a room full of dignitaries. When Michael's gaze connected with Paige, she smiled and rolled her eyes behind the back of her father who gestured as he made an emphatic point in the conversation he was having with the dean, the District of Columbia police chief, the junior senator from Maryland, and the state's attorney from Baltimore City.

Michael tipped his head toward the bar, inviting her to join him for a drink. He watched her whisper to her father, who nodded without missing a beat in his conversation.

"Whew," she said when they met at the bar. "Thanks for the lifeline."

Michael chuckled. "My pleasure. Buy you a drink?"

"White wine, please," she said to the bartender.

Michael ordered another beer. "Michael Maguire."

She shook his hand. "Paige Simpson."

They moved out of the party fray to sit by the fire.

She slid off her black pumps. "It feels good to sit down."

Watching transfixed as she stretched her long legs, he was startled when his penis sprang to life. *Holy junior high!* He quickly shifted his eyes up to find that her porcelain complexion had grown rosy from the heat of the fire. In her blue eyes he saw intelligence, laughter, and a touch of mischief. He cleared his throat. "So what brings you to our exciting shindig?"

"My father." She nodded to the Admiral. "My mother had a meeting, so he asked me to come along."

"Is he stationed at the Pentagon?"

"No, the Naval Academy. He's the superintendent."

Michael released a low whistle. "That must be nice."

She smiled. "It's not bad."

"What about you? What do you do?"

"My father says I'm a professional student. I'm an undergrad here at Georgetown. I've switched majors a few times, so I'm on the six-year plan. I'll finally be getting an art history degree in May."

That made her twenty-four, Michael figured. She seemed both older than that and younger at the same time. The face was that of a child but the eyes were those of a woman, and they were studying him with interest.

"And you're at the law school?"

"Yes. Almost done, thank God. Just a few more months to go."

"Then what?"

"I don't know yet. I think about going home to Rhode Island to open a practice. That's what I've always wanted to do, but I love living in D.C. So the jury's still out."

She smiled at the legal pun.

"Paige, honey, there you are," a voice boomed from behind them.

"Dad, this is Michael Maguire, a third year at the law school."

Michael stood to shake his hand. "Pleased to meet you, Admiral."

"Yes, likewise." The Admiral turned to his daughter. "We need to be getting back to Annapolis. I have a faculty meeting tonight."

"But my new friend Michael just asked me to have dinner with him, so I can't leave yet," she said with a sly smile and wink for Michael.

"You don't have your car."

"I'd be happy to bring her home after dinner, sir," Michael said. He was rewarded with a bright smile from Paige that once again caught the attention of another part of his anatomy. *Christ!*

"Well, then, I guess that's fine." The Admiral kissed his daughter's forehead. "Don't be out too late. You know how your mother worries. It was nice to meet you, Michael. Drive carefully with my daughter."

Michael shook his hand again. "Yes, sir."

They watched the Admiral consult with his friend the dean and saw him nod with approval.

"Looks like you just got the okay from the dean," Paige whispered.

"It's a good thing because I was thinking about asking you to have dinner with me."

She laughed. "That's a wonderful idea. I'd love to."

A soft knock on the guest room door brought Michael back to the present. Opening the door, he found Paige wearing a pale pink strapless silk gown, her hair in a sleek French twist.

"You look stunning." Michael stepped aside to let her in.

"Thank you. Are you ready?"

They had exchanged only a few tense words since their argument in the mall.

"Well, you know the tie always gives me trouble."

"Let me," she said, ushering him toward the bathroom mirror.

He squatted down so she could wrap her arms around him from behind.

She knotted the tie with quick, confident movements and then rested her hands on his shoulders.

"I don't know how you do that." He adjusted the tie into place on his tuxedo shirt. Catching her gaze in the mirror, he noticed tears in her eyes and turned to her. "What's this?" He brushed at a tear before it could mar her eye makeup.

She shrugged.

"Paige?"

"I can't stop thinking about what you said before. Did you mean it?"

"I've been having some worries lately. I won't deny that."

"About us?"

He nodded.

"And you wait until the day of our engagement party to mention them to me?"

"Actually, I tried to mention them last night," he reminded her.

She clutched her stomach. "I think I'm going to be sick."

"Paige! Michael! Are you coming? We need to go," Eleanor called from downstairs.

"Just a minute," Michael replied before he turned back to Paige. "Let's enjoy the party. There'll be time to talk later." He held out a hand to her.

"Do you still love me, Michael?" Her blue eyes glistened with new tears as she held her breath and waited for his reply.

Leaning in to kiss her, he suddenly thought of Juliana and her soft, captivating brown eyes. Unsettled, he said, "Of course I do. Come on, your parents are waiting for us."

Chapter 6

AFTER THEIR EMOTIONAL DISCUSSION ON THE BEACH, Jeremy devoted himself to showing the reluctant Juliana a good time. They drove south along A1A to Saint Augustine where they walked through the Spanish Quarter. He tugged her over to look at rings in a jewelry store window.

"If you could have any one of them, which one would you choose?" he asked with a playful smile.

She pulled her hand free. "Don't, Jer."

"Come on." He brought her back. "Just look."

The diamonds glittered in the late afternoon sun. Only yesterday this discussion would have made Juliana's heart dance with excitement, but now she just felt dead inside.

"Which one do you like? How about the square one? That's cool, isn't it?"

She shrugged. "I guess."

"Let's go in so you can try it on."

"No."

"Jule—"

"I said *no.*"

"Is there *anything* I can do?" he pleaded. "I want to take back everything I said this morning. I want to go back to where we were before."

"You can't take it back, and you shouldn't have to. You were honest about how you feel."

"Then tell me how *you* feel," he said with quiet desperation.

She looked straight into his eyes. "I hurt," she whispered. "Everywhere."

"I'm sorry." He took a sudden interest in his feet. "I love you so much. That I could've hurt you like this kills me."

"Can we go back to the hotel? I don't want to be here."

"Sure." He put his arm around her and led her to the car.

Back in their room, Juliana still didn't feel up to talking, so she decided to take a nap.

"Do you mind if I go for a run on the beach?"

"No, that's fine."

After he left, Juliana stretched out on the big bed and turned so she could see the ocean. Would the sound of waves crashing on the beach always remind her now of Jeremy telling her he wanted other women? She ached when she thought about life without him—a life that revolved around her mother, her job, and her endless responsibilities. But how could she stay with him knowing what she did?

Losing him would be like severing a limb, only more painful. For so long he had been her refuge, her sanctuary, her place of peace in the storm of her life. She closed her eyes and must have dozed off because she awoke with a start when Jeremy returned from running.

"Babe," he whispered. "Are you sleeping?"

Juliana kept her eyes closed so he would think she was asleep. She couldn't deal with any more just then. When she didn't answer him, he went into the bathroom to shower. At home he sang—badly—in the shower, but here he was quiet.

He came out a short time later and squatted down next to her, brushing the hair off her face and kissing her forehead. A few minutes later, he stood up.

Juliana opened her eyes. He had a towel around his waist and was slumped against the big window.

"Jer?"

Turning to her, his face a picture of devastation, he said, "I'm sorry, Juliana. I'm so sorry."

She held out her arms to him.

He sat on the edge of the bed and leaned into her embrace. "I don't know how to fix this."

Touched by his raw despair, she brought him down for a soft kiss.

He wrapped his arms around her and shifted her under him in the middle of the big bed. "Jule," he whispered against her lips, "I love you so much. Let me show you."

She arched into him, her arms tightening around him in surrender to the familiar dance.

He pulled back to gaze down at her before he tugged the shirt over her head. Capturing her hands, he left a lingering kiss on each palm and put them on the pillows.

"Leave them there," he whispered, running his index finger straight down the middle of her, between her breasts and over her belly.

She trembled and fought the urge to reach for him.

Unbuttoning her shorts, he slid them and her panties over her hips and tossed them aside, all the while keeping his eyes fixed on hers.

He gave her ear his full attention then left wet, hot kisses on her forehead, her cheeks, and the end of her nose.

She tried to capture his lips, but he shifted to focus on her neck.

She moaned.

With the flip of two fingers over the front clasp of her bra, he freed her breasts and kissed her everywhere but where she craved him most. When he finally rolled her nipple between his teeth, she lifted off into a soaring climax that shook them both to the core. In all their years together, it had never happened like that for her.

He rested against her until she caught her breath and then devoured her mouth in a series of kisses that left her weak with desire. Cupping her, his fingers coasted through her slickness. As another orgasm rolled through her in soft waves, he raised himself to enter her. He gave her everything he had, as if it was their first time—or maybe their last.

And when it was over, he lay gasping on top of her, his eyes bright with emotion. "I love you, Juliana. I'll love you forever."

She closed her eyes tight against the burn of tears and held him close to her as the sun set over the beach.

Chapter 7

THE AMELIA ISLAND COUNTRY CLUB SPARKLED WITH white lights, crystal champagne glasses, chandeliers, and candles floating in elaborate floral centerpieces. A small orchestra provided background music while the Simpson's guests mingled over cocktails.

When Michael was introduced to the governor of Florida, the attorney general, and the state's senior senator, he realized the Admiral was killing several birds with this party. A staunch Republican, he was considering a run for the House of Representatives from Florida's fourth district.

"Meet my future son-in-law, Michael Maguire," the Admiral said to the governor and the attorney general as he slapped Michael on the back. "He's a prosecutor on Tom Houlihan's team up in Baltimore. Michael's first chair on a murder trial that starts next week."

The attorney general, Derek Gantley, clasped Michael's hand. "Gang shooting?"

"Yes, sir," Michael said.

"I've read about that case. Looks good for conviction."

"We like our odds."

"Best of luck," Gantley said.

The Admiral whisked him and the governor away to meet other guests.

Michael grabbed a glass of champagne off a passing tray and had downed half of it when he located Paige across the room surrounded by her high school friends. Before the Admiral transferred to the Pentagon and then the Naval Academy, she attended the exclusive Bolles School in Jacksonville while her father served as the commanding officer of Naval Air Station Jacksonville. Many of her friends still lived in the area, which was one of the reasons she had been so anxious to move back to Florida when her father retired from the Navy.

Michael was working on a third glass of champagne when Paige came to find him.

"Having a good time?"

"Yes," she answered without looking at him. "They're ready to serve dinner so we need to be seated."

Michael followed her to the large head table where they sat with her parents, the bridesmaids, and their dates. He attempted to make conversation with the matron of honor's husband, a big blond guy named Brad.

"You know how it is in marketing," Brad was saying when Michael tuned back in minutes later. "You're lucky to stay one step ahead of the changing times. That's why focus groups are so critical."

"Uh huh." Michael preferred to focus on his prime rib. Out of the corner of his eye he noticed Paige pushing shrimp around on her plate without actually eating anything.

Brad prattled on about market influences, direct mail, and the latest consumer buying trends. He seemed satisfied with Michael's occasional nod.

After the waiters cleared the dinner dishes from their table, the orchestra leader called Michael and Paige to the dance floor. "Please join me in a round of applause for the happy couple—Michael and Paige."

The applause embarrassed Michael. This whole thing was so over the top. But he took Paige into his arms and went through the expected motions as the orchestra played "What Are You Doing the Rest of Your Life?"

Paige looked up at him with a sad smile. "Remember?"

After they had dinner in a Georgetown bistro the night they met, they walked slowly back to his apartment to get his car. In just three hours with her, he felt like he'd known her forever.

She tucked her hand into the crook of his arm as they strolled through the quaint, eclectic neighborhood.

"Oh, look, Michael! They're dancing. Can we go in?"

He gazed into the jazz club. "Don't you need to get home? It's a long ride to Annapolis," he said, trying not to think about the two hundred pages he had planned to read that night.

She grinned. "I don't have an official curfew anymore."

He was already beguiled by that hint of mischief in her eyes and could feel himself drifting into something that had the potential to be important. Powerless against the urge to frame that flawless face with his hands, he hadn't expected the desire to roar through him when her breath hitched in the instant before he kissed her. He felt her arms go around him as her eager mouth opened under his.

Long, passionate minutes passed before a group of college kids brushed against them, reminding Michael of where he was and what he was doing. Someone muttered, "Get a room."

Paige giggled.

Still trying to get his head to stop spinning, Michael decided that no kiss had ever affected him quite like that one.

"Does that mean you want to dance, or what?" she asked with a teasing grin.

"Yeah." He opened the door to the club for her. "Let's dance."

On a dance floor packed with couples swaying to the jazz band's sultry sound, Michael took her into his arms like he had done it a million times before. He couldn't help but notice how well she fit against him.

After they danced for a long while, a woman who sounded just like Ella Fitzgerald stepped up to the microphone to sing "What Are You Doing the Rest of Your Life?"

Michael looked down at Paige, wanting more than anything to kiss her again.

She tilted her face in invitation.

Swamped with tenderness and need and a kind of wild desire totally unfamiliar to him, he touched his lips to hers.

"Paige," he whispered when the song ended. "We should go."

She nodded and followed him through the crowded club.

Back on the street, he took a deep breath of the cool winter air, hoping to regain control of his rampaging hormones. They were quiet on the short walk to his building where he helped her into his Toyota Camry for the ride to Annapolis. He got in next to her, looked over, and wondered what it was about her that had him so bewitched after spending just one evening with her.

She reached out to caress his face. "Michael," she said in that breathy voice of hers.

This time when he kissed her neither of them held anything back, and the punch was twice as powerful as it had been on the busy sidewalk. He hauled her into his arms and plundered.

Her fingers tunneled into his hair as she responded with equal ardor.

"Paige," he sighed after what seemed like a lifetime had passed. He kissed her neck and throat while his hand found the soft skin of her back under her sweater. "This is crazy."

"Uh huh."

"I want to take you upstairs and—" She traced his bottom lip with her tongue, and his mind went blank.

"And what?" Her innocent expression was in sharp contrast to the way she had kissed him.

He whispered in her ear all the things he wanted to do with her—and to her.

She shuddered. "Oh *God*. I want you so much. I've never behaved like this before, Michael. This isn't like me."

"It's not exactly my usual routine, either." He kissed her again and caressed her back. "But I should get you home. It's getting late, and the Admiral isn't going to be happy with me."

She chuckled. "The Admiral would kill you if he could see us right now."

"Well, isn't that as effective as a cold shower?" With great reluctance he removed his hand from her back and drew her sweater down.

She shifted into the passenger seat to put on her seatbelt.

Michael opened the window to let in the cold air to clear both his head and the steam on the windows. As they drove out of the District on Massachusetts Avenue, he reached for her hand. "I'm glad your mother had a meeting today."

She smiled. "So am I."

He merged onto Route 50 and headed east to Annapolis. "I want to see you again."

"I think that can be arranged."

"How often are you in the city?"

"I have class on Monday, Wednesday, and Friday this semester, and I volunteer at the Smithsonian on Thursdays."

"You've made me forget what day it is today."

She giggled. "Friday."

"That's what I would've guessed. What are you doing tomorrow?" A mental alarm sounded, reminding him of the studying he planned to do all weekend.

She groaned. "I have to study. I have two exams on Monday."

"I do, too. Maybe we could study together?"

"I don't know. I think you'd be too much of a distraction."

"You're probably right. I can't imagine tort law would hold my attention if you're in the room."

"There's a compliment in there somewhere."

He laughed. "What about Sunday?"

"My parents and I go to brunch at the officer's club on Sundays. Would you like to come with us?"

"Will they mind?" Michael asked.

"Of course not."

"Okay, but I don't think I can wait that long to talk to you again." He let go of her hand to reach for a piece of paper and a pen. "Will you write down your number?"

She smiled. "Sure."

At the gates to the Naval Academy, Paige showed the guard her identification card.

"Good evening, Ms. Simpson," the guard said, waving them on to the base.

"Did we just get V.I.P. treatment?"

"Sort of. You're supposed to get a pass for your car, but they're good to us. I'll have my dad put you on our guest list so you can come in on Sunday." She directed him through the campus to the superintendent's large white house on the banks of the Severn River. A light over the front door cast a glow over the sweeping front porch.

"Military housing is so pathetic," he joked.

"We make do," she said with a smile as she turned to him. "Thank you for dinner."

"You're welcome." He brushed his thumb over her cheek. "I'll walk you in."

"You don't have to."

"Yes, I do." He went around to open her door. Before they reached the bright lights of the porch, he stopped her and could tell he caught her off guard with the gentle, easy kiss. When she expected flame, he gave smolder. And when she reached for more, he held back, leaving them both breathless by the time he finally pulled away. "Good night," he said.

Her eyes were wide, her lips swollen, and it was all he could do not to drag her back against him for more.

"Good night."

He waited until she was inside before he returned to the car. Arriving at home nearly an hour later, he could still taste her on his lips. *What was it about her?*

A second round of applause pulled Michael back to the engagement party. He looked down at Paige and was surprised by a flood of tenderness. Thinking back to the day they met reminded him of why he was here tonight celebrating their engagement. He had loved her since that first day, maybe even from that first moment when their eyes met across the crowded room at the dean's house.

He kissed her as the orchestra played the final notes of the song he quoted in his proposal when he'd asked her what she was doing the rest of her life.

Responding to his unexpected kiss, Paige seemed almost startled.

The Admiral's booming voice ended the moment. "Don't they make a fine-looking couple?"

Their guests applauded.

Eleanor, lovely in a mauve evening gown, stood next to her husband.

"Paige's mother and I would like to propose a toast to our daughter and future son-in-law. I'm proud to say I was with Paige when she met Michael four years ago. He's a fine young man, and we look forward to welcoming him into our family. Eleanor and I were delighted by their engagement, and we're pleased you all could join us tonight to celebrate. Now, you know Paige is our only child, so we've been known to dote on her a bit."

That's putting it mildly, Michael thought, keeping an arm around her.

"The idea of her getting married and moving away breaks our hearts, especially when there are sure to be grandchildren before too long," the Admiral said with a guffaw. The guests applauded again.

Michael looked down to find Paige's cheeks pink with embarrassment.

"Anyway, I think we might have a solution to this geographical problem, but before we get into that, I ask you to raise your glasses in a toast to Paige and Michael. We wish you a long and happy marriage that's blessed with many, many children!"

"Hear, hear," the guests chimed in.

Because he knew he was expected to, Michael touched his champagne glass to Paige's and kissed her. His stomach took a nervous dip when the attorney general joined Admiral and Mrs. Simpson on the stage. *What's this?*

Derek Gantley shook hands with the Admiral and stepped up to the microphone. "Congratulations to the happy couple. Michael, I've been impressed with your work in Maryland, especially on the Benedetti case. There's an assistant attorney general position opening up in Jacksonville, and I'd love to have you come to work with me. What do we think? Wouldn't Michael make a fine addition to the Florida team?"

As the guests applauded, Michael's arm dropped from Paige's shoulders.

"I know you've got more important things on your mind tonight, Michael, but I look forward to talking with you soon," Gantley said, shaking hands again with the Admiral.

"How about that?" the Admiral asked with glee.

Michael heard nothing but the roar of anger. "Did you know about this?" he asked Paige.

"I thought you'd be happy about it."

"You thought wrong," he said, making no effort to hide his fury. "I need some air." He headed for the French doors that led to a terrace overlooking the golf course. One person after another called out their congratulations. Nodding politely, he didn't stop until he was outside. On the terrace he paced back and forth, trying to control the anger. *Goddamn it! What a fucking operator the Admiral is! He knew that by having the A.G. offer the job publicly, he made it all but impossible for me to say no.*

Paige joined him on the terrace. "Michael? Michael, honey, please don't be mad."

He shook her hand off his shoulder. "This is how it's going to be, isn't it?"

"What do you mean?"

"Your father will say 'jump,' and I'll be expected to ask, 'how high?'"

"You don't have to take the job."

"Yeah, right. If I say no your father will be embarrassed in front of the same people he's counting on to put him in Congress. I'm sure my future father-in-law would be *delighted* to welcome me into his family then."

"You don't have to do anything you don't want to do." Paige reached for his hand. "I don't care where we live as long as we live together."

He pulled his hand free. "I've already let him push me into one job I didn't want. I've given that one my all, and I've grown to like it. I don't want the job with the A.G., but more than that, I don't want your father thinking he can make career decisions for me. I'm not one of his sailors he can just order around."

"I'm sorry."

"I'm sorry you didn't put a stop to it when you found out about it."

Tears spilled from her eyes. "I just wanted you to be happy."

"Give me a break, Paige! You weren't thinking of me when you let this happen." He shook his head in frustration and anger. "I need to get out of here."

"You can't leave your own party," she said frantically.

"I can't trust myself to be civil right now."

"You'll embarrass me if you leave me here alone. This is our *engagement party,* Michael."

"Our engagement is off. I can't marry you. It'd never work. I'm sorry."

"*Michael!*" she cried as he walked to the terrace stairs. "Michael, please. I'm sorry." When he didn't stop, she screamed, "*Michael, I love you! I love you!*"

Moving through the darkness, his heart raced. After he walked for several minutes, he finally left the sound of her choking sobs behind. *Did I really just break up with her?* His hands felt clammy, and his stomach lurched. Cutting through the golf course, he recalled making love with her the summer before in a dark corner near the sixteenth fairway.

At the Simpson's house, he found the key they kept hidden in the lanai that covered the pool. He punched Paige's birth date into the security system to shut off the alarm. In the great room he poured a shot of whiskey and downed it. After two more shots, the liquor finally did its job, and his heart stopped racing. Reaching up to his collar, he tore off the bow tie and went into the kitchen to use the phone.

Ten minutes later, he slammed the phone down after learning he had missed the last flight out that night and the next day was booked solid. "Shit," he said on the way upstairs to the guest room where he shed the monkey suit and took a long shower. With a towel tied around his waist, he lay down on the bed. The whiskey and champagne had given him a buzz, and the room tilted in a nausea-inducing spin. He had ended it with Paige, and now he was trapped in her parents' house. *What a nightmare,* he thought, resting his arm on his forehead.

Once the shock of the night's events lifted, the numbness wore off and Michael began to hurt. They'd had their problems, but he did love her, and suddenly all he could think about was just how much he had once loved her.

The Sunday after they met, he went to Annapolis for brunch with her parents. Afterward, they walked through the Academy campus and along the waterfront in downtown Annapolis. On the way back, Michael stopped her on a quiet sidewalk near the state capital.

"What time did I get here?"

"At eleven. Why?"

He looked at his watch. "Three hours ago."

"Yes," she said, confused. "Do you need to leave?"

"No, but I can't wait one more minute for this." Bringing her into his arms, he kissed her with abandon. He had done more kissing in public with her than in his whole life before her.

She shuddered. "*Michael.*"

"I love that shudder," he whispered in her ear. "I love knowing I can do that to you."

"That's not all you do to me."

Michael's mouth went dry. "What else?"

"My stomach flips, my hands sweat, and I—"

He tightened his hold on her. "What?"

"I ache for you," she said shyly.

"Where?" His voice was hoarse and rough.

She held his eyes with hers and tilted her hips against his erection. "Here."

With a fierce groan, Michael buried his face in her fragrant hair. "Come home with me. Now."

"It's too soon. We can't."

"I've never wanted anyone the way I want you. I haven't slept since I met you, Paige. You're all I think about. I can't study. I can't work. I can't do anything but want you." He steered her into an alley between two colonial houses and pressed her against one of them to kiss her again, leaving her with no doubt as to how much he wanted her. "Please," he said, kissing her neck. "Come home with me. Let me make love to you."

"Yes," she panted, clinging to him. "Yes, take me home with you, Michael."

He kissed her again and took her hand to run back to his car at her parents' house. They were breathless by the time they got there, and he waited with impatience while she hurried in to tell her mother they were going for a drive. When she got in the car, he broke speed records driving to Georgetown. In the elevator, he was almost afraid to touch her on the way to his sixth-floor apartment.

But once the door closed behind them, they were both hit with nerves they hadn't expected.

"Can I get you anything?"

"No, I'm fine."

She startled when he came up behind her. "Relax, honey. I was just going to take your coat."

"I'm sorry." She shrugged off her coat. "I like your place."

"Thanks."

"You're a neat-nik."

He shrugged. "I guess. Law school keeps me disciplined. I'm afraid if I let things slide, it'll snowball on me."

She picked up one of the textbooks on his desk. "Is it as hard as they say it is?"

"Harder."

The word hung in the air between them.

She put the book down and turned to him.

"Come here," he said. When her cheeks flushed with color, any doubt he had that he'd fallen in love with her faded away as she took the first tentative step toward him.

He met her halfway, put his arms around her, and held her tight against him.

She turned her face up, and their mouths met in a hot and hungry frenzy.

Michael trembled at the feel of her hands on his back under his sweater. When he couldn't bear the pain of wanting her another minute, he swept her up into his arms to carry her to his bedroom. But as he brought her down onto the bed, something flashed through her eyes that stopped him cold.

He caressed her face. "Paige? What is it? Are you afraid?"

"A little."

"Of me?"

"No," she whispered.

"Then what?"

"This. All of it."

"Why?"

She looked away from him, and his stomach knotted with understanding. With a finger to her chin, he brought her back to him. "Is this your first time?"

Again her cheeks flushed with color as she nodded.

"*Oh*." He fell onto his back when all the oxygen seemed to leave his body in one big rush. "Oh God, and I've been like a lunatic with you. Jesus."

"You haven't. Don't say that, Michael."

Seeing that she was on the verge of tears, he turned onto his side and put an arm around her.

"I'm sorry. I didn't realize. The way you kiss me—"

She ran a finger over his lips. "I've never kissed anyone quite the way I kiss you. It's like I'm someone else with you."

And there it was again, the dizzying rush of lust that obliterated every rational thought in his mind.

"How come you've never done this before? Surely you've had boyfriends. Lots of them."

She shrugged. "I've never loved any of them."

With his heart in his throat, he asked, "And do you love me?"

"Yes." Her eyes full of wonder, she reached up to caress his face. "I really do."

"I can't believe it, but I love you, too. And I want you so much." He kissed each of her fingers. "But not until you're ready. I don't want you to be afraid."

"I'm ready, Michael. I want it to be with you. Now."

"You're sure?" His heart pounded as he worked to summon the tenderness he would need for her.

Her eager hands moved on his chest under his sweater. "Show me. Show me what to do."

He undressed her slowly, taking the time to worship each new discovery. Their clothes were soon in a pile on the floor. Her breathless sighs and gasps were driving him mad, but he held back the need to devour. Sliding his fingers through the dampness between her legs, he carefully prepared her and then focused on the spot that throbbed for him.

She came with a shriek that startled both of them.

Gasping, she clutched his shoulders. "God," she whispered, aftershocks rippling through her.

With a chuckle, he said, "You're a screamer."

"That's news to me."

He turned away from her to roll on a condom. "I don't want to hurt you."

"I hear it's only bad for a second."

"Stop me if it hurts."

She tensed as he pushed into her.

"Try to relax, honey," he whispered.

When she wrapped her legs around him, he again struggled to hold back urges he'd never felt quite so strongly before.

She, on the other hand, held nothing back as she moved beneath him. Before long her breathing became more frantic. "Oh!" she cried. "Oh, *Michael*, don't stop!" She came again with another scream that snapped his control and sent him into a devastating release that left him completely drained.

Michael ached when he thought of that first time with her. In the months leading up to graduation, they spent every minute they could in his bed where her eagerness more than made up for her lack of experience. It had been madness and passion and lust. And love. Definitely love. But the madness never really abated.

They hit the first of many bumps the weekend of graduation when Admiral Simpson announced he had arranged a job for Michael with his friend, the state's attorney in Baltimore City. Michael had been furious, and the moment he was alone in the car with Paige he told her so.

"I just wanted you to stay here, so when Daddy told me about the job in Baltimore it seemed like the perfect solution."

"Damn it, Paige, don't give me that pout face. It might work with 'Daddy,' but it does nothing for me."

With a coy smile, she ran a hand up his leg. "It doesn't do *anything* for you?"

He pushed her hand away. "Stop." He'd fumed about the interference for a week before he took the job, which was the only offer he received in the capital area. Truth be told, he wanted to stay near Paige as much as she wanted to keep him close. But the Admiral's meddling rankled, especially since he never missed an opportunity to remind Michael of how he got his job.

The next bump occurred at graduation when Michael's mother and sisters took an immediate and intense dislike to Paige—an opinion they never wavered from in four years. "She's not for you," his mother had said.

As Michael fell into a restless sleep in the Simpson's guestroom, he heard his mother saying, "She's not for you." He dreamed of Paige, and as usual, they were making love. Her hands and lips were everywhere on his fevered skin. Then he was inside her, moving with the abandon that overtook him every time they made love. Only when he reached an explosive climax did he realize he wasn't dreaming. As if he'd been scalded, he pulled out of her and rolled away. "*What the fuck? What are you doing?*"

"I love you." Sobs rattled her petite frame. "I just needed you so much."

"Jesus Christ, I was asleep." Another realization settled in on him. "No condom, Paige! What the *fuck?*" They had never taken any chances in that department. His head spun, and his stomach lurched from the booze.

She reached for him. "Michael, please. Talk to me."

He pulled away from her, got up, went into the bathroom, and slammed the door behind him. *Goddamn it!* Splashing cold water on his face, he tried to contain the urge to choke the life out of her. When he came out of the bathroom, he pulled on sweats.

"Aren't you going to talk to me?" she asked between sobs.

"I'm all done talking. You need to go to your room."

"You're not breaking off this engagement, Michael."

"I'm quite certain I already did."

"*You can't!*" she wailed.

He picked up her robe off the floor and threw it at her. "Get dressed. Right now. I've had enough for tonight." He watched her work up a head of steam as she pulled on the robe.

"I don't know who you think you're dealing with, but you are *not* just walking away from me after four years like I mean nothing to you."

"I know *exactly* who I'm dealing with—a spoiled, pampered brat. You're not going to push me around or push me into a job I don't want. And you're *certainly* not going to push me into a marriage I no longer want."

She slapped his face. Hard. "You son of a bitch."

His hand rolled into a fist at his side. "Get out," he said in a low tone that left no room for negotiation. "*Get the fuck out!*"

After she slammed the door behind her, he did something he should have done earlier: he reached for his cell phone to call a cab. He threw on clothes, packed his bag, and went down the stairs into the quiet house.

Admiral Simpson appeared in the darkness. "Going somewhere, Michael?"

"I'm going home."

"Are you sure you want to do that?"

"I'm positive."

"So when Paige said you'd called off the engagement she wasn't being dramatic?"

"No."

"You might want to think twice about that."

"Are you threatening me?"

"Of course not. I'm just wondering if you're seeing the big picture."

"And what would that be?"

"What will Tom Houlihan think of having a man on his team who doesn't keep his promises? Have you thought about that?"

"You know what? I don't give a rat's ass what Tom Houlihan thinks about my private life. Feel free to give him a call."

The cab driver tooted the horn.

The Admiral gave Michael the steely stare that had intimidated legions of sailors, but it had no effect on him. Not anymore. "You're not the man I thought you were, Michael."

"That's funny because you're *exactly* the man I thought you were. Take care, Admiral."

Michael checked into a hotel near the airport and fell into a deep, dreamless sleep. He woke up late the next morning, the events of the day before replaying in his mind. And then he smiled. He was free—of Paige and her parents and their endless manipulation. Imagining his mother dancing a jig at the news of his broken engagement, he laughed.

Chapter 8

ON THE WAY TO THE AIRPORT ON SUNDAY AFTERNOON, Jeremy and Juliana stopped for seafood in Jacksonville Beach. The day was warm so they sat on a deck overlooking the ocean.

After they ate, Jeremy reached across the table for her hand. "What are we going to do, babe?"

Juliana took a long sip of her wine, put the glass down on the table, and met his gaze. "We're breaking up. For now." She had promised herself she wouldn't cry.

"What?" he asked, startled.

"Three months. We won't talk to or see each other for three months."

"Juliana—"

"I've thought about what you said."

"I want you to forget what I said."

"I can't. And we can't go forward with it between us. You were right about something yesterday."

"What's that?"

"Neither of us has ever been with anyone else, so how can we know for sure that what we have will last?"

"It's lasted ten years. That has to count for something."

She squeezed his hand. "It does. But like you said, how do we even know that we're having good sex?"

"You can say that after last night?"

"I'm just agreeing with you, Jer. That's all."

"Why three months? Why not one or two?"

"Because anything less wouldn't be enough time."

He thought it over for a moment. "Supposing I agree to this, what are the rules?"

"No rules. We're both single and can do whatever we want."

He raised an eyebrow. "But you're not going to, you know—"

"You can, but I can't?"

"You said you never wanted to."

"That was before I knew you did."

He dropped her hand. "This is bullshit. I'm not agreeing to this."

"Then we're done. I won't spend my life with you wondering if you're unsatisfied or unfulfilled, or worse yet, unfaithful. I watched my father cheat on my mother for years before he finally left. I won't live like that."

"So either we break up for three months or we break up forever? That's a hell of a choice."

"It's up to you."

"What would happen at the end of the three months?"

"We either end it for good or we get married."

"And would we discuss what happened during the three months?"

"Never."

With a deep sigh, he sat back in his chair. "This is a pretty high-stakes game you're playing here, Jule."

"It's no game, and it's the hardest thing I've ever done. I can't imagine a day without talking to you, let alone ninety of them. But I don't know what else to do." Her stiff resolve crumbled, and her eyes filled.

"This is all my fault." His face tightened with tension. "The idea of you with someone else…"

"I know."

He checked his watch. "Damn it. We have to go."

"So what do you say?"

"You haven't given me much of a choice. Since I'm not prepared to lose you forever, I guess we're breaking up for three months." He threw some cash on the table and guided her from the restaurant.

They drove to the airport in silence, but he kept a firm grip on her hand. He walked her in, and when he couldn't go any further with her, he folded her into a long hug. "I'll miss you. Every minute of every day, I'll be thinking about you."

The huge lump in her throat made it impossible for her to speak so she just nodded.

"Three months," he said with tears in his eyes. "Not one minute more."

"Okay."

"I'll call you three months from today."

She nodded.

He tilted her chin up and kissed her with a fierce, possessive passion that left her breathless and then despondent when it ended. "Don't go falling in love with someone else."

"I won't. I couldn't. Don't you, either."

"Never," he said, letting her go with great reluctance.

"Three months," she said one last time as she moved into the security line.

"Not one minute more." He watched her until she was through to the other side.

She waved, blew a kiss, and walked away.

Michael found her halfway down the long concourse twenty minutes later. She sat on the floor against a wall with her face pressed into her arms, but he remembered that shiny dark hair. He sat down next to her. "Hey."

Startled, she looked over at him and didn't seem to recognize him for a second, probably because he was wearing a sweater and jeans rather than a suit. "Oh, hi," she said, wiping tears from her face.

"I take it things didn't go well." Even with her soft brown eyes swollen from crying, Michael thought she was nothing short of exotic.

She shook her head as a fresh wave of sobs overtook her.

Her misery touched him, and with only the slightest of hesitations he put his arm around her.

For a few minutes she rested against him and then seemed to realize she was crying all over someone she hardly knew. She sat up. "I'm sorry."

"Don't be. Do you want to talk about it?"

She shrugged.

"You might feel better unloading on a stranger you'll never see again."

"That's true."

"I have three sisters," he said with a coaxing grin. "I'm a good listener."

She returned his grin with a weak one of her own.

He stood up and offered her a hand. "First we have to get to the gate, or we're going to miss our plane."

"Good thing you came along." She wiped her face. "I probably would've still been here when it took off."

"Maguire to the rescue." He pulled her up and tossed her carry-on bag over his shoulder with his own bag.

"How was your weekend?" she asked on the way to the gate where the plane was boarding.

He smiled. "Total disaster, but you first. What happened?"

While they stood in line to board the plane, she told him the whole story.

"Hmm." He scratched at the stubble on his chin. "So what happens at the end of the three months?" Michael took her boarding pass and handed both of them to the gate agent.

"I told him we'll either break up for good or get married."

"What if he meets someone else?"

Juliana winced.

"Sorry."

"I know it's a big gamble, but how could I marry him knowing he has all this curiosity about other women?"

"How will you marry him without knowing if he acted on it?"

They found seats together on the plane. "Why couldn't I have just let it go? Why did I have to make such a big deal out of it? He said if it was a choice between me and sowing his wild oats, he'd choose me."

"So then why'd you insist on the separation?"

Juliana looked out the window for a moment before she answered him. "My father cheated on my mother for years. Everyone knew it. Even she knew, but she ignored it because he always came back. Then I guess he fell for one of them because we haven't seen him in five years."

"I'm sorry."

She shrugged. "It's old news now, but that's not how I want to live. Just the idea of it…"

"Then you did the right thing. At the end of the three months you'll know where you stand with each other, and you can figure out where to go from there."

Her eyes sparkled with tears. "There hasn't been a day in the last ten years that I haven't talked to him. Not one day."

Michael reached for her hand. "You'll be okay. I'll bet you're tougher than you think. The time will just fly by."

"Yeah, sure."

Michael kept her hand between both of his as the plane raced down the runway and took off into a sky streaked by the setting sun.

"Thank you," she said when they were airborne.

"For what?"

"Listening and offering comfort. I'll bet you'd make a good friend."

"I wish there was something I could say to make you feel better."

"You're helping. You got me on the plane, right?"

He laughed. "Yes, I guess I did."

"Tell me about your disaster. Give me something else to think about."

He sighed and released her hand.

"That bad?"

"Thermonuclear meltdown."

She turned to him. "What happened?"

"I broke off the engagement."

She gasped. "Oh my God! Before or after the party?"

"During," he said with a sheepish grin.

"No way. *You did not!*"

"I did," he said, relaying the story of the weekend from hell.

"Jeez," she said when he was done. "We should've started with you. I don't know what to say. Are you okay?"

"I think I am. Maybe in a day or two when it has time to register I won't be, but I know I did the right thing. I can't be marching to her father's drum my whole life. It wouldn't have bothered me half as much if she'd tried to stop it, but she was only thinking of herself. Nothing new there."

"It's always disappointing when someone turns out to be less than you thought they were."

He appreciated that she understood completely. "Yes, it is. But it's my own fault. I've pushed aside doubts for a long time because underneath it all, I was crazy about her. I proposed to her when her parents were moving, hoping she'd stay in Maryland with me. She accepted the proposal and moved anyway. That should've been a sign of where her priorities were—or where they *weren't*."

Juliana rested a comforting hand on his arm.

The stewardess came by to offer drinks.

"This time it's on me," Juliana insisted, ordering him the same kind of beer he had gotten on the first flight and a gin and tonic for herself. "Make it a double," she added.

He laughed. "When in pain, drink."

"That's my mother's philosophy of life. Unfortunately for us, she's in constant pain."

"Ouch," he winced. "Sorry."

She shrugged. "It is what it is."

He lifted his beer can in to toast her. "Here's to a disastrous weekend and new friends."

"To new friends."

The plane landed at Baltimore/Washington International Airport just after nine. They walked through the terminal to catch a shuttle bus to the parking lot.

"Which lot are you in?" he asked.

"Long-term A."

He chuckled. "Me, too."

"Of course you are," she said with a smile.

On the shuttle, Michael reached for his wallet and dug out a business card, which he handed to Juliana. "Call me if you need a friendly ear. My cell number is on there, too."

"Thank you. Stop by the salon if you decide to cut that mop of yours."

He ran a hand through his hair. "You think it needs it?"

"Uh, *yeah*. Now that you're back on the market, the ladies will think you're hot without all that hair."

Flustered, he said, "You think so?"

"Uh huh," she said, making a scissor gesture with her fingers.

"I just might take you up on that."

"I hope you do. I really am sorry about your fiancée."

"Thanks. Things work out the way they're supposed to, you know?"

"I guess I'll find out in three months. Oh, this is where I get off."

He looked up with a grin. "Me, too."

As they were getting off the shuttle, his cell phone rang. He was relieved to see it wasn't Paige calling again. He had been ignoring her calls all day. "I've got to take this," he said reluctantly. "It's work."

"Good luck with the trial. I'll be pulling for you."

He gave her a quick one-armed hug and answered the phone. "Hey," he said into the phone. "Hang on a sec." Holding the phone aside, he turned back to Juliana. "Take care of yourself."

"You, too. Thanks. For listening and everything."

"My pleasure."

Waving, she unlocked her battered Toyota Tercel and tossed her bag into the backseat.

Chapter 9

On the way to his car, Michael took the call. "What's up?"

"We've got a problem in the District." His co-worker and second chair George Samuels sounded aggravated.

Michael stopped walking. "What kind of problem?"

"She's having a hissy fit. Wants to see you and only you."

"Oh, come on! Can't you guys settle her down? What about her mother? Has she been there today?"

"From what I hear, the mother's being an even bigger pain in the ass. You'd better get down there, Michael."

"For Christ's sake, I just got back from Florida."

"She's been acting up since Friday, but the boss told us to leave you alone this weekend."

"Fine. I'll be there in an hour." He flipped his phone closed. "Damn it!" All he wanted was to go home, put his feet up, and catch his breath after everything that had happened. Just then he heard a clicking noise and turned to see where it was coming from.

Juliana's forehead rested against the steering wheel of a car that wouldn't start.

Michael walked over to her open window. "This day just gets better and better, huh?"

"You said it."

"Can I give you a jump?"

"I don't think it'll help. I was supposed to buy a new battery but never got around to it."

"Then let me give you a lift."

"Are you sure you don't mind?"

"Not at all, but I have to go into D.C. before I go home. Will it screw you up to get home pretty late?"

She shook her head. "I don't have to work tomorrow, so I'm in no rush. I came home tonight because Jeremy has to work tomorrow. I guess I can deal with this in the morning," she said with a frustrated gesture at the old car. "Just another insult in an insulting day."

Grinning, he said, "Grab your bag."

After she locked her car, he led her to his silver Audi TT coupe.

"*Oh*, is that yours?" she asked with wide-eyed admiration.

"My one major splurge," he confessed.

"It's gorgeous."

"Thanks." He tossed their bags into the trunk and walked around to open the passenger door for her.

"Why do you have to go to D.C.?"

He leaned against the open car door. "Well, here's the thing: I'll tell you, but it's imperative you don't tell anyone you went there with me, okay? Someone's life depends on it."

"Of course. I won't tell anyone."

Hesitating, he realized he was about to take a woman he met on an airplane to see a witness in protective custody. But his gut told him he could trust her, and he trusted his gut.

She looked up at him with those captivating eyes. "I won't tell anyone, Michael. You have my word."

He nodded, closed her door, and walked around to get in.

"The witness to the Benedetti shootings is fifteen years old and a handful," he explained as they left the airport parking lot and headed south. "We have her in protective custody in D.C. She's giving our guys some trouble, and they need me to talk to her. She has, well, how can I put this…"

Juliana laughed at his pained expression. "She has a crush on you, does she?"

"She seems to have a soft spot for me. That's all I'll admit to."

"I love it," she said with a giggle.

"I'm glad you're entertained. She's a pain in my ass." Exiting the Baltimore-Washington Parkway, Michael cut down New York Avenue on the way to Interstate 395.

"Why do you keep looking in the mirror?" Juliana asked.

"We have to be careful we don't lead anyone to her. There're people who we believe would harm her to keep her from testifying."

"Oh." Juliana turned around to look behind them. "I don't see anyone."

"Yeah, it's late on a Sunday. I think we're good. Besides, they think I'm out of town."

"They watch *you?*" Juliana asked, horrified.

"I've sensed a presence lately, but I haven't actually seen anyone."

"God," she sighed. "Your job is dangerous. I never would've thought that."

"It's not usually. This trial has gotten a lot of attention, which has thrust me into the spotlight—against my will, I might add. I hate all the media crap that goes along with this kind of case. All I care about is keeping Rachelle safe."

"What happens to her after the trial?"

"Witness protection. We've already put her family in the wind. Since she's a minor, we've kept her mother close by until the trial, but the rest of them are gone."

"Wow. I just cut hair."

He laughed. "Right about now, I think that would be a wonderful profession."

"I'll bet you do. What's she like?"

"Rachelle?"

Juliana nodded.

"She's a great kid who was in the wrong place at the wrong time. Her aunt lives in the apartment complex where the shootings went down. She was there visiting and ran out to her mother's car to get something. She saw the whole thing."

"And suddenly my troubles seem so insignificant."

"It does have that effect, doesn't it?" He pulled into the parking lot of a 7–11. "I'll be right back. Do you need anything?"

"No, I'm good. Thanks."

He came back a few minutes later. "Blackmail," he said, handing her the bag so she could see that he had bought all the latest gossip magazines, a *Glamour,* a *Cosmo,* four candy bars, two packs of gum, and six scratch-off lottery tickets.

"That's quite a care package."

"I spoil her. That's why she likes me."

"If that's what you have to tell yourself."

"What does that mean?"

"She thinks you're *cute*," Juliana said in a singsong voice.

"Oh, shut up."

She was still laughing when he pulled up to the J.W. Marriott on the corner of Fourteenth Street and Pennsylvania Avenue. "How close are we to the White House?" she asked.

"A few blocks that way."

"I don't know why I never think to spend a day here. It's only an hour from Baltimore."

Michael showed the hotel security his I.D. card, and they were waved in. "I loved living here when I was in law school. It's my favorite city."

A police officer stood guard in the fifth-floor hallway.

"Hey, Michael." The cop grimaced. "The brat's on fire."

"So I hear. I'll see what I can do to settle her down."

"We'd all appreciate it." Using his key card to open the door, the cop nodded at Juliana. "Who's she?"

"She's with me. It's cool."

The hotel room looked like a teenager's closet had exploded in it.

Michael groaned at the mess. "Rachelle!"

Through the door from the adjoining room came a tall, gorgeous girl with coffee-colored skin and a wild mass of dark curly hair. She wore skin-tight jeans and a hot pink T-shirt with sequins that spelled "Queen Bee" across her small breasts. Her face lit up when she saw Michael. "You're here! What'd you bring me?"

He kept the bag hidden behind his back. "Girls who can't behave don't get presents. And from what I hear, that's a very appropriate shirt for you, Queen Bee."

Rachelle reached behind him to see what he had for her. "Give it up!"

"Ah!" Michael held the bag out of reach. "What are you going to do for me?"

"Who's she?" Rachelle asked with a sullen glance at Juliana.

"My friend, Juliana. Be polite and shake her hand."

"Pleased to meet you," Juliana said.

Rachelle did as she was told and shook Juliana's hand. "Is she the *fiancée?*"

Michael tweaked her nose. "No, busybody, she's not."

Rachelle gave him a saucy smile. "Does *the fiancée* know you have *friends?*"

Michael sent Juliana an exasperated glance, which cracked her up.

"Let's focus on your behavior, not mine, okay?" Michael said.

"I'd rather talk about yours," Rachelle pouted.

"Why are you giving everyone such a hard time?"

"I'm so bored! This place *sucks!* I'm sick of being here. I miss my friends. I miss my family. I even miss school. It *sucks.*"

He put an arm around her and brought her to sit with him on the bed. "I know. It totally sucks. But the trial starts in one more week, and I'm going to get you in there just as soon as I can, okay?"

"I heard them talking today. It can take weeks just to pick the jury."

Michael swore under his breath. "They aren't supposed to be talking about the trial where you can hear them."

"I hear everything. I want to see my dad and my brothers."

"We've talked about that. As soon as you testify, we'll reunite you all. I promise."

She kicked at the carpet. "I wish you came to visit more often."

"I'll try to get down here again this week if you promise to behave. You're not the only one who doesn't want to be here, okay?"

She nodded. "I'm very sorry, and I promise to behave. So what's in the bag?"

He chuckled and handed it to her. "That was *so* sincere."

Reacting with glee, she examined everything he had brought her and then embarrassed him when she kissed his cheek. "Thank you."

"You're welcome. If you win anything on the scratch-offs, I get half."

"Bite me. A gift's a gift."

He laughed and looked up at Juliana to share the amusement.

"You know what might be fun?" she asked.

"What's that?" Michael said.

"I could do your hair for you, Rachelle. I'm a stylist, and I'd be happy to give you a wash and blow dry if you want."

Rachelle's eyes lit up. "Really? Like now?"

Juliana glanced at Michael. "Thirty minutes?"

With a grateful smile he gestured for her to have at it and went into the adjoining room to talk to the other cops on Rachelle's detail.

Juliana took the girl into the bathroom to wash her hair in the sink. She gave her the full treatment with a scalp massage and deep conditioning, making use of the products scattered about on the cluttered vanity. "Feel good?" Juliana asked.

"Mmm. Really good. Where do you work?"

"At Panache in Baltimore."

"I went there once with my aunt. It was awesome. Is it a fun place to work?"

"It is. I like it."

"I love your jeans. Are they Juicy Couture?"

"As a matter of fact, they are," Juliana said, amused.

"How do you know Michael?"

"You won't believe it, but we met on an airplane."

"So are you guys going out?"

Juliana smiled at the jealousy she detected from the girl. "No, we're really just friends." For the first time in two hours she thought of Jeremy and their mess. If she hadn't come with Michael she would probably be home alone crying. "I have a boyfriend."

"You'll have to tell me all about him. I can't wait to have a boyfriend."

Hardly anxious to talk about Jeremy at the moment, Juliana rolled a thick towel around Rachelle's hair and helped her stand up. "Have a seat at my station." Juliana gestured to the closed toilet.

"Very classy."

"Only the best. Which side do you part it on?"

Rachelle laughed. "I have no idea. It's totally out of control."

Juliana grabbed a large-toothed comb and a round brush from the chaos on the countertop. "Let's see what we can do about that."

Thirty minutes later Michael came looking for them and stopped short in the doorway to the bathroom. "Where's Rachelle?"

The girl giggled. "I don't know what she did. It's a miracle."

The curls had been tamed into flowing waves that softly framed her face and cascaded down past her shoulders.

"You look beautiful," Michael said. "Really, really beautiful."

Rachelle blushed at the compliment from her favorite guy.

Juliana applied one last squirt of hair spray. "You're all done."

Rachelle gazed into the mirror for another minute before she gripped Juliana in a spontaneous hug. "Thank you so much. I *love* it!"

"My pleasure."

"I wish I had a camera. My mom won't believe this, and I'll never get it to look this good again in my life."

Juliana laughed. "Just do like I showed you with the round brush and the hair dryer. You'll get the hang of it."

"Will you come again?" Rachelle asked. "Michael, will you bring her with you again? We could do our nails or something next time."

Juliana glanced at Michael.

"Sure," he said.

"I'd love to." Juliana gave the girl a quick kiss on the cheek. "It's getting late. You need to get to bed, and we've got to get to Baltimore. I'll only come again if I hear you're being good, all right?"

Rachelle nodded. "I promise."

"Behave, brat." Michael bopped her lightly on the shoulder. "I mean it."

"Again you force me to say bite me!"

"Go to bed," Michael ordered as he closed the door.

"How'd you make out?" the police officer in the hall asked.

"I think we settled her down," Michael said. "But go easy on her, okay? This is tough on her, and our case is riding on her."

"You've got it, Michael. Don't worry."

Michael shook his hand. "Thanks."

"Are they Baltimore cops or D.C.?" Juliana asked while they waited for the elevator.

Michael held the door for her and then stepped in behind her. "Baltimore. They're all on special assignment, but the District cops know they're here in case they need backup."

"She's adorable."

"I know."

"She's got you firmly wrapped around her little finger. You're aware of that, right?"

"Yes," he said with a sigh. "I'm way more involved with her than I should be."

"It would be hard to stay detached from her."

"Thank you, Juliana. You did such a wonderful thing for her."

"I enjoyed it."

"Yes, I could see that." When he walked in on them in the bathroom, Juliana had been totally engrossed in

Rachelle. He couldn't imagine Paige ever being so self-less. "I really appreciate it."

"It was fun," she insisted. "You don't have to thank me."

"I don't know about you, but I haven't thought about any of my problems for a few hours."

She smiled at him. "Neither have I."

Chapter 10

THEY HAD THE USUALLY CLOGGED BALTIMORE-Washington Parkway all to themselves on the way back to Baltimore. The closer they got to the city, the quieter Juliana became.

"How're you doing over there?"

She shrugged.

"You should probably tell me where you live."

"Butchers Hill. Collington Street."

He laughed. "You do *not!*"

"Why?

"I live on Chester."

"You're kidding me! I can't believe we've never seen each other in the neighborhood."

"I know. How long have you lived there?"

"Four years. It used to be Jeremy's mother's house, but she got remarried and moved to Texas. He bought the house from her. What about you?"

"I lucked into an amazing rowhouse about a year ago. I lived in an apartment across the street, and I got to be friends with the guy who owned the rowhouse when he was renovating it. He got transferred unexpectedly and needed to sell it fast, so he gave me a sweet deal on it. He said he wanted it to go to someone who would take good care of it."

"What a great story."

"It's way too big for just me, but when I bought it

I thought Paige would live there with me eventually. Oh well."

"You wouldn't be interested in…" Juliana stopped herself with a shake of her head.

"What?"

"Nothing. Just a ridiculous thought."

"Tell me. Come on."

"I was going to ask if you might be interested in a roommate, but that's insane."

"Why?"

"We barely know each other."

"I meant why do you want to live somewhere else?"

"With everything that's going on now with Jeremy, I can't stand the thought of spending even one night in the house he pays for. If I went to stay with one of my friends, I'd have to explain why I'd left our place."

"I'm sure you contribute your share."

She looked down at her hands. "Here and there. I pay my mother's mortgage, so I don't have a lot of extra money. That's why I shouldn't have mentioned being roommates. I can't afford it."

"Why do you pay your mother's mortgage?"

"It's a long story," she said, hesitating. "Basically it's either that or she ends up homeless. When my father split, he cleaned out the bank account. We hired an investigator to try to find him, but he's long gone."

"For what it's worth, I'd love to have you as my roommate," Michael said, sensing she didn't want to talk about her deadbeat father. "We already get along better than most of the people I've lived with, and I'm hardly ever there anyway. I've got a big place, and I only use a fraction of it. You're welcome to it if it would help you out for a while."

"You're sweet, but it's a crazy idea. Besides, I really can't afford it."

"I don't need the money, but I wouldn't mind the company."

She turned to look at him. "You're serious."

"Sure I am," he said, taking the Inner Harbor exit off Interstate 95.

"I'd have to pay you something."

He shrugged. "Whatever. I don't care. So is that a yes?"

After a long moment of silence, she suddenly said, "Yes. Yes, I'd love that."

"What's wrong now?" he asked when her smile faded.

"It's kind of... you know... embarrassing."

"What is?"

"The reason Jeremy and I are taking this break. I've decided not to tell anyone about it because then people would know I wasn't... well... enough for him," she ended on a whisper.

Michael reached over to squeeze her hand. "He's a fool."

"Maybe I'm the one who's been the fool."

"I don't think so. Shall we go home?"

"Now?"

"Why not? You've got stuff with you, right? Will anyone be trying to get in touch with you tonight?"

"No, we both have cell phones. We don't have a phone in the house."

"Cool. You can get whatever else you need tomorrow then. And after work we can go get your car."

She laughed.

"What's so funny?"

"I just feel better all of a sudden."

"Good."

"Oh, Michael, this place is amazing!" Juliana ran a hand over the exposed brick wall in the living room. Like most rowhouses, it was tall and deep. The living room fed into the dining room, which led to the kitchen. There were gleaming hardwood floors and a fireplace with a mahogany mantle.

"Thanks, but I can't take any of the credit. The guy who owned it before me did all the work. Check this out." He opened a door where three stairs led to a small bathroom with dark red walls and the tiniest pedestal sink Juliana had ever seen.

"It's so cute!" She did a double take. "Is that a *phone?*"

Michael chuckled. "He put one in every bathroom. You'll never miss a call in this house." He led her to the kitchen where cabinets were suspended from the ceiling over slate countertops.

"Oh, wow! What a great kitchen."

"Isn't it?" He opened the stainless steel fridge and peered inside. "I have beer, water, and beer."

"Um, I'll have a beer."

"Good choice."

He opened two of them and handed one to her.

"Don't feel like you have to entertain me. I'm sure you want to get to bed."

"I'm kind of keyed up, actually. Let's go upstairs."

The stairs were in the living room. On the second floor,

he showed her to a guestroom with a bathroom. "The sheets are clean, and there're towels in the bathroom."

She dropped her bag on the bed. "Thanks."

The second bedroom was a combination home office and gym.

"Do you use the Bowflex or does it collect dust like ours does?"

"I haven't used it much lately," he confessed. "Come see my view."

She followed him up another flight of stairs to his bedroom on the top floor. The room and adjoining bathroom took up the entire third floor. "This is beautiful."

"It's my favorite part of the house." He walked over to slide open the door to a deck and gestured for her to come out with him.

"You can see the whole city!"

"It gets better." He pointed to wooden stairs and took her up to the roof deck.

Gazing down at the lights of Fell's Point and the Inner Harbor, she said, "What a view."

"Sometimes I still can't believe I live here. I grew up in a tiny house crammed with people. I feel like I can breathe here." He stretched out on one of the lounge chairs and invited her to take the other.

She kicked off her shoes and sat down. "Having something like this to show for it must make all your hard work in law school and now with your job worth it."

"Yes," he said. "It does." He took a long drink from his beer. "Do you know what Paige said the first time she saw this place?"

"What?"

"That the basement was smelly and the carpet was ugly, but she could make it work if she had to."

"And you didn't smack her?"

"She never would've seen it the way you did, how having something like this makes all the hard work worth it." He picked at the label on his beer bottle. "She's never had to work for anything in her life, so she doesn't appreciate anything. Sometimes I felt like I was just another *thing* she had to have."

"Seems like you did the right thing calling it off with her."

"I know I did. All day today I tried not to think about what happened last night, but then it would come back to me with this rush of pain. It's strange. She made me so mad, yet still it hurts so much. Why do you suppose that is?"

"Because you loved her, and she let you down. You're probably disappointed more than anything."

"Probably." He finished his beer in one long swallow. "She hit me."

"*What?* She *hit* you?"

"After the party when she finally got that I meant it when I said it was over between us." He brushed a hand over his face. "I can almost still feel it."

"Someone needs to smack her," Juliana said with indignation.

"We're quite a pair, huh?"

She laughed. "We're a two-person support group for losers in love."

He rested his head back against the lounge chair and smiled at her. "I'm glad you're here."

"I am, too."

Juliana woke up disoriented the next morning in the strange bedroom with the blue walls and curtains—until the events of the day before came rushing back to her. *What am I doing here? I can't stay with a guy I met on an airplane! I must've lost my mind while I was in Florida.* She got up to make the bed, straighten the room, and get dressed. Tossing the last of her belongings into her bag, her hand brushed against the ivory silk nightgown she bought just last week with Jeremy in mind. An intense ache streaked through her when she imagined him with the faceless Sherrie. Had he acted yet on his newfound freedom?

Juliana sat on the bed to catch her breath and fought the urge to call him. Was it too much to want to hear his voice like she had every morning for so long? "You will *not* call him." Determined, she stood up, zipped her bag, and went downstairs. In the kitchen she looked for some paper to leave a note for Michael and instead found one from him sitting next to a key on the counter.

"Good morning! I made coffee for you. All you have to do is press start on the coffeemaker. There's cereal in the cabinet over the stove, otherwise it's slim pickings. Here's a key for the front door. Make yourself at home. Feel free to use the roof deck and anything else you want or need. I should be home by eight, and we can deal with your car then. Call my cell phone if you need anything (the number is on the card I gave you). Have a good day! M"

Juliana read it again. He was such a nice guy, and it made her mad all over again to imagine his fiancée hitting him. He didn't deserve that. What he *did* deserve was a friend. Standing there with his note in her hand, she thought of some things she could do to help him out while he was working crazy hours. Since she couldn't pay him much rent, she could do the grocery shopping, cooking, and laundry. Maybe this would work out well for both of them. He'd give her a place to hide out for a while, and she would make his life easier during the trial. She put the key in her pocket and hit "start" on the coffeemaker.

Michael's day began at seven in a meeting with the jury consultants they'd hired to help them empanel the twelve citizens most likely to convict the Benedettis. They pored over demographic reports, census information, and a PowerPoint presentation that outlined the consultants' idea of the perfect jury.

We'll never get it, Michael thought.

The defense had an ideal jury of its own, and he could guarantee it looked nothing like the one on the screen. In one week, the battle would begin. If they were lucky, they would get half the ideal citizens the consultants identified.

With the meeting heading into a fourth hour, Michael excused himself and left it in the capable hands of his second chair, George Samuels.

Michael had just returned to his office when Tom Houlihan knocked on the door. The picture of an up-and-coming politician, Tom had close-cropped blond hair, blue eyes, and a boyish face that made him look much younger than his fifty years. Michael respected the hell out of the guy and didn't like the expression on Tom's face as he closed the door.

"What's up?" Michael leaned back in his desk chair and gestured for his boss to take a seat.

"I heard you had quite a weekend."

"He didn't waste any time," Michael said through gritted teeth.

"He's upset. His daughter's upset. His wife's upset."

Michael hated having this conversation with his boss, of all people.

Tom put both hands on Michael's desk. "Here's the deal, Michael. Your personal life is none of my business, and I told the Admiral the same thing. What *is* my business is the trial you're starting one week from today. You've just broken up with your fiancée, and I wouldn't be doing my job if I didn't ask whether your head's in the game the way it needs to be right now."

Michael didn't blink when he replied. "It is. The trial is all I'm thinking about. You don't need to give it another thought."

Tom studied him for a long moment before he said, "Good. You know my door's always open if there's anything I can do for you in the next few weeks."

"Thanks, Tom."

"Oh, just one other thing. I saw the report this morning from Rachelle's detail. You had someone with you last night who wasn't on the list. What's up with that?"

"She's a friend who was with me when George called me in. Rachelle took a liking to her and wants me to bring her again. I'll get her on the list."

"I don't have to remind you to be careful."

"I'd never do anything to endanger her, Tom."

"I know." Tom hesitated before he added, "Are you all right? You know, the thing with Paige and all…"

"I'm fine. Thanks for asking."

Tom nodded. "Carry on then."

As Michael watched him leave, his cell phone vibrated on his desk. He checked the caller ID to find that Paige was calling again and ignored it. She had left six hysterical messages on his voice mail since he left her house on Saturday night, and he had no plans to call her back. He had twenty minutes until a meeting with his ballistics witness, which was just enough time to review the report one more time.

The phone on his desk rang. "Maguire." He pulled the file he needed from a sloping pile.

"Michael."

He groaned. "Not now, Paige."

"You have to talk to me."

"I don't *have* to do anything."

"But we're engaged…"

"We're *not* engaged. Not any more. The wedding is off. I'll talk to you, but not until the trial's over. Not one second before. Am I clear?"

"*What am I supposed to do until then?*"

"Maybe you should spend the time thinking about what you're going to do with your life. It's time you figured that out, don't you think? Now, I have a meeting, and I have to go. Do *not* call me at work again. I mean it, Paige."

"Michael, *please.*"

With a vicious swear, he slammed down the phone.

"Everything all right in there?" his assistant called.

"Yes," he hissed.

❖ ❖ ❖

Juliana let herself into the house on Collington Street
that had been her home for the last four years. As she
shut off the alarm, she almost felt like she was breaking
into Jeremy's house and was amazed at how discon-
nected she felt from him on just her first full day without
him. She checked the mail and paid a few bills from a
joint account they opened when he was sent to Florida.
He provided the money, she wrote the checks.

After the chaos of her family life, Juliana had always
loved this house. Jeremy's mother had taken impeccable
care of it, and they put their own stamp on it. But after
seeing Michael's home, it just seemed boring in compar-
ison. It had none of the charm or style of his place.

Juliana went upstairs to the bedroom and moved fast to
pack what she wanted to take to Michael's. The bedroom
was full of memories—the candles on the bedside table,
the framed photos of her and Jeremy, his clothes hanging
next to hers in the closet. She picked up a photo of them
taken at the beach the summer before. Studying his
tanned, smiling face, she wondered if he had wanted other
women then, too. Breathless from the pain, she put down
the photo and hurried through the packing.

She rushed back downstairs with two bags, weak
with relief that she had found somewhere else to live
for the time being since there was no way she would've
been able to stay in their place after what happened. She
reset the alarm and locked the door. On the walk back to
Michael's house, she took several deep breaths to settle
her rattled nerves.

Making her way up Chester Street, she noticed a man
standing outside of Michael's house, looking up at the front
door. He was young and might have been Hispanic.

"May I help you?" she asked, startling him.

"You live here?"

She nodded.

His eyes narrowed. "Just you?"

A prickle of fear crept down Juliana's spine. "Yes," she said since there were people close enough on the sidewalk to come to her rescue if necessary.

He looked her over again and then walked away.

Juliana hurried up the stairs, her hands shaking as she used the key. Inside, she locked the door, dug Michael's business card out of her purse, and called his cell phone.

"Hi," he said. "Everything going okay?"

"Yes, thanks." She hesitated, wondering if she was overreacting.

"Juliana? What is it?"

"I, um… I had kind of an odd encounter on the street a minute ago, and I thought you should know about it."

"What kind of encounter?"

She relayed the conversation with the man on the street. "I thought of what you said about them watching you, so that's why I told him I live here alone."

"Juliana!" His distress came right through the phone. "I appreciate you trying to protect me, but you shouldn't have put yourself in jeopardy like that! What if he had grabbed you or something? Are you all right?"

"I am now."

"What did he look like?"

She described him.

"Doesn't sound like any of the Benedetti's known associates. Since he didn't really do anything threatening, I can't see the point of calling the cops."

"I guess not. I just thought you should know. Sorry to bother you."

"It's no bother," he said, still sounding rattled. "You were right to call me. Thanks for what you did, but don't do anything like that again. I want you to be careful."

"I will be. Don't worry."

"I'll see you tonight."

Michael hung up with her, picked up his office phone, and dialed Tom Houlihan's direct line.

"Hey, it's Michael. I need you to authorize a cop at my house until the trial is over."

"I thought you'd turned down protection."

"A guy on the street outside my house just asked my roommate if she lives there alone. He gave her the creeps. And I've had the feeling I was being watched a couple of times lately when I was on the street."

"Consider it done," Tom said.

"Thanks."

Chapter 11

AFTER SHE TALKED TO MICHAEL, JULIANA CALLED HER brother Vincent.

"Hey," he said. "Are you back?"

"Sort of."

"What does that mean?"

"My stupid car is dead at the airport. Can you do one more day with Ma? I'll get over there before work tomorrow."

"*Do I have to?* She's been a bear all weekend."

"She's a bear every day. You just don't see it most days. Will you do it?"

"I guess so."

"Thanks," Juliana said, relieved.

"You owe me."

"Don't go there, Vin."

He laughed. "So how's Mr. Wonderful?"

"He's fine."

"Still no ring?"

"Don't go there, either," she said, shutting down one of her brother's favorite subjects. He couldn't understand why Juliana hadn't pushed Jeremy into marriage, which she found ironic since Vincent had been pushed into two disastrous marriages of his own.

"Hey, you know what I always say: if he's getting the milk for free, why buy the cow?" He laughed at his own joke. "Moo."

"That's enough, Vin," she said softly.

"Strike a nerve?"

"I've got to go. Don't forget about Ma."

"Don't forget you owe me. Hey, do you need help with your car?"

Juliana's anger faded a bit at that. "No, thanks. A friend's going to help me. I'll talk to you later."

After she hung up, his words echoed in her mind: why should he buy the cow when he's getting the milk for free? "Yeah, well, it's not my milk he wants!" Juliana shouted to the quiet house. "How does that grab you, Vin? It's not my milk he wants." She'd heard that stupid line from Vincent a million times over the last ten years, but it took on a whole new meaning now.

"I'm not going to do this." Furious with herself, she stood up. "That's enough."

Michael got home just after seven and was greeted by music pulsing through the house and an aroma that made his mouth water. He followed the noise and the smell to the kitchen where Juliana danced about as she tended to a pot on the stove. She moved with the abandon of someone who didn't know she was being watched. Her dark hair, in a high ponytail, swayed in time with the music. Watching her, something stirred deep inside him, the same curious thing he felt when he'd looked over to find her sitting next to him in the airport.

"Hey," he finally said from his post against the door-frame. She didn't hear him so he said it louder.

She startled. "*Oh!* Michael! You scared me!"

"Sorry."

Her face flushed with embarrassment as she turned down the radio. "How long have you been there?"

He smiled and pulled off his tie. "Long enough. What are you making? It smells fabulous."

"Chicken parmesan. Are you hungry?"

"I'm starving. This is a nice treat. I haven't had a home-cooked meal since the last time I was in Rhode Island."

She took a taste of the sauce. "It's ready."

They sat down to eat, and Michael moaned when he took the first bite of tender chicken. "*Oh my God.* This is unbelievable. Where'd you learn to cook like this?"

"I grew up with an Italian grandmother. She taught me."

"She taught you well. Thank you."

"You're welcome."

When they were finished eating, he said, "Let's clean up and go get your car."

"I'll clean up."

"No way. My mother might find out I didn't help, and that wouldn't be good for me."

Juliana laughed. "I'll never tell. Go get changed. You can help next time."

On the way to the airport, they stopped at Wal-Mart where she bought a new car battery. Michael installed it for her, and when she started the car, he dropped the hood.

"Good to go," he said after he put the old battery in her trunk. "I'll see you at home."

The easy familiarity of the statement hung in the air between them. Juliana finally looked away from him. "Thanks for the help."

"No problem."

She parked behind him across the street from the house.

"Come here for a minute." He gestured her over to a car parked further up the street, tapped on the car window, and when it was rolled down he extended his hand to the man inside the car. "Michael Maguire."

"John Tanner."

They shook hands.

"This is my roommate, Juliana Gregorio. Juliana, John's a police officer. He and some of his colleagues will be keeping an eye on us until the trial is over."

Juliana shook his hand. "Nice to meet you."

"Let me know if you need anything, Mr. Maguire."

"Thanks. Have a good night."

As they crossed the street, Juliana asked, "Is that because of what happened today?"

"That and a few other things. They wanted me to have protection anyway, but I refused it."

"You asked for it because of me." She followed him inside. "Maybe I should go home. You don't need to be worrying about me right now."

"I don't want you to go home. I just want you to be careful."

"I almost left this morning anyway."

He stopped and turned to her. "Why?"

She shrugged. "The whole thing seemed so bizarre in the bright light of day. I mean, I met you on an airplane on Friday, and now I'm living with you?"

"It's temporary, right?"

She nodded.

"Did you go to your place today?"

"Yeah."

"How was that?"

"I was glad I had somewhere else to live," she confessed.

"See? There you go. Don't make it into something it's not. We're friends, right?"

"Right."

"And friends help each other out. Like that dinner you made." He rubbed his stomach. "I'll be thinking about that for *days*."

She smiled. "You're easy."

"Yes, I am," he said, feigning insult. "Do you have a problem with that?"

She held up her hands and laughed as she sat on the sofa. "No, no problem. I was thinking about Rachelle. I promised her I'd go back to see her again this week. I could do it after work on Wednesday if that's good for you."

"Sure. I should be able to do that." He started up the stairs. "I need to finish some work."

"Thanks again for helping with my car."

"You're welcome." He hesitated on the stairs as if there was something else he wanted to say.

"What's wrong?"

"Paige called me at work today."

"Did you talk to her?"

"Not really. Of course her father also called my boss. Fortunately, Tom's a good guy, and he didn't really say too much about it other than to ask if my mind was on the trial. It just pisses me off that her father thinks he can call my boss about my personal life."

Juliana shook her head. "That sucks. I'm sorry."

"The timing couldn't be worse. It's the last thing I need to be dealing with right now." He rubbed his face wearily. "I have a bad feeling that things with her could get ugly before all is said and done."

"It got ugly when she hit you."

Michael stared at her. "Yes, you're right. It did."

He looked so tired and sad that Juliana had to resist the sudden urge to hug him. She swallowed hard. "Try to get some sleep tonight. You need it."

He nodded. "Good night."

"Night."

Early the next morning Juliana took the extra chicken parm to her mother's house in Highlandtown. She had made that drive almost every day for four years and could just about do it in her sleep. Outside her mother's dingy rowhouse, Juliana took a moment to work up the fortitude it took to walk into the house where she'd grown up. She didn't have many happy memories of the years when there'd never been enough of anything—money, love, affection… At twelve, she began babysitting the neighborhood kids so she could pay for her own clothes, and she'd been working ever since.

Realizing time was getting away from her, she got out of the car and went inside.

"Ma?"

Juliana put the food in the refrigerator and went in search of her mother. She found her still sleeping and nudged her awake.

"What do you want?" Paullina asked with a nasty sweep of her hand.

"I just stopped by to bring you some dinner for later," Juliana said, attempting to straighten up the messy bedroom. Clothes and newspapers were strewn about, an ashtray overflowed, and the remnants of an all-night happy hour were on the bedside table. *I'm so glad half my monthly income goes to pay for this dump.* "Have you been smoking in bed again, Ma? What've we told you about that? You're going to burn the house down."

Paullina sat up and defiantly lit a cigarette. "What the hell time is it anyway?"

"Eight."

She groaned and rubbed her head. "That's too goddamned early."

"I have to work at nine, and it would be too late for dinner by the time I got here after. It was now or never." Juliana almost gagged as she picked up the ashtray and dirty glass off the table and took them into the kitchen. Somehow a woman who couldn't get around to feeding herself managed to have no trouble keeping up a steady supply of booze and cigarettes. Despite numerous attempts, her children had been unable to identify her supplier.

"How was your *romantic* weekend," Paullina asked with a sneer as she took a long drag on her cigarette.

Juliana returned the empty ashtray to the bedside table. "It was great," she said with a forced smile.

"I don't know why you stay with that loser. He's never going to marry you."

"Then it's a good thing I don't care about being married," Juliana snapped and then was mad at herself for taking the bait. So many years of bitterness and booze had made her once beautiful mother into an ugly person. Juliana waged a daily battle to keep from being sucked into her web of misery.

Juliana's cell phone rang, and she saw it was Mrs. Romanello, who lived next door to her and Jeremy. If Paullina was Juliana's mother by birth, Mrs. R was the mother of her heart.

Juliana went into the living room to take the call. "Good morning."

"Hello, hon. Where are you hiding out? I have something here for you."

"What is it?"

"A delivery. You'll have to come see."

Juliana checked her watch. "I'm at my mother's. I'll stop by on my way to the salon."

"See you then."

She went back into the bedroom. "I've got to go."

"Don't let me keep you."

"Do you need anything?"

Paullina waved her hand. "With all this? What more could I want?"

"I have something to do tomorrow after work. Do you still have the money I gave you last week? You could order a pizza for dinner." Juliana doubted she would bother. If someone wasn't there to make sure she ate, all she did was drink.

"Stop hovering."

"There's chicken parm for tonight. I want you to eat it, do you hear me?"

"Go to work, Juliana."

Juliana turned and left the room without another word. *Why do I bother? If she wants to drink herself to death, maybe I should just let her. No one else cares if she does. Why do I?*

Driving back to Butchers Hill on Eastern Avenue, Juliana pondered those questions. Born eight years after Vincent, Juliana knew she had been an accident. Her oldest sister and brother, Serena and Domenic, fled the moment they graduated from high school. Both had families on the West Coast that Juliana barely knew. Hell, she barely knew *them*. They moved out before she was six. She couldn't blame them for running for their lives after they endured some of the worst years of their parents' marriage. Donatella and Vincent lived in Baltimore but only bothered with their mother when Juliana guilted them into it.

All her life Juliana had been the adult in her relationship with her mother. *Maybe it's my fault she can't do anything for herself. Maybe if I just stopped she would have to deal with the mess she's made of her life.* Even as she thought it, though, Juliana knew she could never act on it.

Her mood lifted when she parked on Collington Street. Without even a glance at her own front door, Juliana walked into Mrs. Romanello's cluttered house. "Hello!"

"Back here!"

The first thing Juliana saw when she walked into the kitchen was the huge vase of at least two-dozen fragrant red roses. "Oh, wow! Who sent you flowers?"

Mrs. Romanello kissed Juliana's cheek. "They're not for me, hon." She handed the card to Juliana.

Startled, Juliana said, "For me?"

Mrs. R nodded. "Open it."

Juliana fumbled with the envelope and pulled out the card. "88 days. I love you. Jeremy."

"Jeremy?" Mrs. R asked.

Juliana nodded and blinked back tears.

Mrs. R reached for Juliana's hand. "Did something happen this weekend?"

"Why do you ask?"

"Tears and two dozen roses? Something happened."

"I really don't want to talk about it, okay?"

"Of course. How about some coffee or breakfast?"

Mrs. R, who was widowed with four children scattered around the country, loved to feed her and Jeremy. "I'm good, thanks," Juliana said with a smile for her friend. "I need to get to work. Why don't you keep the flowers and enjoy them?"

"Don't be foolish. Take them over to your house."

"Um, I'm actually staying with a friend right now."

Mrs. R's eyes narrowed. "What friend are you staying with? What's going on, Juliana?"

"Jeremy and I are taking a break. It's nothing, really. We just need a breather to figure some things out."

"I don't like the sound of that. People who love each other don't take breaks."

Ouch. "It'll be fine," Juliana said with more certainty than she felt. "I'll take the flowers to the salon." She tipped the vase over the sink to dump out the water.

"Where are you staying?"

"With a friend. I'm fine. I promise." Juliana kissed her. "I've got to go."

Mrs. R took hold of Juliana's chin, her wise old eyes scanning Juliana's face. "You're *not* fine. I know you. But I won't push. You know where I am if you need me."

"Yes. Thank you." Juliana hugged her, picked up the roses, and left.

At the salon she deposited the roses on the reception desk. The salon was all glass, track lighting, mirrors, light wood floors, and modern art. Juliana loved the clean, stylish look of the place and the fragrant scent of the beauty in the air.

"Where'd you get them?" her friend Carol asked. "Jeremy?"

Juliana nodded.

"Uh oh. What'd he do?"

"Since when do roses mean trouble?"

"A dozen red roses means I love you," Carol said, following Juliana to the break room to stash their coats and purses. "Two dozen means I'm sorry for something."

"Have you been reading *Glamour* again?" Juliana asked with amusement, which faded when she thought of the other thing she needed to tell her friend. "Hey, so, you won't believe who I met on the plane."

"Who?" Carol filled two mugs with coffee. Her short red hair was stylishly teased into spikes that would have looked ridiculous on anyone else. On her the style was avant-garde.

"The Benedetti prosecutor."

Carol paled. The loss of her young cousin was still a raw wound. "Michael Maguire?"

Juliana nodded.

"I've met him a few times at my aunt and uncle's house. He's very good about keeping them informed."

Juliana wasn't surprised to hear that. She took the cup of coffee from Carol and squeezed her arm. "He says they're going to get them, Car. He has no doubt."

Carol nodded and dabbed at her eyes before tears could ruin her makeup.

"Juliana, your nine fifteen is here," the receptionist announced through the intercom.

"Are you okay?" Juliana asked Carol.

"Yeah. I'll just be glad when the trial's over. We all will."

"I'm sure."

"We'd better get to work, but I still want to know why Jeremy's in the doghouse."

"You're imagining things," Juliana said, and they walked out to greet their clients.

Chapter 12

On Wednesday, Michael picked Juliana up at the salon just after six.

Once she was in the car, she kicked off her shoes and groaned. "God, my feet are *killing* me."

"I don't know how you stand up for nine straight hours."

"I'm used to it, but sometimes my feet let me down," she said, rubbing one of them.

"What's in the bag?"

"Shampoo samples for Rachelle."

"She'll love that."

"I brought my scissors, too. I thought she might like a trim."

"Thanks, Jule."

Startled, she looked over at him.

"What?"

"That's what Jeremy calls me," she said softly.

Michael cringed. "I'm sorry."

"No, don't be. I don't mind. It's just that no one else calls me that."

"How are you holding up? What is it? Day three?"

She nodded. "Three down, eighty-seven to go, but who's counting?"

"Not you of course."

"Can I ask your opinion on something?"

"Shoot."

"If a guy sends a girl two dozen roses, what's he saying?"

"What color?"

"Red."

"That he screwed up. Definitely."

Juliana laughed. "Am I the only one who's never heard that before?"

"Why do you ask?"

"Jeremy sent them to me yesterday."

"So people are wondering what he did?"

"Yes!"

"It was a nice thing for him to do," Michael conceded. "He didn't have to."

"I just wonder what else he's doing," Juliana said, biting on a thumbnail.

Michael kept an eye on the rearview mirror as they sat in heavy traffic in the southbound lane of the Baltimore-Washington Parkway. "Try not to think about it."

"It's *all* I think about. I just wonder, you know, is he doing it with someone else right now? Right at this very moment?"

"You're going to drive yourself crazy with that."

She sighed and rested her head back. "I know." Glancing over at him, she noticed how handsome he was in a dark pinstriped suit. They hadn't even known each other a week ago, yet there seemed to be nothing she couldn't talk to him about. "Have you heard any more from Paige?"

"She's been oddly, strangely quiet. I'm not complaining, but I'm wondering when the other shoe's going to drop."

"Maybe she's given up."

"I doubt it. I just hope she leaves me alone during the trial."

After more than an hour of crawling through rush hour traffic, Michael drove past the hotel to make sure he wasn't being followed. It was almost seven thirty when they finally pulled up to the J.W. Marriott.

Rachelle was delighted to see them and thrilled with Juliana's gifts as well as her plans for a haircut.

"Don't let me keep you ladies," Michael said. "I'll order us some dinner. Any preferences?"

"Whatever you're having," Juliana said.

"I already ate," Rachelle told him and then turned to Juliana. "You look so cool all in black."

"It's what we wear to work at the salon. Keeps it easy." Juliana draped the cape she had brought from the salon around the girl's slender shoulders and ran her fingers through her hair. "You did a good job with the round brush."

Rachelle's face lit up. "Do you think? I spent extra time on it today when I heard you were coming."

Juliana smiled at her in the mirror. "So how about some layers and bangs?"

"You're the expert. Whatever you say."

"Let's wash it first."

Combing out Rachelle's wet hair, Juliana noticed the girl wasn't as animated as she had been the other night. "What's wrong?"

"Nothing."

"Are you sure?"

Rachelle shrugged. "I'll have to testify soon."

"Are you nervous about it?"

"Sort of. They're really bad dudes, you know? Michael

told me they'll try to scare me when I'm on the witness stand, so I shouldn't look at them except for when I have to identify them. I just need to tell the truth."

"That's right," Juliana said, her heart aching for Rachelle.

"Those kids weren't doing anything wrong," Rachelle said softly, her eyes a million miles away.

Juliana continued to brush her hair.

"They were riding their skateboards in the parking lot when the car pulled up. I saw they were scared when they realized who was in the car. That's how I could tell they knew them. The two guys started yelling, and then they were shooting. They didn't see me, or they probably would've shot me, too."

"Thank God they didn't see you. What did you do?" Juliana rested her hands on Rachelle's shoulders and talked to her in the mirror.

"For a few minutes after they drove off, I was just frozen. I couldn't move. And then I ran back to my aunt's apartment. My mom said I was screaming. I don't remember that. The cops came, but I couldn't talk. For like three days, I couldn't talk. The doctors said I was in shock."

"Of course you were." While Rachelle talked, Juliana began to cut and shape her hair. "It must've been very scary when you were finally able to talk to the police."

Michael came to the door.

Juliana shook her head and used her eyes to tell him he was interrupting an intense moment.

He nodded and backed away.

"I guess the Benedettis had a big argument with the kids at an arcade that day. Some of the kids' other friends were with them when it happened. They described the Benedettis, so after they were arrested I just had to pick them out of a lineup."

"You're doing a good thing, Rachelle, by seeing to it that they can't do this to anyone else. You're making so many sacrifices, but you know that's why, right?"

Rachelle nodded. "I just wish we didn't have to move. I wish I'd never gone outside that night. I think about that, you know? If I hadn't forgotten my purse in the car, none of this would've happened to me or my family."

"But the Benedettis still would've killed those kids, only they might've gotten away with it if you hadn't seen it."

Their eyes met in the mirror. "That's true. Michael says I'm his slam dunk," Rachelle said with a small smile as she finally noticed the haircut Juliana had given her while they talked. She reached up to touch hair that was now three inches shorter. "Wow."

"Let me dry it, so you can see the full effect." Juliana turned Rachelle away from the mirror and worked for fifteen minutes with the hair dryer and brush. "Okay, are you ready?"

"I'm dying to see it!"

When Juliana spun her around, Rachelle gasped. "Oh my God! Is that *me?*"

Juliana chuckled. "That's you."

Rachelle ran her fingers through the layered tendrils. "I love it! Thank you."

"I'm glad. I've had this in mind for you since the other night." Juliana styled Rachelle's hair for another moment before she said, "You know who *really* needs a haircut?"

"Michael," they said together.

"Want to help me talk him into it?" Juliana asked.

"I'm on it."

They ventured into the adjoining room where Rachelle's detail of police officers made a big fuss over her new look. Juliana watched Rachelle seek Michael's approval.

"It's perfect," he said. "You look fantastic."

Rachelle blushed. "Thanks."

As Juliana ate the burger Michael ordered for her from room service, Rachelle went to work on him.

"You ought to let Juliana do something with your hair," she said, stealing a French fry from Juliana's plate.

"I don't know." He glanced from Rachelle to Juliana. "Why do I feel like I'm being ganged up on?"

"*Please*, Michael?" Rachelle pleaded. "Let her cut your hair."

"If you don't do it, Maguire, I might," one of the cops said as she reclined on a bed with the newspaper.

"What's in it for you?" Michael asked Rachelle.

"Entertainment," she said with a big smile.

"Oh, all right."

"Caved right in, didn't he?" the same cop said to one of the other female officers, and they shared a laugh.

"Shut up," Michael said under his breath to the cops as he let Rachelle tug him into the bathroom in her room.

Juliana followed them.

"Just a trim. I mean it. I like my hair long."

"Let her do what she wants," Rachelle said. "She's the expert."

"*A trim.* That's all I'm agreeing to."

Rachelle rolled her eyes at Juliana. "Sheesh, what a baby he is."

Juliana smiled and draped the cape around his shoulders. He had taken off his suit coat and tie and rolled up his shirtsleeves. She ran her fingers through his hair for a few minutes while she thought about what she wanted to do. When her eyes met his in the mirror, she was startled to find awareness and desire in his. For a long moment neither of them looked away.

"Come on!" Rachelle prodded from the doorway, breaking the spell. "Start chopping."

Juliana took a deep breath and went to work. When she was done, she discovered he *was* hot underneath all that hair, and suddenly the walls of the tiny bathroom seemed to close in on her.

"You look, so... so different," Rachelle said with a love-struck sigh.

"Is that good or bad?" Michael asked, looking himself over in the mirror.

"Good." Rachelle gazed at him with her heart in her eyes. "Definitely good."

Michael brushed the hair off his neck. "Definitely good. I guess that's better than butt ugly."

Juliana shared a smile with Rachelle.

"We'd better hit the road," Michael said. "It's getting late."

"Let me clean up the hair first," Juliana said.

"Housekeeping can do it," he said. "I'll ask one of the cops to call them."

"Are you sure? I hate to leave a mess." Juliana couldn't get over how different he looked with short hair.

"It's fine," Rachelle assured her. "They send someone right up whenever we call them."

"Okay," Juliana said. "Well, I guess we'll see you soon." She gave Rachelle a hug. "Hang in there, honey."

"Thank you. For the haircut and all the stuff."

"You're welcome."

"We'll try to come back this weekend." Michael hugged the girl. "Keep up the good behavior."

"Yeah, yeah."

They gathered their belongings, and Michael had a word with the cops before they left the adjoining room. In the hallway, the police officer on duty whistled at Michael. "Nice 'do, Maguire," he said. "Did you *girls* have fun playing haircut?"

Juliana smiled at Michael's furious scowl.

The police officer's laughter followed them to the elevator.

"I said a *trim,* Juliana." Michael punched the down arrow. "What does that word mean to you?"

Her smile faded. "Oh. You really don't like it."

"Did I say that?"

"You don't seem too happy with it."

"Will you or will you not admit that what we have here is more than a trim?"

"Jeez, I feel like I'm on the witness stand or something. I'm sorry. I just got into my zone."

He smiled. "I know. I was watching."

Her face heated with embarrassment. "You were?"

"Uh huh. I could've stopped you."

Again that flash of awareness mixed with a hint of what was definitely desire.

Since she was unable to process all that she saw, she looked away from him. "So why didn't you?" she asked when they were in the elevator.

"Because you were in your zone, and I enjoyed watching you."

She almost gasped when he reached out to touch her hair.

"Seems only fair."

"What does?" She reminded herself to breathe.

"You got to run your fingers through mine. I've wondered if yours is as soft as it looks." When he twisted a lock of long hair around his finger and brought it close enough to smell, she did gasp. "It's even softer than it looks. You always smell so good."

She moved away from him just before the elevator doors opened to the lobby. "What are you doing?" she whispered. "Why are you doing this?"

"What am I doing?"

"If you're looking for a rebound, you've got the wrong girl."

He stopped walking. "Is *that* what you think?"

"I don't know what to think. I thought we were friends," Juliana said, mortified when her eyes flooded with tears. She was like a faucet lately.

He put his arms around her and pulled her tight against him.

Suddenly, the strain, the uncertainty, and the agony of the last few days caught up to her, and before she knew it she was sobbing in Michael's arms right in the middle of the busy hotel lobby.

"I'm sorry," she whispered after several minutes passed. She tried not to notice how safe and comfortable she felt in the sanctuary of his embrace or that her arms were wrapped around him, too.

He didn't say anything, but he didn't let her go, either.

"I'm okay," she said when she finally pulled back from him.

He kept an arm around her as they went outside. Once they were in the car, he turned to her. "I'm not looking for a rebound, Juliana. That's not what this is."

"Then what is it?" she asked softly.

He ran a finger over her cheek to brush away a lone tear. "It's *not* a rebound."

"I don't want it, Michael. Whatever it is. I love Jeremy."

"I know you do, but you see, the thing is, I'm falling for you, Juliana."

"*What?*" she asked, flabbergasted. She pushed his hand away from her face. "You can't mean that!"

He kept his eyes locked on hers. "In the five days I've known you, you've given me more, been there for me more, done more for me than Paige did in four years. I knew I would care for you from almost the first moment I saw you. When I found you crying in the airport on Sunday, all I wanted to do was scoop you up and take you home with me."

New tears wet Juliana's cheeks. "You don't know what you're saying."

He took her hand. "On Friday night I tried to get Paige to marry me right away. Do you know why?"

Juliana shook her head.

"Because I was terrified after I met you. I already knew everything was about to change, and I guess a part of me thought I should try to stop it. But I was power-less to stop it. In those first moments with you, I knew I wouldn't marry her."

"Michael," she sobbed. "Stop. Stop saying these things."

"Juliana, any man who would let you think, for even

one minute, that you aren't enough for him doesn't deserve you."

"Please," she whimpered. "Please stop."

With a hand to her chin, he turned her to him. "I knew I was falling for you when you jumped right in with Rachelle on Sunday night and did her hair. I knew it when I found you dancing in the kitchen when you were making me dinner. I knew it because my heart almost stopped when you told me someone hassled you on the street. I knew it when I heard you talking to Rachelle about what she saw, and you said all the right things—all the things she needed to hear." He ran his thumb along her jaw. "And when I felt your fingers in my hair I knew I wanted them there always. Don't tell me I don't know what I'm saying."

He leaned over to kiss her gently, without demand, and for one breathless moment, she let him. Then she pulled away. "Michael. My head is spinning. Please don't."

"I'm sorry. I know this isn't a good time for you to be hearing this, but I couldn't let you think this was about rebounds. I'm not going to pressure you or push you, so you don't have to worry about that. I'm going to be so wrapped up in this trial for the next month or two I won't have time for anything else. I just wanted you to know."

"I can't stay with you anymore. Not now."

"Why? I just said I'm not going to do anything about it."

"Because everything's going to be weird between us."

He took her hand again. "It won't be weird because you'll hardly see me. I don't want you to go."

"I don't know… I'll only stay if you promise not to mention any of this again. I can't deal with it on top of everything else."

"I promise I won't say another word about it until you do."

She pulled her hand out of his grasp. "That's not going to happen."

"We'll see," he said, starting the car to drive them home. "We'll just see about that."

Chapter 13

THE NEXT MORNING MICHAEL SAT AT HIS DESK LOST IN thought. He couldn't believe the way he had bared his soul to Juliana the night before. He didn't regret anything, though. Everything he told her was true.

She hadn't said a word to him on the way home. Once they arrived she went straight up to her room and closed the door. Despite her silence, Michael knew she had feelings for him, too. He could see it in the way she looked at him when she thought he wasn't paying attention.

That she was still mired in a ten-year relationship gave him pause. "But hey," he said out loud, "she's living in *my* house and not even talking to *him*." The thought made Michael feel better about his chances with her until he remembered how wrong he'd been about Paige. But Juliana was different from Paige in every possible way. "That's one thing I know for sure."

His assistant, Angela, came to the door. "Talking to yourself, Michael?"

"Huh?"

"Your mother's on line two." The demands from the press had gotten so out of hand in the last few days that Angela was screening his calls.

"Thanks."

Angela left him to take the call.

"Hi, Mom."

"How are you, Michael? They mentioned your trial on the *Today* show this morning."

"We're getting a lot of attention. Too much."

"How're you holding up, sweetheart?"

"Good. I'm ready to go."

"You know we're all pulling for you. So how was the cotillion in Dixie last weekend?" His mother had long ago stopped pretending to approve of the Simpsons or their lifestyle.

"It was interesting. I've actually been meaning to call you since I got home."

"Oh? Why?"

"Well, I'm sorry to report the engagement is off."

"*What? Are you serious?*"

"Try to contain your euphoria, Mother," Michael said with a dry chuckle.

"What happened?"

"It's a long story. Suffice it to say I finally saw the light."

"Hallelujah! Your sisters will be thrilled to hear this."

"I'm sure."

"Are you all right, Michael? I know you loved her. I'll never understand why, but I'm sure you must be upset. I don't mean to make light of it."

Michael laughed. "Yes, you do. I'm fine. Believe me, by the time the whole thing blew up, I could hardly remember what it was I loved about her."

"She must've taken it well." Maureen's voice dripped with sarcasm.

"Yeah, not so much. In fact, I'm quite certain I haven't seen the last of her. But right now all I'm thinking about is the trial." *Well, not all,* but he wasn't ready to tell his mother about Juliana. Not yet.

"I know you're busy, so I won't keep you. I'm sorry if you're hurting, Michael."

"I'm fine. Really."

"Keep us posted on the trial. We'll have our fingers crossed for you."

"Thanks, Mom. Give my love to everyone."

"I will. You know you have ours."

She ended the call promising to check on him in a week or so. He smiled when he imagined the news of his broken engagement burning up the phone lines in Newport's Fifth Ward and had no doubt he would hear from his sisters before the day was out.

On her way home from her mother's that evening, Juliana stopped at Collington Street where she cleaned out the fridge, took out the trash, and stashed the mail in her purse to deal with later. She was in and out of there in ten minutes. Even after the emotional exchange with Michael the night before, she still couldn't bear to be in the house she had shared with Jeremy.

Michael's words had haunted her all day as she made polite small talk with her clients. *How could he be falling for me? It's preposterous. We haven't even known each other a week!*

But there was something, Juliana acknowledged. She had felt it herself. More than once. It wasn't love, though. No way. Things like that happened in the movies, not to real people.

At times she wondered if her head would just explode from thinking too much. Ironically, though, she hadn't had the urge to call Jeremy all day.

Letting herself into Michael's house, she flipped on the lights. She supposed she should consider it her house, too, since she had written him a check for two hundred and fifty dollars. It wasn't much, but it was all she could afford. He took the check only when she insisted.

In the microwave, she defrosted the pork chops she brought from the freezer on Collington Street and put two potatoes in the oven. While the chops defrosted, she went upstairs to gather clothes from both their bedrooms and threw in a load of darks. All the while she tried not to think about anything other than what she was doing. Her brain was tired and overtaxed.

Back downstairs she put the seasoned pork chops under the broiler, tossed a salad, and went through the mail she had picked up earlier. Mixed in with the junk mail and bills was a letter from Jeremy.

She sat on one of the kitchen stools and opened it with shaking hands. Just the sight of his familiar handwriting made her heart beat faster as anticipation battled with anxiety and dread.

Dear Jule,

I haven't spoken to you in two days—the longest two days of my life. You said we couldn't talk to each other, but you never mentioned writing. I hope you'll read this and not just throw it away. I can't believe I agreed to this foolish plan of yours, but I also can't believe how stupid I was. If I could hit rewind and undo anything in my life it would be that conversation we had on the beach.

I've discovered since you left that freedom is a funny thing. Last week I longed for it. This week I'm terrified of it. I don't want anyone but you. I know you won't believe me because of what an ass I've been, but it's true. I tried to go out with someone else. We went to dinner, but everything was wrong because she wasn't you. I didn't care about what she was saying, I didn't want to kiss her, and I certainly didn't want to have sex with her. I only want you. I've made a terrible mistake, Jule, and I know if I lose you I'll be sorry about it for the rest of my life.

All I think about is that you're going to meet someone else. I worry about that constantly. It keeps me awake at night. Please don't meet someone you like better than me. I think that would kill me. I've let my boss know I'm leaving here in three months whether the install is done or not. Even if I have to quit my job, I'm coming home to you.

I've made mistakes. I know I have. We should've been married years ago. It's my fault we aren't, but I plan to rectify that as soon as we're together again. Until then, I want you to know I'm thinking about you all the time.

All my love,
Jeremy

Juliana read the letter again. All the things she had waited years to hear, mixed in with a few things she could have lived forever without knowing. He had longed to be free. Free of her. And it had taken him just two days to go out with someone else—the same day he sent the roses. He sure had been busy that day.

After several minutes spent processing the letter, she got up to flip the chops and pour a glass of wine. When everything was ready, she pushed the food around on her plate without really eating much of it. She made a plate for Michael, wrapped it in foil, and left it in the oven on warm. The doorbell rang just as she finished cleaning up the kitchen.

Looking through the peephole, she swallowed hard and had to think for a second about what she should do. Reluctantly, she opened the door.

"Who are you?" Paige asked, pushing past Juliana. She carried a large shoulder bag and disregarded Juliana the way she would the hired help.

Juliana cleared her throat and extended her hand to the other woman. "I'm Michael's roommate, Juliana."

Paige ignored her outstretched hand. "Michael doesn't have a roommate."

Juliana dropped her hand. "He does now."

"Where is he?"

"At work." Juliana noticed that Paige still wore her enormous diamond engagement ring.

"Fine." Paige took off her coat and plopped down on the sofa. "I'll wait."

"Suit yourself," Juliana said on her way upstairs.

"Thank you, I will," Paige said in a bitchy tone.

Juliana closed the bedroom door and reached for her cell phone.

"Hey," she said when Michael answered. "Where are you?"

"Why? Do you miss me?"

"Really. Where are you?"

"Juliana? What's wrong?"

"Um, Paige is here."

He groaned. "*Tell me you're kidding me!*"

"Sorry."

"Oh, God, that's the *last* thing I feel like dealing with tonight."

"I shouldn't have let her in, but I didn't know what to do."

"It's fine. She would've waited for me. At least this way I'm warned. Are you okay? Was she nasty to you?"

"She wasn't thrilled to discover you have a roommate, especially a *female* roommate."

He laughed. "I don't imagine she was. I'll be home in about fifteen minutes."

"Should I make popcorn?"

"I'm glad you're enjoying this," he joked.

"I'm only kidding. I'm not enjoying it."

"I know."

"Michael?"

"Yeah?"

"Don't let her hit you again."

After a long moment of silence, he said, "I won't."

Michael parked on the street and rested his head on the steering wheel. He had put in a fourteen-hour day, and all he wanted was to have some dinner, put his feet up, and just *be* with Juliana. Instead he was steeling himself for yet another showdown with Paige.

Crossing the street and giving himself one last moment to prepare, he stepped into the living room.

Paige jumped up. "Oh *God,* Michael! What did you do to your hair?" She made a face. "Well, it'll grow back before the wedding."

He counted to ten before he allowed himself to speak. "What are you doing here?" Inside the front door, he dropped the bag of work he hoped to get to that night and pulled off his coat.

Paige followed him into the kitchen. "Who's that girl who says she's your roommate?"

"My roommate." Reaching for the phone book, he smelled something mouthwatering coming from the oven, and his stomach let out a hungry growl. In the yellow pages, he found what he was looking for and picked up the phone. "Yes, I need a taxi at 8 South Chester Street. Thirty minutes? Okay. Thanks."

"Michael, what are you doing? We need to talk."

"We're not going to talk, but you *are* going to listen." He took a deep breath to summon the calm he needed to get through this. "I'm starting what'll probably be the biggest trial of my career on Monday. Today's Thursday. That means the trial starts in *three* days. *I do not need this right now!* So you're leaving in…" He checked his watch. "Twenty-eight minutes. Go home and leave me alone. Am I clear? Is there *any* part of that you didn't understand?"

"Where am I supposed to go at nine o'clock at night?"

Michael shrugged. "Not my problem."

"I'm not leaving. The least you can do is let me spend the night here."

"You're not spending the night. Check into a hotel. I don't care what you do, but you *are* leaving."

Her eyes widened. "*Oh my God!* You've got someone

else! All this time I've been in Florida, you've been seeing someone else. She's living here!"

Michael forced himself to remain calm. "I have *not* been seeing someone else."

She ignored him and stormed into the living room. "Get her down here! I want a better look at the woman who's been fucking my fiancé!"

"That's enough!" Michael's control finally snapped. "This is my home, and I don't want you here!" He opened the front door and tossed her bag onto the sidewalk. "I want you out. *Right now!*"

"Why? So you can fuck your whore?"

This time Michael saw it coming and grabbed her arm in midair before her hand could make contact with his face. "I don't think so, Paige. I let you get away with that once but not twice." While he had her hand he slid the engagement ring off her finger and put it in his pocket. "I'll take that back, just so you're absolutely clear on where we stand. Now get out." He released her arm.

She snatched her coat off the sofa. "You'll be sorry, Michael! You're going to regret this!"

"No, I won't."

"Everything all right, Mr. Maguire?" Officer Tanner asked from the sidewalk.

"It is now. Ms. Simpson was just leaving. A taxi will be coming to get her in a few minutes."

Paige brushed by him.

The moment she was outside Michael slammed the door closed and leaned his head against it for a minute. He turned around to find Juliana coming down the stairs.

She held out her arms to him.

Like a man who had found water after forty days in the desert, he went to her.

Standing on the second stair from the bottom, she held him close to her.

When he pulled back after several minutes, he was able to look directly into her eyes. His hand curled around the back of her neck, and this time when he kissed her he held nothing back. If kissing Paige had been about fire and heat, kissing Juliana felt like coming home. The heat was there, too, but it was almost secondary to everything else he felt when she responded with equal ardor. Coaxing her mouth open, his heart almost burst as her tongue tangled with his. He only ended the kiss when he remembered what she had said about him looking for a rebound. That was the last thing he wanted her to think.

"I'm sorry." He leaned his forehead against hers. "I didn't mean to do that."

She caressed his face. "She was so horrible to you."

"To both of us."

"I know. I heard."

He winced. "I'm sorry you had to hear that. I never saw how truly awful she can be until this last week."

"She hid it from you." Juliana kept her arms around him.

"Either that or maybe I just chose not to see it."

"She'll get the message after tonight. Are you all right?"

"I was all right the moment I turned around and saw you coming down to me." He tightened his hold on her and buried his face in her hair.

"Michael," Juliana said breathlessly. "I made you some dinner."

"I know. It smells good." But he didn't release her. Five minutes passed or maybe ten before he was ready to let go. "Thank you."

"For what?"

"For being here, for offering comfort." He kept an arm around her as they walked into the kitchen.

She retrieved his dinner and shut off the oven.

"What's this?" He picked up Jeremy's letter from the counter.

"Oh. A letter. From Jeremy."

Michael handed it to her without looking at it and sat down to eat. "He's not giving up either, huh?"

Juliana shook her head. "He feels really bad about what happened last weekend."

"It'll seem self-serving for me to say he *should* feel bad about it. This is fabulous, by the way. Thanks."

"I'm glad you like it." She brought two glasses of wine to the table and sat with him. "He went out with someone else."

Michael's fork froze in midair. "He *told* you that?"

"I figured out from when the letter was written that he went on a date the same day he sent me the roses. He said the date was awful because it wasn't with me."

Michael took a long sip of his wine. "I can't be a good friend to you in this situation. I can't say what I really want to."

"It's all right. There's nothing you could say that I'm not already telling myself."

He took her hand. "I'm sorry."

"Are you?" she asked as she laced her fingers through his and flipped her soft brown eyes up to meet his.

Michael tugged on her hand and brought her to sit on

his lap. He wrapped his arms around her. "Not really. He's a fool. I already told you that."

Juliana rested her head on his shoulder. "He said he wants to fix this before I meet someone else."

Michael kissed the top of her head. "Too late."

Chapter 14

"TELL ME MORE ABOUT YOUR FAMILY," JULIANA SAID. They had folded the laundry she'd done earlier and were finishing the bottle of wine from dinner.

Michael stretched and rested his head against the back of the sofa. He had changed into a Red Sox T-shirt and sweats. "I told you I have three sisters, right?"

"Uh huh. Where are they now?"

"They all still live within blocks of my parents' house in Newport, and they married guys we grew up with. Let's see, Mary Frances is the oldest. She married John Doncaster. They have five kids—Connor, Colm, Cormac, Catherine, and Clara," he said, ticking off the names on five fingers.

"I love the Irish names."

"There're more coming. Maggie married Luke O'Shea, and they have three kids, Patrick, Sean, and Emma. Then my sister Shannon married Hughie Sullivan, but we're not supposed to call him Hughie anymore. They have Lauren, Ailish, Hannah, and Grace."

"Wow, four girls!"

Michael laughed. "I know. Hughie—I mean Hugh—is totally overwhelmed by them. He was the roughest kid. It's so funny to see him with all those women."

"What are your parents like?"

"My mother, Maureen, loves being a grandmother. She has at least three kids trailing behind her whenever she's not working as a housekeeper for the Preservation Society. They take care of Newport's famous mansions. My dad, Sean, is the city's deputy fire chief."

"They must be so proud of you."

"They are, but I think they wish I'd married a girl from the neighborhood and stayed close by like the others did."

"And had six Irish kids?" Juliana asked with a teasing smile.

"I'm more than happy to let my sisters produce the grandchildren. My dad was disappointed that I didn't follow him into the fire department. His father, his brothers, and their sons are all firefighters, but it just wasn't for me. I wanted to go to school."

"Where did you go?"

"Boston College. Then I worked in Boston for a few years to save some money before I went to law school."

"Did you always want to be a lawyer?"

"For as long as I can remember. And I always wanted to go to Georgetown. A recruiter came to my high school when I was a junior, and from then on I was just hooked on Georgetown and the idea of living in the District. I didn't get in as an undergraduate, which was bitterly disappointing. But I kicked ass on the LSATs—the test you have to take for law school—and got in."

"Did it live up to your expectations?"

"Totally. I loved every minute of it. Well, except for the nonstop studying. That got old fast, especially since I'd had a few years off from school by then and had lost all my discipline."

"I always wanted to go to college," she said wistfully.

"Why didn't you?"

LOVE AT FIRST FLIGHT   135

"No money," she said with a shrug. "My dad was a bus driver for the city, so we barely had enough to make ends meet. It also didn't help that my brother Vincent flunked out of Towson, which made my father crazy. He would go on and on about the money he wasted. After that, I knew he'd never pay for me to go."

"You can still go, you know. It's never too late."

"There's still no money," she said with a sad smile.

"There're lots of options—financial aid, scholarships. You could do it."

"I think that ship has sailed for me. Besides, I like my job, and I feel lucky to have it. Panache is one of the best salons in the city. I've built up a pretty decent following and hardly ever have an open appointment anymore."

"You're good at it. I've seen your work, remember?" He ran a hand through his hair to make his point.

"I'd hate to think of you as one of my few unsatisfied customers."

"I'm a very satisfied customer. The women in my office went crazy over it today."

Juliana raised an eyebrow. "Did they?"

"Uh huh," he said, grinning. "And Paige *hated* it, so good job."

Juliana threw a sofa pillow at him. "Glad I could help." She reached for her wineglass. "You're lucky, you know?"

He covered her free hand with both of his. "Because I'm here with you?"

She gave him a withering look. "*No*. Because you have such a nice family. Mine's a disaster area. Yours sounds so normal."

His handsome face grew somber. "We've had our challenges." After a long pause, he said, "I had a brother."

"You did?"

"Patrick. He died when he was twelve and I was seven."

Juliana squeezed his hand. "Oh, Michael. I'm sorry."

"He had leukemia. He got sick in the middle of the summer and was dead by October."

"It must've been so shocking."

"Yeah, my parents were never quite the same after."

"Of course they weren't."

"The worst part was after he died, we never talked about him. It was like we were all afraid to mention his name because we didn't want to upset my mother, so we just stopped talking about him."

Juliana's eyes filled with tears.

"He was the most important person in the world to me and then, in the blink of an eye, he was gone, and I had to act like he never existed."

Juliana rested her head on Michael's shoulder and held his hand. "What was he like?"

"He was a great athlete—an all-star baseball and football player. The coaches used to tell my dad he was going to be a pro. It was just a matter of which sport. But I think he would've been a firefighter. He used to take me with him everywhere he went, and he never complained about having me around. He called me Mikey."

"That's cute."

"I've never let anyone else call me that. He's been gone twenty-five years, and I still miss him." Michael raised his arm and put it around her. "Can I be self-serving again for a minute?"

She smiled up at him. "If you must."

"In all the years I was with Paige, I never told her about Pat. There was just never a time when I felt comfortable telling her."

"Thank you for telling me," Juliana said, touched by his confession.

"It's not just me, is it?"

"What?"

He held her eyes with his. "You feel it, too, don't you? Even just a little bit?"

She couldn't look away. After a long moment of silence, she bit her lip and nodded.

He leaned in to kiss her.

Under the hand she had on his chest she felt his heart begin to pound and told herself she should stop, that kissing him like this was wrong because she was still involved with Jeremy. But then she remembered that she wasn't *with* Jeremy now, so technically this wasn't wrong. And, *damn,* it felt so good to be in Michael's arms, to feel the weight of him resting against her as he kissed her with wild abandon.

"Juliana," he whispered against her ear. "God, you smell so good. I can't get enough of you." He kissed her again and groaned when her arms closed tight around him. As his tongue teased hers, he caressed her back under the black T-shirt she had worn to work.

"Michael, wait," she said, tearing her lips free of his. "This is happening too fast for me."

He took her hand and put it over his pounding heart. "Feel that? You did that."

"Please." Her own heart skipped an unsteady beat. "I can't do this. I can't jump from one guy to another. It's just not who I am."

"I know. I'm sorry." He helped her sit up next to him and dropped his head into his hands. "I said I wouldn't push you."

"You haven't." She rested her arm on his back. "It's just that things are so complicated right now—for both of us. If we let this get out of hand, someone's going to get hurt."

"You're right."

"I'm not going to deny there's something between us," she said, smiling when he brightened at her admission. "But we need some time. You've just ended an engagement, and I'm still involved with Jeremy. We're having some problems right now, but it's far from over between us."

"We'll take it slow and see what happens."

"Promise?"

He kissed her hand. "I promise."

Juliana had to work at noon the next day, so she slept until nine thirty. She lay in bed for a long time wishing there was someone she could talk to about everything that had happened in the last week. Most of her girlfriends were part of couples she and Jeremy were friends with, so there was no way she could share this with them. She could talk to Carol at work, but with the trial starting she hated to burden Carol with her problems. Her sister Dona would take far too much pleasure in hearing there was trouble between her and "Mr. Wonderful"—the sarcastic nickname she and Vincent bestowed upon Jeremy years ago.

Juliana was almost startled to realize there was no one else. She had turned to Jeremy for everything she needed for so long that she had isolated herself from other relationships. *Interesting,* she thought as she got up to shower. When she was drying her hair, it occurred to her that there was one person she could talk to who wouldn't pass judgment on her—or Jeremy. The last thing she wanted was anyone treating him differently if they managed to work things out.

She got dressed for work and walked the short distance to Collington Street. Mrs. Romanello's door was never locked, and Juliana went in calling out, "Hello? It's just me."

"Come on in!" Mrs. R called from upstairs. "I'll be right down. There's coffee on if you want some."

The television blared on the counter as Juliana poured herself a cup of coffee. Jeremy always said Mrs. R's coffee was better than any coffee shop's. When he was home he went next door on many a morning to fill his mug—and his stomach—before work. The memory made Juliana sad. Suddenly, it seemed like a hundred years had gone by since they lived happily next door.

"This is a nice surprise," Mrs. R said with a kiss to Juliana's cheek. She wore one of the stylish sweat suits Juliana had given her for Christmas the year before.

"Coffee?" When the older woman nodded, Juliana filled a second mug.

"You're all in funeral colors, so you must be working today," Mrs. R said, turning the television down to a normal decibel.

"I know, I know: young girls don't belong all in black. You don't have to say it."

"It's ridiculous. The owners of that salon of yours need to have their heads examined."

"Think of it this way—I never have to spend even one second wondering what to wear to work."

"That's true, but you're not here to have this old argument with me, are you? What's on your mind, hon?"

Juliana shrugged and sat down at the kitchen table. "I seem to have gotten myself into a bit of a mess."

"What kind of mess?"

Juliana poured out the whole story—from meeting Michael in the airport, to Jeremy's desire to be with other women and their decision to separate for a few months, to moving in with Michael, his broken engagement, his confession that he was falling for her, her growing feelings for him, and Jeremy's campaign to keep her in his life. Remembering her promise to Michael, the only thing she left out was the part about Rachelle.

"Well," Mrs. R said with a stunned expression, "all this in one week?"

"I know! It's too much. I can't process it. What should I do, Mrs. R? *I'm so confused.*"

"I'm going to be honest with you, hon. I'm disappointed in Jeremy. I can't imagine what he's thinking. If you fall for this Michael fellow or someone else for that matter, Jeremy's going to have to acknowledge that he let it happen."

"Don't be mad with Jeremy," Juliana pleaded. "I don't want you to hate him if we manage to get through this and stay together."

"I could never hate him. I love you both like my own. You know that, Juliana."

"Yes," she whispered.

"I love him, but I'm disappointed in him, too. He's put you in a terrible position by telling you his most private thoughts."

"But wouldn't it have been worse if he'd acted on

them and kept it from me? I mean, he could've gotten away with it, right? I never would've known."

"You would've known. You know him better than anyone on this earth, and he knows there's no way he would've gotten away with cheating on you. I have to give him a few points for respecting you enough not to do that." She took a sip of her coffee.

The local newscast at the top of the hour led with the Benedetti trial.

"Listen. They're talking about the trial—Michael's trial."

"Attorneys met today in a pre-trial conference with Judge Harvey Stein," the anchorman reported. "Jury selection gets under way on Monday in what promises to be the contentious trial of Marco and Steven Benedetti, accused in the shotgun slayings of Baltimore teenagers Jose Borges, Timothy Sargant, and Mark Domingos." The news shifted to a shot of the courthouse steps where reporters surrounded Michael and several other men in suits.

"Oh, look! That's him. That's Michael."

"Mr. Maguire!"

The reporters all talked at once.

"What can you tell us about your trial strategy?"

"Not much," Michael replied confidently. "Except that we're ready to go for Monday and looking forward to seeing justice served on behalf of the Borges, Sargant, and Domingos families. That's all I'm going to say at this time."

"Mr. Maguire, is it true your case rides on the witness you have in protective custody?"

"No comment."

Juliana watched him push his way through the crowd of reporters. When the news shifted back to the anchor, she noticed Mrs. R watching her with an odd expression on her face.

"Oh, my," Mrs. R said.

"What?"

"You're in love with him. It's all over your face. You couldn't take your eyes off him."

"I am *not* in love with him," Juliana protested, her heart beating hard. "I like him, though. A lot."

"You could be in danger living with him during all this craziness."

Juliana reached across the table for Mrs. R's hand. "It's safe. They have a cop watching the house. There's nothing to worry about."

"I don't like this, Juliana. Not one bit. Will you promise me if you're ever scared there you'll come stay here with me?"

"I promise, but you don't have to worry. Besides, I've got bigger problems. *What am I going to do?*"

Mrs. R appeared to give Juliana's question considerable thought before she answered. "My Tony and I, bless his soul, were married for fifty-three years. Fifty-three beautiful years." A soft look of love fell over her wrinkled face. "In all that time, I never once wondered if he was thinking of someone else. Not once."

Juliana looked down at her coffee cup.

"Jeremy loves you. I know he does. But what he's asked of you is almost too much. I've wondered why the two of you never married."

Juliana shrugged. "We just never got around to it."

"You need to think about why that is."

"Vincent says it's because Jeremy doesn't need to buy the cow when he's getting the milk for free," Juliana said, blushing.

Mrs. R raised an eyebrow. "Vincent's an idiot, but he's got a point. Maybe you were too good to Jeremy, and he began to take you for granted. But you have to ask yourself: if you're able to work all this out and he manages to win you back, is he going to get itchy feet again a year or two down the road when you're married and maybe have a baby on the way?"

"I don't know how to *be* without him. He's been everything to me, you know? He rescued me from the hell of my family, and gave me this safe place to be for so many years. How do I just walk away from that?"

"You did the right thing taking this break, hon. You both need to figure out what you want. Just because you've been with him for ten years doesn't mean you're meant to be with him forever. Why don't you give yourself this time to learn how to be without him? When the three months are up, you can see how you feel about it and decide what to do then."

"What about Michael?"

"What about him?"

"I have feelings for him, but I don't want to be one of those girls who goes from guy to guy like they don't know how to function on their own."

Mrs. R laughed. "You've been with the same guy for *ten years*, Juliana. You're hardly setting a pattern by exploring your feelings for *one* other guy. Besides, the way you've taken care of your mother all these years proves you don't need a man to take care of you. There's no doubt in my mind that you're capable of standing on your own two feet in any situation."

Juliana reached over to hug her. "Thank you," she whispered.

"Any time." Mrs. R tilted Juliana's chin up, wise old eyes zeroing in. "You do know if you let yourself become involved with Michael that eventually it's going to come down to a choice, right? You'll have to choose between them. Are you prepared to do that?"

"I'm already involved with Michael," Juliana admitted.

She hugged Juliana close to her. "Then be true to your own heart, Juliana. Only your own."

Juliana nodded and rested for another moment in the warm comfort of Mrs. Romanello's embrace.

Chapter 15

IT TOOK EIGHT TEDIOUS, PAINFUL, ENDLESS DAYS TO empanel the jury. In the end, Michael got exactly what he expected—six jurors perfectly suited to the prosecution, six perfectly suited to the defense, and two alternates who could go either way. He worried about the Italian grandmother the defense managed to secure. If she saw one of her own precious grandsons in either of the Benedettis, she could be enough to hang the jury.

But whenever he felt the need to worry, Michael reminded himself of how strong their case was. Regardless of their ages, races, occupations, or built-in biases, the jurors were most likely rational people who, when presented with the facts of the case and Rachelle's eyewitness testimony, would have no choice but to convict. At least he hoped so.

He always experienced these jitters on the eve of a trial, but this one was different and had been from the beginning. It wasn't just that it had received national media attention. No, it was that the hopes of a lot of people were resting on his shoulders. Three devastated families and the larger community were looking to him for closure. He wanted that for the families and for Rachelle, who lost her childhood on that fateful night. But Michael wanted it for himself, too. He wanted to win every case he tried and for the most part he had, but he wanted this one badly. At times, he felt like everything in his life had led him to this moment, and he hoped he was up to the awesome task.

The Sunday afternoon before he was due to deliver his opening, Michael and Juliana went to meet with Rachelle and her mother. Rachelle had been moved to a hotel in Annapolis to put her in closer proximity to the courthouse. This visit was business, and Juliana had been uncomfortable about joining him until he told her Rachelle had asked for her.

"Guess who called me today?" Michael said as they traveled south on Interstate 97 to Annapolis. The fall foliage was at its peak in the late afternoon sunlight.

"Larry King? Nancy Grace?"

"Yes to both, but that's not who I mean. Derek Gantley, the Florida attorney general."

"Oh, he's the one who offered you the job, right?"

"Uh huh."

"What did he want?"

"Just to wish me luck with the trial and to remind me of his offer. Imagine his surprise when I mentioned I'm no longer engaged to Paige."

"He didn't know?"

"Nope. He surprised *me,* though, when he said the offer's still on the table."

"That must've made you feel good."

Michael shrugged. "I guess. I told him I'm hardly thinking about my career right now, but thanks for calling, blah, blah, blah." As he took the Annapolis exit, Michael was hit with a slew of memories of all the time he spent there with Paige. It must have shown on his face.

"What's wrong?"

"Nothing."

She reached for his hand. "Tell me."

"I spent a lot of time here with Paige when her father was at the Naval Academy."

Juliana put her other hand on top of his.

He appreciated that she knew when to say nothing.

"You know, I've been thinking," Michael said, wanting to change the subject. "I don't have court next Friday because Judge Stein has to deal with some procedural stuff in the trial he has after this one. Barring any unforeseen crises, I may have three whole days off. I was thinking about a quick trip home to Rhode Island."

"That sounds like a good idea."

"Will you come with me?"

Startled, Juliana looked over at him. "I don't know, Michael…"

"Please? I won't go if you don't come with me."

"That's crazy! Why not?"

"I'm not leaving you alone at my house for three days during this trial. No way."

"I thought you weren't worried about any trouble."

"I'm not leaving you there, Juliana. Come with me. Come on."

She smiled at the face he made as he pleaded with her. "I am not saying yes, but I will tell you I'm off next Friday and Saturday because Jeremy was supposed to be home."

"Yes! You're coming."

"I didn't say yes!" she said, laughing.

He pulled the car off the road.

"What are you doing?"

"This." He reached for her and kissed her with the frustration that came from ten days of doing his best to keep his distance from her. Weaving his fingers into her hair to keep her still, he sent his tongue to find hers.

Her arms closed around him.

"I tried, Juliana," he whispered. "But I can't resist you. I think about you all the time. I *dream* about you."

"*Michael.*" This time she reached for him.

After several long, hot minutes, he pulled away from her with great regret. "I've never wished for a backseat in this car as much as I do right at this moment."

"And what do you think would be happening by the side of the road in broad daylight if you had a backseat?"

He gave her a meaningful look as he kissed her hand and then her mouth. "You make my heart *pound,*" he said against her lips. "And you've succeeded in changing my memories of Annapolis."

With a chuckle, she pushed him back into the driver's seat. "You have a meeting. Drive."

He exhaled a long, frustrated deep breath and eased the car onto the highway.

Juliana sat next to Rachelle as Michael spelled out a change in their trial strategy. "We're putting the victims' friends who saw the fight in the arcade on first, followed by the detectives, and then the ballistics guy. We've decided to put you on last, Rachelle."

"I thought you said she'd be first," said Rachelle's mother, Monique, her stunning black face tight with aggravation.

"We've given this a lot of thought," Michael

explained. "We think the case is stronger if Rachelle's testimony is the last thing the jurors hear before the prosecution rests."

Knowing Monique's histrionics got on his nerves, Juliana gave him credit for being so patient with her. When Monique stood up to pace the room, Juliana squeezed Rachelle's hand. She had noticed in previous visits that Rachelle lost some of her sparkle when her overwrought mother was around.

"I haven't seen my husband and sons in seven weeks," Monique complained. "It's been even longer for Rachelle. You're sure we have to do it this way? You could call her first and we'd be out of here tomorrow."

Michael stood up to face her. "I wouldn't ask it of you—either of you—if I wasn't sure it was the best way to proceed." He moved over to squat down in front of Rachelle, taking both of her hands in his. "Sweetheart, I know this has been so hard, and you've been incredibly brave. I'm asking for just a little while longer—one more week, maybe two. Can you do that for me?"

Watching him handle the teenager with such infinite gentleness, Juliana felt all her defenses slip away and the door to her heart open to him. She loved him. It was suddenly as clear to her as anything she had ever known in her life.

Rachelle's big brown eyes were bright with tears, but she nodded. "I can do it for you."

"That's my girl."

They visited with Rachelle for another half hour before Michael said they had to go. He hugged Rachelle and told her the next time he saw her would be in court. "Just remember what we've talked about. Answer only the questions you're asked, don't offer anything extra, and don't look at them except for when I ask you to identify them, okay?"

She nodded.

He kissed her cheek. "You're going to be just fine. You're my slam dunk, and don't you forget it."

"I won't," she said with a smile. "Michael?"

"Yeah?"

"Get 'em," she said softly. "Just make sure you get 'em."

"I will."

Juliana hugged the girl. "I'm so glad I got to know you, Rachelle."

"Thank you," Rachelle said. "Thank you so much for being my friend."

"I'm proud to call you my friend." Juliana folded the girl into one more hug before Michael took her hand to lead her from the room.

Monique followed them into the hallway, closing the door to Rachelle's room behind her. "Michael?"

He dropped Juliana's hand and turned to Monique.

"Promise me nothing's going to happen to my baby," Monique said, blinking back tears.

Michael put his hand on her arm. "The Baltimore Police chief has made the full resources of the department available to us during the trial. You have my word that nothing's going to happen to her."

Monique squeezed his hand. "Thank you."

"I'm sorry for what your family's been through. I'm going to do everything in my power to make sure it was worth it."

She nodded. "Okay."

"It'll be over soon. Stay strong for her, Monique."

"I'm doing my best."

When they got back to his car, Michael surprised Juliana when he said, "Let's go out to dinner."

"Do you have time?"

"I need to get my mind off it for a while. Help me?"

"Of course. But before we change the subject, I have to tell you that you handled them beautifully. Both of them."

"Do you think so?"

The insecurity on his face touched her. "I do."

"Thanks."

"No trial talk for…" she checked her watch, "three hours. Deal?"

He leaned over to kiss her. "Deal."

They went to the Chart House on the Annapolis waterfront and talked about everything but the trial and even managed to avoid talking about Jeremy and Paige. Michael was putting his credit card back in his wallet when an elderly couple approached their table.

"Mr. Maguire?" the woman asked.

"Yes." He stood up to shake their outstretched hands.

"We just wanted to wish you well with the trial," the man said. "All of Maryland is pulling for you, young man."

"I appreciate that."

"Enjoy your dinner and your pretty young lady," the woman added.

Michael smiled. "I will, thank you." After they walked away, he extended his hand to Juliana to help her up.

"I'm dining with a celebrity," Juliana teased.

He put his arm around her. "Shut up."

They were still laughing as they walked the dock that led to the parking lot.

"Juliana?"

She looked away from Michael and came face-to-face with Pam and David Newman, close friends of hers and Jeremy's who were stunned to see her with another man's arm around her.

"Pam, David." She tried to hide her shock. *Oh God. They'll tell Jeremy they saw me with Michael.*

They both kissed her cheek while trying not to stare at Michael.

"This is my friend, Michael." She made a huge effort to keep her voice normal as she introduced them. "This is Pam and David Newman, friends from high school."

With what appeared to be great reluctance, David shook Michael's hand.

"What brings you guys to Annapolis?" Juliana asked a little too brightly.

"It's our anniversary," Pam said, looking Michael over with interest. "Three years."

"Already? That seems hard to believe."

"How's Jeremy?" David made no attempt to hide his annoyance at seeing her with Michael.

"He's doing great. Working hard in Florida. I was down there a few weeks ago."

"Be sure to tell him we said hello," David said. "We'll have to get together when he gets home."

"Do I know you from somewhere?" Pam asked Michael.

"No, I don't think so. We need to get going, Juliana."

"Well, it was nice to see you guys." She hugged and kissed them both. "Happy anniversary."

"Thanks," Pam said, studying Michael again before David led her away.

"Oh my God," Juliana whispered, trying to catch her breath. "Oh God."

Michael put his arm around her and led her to the parking lot. "Hey," he said once they were in the car. "You haven't done anything wrong."

"David will go right home and call Jeremy. He might not even wait that long. Jeremy was David's best man. I was a bridesmaid. This is really bad."

"Juliana, look at me." When she turned her eyes to him, he said, "You aren't doing anything that he's not doing, too. Surely if David calls him, Jeremy will tell him that."

"No," she whispered. "Jeremy will just freak out. He won't tell David we're not seeing each other. He'd never tell him that. They're going to think I'm cheating on him while he's out of town."

"But you're not. Come on. Don't do this to yourself. You know the truth."

She dissolved into tears.

He brought her into his arms. "Oh, Juliana, don't. You're breaking my heart here."

"I'm sorry," she sniffed. "It's not that I'm ashamed to be seen with you, Michael. I'm so proud to be with you."

"You are?"

"Of course I am. I just don't want them to think I'm cheating on him. I couldn't bear that."

"Then maybe you need to tell them what's going on."

"Yes," she agreed. "I'll have to." She turned to him.

"I'm sorry to ruin our evening. Thank you for dinner."

He kissed her cheek. "Thank *you* for taking my mind off the trial."

"Can we go home? Please?"

"Absolutely."

They were quiet on the ride, but he kept his hand wrapped around hers. At home, he asked for her opinion on which suit and tie he should wear to court the next day. He laid the two options on his bed. "What do you think? The navy suit and red tie or the gray suit with the blue tie?"

Juliana studied the choices. "Blue suit, red tie," she said. "Definitely."

"How come?"

"You're representing the government, right?"

"Right."

"Red and blue is patriotic."

"Good point. Thanks."

"I'm going to bed."

He put his arms around her. "Are you sure you're all right?"

With her hands on his chest, she nodded. "Good luck with everything tomorrow. I'll be thinking of you."

"I'll be thinking of you, too," he said, kissing her lightly.

"Think about your work. Don't think about me."

"Impossible."

"Good night."

"Night."

Hours later Juliana lay awake, her mind racing with unpleasant scenarios. Running into Pam and David had thrown her. She wasn't prepared to explain her relationship with Michael to them or anyone else. Hell, she couldn't even explain it to herself.

When the ceiling above her bed creaked a couple of times, she realized he was pacing. She got up, pulled on her robe, and tied it around her waist on the way upstairs.

Moving back and forth across his big bedroom lost in thought, he wore only a pair of loose-fitting pajama bottoms that hung low on his narrow hips.

Juliana tried not to stare at his muscular chest and washboard stomach. "Michael?"

"Hey," he said, surprised. "What are you doing up?"

"Couldn't sleep. What about you?"

"I can't." He tapped his head. "Can't turn it off."

She went over to him and took his hand. A perplexed look crossed his face when she tugged him toward his bed. "Lie down." He did what she asked, and she could tell she shocked him again when she lay down next to him.

He groaned. "Is this supposed to be helping?"

"Turn over."

Keeping his eyes trained on her, he shifted onto his side.

"All the way."

Face down on the bed, he turned his head so he could see her.

She reached over to massage his back, her mouth going dry as her hand made contact with his warm skin.

He sighed.

"Close your eyes." She moved to her knees so she could massage him with both hands. "Feel good?"

"Mmm."

"Go to sleep."

"Yeah, right. I've got the most beautiful girl in the whole world in my bed, and you expect me to sleep through it?"

His words shot straight to her heart—and a few other places. When she leaned over to kiss his cheek, his eyes flew open. "Sleep," she said, brushing a hand over his eyes to close them again. She kneaded the tension out of his shoulders before she worked her way down his back. As his breathing became slow and steady, she applied less and less pressure until she was certain he was almost asleep. She started to move off the bed, but his arm encircled her hips to draw her down next to him. Since it was either fight him and wake him up or stay with him, she chose to stay.

Chapter 16

MICHAEL WOKE UP THIRTY MINUTES AHEAD OF THE three alarms he had set. Turning to find Juliana in bed with him, he thought he was dreaming. Then he remembered the way she had cared for him the night before and was filled with a whole new surge of love for her. Her silky dark hair was spread out on the pillow and one arm was tossed over her head. Michael studied her exquisite face, realizing he wanted to wake up with her forever. He knew it with a certainty he had never felt with Paige and didn't have a single doubt he could spend his life with Juliana and be completely content.

After he watched her sleep for at least ten minutes, he remembered the trial was starting today and he needed to get moving. Amused to acknowledge that only waking up to Juliana in his bed could have pushed the trial from his mind on this of all days, he leaned over to kiss her cheek before he got up to shut off the alarms and take a shower.

He was knotting the red tie she had chosen for him when she stirred.

"Hey," she said with a yawn. "What time is it?"

Tugging on his suit coat, he sat down next to her on the bed to tie his shoes. "Six thirty. Go back to sleep."

She ran his silk tie through her fingers. "Are you okay?"

Dumbstruck, he watched her fingers slide over his tie. "Yeah," he was finally able to say.

She held out her arms to him, and he sank into her tight embrace. "Get 'em," she whispered, using Rachelle's words for encouragement.

He pulled back to look at her. Trailing a hand down her face, he brushed back her hair and kissed her. "I'll call you when I get out of court."

"I'll be waiting."

He left her with one last kiss.

Juliana went back to sleep for a couple of hours. When she got up, she made Michael's bed and threw in a load of laundry before she went downstairs to flip on the television and find her cell phone.

On the local news at the top of the hour, she caught a glimpse of Michael going into the courthouse. A pack of reporters followed in hot pursuit as he moved quickly up the stairs. The camera cut to a standup shot of a blonde reporter gesturing to a fleet of media trucks with large satellite dishes on top. "As you can see, it's quite a circus here at the courthouse. Back to you in the studio."

Juliana put the television on mute and dialed Pam's number at work.

"Pam Newman."

"Pam, it's Juliana."

"Oh. Hi."

"Um, listen, about last night…"

"If you're worried David's going to tell Jeremy, I think I talked him out of it."

"I appreciate that, but there's something you should know."

"What's that?"

"Jeremy and I are… well… we're—"

"Spit it out, Juliana."

"We're not seeing each other right now."

"*Since when?* What happened?"

"Almost a month," Juliana said, finding that hard to believe.

"Because you're seeing that other guy? He's the prosecutor who's been on the news with the Benedetti trial. I figured that out this morning."

"Yes, he is, but he's not the reason Jeremy and I aren't together. I swear to God, Pam. That's not it."

"Then what? I can't imagine this world without you and Jeremy together. What happened?"

"Have you ever had a fight with David that you tell everyone about and then wish you hadn't when he does something wonderful to make it up to you?"

"Of course. All the time, actually."

"Well, I'd rather not get into the why and how of it, if that's all right. I just didn't want you and David to think I'm fooling around on Jeremy while he's away. That's not the case."

"What's going on with you and that sexy lawyer, Juliana? You two were awfully cozy."

"I'm not sure. But I wouldn't want Jeremy to hear about it through the grapevine because it would upset him."

"He won't hear it from me, but I can't make any promises about David. He was pretty spun up about it last night."

Juliana winced. "I'm sorry. It was your anniversary."

"Don't worry about it. Do you need anything, Juliana? Are you okay?"

"I'm just fine. Thanks."

"Call me soon, will you? I want to know what's going on."

"I will," Juliana promised and ended the call. She had done what she could to put the lid on that situation. Turning off the television, she went upstairs to shower and get dressed so she could spend her day off cleaning her mother's house.

Juliana was riveted to the lengthy coverage of the trial's fourth day on the six o'clock news, which included the daily interview with Michael on the courthouse steps. According to his reports to her each night, the trial was going as well as he could hope for so far, but he was frustrated by the defense team's propensity to drag everything out. One witness he hoped to get in and out in half a day spent two full days on the stand.

He had called a short time ago to say he would be home around eight and to pester her once more about going with him to Rhode Island the next day. Juliana put him off yet again because she didn't feel right about going. What would his family think when he brought home someone new just a few weeks after he broke up with his fiancée? Not to mention someone who wasn't quite free of her boyfriend of ten years?

Because she hadn't heard from Jeremy she was hopeful that David had resisted the urge to report in to him. Imagining Jeremy's reaction to hearing she had been out on a cozy date with another man, she shuddered. No matter what else happened, she didn't want to hurt him if she could avoid it.

Leaning forward from the sofa, she reached for the clicker to change the channel as the news ended. She had just sat back when she was startled by the sound of glass breaking and tires squealing in the street. Before she could move to see what was going on, the glass coffee table in front of her shattered. Juliana sat frozen in shock for several seconds until she felt something dripping on her face. Reaching up, her hand came back covered in blood.

She screamed.

Someone pounded on the door. "Juliana, open up! It's Officer Tanner." He banged on the door again. "Juliana!"

She crawled over the back of the sofa to avoid the glass that seemed to be everywhere and opened the door.

"Are you all right? Oh, Christ, you're bleeding. *Shit!* I went around the corner for one minute to take a leak." He called for backup and an ambulance and dug a handkerchief out of his pocket. "Sit down. Here, on the stairs." He pressed the cloth to her forehead, which seemed to be the source of the blood coursing down her face.

Stars danced in her eyes, and sirens wailed in the distance as she fought to stay conscious. In a matter of minutes, the house was full of cops and paramedics. They carried her into the dining room to lay her down so they could clean her wound and apply a butterfly bandage to her forehead.

The cops scoured the room for evidence. Under the remains of Michael's coffee table they found a large rock. Juliana swallowed hard when she realized that if she had leaned forward to change the channel one second later the rock might have hit her rather than the table. The thought made her sick.

A buzz went through the room when the cops discovered a message painted in red on the rock. "What does it say?" one of them asked.

"'We'll find her.'"

"What the hell does that mean? 'We'll find her?'"

"Rachelle," Juliana whispered in a panic. "They're talking about Rachelle, the witness in protective custody. Someone needs to call Michael. Right now." She tried to push herself up but the room spun, making her nauseous. "Call Michael," she begged Tanner.

He unclipped his cell phone from his belt. "What's the number?"

Juliana gave him Michael's cell number and then squeezed her eyes shut as her head began to throb.

"Mr. Maguire, Officer John Tanner. We've had some trouble at your house. You need to come home right away."

Juliana could hear the muffled sound of Michael yelling into the phone.

"She's hurt, but she's okay." He told Michael about the rock, the message, and Juliana's worries about Rachelle. "Yes, of course. I'll be right here with her." He ended the call and turned back to Juliana. "He's coming."

Michael's heart lodged in his throat. *Hurt but okay. What the hell does that mean? Hurt how?* He drove like a maniac through the city. When he turned on to Chester Street, the police lights, ambulance, and crowd gathered on the sidewalk in front of his house turned his blood to ice.

He pulled his car into the first available spot on the street and didn't care that he left the car door hanging open in his haste. All he could think about was getting to Juliana. "*Let me through!*" he yelled when he reached the outer edge of the crowd. "*Goddamn it! Let me through!*"

The crowd parted, and a police officer who recognized Michael lifted the yellow crime scene tape for him. He flew up the stairs and into the house, stopping dead in his tracks when he saw Juliana lying on the dining room floor covered in blood. "Oh my God," he gasped. For a brief nauseating moment he thought he was going to faint.

She raised a hand to him. "I'm okay. It looks worse than it is."

He dropped to his knees next to her and rested his head on her chest. "Oh, baby, what did they do to you?"

"We think a piece of glass from the coffee table nicked her forehead," Officer Tanner said.

"*Where the fuck were you? She could've been killed!*"

The young officer paled. "I'm sorry, Mr. Maguire. I left for five minutes to go to the bathroom. They must've been watching me."

"Do you *think?*"

"Michael, please." Juliana's fingers combed through his hair. "Don't yell at him. It's not his fault."

Michael fought back tears, and as he gathered her into his arms he was hit with the shakes. "You could've been killed," he whispered.

"Michael, the message on the rock. What about Rachelle?"

"I took care of it. We've doubled her detail. Don't worry about her."

A police lieutenant approached them. "Mr. Maguire?" Michael looked up at him.

"We're going to be here a while, so we'll put you two up in a hotel for the night."

"She needs to go to the hospital," Michael said.

"We treated her," one of the paramedics said. "It was a surface cut, but head wounds bleed like crazy."

"I'm fine, Michael, really. Just shook up. I don't need the hospital."

"Why don't you pack a bag so we can get you settled?" the lieutenant suggested to Michael.

"Will you be all right for a few minutes?" Michael asked her, afraid that if he let her go for even a minute, he might come back to find that she wasn't fine, that she had been hit by the rock rather than a piece of glass. He trembled at the thought of how close it must have been.

She caressed his face. "I'm fine. Go ahead and pack us a bag. Can you grab me a shirt to change into?" The one she had on was soaked with blood.

He nodded and kissed her before he went upstairs to pack. When he returned a few minutes later, the lieutenant ordered Tanner to drive them to the Hyatt at the Inner Harbor.

"I've arranged to have two men posted outside your door," the lieutenant said.

Michael helped Juliana up from the floor and held her until she was steady. "Do you need help?"

"No, I can do it." She took the shirt he had brought her into the tiny bathroom off the dining room.

"Can you clear the street?" Michael asked the cops. "I don't want her photographed." When she emerged from the bathroom, he produced a large, hooded Georgetown sweatshirt and helped her into it. "I don't want them to know your face," he whispered, pulling the hood up around her head.

They were whisked down the stairs and into a waiting cruiser for the ride downtown. In the back of the car, Michael held her close to him and struggled to contain the riot of emotions that coursed through him—rage, relief, love, and fear. For the first time in his career he was afraid but not for himself. "I need to call my boss, honey." He reached for his cell phone while keeping his other arm wrapped around her as she rested her head on his shoulder. "I'm sorry. I want to focus only on you, but I have to tell him about this."

"Of course you do."

Michael called Tom Houlihan at home and filled him in.

"This is outrageous!" Tom said. "When I hang up with you I'm calling Judge Stein. Are you sure your friend is okay?"

"Yes, she's shaken up and a piece of the coffee table cut her forehead, but the paramedics said she's okay. They're putting us in the Hyatt for the night while crime scene does their thing at my house."

"Call me if there's anything at all you need."

"I want you to keep her name out of the papers, Tom. I mean it. I don't want them having her name."

"I'll see to that personally. I'm sure the trial will be in recess until this is sorted out."

"I'd like to avoid that if we can," Michael said. "The longer this goes on, the more danger Rachelle is in. Try to talk him into moving forward on Monday."

"I'll see what I can do, and I'll call you in the morning. I'm sorry about this, Michael."

"Thanks. I'll talk to you tomorrow."

"Do you really think Rachelle is in danger, Michael?" Juliana asked in a small voice. "I'm so afraid for her."

"She's fine. She has seven cops with her. I don't want you to worry." He released a ragged deep breath. "What the hell was I thinking letting you become involved in all this?"

Juliana raised her head to look him in the eye. "I didn't become involved in all of this. I became involved with you."

Overwhelmed by her, Michael guided her head back to his shoulder.

Chapter 17

THEY PULLED UP TO THE HYATT, AND OFFICER TANNER turned to them. "One room or two?"

Michael glanced down at Juliana.

"One," she said.

"Coming right up. I'll be back for you in a few minutes."

"I've always wanted to stay here," Juliana said. The sleek black-glass hotel overlooked Baltimore's famous Inner Harbor where the bombs bursting over Fort McHenry during the War of 1812 inspired Francis Scott Key to write the poem that later became the "Star Spangled Banner." "But it's hard to justify a night in the Hyatt when you live in the city."

"Too bad you had to be nearly killed to get here."

"Michael, stop." She ran a finger along his jaw, which was tight with tension. "I'm fine."

Tanner returned and escorted them to a room on the hotel's seventh floor.

"We'll be right outside, Mr. Maguire. Just holler if you need anything."

"Thank you."

"John?" Juliana walked over to the young policeman.

"Yes?"

"I appreciate all you did back at the house."

"It shouldn't have happened." He looked like he could cry. "I'm sorry."

She put her hand on his arm. "When people are determined to do something like this, they find a way."

"I'm just glad you're okay," he said on his way out the door. "Try to get some sleep."

Juliana attempted to pull the Georgetown sweatshirt over her head and gasped when it rubbed against the cut on her forehead.

Michael came to her side. "Let me help you." He eased the sweatshirt over her forehead and gently removed it. Tossing it aside, he put his arms around her. "It's good of you to be so forgiving."

"It's not his fault, Michael. He didn't throw the rock." She snuggled into his embrace. "I need to take a shower."

He tightened his hold on her. "Wait. Stay here for a minute. Stay with me."

She closed her arms around him and felt a tremble ripple through him.

"When they said you were hurt," he said, his voice hoarse with emotion, "I don't think I've ever been more terrified in my life. And when I saw all that blood…"

"Shh, Michael. Don't."

He looked down at her, his eyes bright with tears. "I love you," he whispered. "Those words seem so insignificant in light of all I feel for you. There just isn't a big enough word, Juliana."

"I love you, too."

He seemed to stop breathing. "You do?"

She reached up to caress his face. "I've known it since the last time we saw Rachelle. The way you were with her… You were amazing, and I just knew."

Releasing a rattling deep breath, Michael closed his eyes and kissed her slowly and deeply, as if he was trying to put all his love for her into that one kiss.

After a long while, she pulled back from him. "I'm going to go wash off the blood. You got some on your shirt."

"I don't care."

She reached up to unbutton the light blue dress shirt he had worn to court that morning. "Take it off. I'll soak it."

"Don't worry about it. Are you hungry?"

"I don't think I could eat."

"Me either."

"I'll be right back."

He stole one more kiss before he let her go. "I'll be right here."

She pushed the shirt off his shoulders and took it with her into the bathroom. In the shower, she winced at the water sliding over the cut on her forehead. She watched the water in the tub turn red when she rinsed her hair and washed it. The pulsating shower helped to ease some of the tension from her shoulders and back. Stepping out of the shower, she wrapped her hair in a towel and pulled on the thick white robe the hotel provided. Wiping the steam off the mirror, she took a close look at the wound on her forehead. The small cut certainly didn't measure up to the amount of blood it had produced. A tinge of black and blue already surrounded it.

As she brushed her hair and then dried it, she shuddered each time she thought about how much worse it could have been. Her legs still felt like they were made of Jell-O.

She had told Michael she loved him, which made her stomach also feel like Jell-O—not only because it was true, but because she still loved Jeremy. However, she wasn't thinking of him just then. No, her thoughts were all about Michael and the way his face had faded to a ghostly pale when he came rushing into the house to find her covered in blood. In that heartbreaking moment, she had *seen* his love for her. And when he said there wasn't a big enough word to describe how he felt about her... That had been, quite simply, the most romantic moment of her life.

Michael ignored his ringing cell phone for a tenth time, turned it off, and went to look out at the full moon hanging over the Inner Harbor. To his right, he could make out the brick walls of Camden Yards, home to the Baltimore Orioles.

After he'd finally managed to stop shaking, he was hit by a wave of rage so deep and so intense it took his breath away. That those fucking *monsters,* those fucking arrogant *bastards* thought they would get away with this...

The hair dryer turned off, and he took a deep breath to calm himself down. He didn't want Juliana to see the rage. That wasn't what she needed from him right now. She loved him. Nothing else mattered. Not tonight.

The bathroom door opened, and he turned to her, deciding instantly that he had never seen anything more beautiful than Juliana in the white bathrobe with her shiny dark hair flowing down around her shoulders. Her usually vibrant olive skin had a pallor to it that made her brown eyes seem even bigger than usual. His gut clenched when he remembered how the bandage on her forehead had gotten there and what might have happened…

Pushing those thoughts aside, he held out his hand to her. "I found some medicine." He pointed to the two small bottles of Sutter Home from the mini-bar.

"Bring it on, but I warn you, it'll go straight to my head."

"Does the cut hurt?"

"No."

"I asked the cops to get you some Tylenol. It's over there if you need it."

"Thanks." She moved to the window to check out the view of the harbor. "I figured your phone would be ringing nonstop."

"I shut it off."

She turned to him. "Can you do that?"

He handed her a glass of wine. "Tom can deal with the media tonight. That's why he's the boss. Feel better after the shower?"

"Much better. Do you think it'll be on the news?"

"It probably already is, but your name won't be mentioned. Tom will see to that."

"What does it mean for the trial?"

"I don't know, and right now I don't care. I don't want to think about that."

She ran a hand over his bare chest and toyed with the St. Christopher medal he wore on a thin gold chain.

He trembled under her caress.

"I'm frightened for you, Michael. What if they hurt you? Or worse? You're trying to put them in prison—"

"Don't." He tipped her chin so he could see her eyes. "Don't bring them into this room with us. I don't want them anywhere near us. Not ever, but especially not tonight." He kissed her. "Not tonight," he whispered. He took the wine glass from her and put it on a table. Running his thumbs along her jaw, he slid his fingers into her hair. His lips glided over hers in a soft, easy caress that quickly became passionate.

She loved him. He didn't have to wonder or hope anymore. And when her arms encircled his neck and her tongue met his in ardent response, he was lost. He picked her up, carried her across the room, and laid her down on the big bed. With his eyes trained on hers, he kicked off his pants, reached for the belt to her robe, and tugged it open.

He ran his hands over her reverently. "Oh, Juliana," he sighed, his lips pressed to her belly. "You're every fantasy I've ever had come to life."

He cupped her breasts and had to remind himself that they had all night. She was so beautiful, so perfect in every way that he resisted the urge to devour and took the time to savor. That she loved him, too, was nothing short of a dream come true. *She* was a dream come true. He rolled his tongue over her pebbled nipple, and she gasped with pleasure.

"You smell so good," he said. "I don't know what it is, but it turns me on like nothing ever has."

She chuckled. "It's Aveda."

"Mmm, I love Aveda." Reluctantly leaving her breasts for the time being, he kissed his way down, nudged her legs apart, and nuzzled her with his lips and then his tongue. He teased her with short caresses that had her panting for more and then deeper strokes that made her moan. He kept it up until she was wild beneath him.

Finally, he focused his tongue on the spot that pulsed with desire and slipped a finger into her.

Releasing another choppy moan, she lifted her hips in encouragement and grabbed a fistful of his hair to keep him there. It took only a few strokes of his tongue and finger to send her flying.

He looked up, startled to find her cheeks wet with tears. "Juliana? Are you all right?"

She nodded and reached out to him.

"What is it?" he whispered against her neck. He felt her fingers tunnel through his hair and was reminded of the first time she had done that, the moment he knew for sure that he loved her. Lifting his head, he found her eyes. "Tell me."

Biting her lip, she studied him. "You know I want this—I want *you*—right?"

"I think so."

"And that I love you? I really love you?"

"I'm still getting used to that one," he said with a smile, the wonder of it hitting him all over again. How had he ever gotten so lucky?

She rested her hands on his face. "It's just that I've never, you know, done… this—"

"With anyone else."

"Yes."

"And you're feeling guilty."

"Kind of."

Afraid she was retreating from him, he leaned down to kiss her softly, gently. Ignoring his own urgent need, he said, "We don't have to, Juliana. Not if it doesn't feel right to you."

"But it does. It feels right. *You* feel right."

Her hands traveled from his face to his back and down to clutch to his backside.

He trembled with want, but still he held back.

"Make love to me, Michael." Lifting her legs up and around his hips, she offered herself to him and smiled as she took him in.

Fully sheathed in her heat, he was swamped with the sensation of being exactly where he belonged. This was it. *She* was it. She was *the one*.

"Look at me, Juliana." Their first time, which could have been awkward, wasn't. They moved in effortless harmony, like a couple together for years rather than weeks. "Don't look away. I want you to see how much I love you." He waited, held off, watched. He saw her eyes flutter with fulfillment even before he felt it, but still he wouldn't let her look away, wouldn't take the chance that she would think of anything—or *anyone*—but him in that moment.

Calling upon every ounce of self-control he could muster, he drove her up and over once more before he let himself join her in the most earth-shattering, mind-altering climax of his life. It left him gasping for air, for reason, for sanity.

So… This was what it meant to make love, to really and truly make love. He'd never before emerged from a sexual encounter feeling so irrevocably changed.

"I love you, Juliana," he whispered against her neck. "There'll never be anyone but you for me. Not ever again."

"I love you, too." Her fingertips trailed over his back as her lips found the sensitive place where his neck met his shoulder.

He shivered. "What if we made a baby?" he asked, unable to believe he hadn't thought of it before now. That, too, was a first.

"I'm on the pill."

"Damn."

She laughed. "I thought you wanted to leave the baby-making to your sisters."

Raising his head so he could see her, he said, "Not anymore." He dropped light kisses on her cheeks, her nose, her chin, and the butterfly on her forehead before he reclaimed her lips. "Tell me again, Juliana. I need to hear it again."

She looked into his eyes. "I love you, Michael. I love you," she whispered, bringing his mouth back to hers.

He rolled them over so she was on top. "Show me."

Her throbbing forehead woke Juliana at five the next morning. As she eased out of Michael's embrace, reached for the robe on the floor, and pulled it on, he sighed but didn't wake up. She found the Tylenol he had gotten for her and swallowed the pills. Taking another long drink from the bottle of water, she went over to the window.

The sunrise flirted with the horizon, casting a warm glow over the Inner Harbor. From this vantage point, she couldn't quite make out the salon on the far end of the shops and restaurants that lined the harbor. The normally bustling waterfront was quiet and still. Juliana had never seen it quite so tranquil.

Off in the distance she noticed one of the party boats that populated the harbor and the Chesapeake Bay and was struck by the memory of attending her senior prom with Jeremy on one of those boats. *Oh, Jer. What am I going to do?*

She turned to look at Michael, and her heart galloped when memories from their night together flashed through her mind. Her body tingled as she recalled his intense lovemaking. She couldn't say exactly why, but being with him had been different than being with Jeremy. Maybe it was because of all they had been through in their short time together, but she'd never felt more cherished in her life than she had in Michael's arms. He made her feel as if she was the answer to every question he'd ever had.

Gazing back out over the harbor, Juliana summoned the courage she would need to face what was ahead. Before much longer, she would disappoint one of the two men she loved—one of the two men who loved her. Mrs. Romanello had warned her that it would come down to a choice, and she was exactly right.

Juliana was startled out of her thoughts when Michael came up behind her and wrapped his arms around her. He nudged her hair aside to gain access to her neck.

"What are you doing up so early?"

Covering his hands with hers, she trembled from what he was doing to her neck. "Couldn't sleep. What about you?"

"I couldn't find you."

Against her back, she felt his arousal.

"Come with me," he whispered.

With a last glance at the sunrise, she let him take her to bed.

Michael held her close to him and tried to catch his breath as his heart hammered in his chest. Would it always be like this with her? What had been hot and passionate with Paige was all of that with Juliana and *so* much more. "It's still early." He kissed the top of her head. "Why don't you try to go back to sleep for a while?"

She laughed softly. "You've got me *wide* awake."

He propped himself up on one elbow. "Let's get the hell out of here for the weekend, Juliana," he pleaded. "I want to take you to Rhode Island. Please go with me?"

After studying him for a moment, she said, "Okay."

"Yeah?"

She brought him down for a kiss. "I'll have to bribe my brother to take care of my mother for the weekend, but he'll do it."

"Why don't we just get up now and go? I have a couple of things I have to do, and then we can hit the road."

"I'm going to take a quick shower."

"I'll order us some breakfast." He gave her one last kiss before he released her. "Any preferences?"

"Whatever you're having is fine."

Once again Michael was struck by the differences between Juliana and Paige, who would've had a very specific request. In just a few weeks with Juliana, the idea of being married to Paige had become preposterous. He pulled on a pair of gym shorts, called in the room service order, and opened the door to the hallway to get the paper.

"Morning, Mr. Maguire," the police officer on duty said. "Everything all right?"

"Yes. I'll need a lift to my house in about an hour if that's okay."

"Sure thing."

"Thanks."

Michael took the paper back into the room and wasn't surprised to find a story about the vandalism to his house above the fold on the front page of the *Baltimore Sun*.

Benedetti Prosecutor Victim of Vandalism

The home of Michael Maguire, lead prosecutor in the ongoing murder trial of Marco and Steven Benedetti, was vandalized on Thursday evening. A large rock was thrown through the window of Maguire's Butchers Hill home. Maguire's roommate suffered minor injuries. He was not home at the time.

The Benedetti brothers face first-degree murder charges in the slayings of three city teenagers a year ago. The trial, in recess today for an unrelated matter, will resume next week in Baltimore City Circuit Court.

Police refused to comment on whether the incident is related to the trial, nor would they release any further details.

A spokesman for Maguire's employer, Baltimore City State's Attorney Tom Houlihan, had no comment.

Calls to Circuit Court Judge Harvey Stein, who is presiding over the trial, were not returned by press time.

Michael was relieved that Tom had succeeded in keeping Juliana's name out of the story.

She came out of the bathroom. "Shower's all yours."

"The story is in the paper." He handed it to her. "No details, though."

"Good." But she winced as she scanned the article. "It mentions your roommate was injured. I need to make a phone call." She dug her cell phone out of her purse. When she turned it on, it beeped with multiple messages. She found the number she was looking for and pressed send. "Hey, Mrs. R, it's me." Pausing, she said, "It's just a tiny cut. Honest." Another pause. "We have cops all around us. There's nothing to worry about. We're going out of town for the weekend, but I'll come by before we go, okay?" Juliana nodded. "I will," she said, closing her phone to end the call.

"What was that all about?" Michael asked on his way to the shower.

"Our neighbor. She's like a mother to me. She's the only one who knows I've been staying with you, so I knew she'd panic when she saw the paper."

"So you told someone about me, huh?" he asked with a satisfied smile.

She grinned. "Go take a shower." After Michael closed the door, she called Vincent.

"*What?*" he roared.

"Sorry. I forgot how early it is."

"What do you want, Juliana?"

"You have to take care of Ma this weekend."

"I don't gotta do nothing."

"I'm going away, so it's you or no one unless you can get Dona to help you."

"As if. Are you off to see Mr. Wonderful again?"

"No. I'll be back Sunday night. Check on her, Vin. She's been worse than usual lately."

"She's living on booze. I can't ever get her to eat anything."

"We're going to have to do something about that one of these days."

"Yeah."

"Thanks for the help."

"I'm going back to sleep."

An hour later, Michael and Juliana were driven home by a police officer.

"Let me go in ahead of you," the cop said.

"The window's already fixed," Michael noticed.

"Your boss took care of that himself. A guy who grew up in Canton with Houlihan was over here at eleven last night to fix it."

"That's good of him," Juliana said.

"Everything seems okay," the cop said. "I'll be right outside if you need anything."

"We'll be leaving town until Sunday night," Michael said.

"I'll need to know where you're going. Houlihan wants someone on both of you until the trial is over. Maybe even beyond that."

"We'll be in Rhode Island, so we won't need coverage there," Michael insisted. "I'll talk to Houlihan. Someone needs to be with Juliana for about an hour while I take care of something, and then we're good until Sunday."

"Okay," the cop said and left them.

Michael watched Juliana fixate on the open space in the room, the coffee table's absence a glaring reminder of what happened the night before.

Michael tugged her hand. "Come on."

"They did a good job cleaning up," she said softly. "You'd never know."

He steered her up the stairs. "Let's pack and get out of here."

Two officers in a police cruiser followed them to Mrs. Romanello's house.

"Will you come in for a minute?" Juliana asked Michael. "I'd like you to meet her."

"Sure."

He wore a black sweater with faded jeans, but Juliana knew that when she pictured him, she would always see him in a suit.

"Where's your house?"

Juliana pointed. "That one."

He glanced at it and followed her up the stairs to Mrs. R's front door.

"Hey," Juliana called when they walked in. They followed the sound of a mixer running in the kitchen. Juliana kissed the older woman's cheek.

"Oh, hon, let me see." Mrs. R turned off the mixer and tipped Juliana's face so she could get a better look at the wound. "It shouldn't leave a scar."

"I'm not worried about it," Juliana said, touched by her friend's concern. "This is Michael Maguire."

Mrs. R sized him up and reached out to shake his hand. "Hello."

"Nice to meet you."

"I'm not pleased about this, young man." She gestured to Juliana's face.

"Believe me, I'm not either."

"You'll come stay here," Mrs. R said to Juliana.

"That's a good idea," Michael agreed. "We're going out of town for a few days, and then Juliana will come stay here until the trial's over."

"Hello, I'm in the room," Juliana protested. "I'm not moving out, Michael, so you can both stop running my life."

"It's not safe at my house."

"Are you staying there?"

"Well… Yeah."

"If you're staying, I'm staying." She gave him a look that let him know the subject was closed. "Go do what you need to do so we can get going," she said with a nudge to get him moving.

"I'll be less than an hour," he told Juliana. To Mrs. R he said, "Nice to meet you."

"You, too. Keep this girl safe, do you hear me?"

"Yes, ma'am," he said, hesitating.

Juliana realized he wanted to kiss her, so she walked him to the front door.

He slipped his arms around her. "While I'm gone, how about you go next door and find something you can bring with you to wear in a place with candles and wine and music, okay? Something you've been saving for a special occasion."

Amused, she asked, "How do you know I have something like that?"

"I know you."

"Hurry back," she said with a lingering kiss.

Groaning, he tore himself away from her. "I will."

Juliana watched him go and then returned to the kitchen.

"Oh, Juliana," Mrs. R said with a hand over her heart. "Oh, hon. What in the world are you going to do?"

"I love him."

"I can see that." Mrs. R put an arm around Juliana, leading her to sit at the kitchen table. "You've been with him. I see that, too."

Juliana's face burned with embarrassment. "Yes," she said in a whisper.

"Where are you going this weekend?"

"To Rhode Island where his family lives."

"Every minute you spend with him gets you deeper into this. You know that, don't you?"

"I just need to be with him right now. Maybe I'll feel differently when I see Jeremy again, but for now, this is what I want. He's what I want."

Mrs. Romanello clutched Juliana's hand. "God bless you, hon. God bless you all."

Chapter 18

JULIANA WENT NEXT DOOR TO PICK UP THE MAIL AND THE dress Michael asked her to bring. She left two more letters from Jeremy unopened on the kitchen table. The house smelled musty and a thin layer of dust covered every surface. She would have to get over here to clean next week.

Michael was back in forty-five minutes. They bid Mrs. Romanello and their police detail good-bye and headed north on Interstate 95 to the Delaware Memorial Bridge. As they left Baltimore and all their troubles behind, Juliana began to relax.

"How long will it take to get there?"

"Six or seven hours, depending on the traffic on the Jersey Turnpike, the Cross Bronx Expressway, and in Connecticut, which is always the worst."

"Do you usually fly or drive?"

"I fly because I never have much time, but I prefer to drive."

"If I had this car, I'd prefer to drive, too."

"Want to?"

Her eyes widened. "Really?"

He pulled over. "Really."

Juliana clapped her hands with glee and jumped out of the car to change places with him. Once in the driver's seat, she put on her seatbelt, shifted the car into first gear, and hit the gas.

"Jesus!" he said, gripping the armrest with alarm.

Juliana smiled at him. "Hold on to your hat, baby."

"I've never gotten to Connecticut this fast—ever," Michael said just over three hours later. "How about giving me a turn?"

Juliana smiled. "Nope. I'm having too much fun."

He cringed when she darted between two semis. "You're stressing me out."

"Don't look."

"The way you're changing lanes, I'll puke if I close my eyes."

"I never knew you were such a wimp."

"You weren't calling me a wimp last night."

She glanced over at him. "Just a tad bit full of yourself, aren't you?"

"Watch the road!"

Cruising along the southern coast of Connecticut, Juliana confessed that she hadn't been to New England before.

"Never?"

"Nope. We didn't really go anywhere when I was growing up. A daytrip to Ocean City was a big deal."

He reached for her hand. "You didn't have an easy go of it as a kid, did you?"

She shrugged. "It was what it was. Most of the time, it was just my parents and me since the next oldest—Vincent—was eight years older than me."

"And your parents were unhappy together?"

"That's putting it mildly. They fought like cats and dogs—when my mother wasn't loaded, that is."

"Your brothers and sisters weren't around?"

"Not unless they had to be. They all moved out as soon as they turned eighteen."

"Why didn't you?"

"Well, by then my father was heavily into his 'extra-curricular activities,' as my mother called them, and she was hitting the bottle pretty hard. I just felt like I needed to be there with her."

"So how did you end up moving out?"

She glanced over at him and then back at the road.

"Juliana?"

"Jeremy kind of put his foot down about it. He hates the way my family treats me, so he insisted I move out of my mother's house and in with him."

"He *insisted?*"

"He gave me the push I needed to do something about a bad situation."

"Like an ultimatum?"

"Of course not."

"I'm sorry."

"He didn't give me an ultimatum, Michael. It wasn't like that."

"It's none of my business," Michael said, looking out the passenger window.

Juliana tugged on his hand. "Hey. Don't check out on me. What're you thinking?"

"I forget sometimes that you're not really free. Then I'll remember all of a sudden, and it just kind of hits me right here." He ran a hand over his gut.

She sighed.

He looked over at her. "What am I going to do if you go back to him?"

"Can we not do this?" she pleaded. "I don't have to make any decisions today, tomorrow, or even the next day. Can we just be together for now?"

He studied her for a long time before he answered. "I guess we can do that." Kissing her hand, he added, "For now."

They stopped for lunch in Mystic, Connecticut, where Michael managed to wrestle the keys away from Juliana.

"It's so pretty," she said an hour later as she looked out over Narragansett Bay from the top of the Newport Bridge. "This bridge reminds me of the Bay Bridge," she said, referring to the span over the Chesapeake Bay that connects the Annapolis area to Maryland's Eastern Shore.

"That bridge looks like it was assembled from a bridge yard sale, like ten different kinds of bridges all in one."

Juliana laughed. "You're right. It does. Oh, look, there's a house sitting on the rocks out there!"

"The house is called 'Clingstone.'"

"I love that!"

He took the Newport exit, and as they drove between two cemeteries, he said, "Guess what the name of this street is?"

"Cemetery Way?"

He shook his head. "Farewell Street."

"Oh," she said with a chuckle. "That's a good one."

"In the summer this road is jam-packed with cars," he said of America's Cup Avenue.

"It seems almost familiar in some ways. I wonder why."

"Annapolis reminds me a lot of Newport. The colonial houses, the gas streetlamps, and the cobblestone streets are so similar."

"And there's a harbor here, too. Just like Annapolis."

He took a right on to Lower Thames Street. "This part of Newport is called the Fifth Ward," Michael said when they had traveled about a mile down Lower Thames. "It's where all the Irish people live."

"Like Little Italy in Baltimore."

"Yes, sort of," he said, pulling into a driveway on Carroll Avenue.

They stretched out the kinks from the long ride.

"This is it." He gestured to the small ranch house. "This is where I grew up. We used to play baseball at the park we passed at the corner."

"Are your parents home?"

"I'm not sure what their schedules are today. I didn't tell them we were coming."

"*What?*"

He laughed, put an arm around her, and kissed her cheek. "Don't sweat it, baby. They'll be thrilled to meet you." He tugged her along with him and used a key on his ring to unlock the door. It took him about five minutes to show her around the small, tidy house that smelled of lemon furniture polish and potpourri.

"Oh, is that you?" Juliana asked, pointing to a faded framed photo in the hallway.

Michael grimaced. "I think that was seventh grade."

"You were so cute!"

"*Were?*"

Giggling, she studied the other photos on the wall. "That's Pat."

"You looked alike."

"That's what people said."

The bedroom that used to be Michael's was now filled with toys belonging to his nieces and nephews. Another bedroom contained twin beds.

"For grandkid sleepovers," Michael explained, leading her back to the kitchen. He went to peek into the garage. Returning to her, his arms circled her waist. "No one's home," he whispered against her lips.

She pushed him away. "Stop it!"

"What?" he asked, his lips quirking with amusement.

"We're in your *parents'* house. Behave."

"Why?" He backed her up against the kitchen counter for a searing kiss.

"Michael, *stop,*" she pleaded when he kissed her again.

"I've needed this for hours." He held her tight against him as he teased and tormented with his lips and hands until she was breathless.

She moaned when he went to work on her neck and throat. "Stop," she whispered.

He cupped her breasts and ran his thumbs over her nipples. "I want you."

Filled with nervous laughter, she said, "I can tell."

He dropped his hands to her bottom, pulled her tight against his erection, and reclaimed her mouth. Even when Juliana's cell phone began to ring, he kept up the mischief until she tore herself away from him to reach for her purse. "It's Mrs. R," she told Michael.

"Juliana?"

"Hi. What's up?"

"Jeremy's in town, and he's looking for you."

"Oh my God! What's he doing there?"

Michael gave her a questioning look. She held up a finger to say just a minute.

"He said he had plane tickets for this weekend and decided to come as planned. He wants to know where you are. What should I tell him?"

"I'll call him."

"Are you sure that's a good idea?"

"Don't worry," Juliana assured her friend. "I'll take care of it."

"He's um, well—"

"What?"

"He's wound up because he can tell you're not living in the house. He's having a fit."

Juliana groaned.

"Did you get there okay?"

"Yes, about half an hour ago."

"Okay. Call me back if you need me for anything."

"I will. Thanks."

"What's going on?" Michael asked when she flipped her phone closed.

"Jeremy's in town. I guess he's raising hell because I'm not there. Mrs. R said he figured out I'm not living in the house. I noticed how dusty the place was this morning when I was there. He knows I'd never let it get like that if I was living there." She paused before she added, "I need to call him."

"Okay."

"I'm sorry."

"Nothing to be sorry about." He kissed her forehead and steered her into the living room. "I'll wait for you in the kitchen."

Juliana took a deep, calming breath and released it before she opened her cell phone to push number one on her speed dial.

"Babe?" Jeremy said, apparently pouncing on the phone. "Where the heck are you?"

"I'm out of town. I needed to get away for a while."

"I really wanted to see you this weekend. I was hoping we could get past all this craziness."

"We said three months. It's only been one."

"Come on, Juliana! This is getting ridiculous."

"I'm sorry you feel that way, but I need this time to figure some stuff out."

"What stuff?"

"I've got to go, Jer. I'll talk to you in two months."

"Where are you living, Juliana? I can tell you're not staying here."

"With a friend."

"You don't have friends that I don't know."

"I do now."

"I miss you, babe," he said, his voice urgent. "It's making me sick. I miss you so much."

"Bye, Jer." Overwhelmed by the emotion and distress she'd heard in his voice, Juliana buried her face in her hands.

"Are you all right?" Michael asked from the doorway.

Making an effort to rally, she forced a smile. "Yeah."

He came into the room and sat next to her, drawing her into his arms.

Juliana relaxed into his embrace, comforted by the strong beat of his heart.

"Better?" he asked after several quiet minutes.

She tilted her face up and kissed him softly. "Much."

He cupped her cheek and was about to kiss her again when they heard the garage door open.

She pulled away from him.

He groaned. "You owe me," he whispered, helping her up from the sofa.

Juliana giggled and followed him into the kitchen.

Michael's mother burst into the room with a huge smile on her pretty face. "I see Maryland license plates in my driveway!" She stopped short when she saw that her son wasn't alone. "Oh, and you finally cut your hair! I love it!"

"Hi, Mom." Michael smiled as he leaned down to kiss and hug her. She was a shorter, rounder version of Michael. Her brown hair was shot through with silver and her blue eyes skipped over her son and his companion. "This is Juliana Gregorio. She's responsible for the haircut."

Maureen extended her hand. "Pleased to meet you, Juliana. Wonderful job on the hair."

Juliana shook her hand. "Thank you, Mrs. Maguire."

"Please, call me Maureen."

"Where's Dad?" Michael asked, helping himself to a beer from the fridge.

Juliana shook her head when he offered her one.

"He's working until five. He'll be thrilled to see you." Maureen swatted Michael. "Why didn't you tell me you were coming? I would've cleaned the house."

"Cleaned what?" Michael asked, looking around at the spotless house.

"Your home is lovely, Maureen."

Maureen looked at Juliana with an almost surprised expression. "Thank you." She turned back to Michael. "How'd you get away? No court today?"

"Nope. The judge had something else to do."

"How's the trial going?" Maureen asked.

"Pretty well."

They had agreed not to mention the trouble at his house to his family since they would worry.

"Your sisters will be delighted that you're here. Are you staying at Maggie's?"

"I hope she has room."

"It's the off-season. She's slow."

"Maggie and Luke own a bed and breakfast inn," Michael explained to Juliana.

"Well, let me call them all," Maureen said. "I'll invite everyone over for pizza, sound good?"

"Sounds perfect," Michael said, looking to Juliana.

She nodded in agreement.

Many hours later, Michael's sister Maggie showed them to a fancy room on the third floor of her home.

A natural blonde who favored their father, Sean, Maggie gestured to a doorway. "The bathroom's right through here, and there're plenty of towels in the closet. Do you need anything else?"

"No, we're good. Thanks, Maggie. Just make sure you tell Mom you gave us two rooms."

She laughed and kissed her brother's cheek. "Do you think I was born yesterday? Very nice to meet you, Juliana. Very, *very* nice."

"You, too, Maggie. Thanks for everything."

"I'll see you in the morning. Come on down whenever you get up."

"Good night." Michael closed the door and turned to Juliana. "My sisters love you."

"They're so nice. And the kids are just adorable."

"How many French braids did you do tonight?"

"How many girls are there again?"

"Seven."

"That sounds about right."

Resting his hands on her shoulders, he leaned in to kiss her. "They all loved you. Almost as much as I do."

"I just can't imagine what it would be like to be part of a family like yours. You can tease and bicker and fight, but it's obvious you all love each other so much. You're really lucky, Michael."

"I know I am. Paige was only here once. It was a total disaster. Her complaints were endless: the kids were too loud, my sisters were bitchy to her, my mother didn't like her. On and on."

"I just don't see how…" Juliana shook her head when she thought better of it.

"What were you going to say?"

"I don't see how you lasted so long with her. I know I shouldn't say that, but I wonder."

"I've come to realize I was killing time with her."

"Until what?"

"Until I found you."

"You say the sweetest things," she said, caressing his cheek.

"I mean it." He hugged her. "You know I do."

She relaxed into his embrace. "Michael?"

"Hmm?"

"Can we go to bed now?"

"I thought you'd never ask."

She giggled as he backed her up to the bed, his eyes hot with intent. "I didn't know I needed to ask."

"You don't." His lips cruised up her neck. "I'm all yours. Any time you want me."

Shivering from what he was doing to her neck, she reached down to cup his straining erection through his jeans. "How about now?"

He moaned. "*Juliana…*"

Trailing a finger up and down the length of him, she said, "Hmm?"

He sprang into action, pulling and pushing at clothes, until he had access to what he wanted.

Delighted to have driven him a little crazy, Juliana laughed at the picture she must've made with her shirt pushed up to her neck, her bra pulled down, and her jeans tangled around her ankles.

"What the hell is so funny?" he asked through gritted teeth as he plunged into her.

Juliana's laughter faded into a gasp. Arching her back to meet his thrusts, she managed to say, "I thought we'd get ready for bed the way civilized people do."

Slowing the pace of his hips, he rolled her earlobe between his teeth. "How do civilized people get ready for bed?"

"Often, they get undressed."

"I uncovered the good parts."

Slipping her hands under his shirt, she eased it up and over his head. "Mmm, more good parts," she said, running her thumbs over his nipples.

He groaned and pushed into her again as she wiggled under him. "What're you *doing?*"

Choked with laughter, Juliana said, "Trying to get my pants all the way off."

With his foot, he swept her jeans away and then hooked her leg over his hip. "Much better."

"*Mmm*," she whispered. "*Michael…*"

"I love the way you say my name." He brushed his lips over hers.

"Don't stop, okay?"

Laughing, he said, "Don't worry, stopping isn't in the plan. Feel good?"

Juliana looped her arms around his neck. "*Amazing.*"

"So there might be something to be said for uncivilized?"

"Oh *yeah…*"

He went deep, and she cried out as an orgasm hit her hard and fast.

"God, *Juliana…*"

She opened her eyes in time to watch him lose himself in her. Moved and astounded by the wonder of it, she held him close to her.

"We can do it your way now," he said after a long moment of quiet.

"How's that?"

"Civilized."

"Why would we want to when your way is so much better?"

Smiling, he brushed the hair back from her face and kissed her.

As he gazed at her with unabashed love, Juliana somehow knew she would never forget this particular moment.

Chapter 19

THE NEXT MORNING, MICHAEL AND JULIANA WATCHED his nephews play against their cousins in a close Little League baseball game.

"Which team are we supposed to be for?" Juliana whispered to him.

"Both. Definitely both."

"Welcome to my world," Maureen said when she overheard their conversation. "Next year the girls are going to try to get them all on the same team. This is too stressful."

After Colm and Cormac's team beat Patrick and Sean's, Michael and Juliana had lunch downtown with his parents. He fought a losing battle with his father for the check, and when his parents left to do some errands, Michael and Juliana walked back to Maggie's. On the way, they window-shopped in the stores and boutiques that lined the waterfront.

"See anything you like?"

"All of it," Juliana said.

He laughed.

An odd expression came over her face.

"What?"

"That guy, across the street. I've seen him somewhere before."

Michael turned to look.

"Which one?"

"The brown jacket. See him?"

Across the street, the man in question took off in the other direction.

"Are you sure you know him?"

"No. He probably just looks like someone I know through work or something. Forget it."

He glanced over one more time, but the man was at least three blocks from them. Michael put his arm around Juliana for the short walk back to Maggie's house.

When they got there, no one was home, so he spirited Juliana up the stairs. Closing the bedroom door and locking it, he turned to her.

"You're going to get tired of me if we keep this up," she said with a shy smile as he eased the coat off her shoulders.

"I will *never* get tired of you." When she looked away, he used a finger on her chin to bring her back to him. "You've heard that before, haven't you?"

She shrugged.

"Juliana, look at me."

Reluctantly, she brought her eyes up to his.

"I will never, ever, *ever* get tired of you—not ten years from now, not fifty years from now." He kissed her and tugged the sweater over her head. "Never." Unhooking her bra, he whispered, "Ever."

"How do you know that?"

Pulling off his shirt, he brought her hand to his chest. "Because you make my heart pound. No one has *ever* made my heart pound, and no one but you ever will. I love you. I'll always love you."

"That frightens me."

"Why?" he asked, tugging her jeans and panties down over her legs.

"What if…" She bit her lip.

He stood up and dropped his own jeans into a pile on the floor. "What if what?"

"What if things don't work out between us?"

"It'll work out," he said with supreme confidence as he brought her into his arms. The feel of her breasts against his chest sent a surge of lust rocketing through him.

"How can you be so certain?"

"I just am." He lifted her and entered her with one sure stroke. "I know it."

Juliana wrapped her arms and legs around him and let her head fall back in surrender. "You're going to hurt yourself," she whispered. "I'm too heavy…"

"Shh." With his hands under her bottom, he moved her ever so slowly up and down. "Mmm," he sighed. "Oh, that's so *good*. Can you feel how deep I am? How far inside you I am?"

"Yes," she said softly. "*Yes*." She clung to him, and when he finally walked them over to the bed, she pulled him down with her.

He filled her with long, deep strokes. "Nothing has ever felt like this, Juliana. I'll never get tired of feeling the way I do when I'm with you." Keeping up the steady thrusting of his hips, he dipped his head and sucked her nipple deep into his mouth.

"*Michael!*" she cried, climaxing with a shudder.

With one last push, he joined her.

❖ ❖ ❖

"Michael."

Through the haze of sleep, Michael heard her but couldn't seem to pull himself out of the fog to reply.

She shook his shoulder.

"Hmm."

"Michael, wake up."

"I'm awake," he said but kept his eyes closed. "What's the matter?"

"The guy I saw today is the same one who talked to me that day outside your house."

His eyes flew open. "What?"

"Remember? When I was first living with you? He asked me if I lived alone?"

Michael sat up and ran his hand over his face as he fought to wake up. "You're sure?"

She nodded.

He reached for his phone.

"What are you doing?"

"Calling Tom." When he got his boss on the phone, he told him about the man Juliana had now seen twice. "We didn't report it the last time because he only asked her if she lived there alone. He didn't threaten her in any way."

"Is she certain it's the same guy?" Tom asked.

Michael looked over at Juliana, who was pale and big-eyed—again. "Yes."

"Do you want me to see about getting you some security up there?"

Michael hesitated. "If I was by myself I'd say no, but I'm not risking her. Set it up." Michael gave him the address. "My sister's got three kids in this house, Tom. Make sure the cops know that."

"I'll take care of it," Tom assured him. "When you get back to Baltimore, bring her in to look at the mug shots for the Red Devils. She might be able to ID him."

"I will."

"Listen, I'm glad you called because we got a print off the rock. You'll never guess who."

"Gee, could it be a Red Devil?" Michael asked, referring to the Benedetti's gang.

"Yes, but it gets even better. Nick Dimitri."

Michael gasped. "Their cousin? What a bunch of idiots they are!"

"They've already picked up Dimitri, but he's not talking. We'll be looking at additional charges against the Benedettis, too, if we can get Dimitri to point to them on the order."

"He won't give them up."

"He might. He apparently almost shit himself when he heard the potential sentence for harassing an officer of the court. I also talked to Judge Stein today. He wants to see all the attorneys in chambers at nine on Monday morning. I'll be there, too."

"Okay, thanks, Tom. For everything."

"Be careful, Michael. The Benedettis know you've got them by the balls. They've got nothing to lose."

"I hear you. I'll see you Monday." Michael hung up and told Juliana the rock thrower was in custody and that Tom was arranging protection for them while they were in Newport. "But that's enough of that. Tonight, we're going out."

"Where are we going?"

"You don't need to know. All you have to do is put on something so sexy I won't be able to think of anything but you, got it?" He kissed her and got up. "I'm taking a shower, and then I've got to go do a few things. Can you be ready in about two hours? Seven thirty?"

"I should be able to throw something together by then."

"Do your best," he said, leaning down to kiss her.

She tried to pull him back into bed with her, and he resisted with a groan. "Release me, woman! I have stuff to do," he said, sinking into the kiss despite himself.

Ten minutes later, she finally let him go.

Michael went out to his car and introduced himself to the police detail that was already positioned outside his sister's house. One police car stayed at Maggie's while another followed him to his parents' house where Maureen waited for him.

She reached up to kiss him and adjust the collar of his shirt. "You look nice."

"Thanks. Where's Dad?"

"At a meeting at the Hibernian Hall." She led him into the kitchen. "I have all the stuff you asked for."

Michael inspected the bag to make sure everything was there. "This is great. Thanks."

"She's lovely, Michael. Really, really lovely."

"I know."

"I'm so happy to see you with someone like her. She's exactly perfect for you."

"I think so, too. I'm glad you like her."

"We all do. Your sisters are crazy about her."

"I figured they would be. It's just, well—"

"What?"

"It's kind of complicated," he said, giving her a brief rundown of Juliana's situation.

Maureen looked like she could cry. "Oh, Michael! And you love her so much! I can just feel that when I'm with the two of you."

"Yes," he said. "It happened fast, but I felt something different for her the first time I ever saw her. Isn't that strange?"

"No, it's not strange, not when it's the real thing. She'll make the right choice, honey. In the end, she will."

"I hope you're right. Well, I'd better get going. Thanks for the help."

"Have a nice time tonight." She stopped short at the front door. "Michael, why are there cops outside my house?"

"Oh, just something to do with the trial. Tom Houlihan ordered it. Nothing to worry about," he said, kissing her forehead.

"Are you sure?"

"Positive. We'll see you tomorrow before we head home."

"Okay," she said with another nervous glance at the police car.

Michael arrived back at Maggie's house to find Juliana reading to his niece, Emma, in the living room. With Emma on her lap, he couldn't get a full visual on what Juliana was wearing, but he saw enough bare shoulder and smooth leg to make his mouth water.

"Uncle Michael," four-year-old Emma said, "Juliana's reading *Goodnight Moon*."

He kissed his niece and sat down next to them. "I see that. And I see you talked her into another braid," he said, tugging on the end of the long blonde braid.

Maggie came into the room. "Come on, Emma, it's bath time."

"Do I *hafta?* Juliana's reading to me."

"Yes, you hafta. Juliana's going out."

Emma made a big production of hugging and kissing Michael and Juliana before she took her mother's outstretched hand.

"You guys have a nice time tonight," Maggie said with a wink for Michael.

"We will."

"What was that all about?" Juliana asked when they were alone.

"I don't know," he said with a shrug. "You look amazing. Stand up and let me see."

She did as he asked.

He made a twirling motion with his index finger.

Juliana spun around so he could get a full view of the sexy peasant-style black dress she wore with open-toed black heels.

"Mmm, mmm, *mmm,*" Michael said, fanning himself. "*Hot.*"

She giggled, and his heart ached with love for her.

"Does that mean you approve?"

Getting up, he wrapped her shawl around her shoulders. "Oh, yeah," he said, kissing her. "I definitely approve." He led her out the front door.

When they passed his car, she asked, "Where are we going?"

"For a short walk," he said, putting his arm around her. "Are you warm enough?"

She nodded.

Crispy fallen leaves littered the sidewalk, and the smell of smoke wafted through the chilly autumn air.

Over his shoulder, Michael noticed two police officers following them at a respectful distance.

They walked along Lower Thames until Michael stopped in front of a three-story Victorian with paper covering the large street-level windows on either side of the front door.

"Where are we?"

He used a key to unlock the door. "My place."

"Yours? I don't get it."

"Come on in, and I'll tell you."

Inside the door, he flipped on lights in a small hallway at the bottom of a stairwell. He led her into the rooms on the left side of the stairs. "When I was fifteen, my grandfather and I bought this place together."

Stunned, Juliana stared at him. "You did not!"

"We did," he said with a grin. "He and I used to take long walks through the neighborhood, and he'd tell me stories about the people who owned all the houses when he was a kid. His father grew up on the third floor of this house, so when it came on the market, he and I hatched a plan to buy it. I'd had a paper route and a lawn mowing business for years, and he knew I'd hung on to every dime I'd ever made."

"I can't believe you bought a house when you were fifteen!"

Enjoying her reaction, he said, "My grandfather used to say, 'Michael, my boy, you can't go wrong with real estate.' So we each put down ten thousand dollars and bought the place for seventy-five thousand. When he died about seven years ago, I found out that he'd paid off the mortgage and left his half to me. Turns out he steered me right. It's worth about three-quarters of a million now."

"That's such an amazing story. What are you going to do with it?"

"Whenever I'm home, I chip away at all the work it needs. I spent a whole weekend last spring refinishing the molding around one of the windows upstairs. On the days when I get sick of dealing with Baltimore's criminal element, I dream about opening a general law practice down here and living upstairs."

"I can see that. I can see you as the neighborhood attorney taking care of everyone's problems."

"Can you? Really?"

"Definitely. You should do it. You'd be great at it."

"Thanks." He shrugged. "Maybe someday. Let's go upstairs."

Back in the vestibule, Juliana asked what was on the other side of the stairwell.

"Another good-sized retail space that I'd lease out in my hypothetical scenario."

The second floor had high ceilings, large windows, an outdated kitchen, two bathrooms, and two big bedrooms. "There's another apartment upstairs."

"Something smells good. Where's it coming from?"

"Go on up and find out." He pointed to the third-floor stairs and gestured for her to lead the way.

Juliana gasped when she walked into a candlelit room with a table set for two in the middle. There were roses on the table and soft music played in the background. "Oh, is this what you were doing?"

"I can't take all the credit. My mother and my sisters helped a little."

"A little?" she asked, raising a skeptical eyebrow.

He smiled. "Okay, a lot. My mother provided all the candles, and Maggie and Shannon did most of the setup."

Juliana put her arms around him. "But it was your idea."

"I wanted to show you this place, and since I wasn't in the mood for a crowded restaurant tonight, I thought this might work."

"It works," she said, kissing him. "Thank you."

"Are you hungry? We've got shrimp scampi from Café Zelda's in the oven."

"I'm starving."

He held her chair, opened a bottle of wine, and poured them each a glass before he went to get their dinner.

"This place has great service," Juliana said when he delivered her dinner. "Very sexy waiters."

"No hitting on the help, please."

"I'll try to restrain myself."

"Don't try too hard."

She laughed. "This is *so* good," she said after the first bite of spicy shrimp.

"I'm glad you like it. Mary Frances said I couldn't go wrong with Zelda's scampi."

"Your sister is very wise. When did you even have a chance to do all this? You've been with me the whole time we've been here."

"Last night while you were playing hair salon with the little girls, I was plotting and scheming with the big girls."

"I'll have to keep a closer eye on you in the future."

"Nothing would please me more."

After dinner, he asked her to dance.

Juliana put her hand in his and followed him to the

middle of the big room where the light from the candles flickered on the bare walls.

They danced for a long while as Michael held her close to him and breathed in the unique scent that had invaded his senses the day he met her and held him captive ever since.

"Who is this?" she asked of the music.

"Allison Krauss," he said, whispering the words to the song. "It's called 'When You Say Nothing at All.'"

"I like it."

"I like *you*." He ran his lips along her bare shoulder and up to her neck. When he glanced over her ear with his tongue, she moaned. "In fact, I love you."

Her arms tightened around him. "I love you, too." She tipped her face up to his for a kiss so hot and so sensual that Michael almost forgot to breathe.

Lightheaded, he pulled back from her. "Come sit with me over here," he said, leading her to a window seat that overlooked Thames Street and the harbor beyond. He sat down and drew her onto his lap. "There was another reason why I wanted to bring you here tonight."

"Oh, really?"

"I have something I want to say to you and something I want to ask you, but you have to let me get through the whole thing before you say anything, okay?"

Her eyes widened, and she nodded.

He took her hand and brought it to his lips. "The other night I said I don't have the words to tell you how I feel about you. I still don't. I doubt I ever will. We haven't known each other long, but it took me all of five minutes to know I could have everything I've ever dreamed of with you. I might not be the last guy who asks, but I wanted to be the first. Will you marry me, Juliana?"

"Michael," she gasped.

"Wait. I'm not finished. I know you're not able to answer me right now, but over the next few weeks when you're going to have to make some big decisions, I wanted you to have no doubt about what I want from you and with you."

He fished a ring out of his pocket. The antique setting seemed perfect for her, and the diamond, while large, was more tasteful than the one he had given Paige. He knew the size of the stone would mean nothing to Juliana. Sliding the ring onto her finger, he kissed her hand. "I just want to see how it looks."

"It's beautiful," she said, wiping tears off her face.

He kissed her hand. "A perfect fit, just like us."

"I don't know what to say."

With great reluctance, Michael slid the ring off her finger and reached for the gold chain that held his St. Christopher medal. He unhooked the chain, slid the ring on with the medal, clasped the chain shut, and dropped it under his shirt. "I'll hold on to it for now. It'll be right here with me until you're ready for it."

"I'm overwhelmed, Michael, and I don't deserve you. You should be with someone who could say yes—without reservation—to such a lovely proposal."

"I don't want anyone but you, and I'll take you any way I can get you."

"I have some things I need to resolve, and it's going to have to happen soon. I know I'm asking so much of you, but I need you to be patient with me. Can you do that?"

"I can do anything for you."

"This was a wonderful evening. I'll never forget it."

"Just don't forget who asked first."

She kissed him. "I won't forget that, either."

Chapter 20

THEY WERE UP EARLY THE NEXT MORNING TO TAKE A walk on Easton's Beach followed by breakfast at Michael's favorite greasy-spoon diner. The police detail was never far from them.

"Oh my God!" Juliana clutched her stomach on the way back to the car. "*Why* did you let me eat so much?"

"You were like a regular truck driver in there."

"I probably gained ten pounds this weekend. When we get home, we're going on a diet."

"Why do I have to?"

"If I have to, so do you."

"Oh, I see," he said, laughing. "Is this what life with you is going to be like?"

Juliana's smile faded.

He took her hand. "I'm sorry."

"Don't be." She reached up to caress his face and gazed into his eyes, which were even bluer than usual under the bright light of the sun. "There are times when I wish…"

He leaned her against the car and put his arms around her. "What, baby? Tell me. What do you wish for?"

"That there was nothing—or no one—standing in our way. I can just see how it would be for us. I think we'd have a happy life together."

"I know we would." Reaching up to his chest, he touched the ring through his shirt. "We can have it,

Juliana. You only have to say the word, and we can have it all."

She touched her lips to his. "I know."

"Come on." He opened the car door for her. "Let's go say good-bye to my parents and get on the road."

At the Maguire's house, Juliana stayed inside with Maureen while Michael went outside with his father, who insisted on checking the oil in the car.

"I'm so glad you came this weekend, Juliana," Maureen said. "I hope we'll see you again."

Something about the way Michael's mother looked at her told Juliana she knew what was going on. "I hope so, too. Thank you for all your hospitality."

Maureen hugged her. "Come again. Any time."

Michael walked in. "Ready?"

Juliana nodded, and Michael hugged his mother.

"Be careful during that trial," Maureen said. "I mean it, Michael."

"I will. Don't worry."

"Yeah, right."

Outside, Sean hugged them both.

As Michael backed the car out of the driveway, his parents waved from the front yard.

Juliana wondered if she would ever see them again.

The closer they got to Baltimore, the quieter Michael became.

"What's wrong?" Juliana asked.

He glanced over at her and then at the road.

"What?"

"You know I want you with me all the time, right?"

She smiled. "You've made that pretty clear."

"I'm so afraid of you staying with me after everything that's happened. I really want you to go to Mrs. R's until the trial's over. Will you do that for me?"

"No."

"Juliana…"

"*No.*"

"They know where I *live,* baby. They know I live with a woman. What better way to get to me than to get to you? If something ever happened to you, I'd go crazy."

She put a comforting hand on his leg. "Nothing's going to happen to me, Michael."

"Just until the trial's over?"

"I'm not leaving you until I have to."

He glanced over at her. "So you see yourself leaving one day?"

"I'm going to have to deal with Jeremy at some point. You know that."

His jaw tightened with tension. "We're talking about the trial. I want you to be safe, and I can't guarantee you will be if you stay with me."

"I'm not going anywhere. Not now."

"How do I go to work tomorrow morning and leave you sleeping there alone? How do I think about anything else but whether you're safe?"

"The house has an alarm system, right?"

He nodded.

"Then we'll use it."

"That won't keep another rock from coming through the window."

"They won't do that again," Juliana said confidently.

"So now you're an expert on criminal behavior?" he asked, amused. "You won't even think about going to Mrs. R's for a few weeks?"

"No."

When they got home, Michael showed her how to use the alarm system. He also let the police know they were back in town. With two officers trailing close behind them, they walked to a neighborhood restaurant for dinner.

"I'm getting used to being followed everywhere," Juliana said as they strolled hand-in-hand back to the house after dinner. The whole time, she kept an anxious eye out for Jeremy in case he hadn't gone back to Florida as scheduled.

"Good, because after what happened the other night, you have your own detail now."

Juliana made a face at that news. "Oh, goodie."

"Tomorrow I want you to come by the office to look at some photos we have of the Red Devils to see if you recognize the guy you saw in Newport, okay?"

She nodded.

"I'll call you at some point to set it up. I have a meeting with the judge at nine. After that, I'm not sure if he'll stay in recess or want to get back to the trial."

"I'm off, so I can come whenever you need me to."

Back at the house, they called to check on Rachelle. Michael talked to her first and told her that depending on what the judge had to say in the morning, he hoped to call her to testify by Thursday—Friday at the latest. "This is it," he said before he turned the phone over to Juliana.

They chatted for a few minutes before Juliana sensed there was something the girl wanted to say to her.

"Honey? What is it?"

"It's none of my business, and I remember you said that you and Michael are just friends because you have a boyfriend and all that, but…"

"What?"

"I think you belong with Michael."

"What makes you say that?" Juliana asked, trying to keep her voice steady.

"I don't know. It's just a feeling I have."

"Well, your opinion means a lot to me, so thank you for telling me. You ought to get some sleep. You've got a big week ahead of you. I'll be thinking of you."

"Thanks," Rachelle said softly. "Good-bye, Juliana."

"Bye, hon."

"What did she say?" Michael asked.

"That you and I belong together." Juliana struggled to define the odd sensation that had come over her during the conversation with Rachelle.

He smiled. "They say kids speak the truth."

"You never miss an opportunity for self-promotion, do you?" she asked with a grin.

"I can't afford to." He stood up and held out a hand to her.

"Where are we going?"

"You'll see."

They went upstairs to his room where he grabbed a heavy blanket and led her to the secluded roof deck. The lights of the city twinkled in the clear night sky as Michael drew her down next to him on the blanket. He tugged the shirt over her head and then did the same with his own.

Her eyes fixated on the engagement ring hanging from the chain around his neck.

"Do you think we could pretend?" he whispered, reaching up to unhook the chain. "That just for tonight you're mine and this belongs right here?" Sliding the ring onto her finger, he kissed his way up her neck. "I want to see you wearing nothing but my ring." He released the clasp on her bra, tossed aside the last of their clothes, and pulled the blanket up around them.

"Let me see." He reached for her hand and kissed each finger but spent extra time on her ring finger. "It's so perfect on you. I bought it on Friday when you were waiting for me at Mrs. R's. Did you know that?"

She shook her head. "I wondered when you'd had the time."

"Make love with me, Juliana. Make love with me like we're engaged and have everything in the world to look forward to."

She pulled him to her. "I love you, Michael. No matter what happens, I love you so much."

"That's all I need."

The next morning Michael left Juliana sleeping in his bed. He set the alarm, locked the front door, and crossed the street to talk to the officers on her detail.

"Juliana is sleeping, and the alarm's on. Stay close to her today, okay?"

"Yes, Mr. Maguire. Don't worry. We're on it."

"Thank you," Michael said.

With one more anxious glance back at the house, Michael got in his car and left for work. Forced to leave her for the first time in days, his stomach churned with nerves. She promised him she would be careful, and since he couldn't see to her safety himself, he could only hope she would be vigilant.

As he drove, he thought about making love with her on the roof deck and then again in his bed after the chilly night air drove them inside. He reached up for the ring and discovered they had forgotten to return it to the chain, which meant it was still on her finger where it belonged. Imagining her going through her day wearing his ring made him smile.

Trailed by two police officers, he arrived at the courthouse with minutes to spare before the meeting with Judge Stein. Michael shook hands with Tom Houlihan in the hallway outside of the judge's chambers. The defense attorneys were huddled on the other side of the corridor.

"Good weekend in R.I.?" Houlihan asked.

"It was great. How was yours?"

"I spent most of it on the phone dealing with the media's feeding frenzy over the rock incident. Rumor has it the judge is on fire over it. This ought to be interesting."

Stein's clerk called everyone in a few minutes later.

The judge paced behind his large mahogany desk, his wiry frame all but bursting with energy. "What the *hell* is going on?" he asked the defense attorneys. "Are your clients out of their minds?"

The lead defense attorney, a heavyset blonde, held up her hands. "They claim to have had no knowledge of what their cousin planned to do."

"Somehow I find that hard to believe." Stein ran his fingers through what was left of his hair, his sharp blue eyes landing on Michael. "Mr. Maguire, your roommate's injuries were minor as reported?"

"Yes, your honor. We were very lucky. She was sitting less than a foot from where the rock landed."

"This is an outrage." He turned to address the defense team. "I want you to tell your clients that I'll tolerate no further harassment of Mr. Maguire or any other member of the prosecution team. You might want to remind them of who'll be determining their sentence should they be convicted. Am I clear?"

"Yes, your honor."

"In light of all the publicity this incident has generated, I'm sequestering the jury for the remainder of the trial. We'll resume tomorrow at nine," he said with a dismissive wave of his hand. "Mr. Maguire."

"Your honor?"

"Be careful. The defendants are already facing three consecutive life sentences. I have absolutely nothing worse than that to threaten them with, and they know it."

Michael nodded. "Yes, sir."

Outside the courthouse, a swarm of reporters and cameras were waiting when Michael emerged from the meeting. They bombarded him with questions as he pushed through the crowd with Tom at his side and two police officers following close behind them.

"Mr. Maguire, what do you have to say about the incident at your house?"

"No comment." He and Tom kept moving in an attempt to break free.

"Mr. Maguire, are you worried about your personal safety?"

"No."

"Mr. Maguire, can you tell us your roommate's name and describe the nature of her injuries?"

"Absolutely no comment."

"Mr. Houlihan, what did the judge have to say this morning?"

"The trial will resume tomorrow."

"Mr. Maguire, is it true you recently left your pregnant fiancée?"

Michael stopped and turned to the reporter who had asked the question. "What did you say?"

A hush fell over the gaggle of reporters.

"Is it true you recently left your pregnant fiancée?"

"No. It's not true. Where did you hear that?"

Tom put a hand on his shoulder. "Michael, come on."

"Wait." Michael struggled to control the urge to punch the reporter in the face. "Where did you hear that?"

The young reporter shrugged. "Word on the street."

"Well, it's not true, and I'd better not see that in print anywhere or hear it on the air, do you hear me?" His eyes circled the group to make sure they knew he meant all of them. "I'll sue your asses so fast you won't know what hit you."

"You can't sue me if it's true," the brazen reporter replied.

Before Michael could act on the urge to punch the guy, Tom pulled him free of the crowd.

"*What the fuck?*" Michael said after they left the

reporters behind. "That's just what the jury needs to hear right about now. My credibility with them will be shot."

"They're being sequestered," Tom reminded him. "Even if it makes it into the news, they won't hear it."

"Son of a *bitch*."

"Is there any chance it could be true? I'm only asking as a friend, Michael."

"No, it's not true." But then the earth seemed to tremble under his feet as he remembered the last time with Paige when they failed to use a condom. "Oh, shit," he whispered. "Oh my God. I've got to go."

Chapter 21

JULIANA EMERGED FROM THE HOUSE AT TEN O'CLOCK and crossed the street to let her detail know she would be going first to Collington Street and then to her mother's in Highlandtown. They followed her as she drove the short distance to Collington Street.

Jeremy would've flown back to Florida the night before, so she planned to get the mail, do a little cleaning, and get out of there as fast as she could.

Since the house was alarmed, they let her go in without them.

Juliana was startled to find the alarm deactivated, which caused her heart to accelerate and anxiety to course through her. She turned to go back for the cops.

"Hello, Juliana," Jeremy said on his way downstairs. "Nice of you to come home."

"Why are you still here?" she sputtered, tucking her left hand into her pocket and working the engagement ring off her finger. "You scared me."

"*You* scared *me* when you didn't come home for three days."

"I told you I was away."

"Who were you with?"

"We aren't seeing each other right now. I don't have to explain myself to you."

"What's going *on,* Jule? Where are you living? I know it isn't here. The place was filthy. When I wasn't trying to figure out where you were this weekend, I was cleaning the house."

"I came to clean today. That's why I'm here."

"*Where* are you living?"

Swallowing hard, she said, "With a friend. No one you know."

"What *friend* do you have who isn't a friend of mine, too?"

"I'm not talking to you about this," she said, her heart racing with anxiety.

He studied her for a long time, a nerve in his cheek pulsing with tension. "What happened to your forehead?"

"I banged it."

He picked up the letters that she had left on the kitchen table. "You're not reading your mail?"

"Look, Jer, I don't know why you're here or what you thought was going to happen when you came home this weekend, but we agreed to spend three months apart. It's only been one. You're not being fair."

"I want out of that stupid agreement." He took a step toward her. "I haven't been with anyone else, and I don't want to be. That was the whole reason we were doing this, right? So the deal's off."

"No, it's not."

"Why are you having so much trouble looking at me, Juliana?"

"I'm not." She tilted her chin to make eye contact with him.

"It's almost like you're guilty about something. Are you seeing someone else?"

"I'm not having this conversation with you. We have

a deal. I'm not giving in on this. I'll talk to you in two months. Not before."

"Something's going on, and I want to know what it is."

"We'll talk in two months," Juliana said, picking up her purse to leave. He had cleaned, so there was no need for her to stay.

He took hold of her arm. "One month, Jule. I'll do one more month. Not two."

She looked up at him, at that oh-so-familiar face, and knew she couldn't deny him this. "Fine. One month from today."

"Meet me here."

"Okay."

"Jule? Will you let me hold you?" He held out his arms. "Just for a minute?"

She bent her head and rested it against his chest as his arms went around her. Her hands rested on his hips, and she felt his lips brush against her hair.

"I miss you, babe," he whispered. "I miss you so much. I'm going crazy without you."

Juliana looked up at him and was startled when his lips came down on hers. When she felt his tongue nudging her mouth open, she pulled back. "Don't, Jer," she said, stepping out of his embrace. "I'll see you in a month." She bolted out the door and drove away before he could notice a police car was following her.

Michael left the courthouse and drove to his office, trying to process the possibility that Paige could be pregnant. He'd ignored a new burst of phone calls from her over the last few days, but she'd made damned sure he wouldn't be able to ignore her anymore. He parked the car and reached for his cell phone.

"Hello, Michael. How good of you to finally call me back."

"What are you trying to pull, Paige? Do you expect me to believe you got pregnant the one time we didn't use protection? Do you think I'm that stupid?"

"You can believe whatever you want to, but I *am* pregnant. Exactly four weeks."

Michael took a ragged deep breath. "I don't believe you."

"Well, you'd better believe it. You're going to be a daddy, Michael, so you can forget all this business about calling off our engagement. It's just as well I never cancelled the wedding plans. We can just proceed as planned."

"Yeah, in your dreams."

"I'm pregnant. You *will* marry me."

"I will *never* marry you. I don't care if you're having triplets. I'm not marrying you."

"Then you'll never see this child. Do you understand me? Never."

Michael laughed. "Have you forgotten I'm a lawyer, Paige? *Bring it on.* By the time I'm through with you, *you'll* never see this phantom kid of ours. Besides, how do I even know it's mine?"

"Go to hell, Michael."

"You're not going to blackmail me into marrying you, and you failed to mess up my trial by leaking this to the media because the judge sequestered the jury. And you're certainly not going to stop me from seeing my kid—the kid I highly doubt even exists. So you may as well give it up. Oh, and it's probably safe to go ahead and cancel those wedding plans. The groom won't be there." He slapped his phone closed.

"Fuck!" he cried within the confines of his car. "Fuck! Fuck! *Fuck!*" As he slammed his hand against the steering wheel in frustration, the phone rang. Expecting it to be Paige calling him back, he flipped it open and roared, *"What?"*

"Michael?" Juliana said.

Just the sound of her voice chased away the rage. "Oh, baby, I'm sorry."

"What's wrong?"

"Nothing now that I'm talking to you. Are you okay?"

"I just had a run-in with Jeremy."

Michael went still. "What kind of run-in? What happened?"

She told him about finding Jeremy at their house and the conversation they'd had.

"Why did you agree to meet him in a month?" Michael asked, despondent to hear their two remaining months had been cut in half. "You said three months."

"I'm sorry, Michael, but I can't let this go on for another two months. I'll work myself into an ulcer by then."

"You could've just told him today that it's over between you guys. Why didn't you?"

"Because it's not over. You know that. Why are you being this way?"

He sighed. "I'm sorry. Paige is pregnant—or at least she's claiming to be."

Juliana gasped. "How, I mean—"

"Meet me at my office, will you? I'll tell you when you get here." He gave her directions.

"I'll be there in ten minutes."

"I'll wait for you in the car."

Ten minutes later, Juliana slid into the passenger seat of Michael's car and reached for him.

He fell into her arms and held her close for a long time. "God, baby, I'm so glad to see you."

When Juliana finally pulled back to look at him, she kept her hands on his face. "How can she be pregnant?"

"That last night, the night of the engagement party, she got in bed with me when I was asleep. I'd had a lot to drink so I thought I was dreaming and didn't realize I wasn't until it was too late, if you know what I mean. I found out about it today when a reporter asked me if it was true that I'd recently left my pregnant fiancée. I didn't return Paige's calls, so she leaked it to the media."

"Oh, Michael. What are you going to do?"

He shrugged helplessly. "First of all, I don't believe her, so I'm not going to do anything. Not now anyway. She said if I don't marry her, I'll never see the kid."

"She can't do that!"

"I know, honey. I told her she's not dealing with an idiot. She's the one who won't see the kid if she wants to play hardball with me."

Juliana put her arms around him again. "I'll never understand a woman who'd stoop to blackmailing a man into marrying her."

"That's because you could never be so evil. She hasn't cancelled any of the wedding plans. Can you believe that?"

"She still thinks it's going to happen?" Juliana asked, incredulous. "After everything?"

"It's not even about marrying me anymore. It's about saving face. If she cancels the plans, she'll have to deal with the humiliation of being dumped. She'd rather blackmail me with a fake pregnancy than be embarrassed."

"I'm sorry. It's just one more thing on your already too full plate."

"Which is exactly why she dropped it on me in the middle of the trial." He reached for her hand. "Where's the ring?"

Juliana found it in her pocket and reached around to unhook his chain to return it to its place next to the St. Christopher medal.

Michael kissed her left hand. "I liked it better here."

She leaned over to press her lips to his and combed her fingers through his hair. The kiss turned hot when Michael tilted her head so he could delve deeper. For a moment they both forgot where they were and that four cops were watching them as they feasted on the comfort only the other could provide.

Michael groaned when he finally pulled away from her. "Why couldn't it be *you* who's pregnant with my baby? I want it to be *you*."

Juliana tightened her hold on him.

After he took a few more minutes to collect himself, Michael led her into his office where several of his co-workers stopped what they were doing to watch them walk by. He knew they were curious about the woman who had been hurt at his house, but he wished they wouldn't stare. Outside his office, he introduced her to his assistant Angela, who handed him a stack of pink message slips. Michael asked Angela to pull the mug shots of the Red Devils. He ushered Juliana into his office and gestured for her to have a seat.

"Nice office."

"Thanks." Michael tossed the messages onto his cluttered desk and draped his suit coat over the back of his chair.

Angela came in with the mug shots. "Here you go. Let me know if you need anything else." She closed the door and left them alone.

Michael sat down next to Juliana and handed her the book. "Take your time, hon. See if you recognize anyone."

Juliana nodded and flipped open the book. "You don't have to sit with me. I'm sure you have work to do."

He glanced at the disaster on his desk. "I've got a few things I could do." With a kiss to her cheek he got up to weed out the messages that needed immediate attention. Then he rolled up his shirtsleeves and turned his attention to his email. When Angela buzzed in with a call from a reporter, he told her to tell him "no comment." He checked on Juliana and found her looking at him. "What?"

She smiled. "I like watching you work. Very sexy."

"The book, Juliana. You're distracting me."

"You're easily distracted."

"I'm always distracted when I'm with you."

"The *computer,* Michael," she said, mocking his tone. "You're distracting me."

He grinned and turned back to his computer.

Juliana went through the book twice but didn't see anyone she recognized. "I'm sorry."

"It's okay. Thanks for trying." He got up and came around to her. "What are you doing the rest of the day?"

"I'm going to clean my mother's house."

"You're good to her. She's lucky to have you."

Juliana shrugged. "You do what you have to."

He hugged and kissed her. "I should be home early."

"Good. I'll make something for dinner."

"Mmm," he said against her lips. "I can't wait."

"Are you okay?"

"I am now that I've seen you. Somehow you manage to make everything better." With one last kiss, he walked her out to meet her police detail.

Chapter 22

THE NIGHT BEFORE RACHELLE WAS DUE TO TESTIFY Michael lay awake while Juliana slept with one arm wrapped around him.

As the clock edged toward four, he thought about how badly he wanted this trial to be over. After tomorrow, the prosecution would rest. The defense would take a week, maybe two, to present its case, followed by closing arguments and jury deliberation.

Everything had gone perfectly so far. The detectives and ballistics witnesses had been unshakable. The kids who witnessed the fight between the victims and the Benedettis in the arcade had been nervous, but they managed to get through their testimony and presented a cohesive, consistent story that established a firm motive.

Based on the reports of the consultants who tracked jurors' body language, Michael had won them over thus far. But it was Rachelle's testimony that would ensure a win. She really was his "slam dunk." No way would the jury fail to convict after they heard her chilling account—or so he hoped.

Michael had spoken to her the previous evening. She had been subdued, but she'd assured him she was ready to testify and to put the whole ordeal behind her. After she appeared in court, a police escort would deliver her and her mother to a private jet that would take them to their new life in St. Louis, Missouri, where they would be reunited with Rachelle's father and brothers.

Juliana stirred and rested her cheek on his shoulder. The T-shirt of his that she had worn to bed had ridden up, so he laid his hand on her warm back and pulled her closer to him.

In her sleep, she curled around him and sighed.

How did I ever live before her? How will I ever live without her if she chooses Jeremy over me? She won't. She can't. Not after everything we've shared and been through together. She'll stay with me. The alternative was unimaginable. He was doing his best not to think at all about Paige and the possibility that she could be pregnant. He would deal with that once the trial was finished and not one minute before. If she was in fact pregnant, she still would be after the trial.

Michael must have dozed off because he was jarred awake by the ringing of the phone just after six.

"Mm, Maguire," he said, struggling to wake up.

"Michael!" His co-worker George Samuels's frantic tone got Michael's full attention.

"George? What's wrong?"

"Jesus Christ, Michael, they've been *poisoned!*" George cried.

Michael sat up. "Who has? What're you talking about?" His gut clenched when he remembered assigning George to stay at the hotel in Annapolis so he could escort Rachelle to court in the morning.

"Rachelle, the cops, all of them," George whispered.

Michael released an anguished wail.

"Michael!" Juliana said. "What is it? What's wrong?"

He fought through growing hysteria to ask, "Is she dead?"

"No, but she's really sick. One of the cops is in a coma."

"Call me as soon as you know more."

Michael put down the phone and dropped his head into his hands. "God," he whispered. "Oh my God."

"Michael, you're scaring me," Juliana said. "What's wrong?"

He reached for her hand. "Rachelle's been poisoned," he said. "George said she's really sick."

Juliana inhaled sharply. "*No!*"

Michael drew her into his arms, and they held each other until the persistent ringing of his cell phone reminded him of the job he still had to do. "I've got to find out what happened." He pulled the covers up over Juliana's trembling body and reached for his cell phone.

"Yeah," he said softly.

"Michael," Tom Houlihan said, his tone grim.

"How did this happen, Tom? *How in the world did they get to her?*"

"Their food was poisoned. Probably arsenic."

"Arsenic?" Michael asked in disbelief.

"Her mother found them, Michael. She's out of her mind."

"Oh, God, I promised her this would never happen! *I gave her my word!*"

Juliana sat up and put her arms around Michael from behind. He reached down to clutch her hand.

"You did everything you could to keep her safe," Tom said. "We all did."

"Clearly, we didn't do enough. Where do I need to be?"

"Stay put for now. I'm on my way to the hospital. I don't want you anywhere near there, not after they've already come at you once."

"She's my witness. I need to be there."

"No. Stay there until you hear from me, you got it?"

"All right." After he hung up Michael lay down next to Juliana. "I should've put her on first. She would've been long gone by now." He blinked back tears. "*Why didn't I put her on first and get her the hell out of here?*"

"Don't do that to yourself, Michael. This isn't your fault."

"I could've prevented it."

"No. They were determined."

"I don't even know what I should do right now."

"Should you go to the office?"

"Tom told me to stay here. He's really scared now. I could hear it in his voice."

"Michael," Juliana whimpered, her lips brushing over his hair. "What if they try to hurt you, too?"

"What if they try to hurt *you?*" He got up abruptly. "This is what I've been trying to tell you was going to happen." Stalking into the bathroom, he slammed the door.

Taken aback, Juliana rolled her face into the pillow and thought about Rachelle who dreamed of having a boyfriend and wanted to see her father and brothers again. Juliana prayed harder than she ever had before for her young friend, a girl who had shown more courage in her fifteen years than most people did in a lifetime.

Michael came out of the bathroom, his hair wet and

his face shaved. He put on a suit and was knotting his tie when he came over to sit next to Juliana on the bed.

"I want you to take a leave of absence from the salon for at least a week," he said in a flat tone she had never heard before. His eyes were dull with shock. "Call your brother and tell him you won't be able to take care of your mother. I want you to stay home until we get a handle on what's happened. I just can't deal with worrying about you right now. If they've been watching us, then they know by now that you're my weak spot. I know it's a big thing for me to ask and that you can't afford it, but I'll take care of anything you need. Will you do this for me, Juliana? Please?"

"Of course. Where are you going?"

"To the hospital."

"But your boss told you to stay here."

His jaw clenched with tension. "I can't just sit here and do nothing."

She reached up to caress his face. "Don't shut me out, Michael. Let me help you."

He got up. "There's nothing you can do. Just stay here. I'll be back."

She heard him go downstairs, activate the alarm, and shut the front door. The phone rang not a minute after he left.

"This is Tom Houlihan. May I speak to Michael, please?

"He went to the hospital."

"Damn it! I told him to stay home."

"He's very upset. He felt like he needed to do something."

"All right."

"Mr. Houlihan?" Juliana swallowed hard. "Is she suffering?"

"She's been vomiting for the last hour, but she seems to be doing better now. They got her to the hospital before any permanent damage was done."

"Oh, thank God."

"I'll call Michael's cell," he said. "Thank you."

Juliana dragged herself out of bed and into the shower. She tugged on sweats and a T-shirt and went downstairs to make coffee. The story was all over the TV news. Reporters and legal analysts predicted Michael would request a continuance of the trial until he figured out how to proceed with his star witness in the hospital.

"Luckily," one talking head said, "the jury was sequestered earlier in the week, so they won't hear about this."

"Will the defense move for a mistrial anyway?"

"I think they'll try, but Judge Stein is tough. If he can find any way to finish this trial he will."

"Will the jury be told of the attack on the witness?" the anchor asked the legal expert.

"Since it would color the current proceedings— unfavorably for the defense—the jury won't hear about today's events until after they've reached a verdict."

"To recap," the anchor said, "the star witness for the prosecution in the Benedetti murder trial was poisoned in an Annapolis hotel room where she was being held in protective custody. A Baltimore police officer is in critical condition from what police believe was arsenic poisoning. The fifteen-year-old city girl is the lone witness to the shootings of three Baltimore teenagers last year. She was due to testify this morning in Baltimore City Circuit Court.

The girl and three members of her police detail, sickened by a poisonous substance, were discovered unconscious by the girl's mother just before six o'clock this morning. Two of the officers are in stable condition. Chief of Police Dennis Noonan and Baltimore City State's Attorney Tom Houlihan will hold a joint press conference within the hour. We'll bring it to you live."

Juliana muted the television and called the salon. Apologizing for all the rescheduling the administrative staff would have to do on her behalf, she explained to one of the owners that she'd had a personal emergency and needed some time off. Since Juliana rarely asked for anything, her boss granted the unusual request.

"Take as much time as you need, Juliana. I hope everything's okay."

"Thank you."

Next she called Mrs. Romanello to assure her that she was safe despite this latest development in the trial.

"Do you know this girl? The one who was poisoned?"

"Yes," Juliana whispered. "She's adorable, the most wonderful kid. Michael and I love her very much."

"I'm so sorry. What a terrible thing. You know you both can come here if you need to, right?"

"Thank you. I'll call you tomorrow, okay?"

"Be safe, hon."

Juliana put the phone down and tuned into the press conference. Michael and Tom stood behind Chief Noonan, their faces grim with fatigue and anger.

"This morning the entire city of Baltimore is praying for three decorated police officers and a fifteen-year-old girl who were attacked while in service to this city." Chief Noonan paid glowing tribute to the careers of the injured police officers. Their photos were shown as the chief talked about them.

Juliana gasped when she recognized Scott Brown, the officer who laughed at Michael's haircut.

The chief paused for a moment to collect himself. "I know there will be a quick rush to judgment in this case, but I urge everyone to let the detectives do their jobs. We'll find the person or persons who perpetrated this crime, and we'll bring them to justice. I'll let Mr. Houlihan give his statement, and then we'll take a few questions."

Tom stepped to the microphone. "The witness to the shootings is a brave, spirited, intelligent girl with an amazing zest for life. Every one of us who has worked with her has been forever touched by her amazing courage under the most trying of circumstances. We know that courage and determination will get her through this crisis as well. The hearts and prayers of everyone in my office are with her and her family this morning."

"Can you give us her name?" a reporter shouted.

"In an effort to protect her and her family from further recrimination, we'll be maintaining her anonymity," Tom replied.

Juliana's heart broke as she watched Michael look down in a failed attempt to hide his anguish.

"We will not rest until justice is served on behalf of these victims."

Reporters began shouting out questions the moment Tom stepped back from the microphone.

"Chief, how do you know it was arsenic?"

"A variety of common symptoms."

"Can you be more specific?"

"No."

"What's the theory on how the poison was delivered to the victims?"

"We're checking the room service and take-out delivery logs to see what they ate, when it was delivered, and by whom. We had video cameras in the hallway and the hotel rooms. Those tapes are currently being reviewed."

"What hospital is the witness in?"

"No comment."

"Do you have any word on her condition?"

"Her injuries are not considered life threatening."

"Do you believe the Benedettis are responsible for this attack?"

"No comment."

"Mr. Houlihan, what're the odds of a mistrial?"

"We don't believe there will be a mistrial, but that'll be up to Judge Stein after he's heard arguments from both sides."

"Mr. Maguire, can you comment on your ability to secure a conviction without the witness's testimony?"

Tom gestured for Michael to take the question. Michael cleared his throat. "I'm hopeful she'll make a full recovery and be able to testify. We'll request a continuance until she's recovered."

"How well do you know the witness, Mr. Maguire?"

"Very well," Michael said softly. The room quieted while the reporters waited for him to go on.

Juliana swiped at tears as she watched him struggle to find the words he needed to pay tribute to his young friend.

"She's a terrific kid. Like Tom said, all of us who've worked with her have grown to care for her very much."

"That's all for now," Chief Noonan said. "We'll keep you informed of any developments."

The news cut away from the press conference for more in-studio analysis, but Juliana had heard enough. She turned off the television, put down her coffee cup, and curled up on the sofa, thinking of Rachelle and her Queen Bee T-shirt, her love of fashion, the way her face had lit up when Juliana cut her hair, the story she had told about the night that changed her life forever, her adorable crush on Michael, and her haunting last words to Juliana. "I think you belong with Michael," she had said before saying good-bye. Not her usual "be cool" or "lata, gata." No, she'd said good-bye, as if she had somehow known that something might happen.

The house phone rang, and Juliana got up to answer it.

"Hello?"

Silence.

"Hello?"

"Your boyfriend's next, Juliana," a raspy voice said. The phone went dead.

Juliana screamed and dropped the phone. She ran for the door, and with shaking fingers she punched in the code to deactivate the alarm. In light of the day's events, her police detail had moved from across the street to the sidewalk outside the front door.

"Juliana, what is it?"

In a halting voice, Juliana told them about the call. She pleaded with them to find Michael and warn him of the threat. One of the officers reached for his shoulder microphone to report it.

"You'll tell Michael's detail?" she asked the officer who escorted her back inside.

"Yes, my partner's taking care of it."

"He knew my name," Juliana whimpered. "They know my name." She jolted when the phone rang again.

The police officer answered it. "Hello? Yes, she's right here." He handed the phone to Juliana. "It's Mr. Maguire."

"Juliana," he said, sounding panic-stricken, "tell me exactly what he said."

"'Your boyfriend's next, Juliana.' He knew my name, Michael."

"I know, baby. I'll be home in a few minutes."

"Be careful." Tears fell from eyes already swollen from crying. "Please be careful."

"I'll be right there."

Chapter 23

MICHAEL RUSHED THROUGH THE DOOR TWENTY minutes later.

Juliana was so relieved to see him that she burst into tears as he wrapped his arms around her.

The police officer who had waited with her returned to his post outside, closing the front door behind him.

"Okay, baby." Michael smoothed a hand over her hair. "It's okay."

"They're going to kill you, Michael!" Juliana knew she sounded hysterical but didn't care.

"Killing me won't stop the trial. They know that."

She wiped her face. "What about the call? What he said?"

"They're just trying to scare me. And you."

"It worked."

The doorbell rang.

Michael went to answer it. "Tom? What are you doing here?" He stepped aside to let his boss in.

"Hi there." Tom extended his hand to Juliana. "Tom Houlihan. Nice to meet you."

"Juliana Gregorio."

Tom cast an admiring eye around the room. "Nice place."

"You have time for social calls today, Tom?"

Tom put his hands in his pockets, his shoulders

stooping as he turned to Michael. "I want to get you out
of here for a while."

"I'm in the middle of a trial. I'm not going anywhere
until those bastards are convicted."

"I'm not asking you."

Michael stared at his boss. "You're *ordering* me out
of town?"

"Either you leave for a week, maybe two, or you're
off the case."

"You can't do this!"

"Yes, I can. Maybe you don't care about your own
safety, but what about hers?" He nodded at Juliana.
"They have her name, Michael. Are you really willing
to risk her just to prove a point?"

Michael sagged as the fight went out of him. "Of
course not."

Tom put a hand on Michael's shoulder. "The trial
is in recess for now while we sort all this out and until
Rachelle gets out of the hospital. Your detail will be
taking you both to my house at Dewey Beach tonight."

"I want to go to the hospital," Michael said. "I need
to see her… And her mother."

"I'll get you over there this afternoon."

"They followed us to Newport. What's to stop them
from following us to Delaware?"

"That's why you're going in the middle of the night."

"And when the trial resumes?"

"I'll bring you back. This is nonnegotiable, Michael."

Juliana watched them lock eyes in a ferocious battle
of wills.

Michael finally looked away. "Fine. We'll go. But
I'm coming back the minute the trial starts up again. No

one else is arguing this case, Tom. It's my case. Do you hear me?"

"Yes."

"And you'll keep me informed of every development?"

"Absolutely."

Michael glanced at Juliana. "I guess we're going to the beach," he said, but she could tell he was still fuming at being exiled.

After Tom left, Juliana told Michael she needed to get a few things from the Collington Street house. The weather had taken a chilly turn in the last week, and she needed a winter coat and some warmer clothes if they were going to the beach. He insisted on accompanying her and her detail for the short ride around the block.

Michael followed her as she unlocked the door and deactivated the alarm. She tossed the mail, including Jeremy's letters, into her purse.

"Have a seat. I'll be just a minute." She dashed upstairs and tried to be quick, knowing the last thing Michael needed today was to be in the home she had shared with Jeremy any longer than he had to be.

A few minutes later she went downstairs and found him holding a framed photo of her and Jeremy taken on a cruise several years earlier. Michael studied the picture with such intensity he didn't hear her approach him.

"Michael?"

He seemed almost surprised to see her as he returned the photo to the shelf next to the TV. "Ready?"

She dropped her bag and went over to put her arms around him.

He went rigid with resistance.

"Please don't check out on me, Michael. I need you."

His arms encircled her, but his embrace lacked its usual warmth. "I don't have a lot to give right now."

"We're going to get through this together."

"How much more do you think we can go through before there's nothing left of us?"

Startled, she pulled back to look at him. "What do you mean?"

"It just seems like the deck's been stacked against us from the very beginning." Gesturing to the photo, he said, "Look at you with him. Anyone could see how much you love him. Paige might be pregnant, Rachelle's sick… Maybe we just weren't meant to be."

Juliana crossed her arms. "So you're giving up? Five days ago you asked me to marry you. Now you're saying we weren't meant to be? Which is it?"

He fixated on the photo. "I don't know how to compete with that, Juliana. I have two months. He's had ten years."

Juliana knew his despondency over what happened to Rachelle was fueling his despair over their relationship. Placing both hands on his face, she drew him down to her and kissed him with all the love and dismay she shared with him.

He whimpered and tried to pull away, but she wouldn't let him.

When he gave up resisting, he hauled her tight against him and poured himself into the kiss.

"I'm right here with you, Michael," she said, kissing his face and then his lips again. "We're going to get through this together. I promise."

Later that afternoon an unmarked police car took them to the hospital where Rachelle's extended family had gathered. Apparently, the media had figured out where she was being treated so Michael and Juliana kept their sunglasses on to hide their red eyes from the cameras.

In the parking lot, several TV reporters went into standup mode in front of cameras when they realized who was paying the family a visit.

Rachelle's cousin greeted them in the waiting room. "I'll let Monique and Curtis know you're here."

When Rachelle's parents came into the room a few minutes later, Juliana was surprised to discover that Rachelle's father was white.

Monique's pretty face was ravaged with fear and rage, which was directed at Michael.

"You gave me your word," Monique said in a barely audible whisper. *"You gave me your word that she'd be safe."*

Michael's shoulders drooped. "I'm so terribly sorry. I don't know what to say…" He shook his head when words failed him.

Juliana introduced herself to Curtis. "How's Rachelle?"

"She's been horribly sick, but thankfully they don't think any organs were damaged," he said. "They're keeping her for a few days to monitor her. And she's freaking out that they actually tried to kill her."

"I'm going to do everything I can to make sure whoever did this doesn't get away with it," Michael said.

"So you catch them, what difference will that make to us, Michael?" Monique asked, swiping furiously at tears. "Can you tell me that? They're in jail, and they still managed to do this. She's always going to be afraid now."

"It might matter to her to know they can't do this to anyone else."

"Whatever," Monique snorted. With one last frosty glance at Michael, she turned and left the room.

"I'm sorry," Curtis said. "She doesn't really blame you, Michael. You know that."

"She has every right to blame me. I promised her that her daughter would be safe, and she ended up poisoned."

"Do you think we could see her?" Juliana asked, contending with the huge knot of anxiety that had settled in her chest. "Just for a minute?"

"Of course," Curtis said, gesturing for them to follow him.

Clutching Michael's hand, Juliana forced her legs forward down a long corridor lined with cops in the intensive care unit.

In the room, she gasped at the sight of Rachelle's petite body hooked to beeping machines.

As they approached the bed, Rachelle opened her eyes. "Hey," she said softly.

"How're you feeling?" Juliana asked.

"Like I've puked my guts up."

"I'm so sorry, Rachelle," Michael said.

"I can't testify, Michael." Her eyes flooded with tears. "I won't."

"Let's see how you feel about it when you get out of here," he said.

Tears spilled down her cheeks. "I can't."

From behind them, Monique said, "We're taking her to St. Louis as soon as the doctors give the okay."

"I understand," Michael said. "I'll make the arrangements to get you out of here when you're released."

"I'm so sorry, Michael," Rachelle said between sobs. "I know I'm letting you down, but I can't take any more of this. They tried to *kill* me."

Michael reached for the girl's hand. "You did great. I'm so proud of you, and don't worry, I'll find a way to get them without you. You need to focus on getting better. That's all that matters."

Michael and Juliana visited with Rachelle until her eyes fluttered closed. They took turns kissing her forehead before stepping into the hallway.

"Thank you for coming." Curtis shook Michael's hand and hugged Juliana. "We appreciate all the time you've spent with her. She thinks the world of you both."

"We'll pray for you all," Juliana said.

"Thank you."

Michael held Juliana's hand as they emerged from the hospital to a burst of flashbulbs and shouted questions from reporters. They kept their heads down and followed the cops back to the car.

Michael stared out the window all the way home.

At two o'clock the next morning, again in an unmarked police car, Michael and Juliana were driven to Tom Houlihan's oceanfront house at Dewey Beach. They arrived just after four, and though they went right to bed in the large master bedroom, neither of them could sleep after the emotional day. Under any other circumstances, Juliana would have been delighted to be staying in a house like the one Tom had made available to them, but her heart was heavy after seeing Rachelle.

She had called Mrs. Romanello to tell her they were leaving town for a week or so, and the older woman was relieved to hear that. Juliana had been almost startled to realize that other than her brother, who agreed to take care of their mother, there was no one else she needed to tell. No one else knew about her relationship with Michael.

That changed the next morning when a photo of them holding hands as they left the hospital appeared with a picture of the injured police officer on the front page of the *Baltimore Sun*. Unfortunately, video of them was also broadcast on CNN.

Before ten o'clock, Juliana fielded phone calls from her mother, her sister Serena in California, her brother Vincent, her co-worker Carol, and her high school friend Pam Newman. Everyone, except for Pam, who had seen her once before with Michael, had the same questions— what was she doing with the prosecutor in the Benedetti trial, where was she now, and what the hell was going on? While Michael dealt with his frantic parents on his cell phone, she evaded the questions from her family and friends, except to tell them she was safely out of town for the time being.

She had just hung up with Pam when the phone rang again. Juliana's gut twisted with nerves when she saw it was Jeremy.

Ending the call with his parents, Michael walked over to her. "Who is it?"

"Jeremy."

"You should talk to him. He's probably freaking out."

"Probably." The phone beeped to indicate a message, which Juliana listened to.

"Juliana, it's me." He sounded frantic. "Jesus, babe, what's going on up there? What are you doing with that guy? Where have I seen him before? Somewhere. I want you to call me. Right away. I'm going to call you every fifteen minutes until I talk to you."

She turned off the phone and wandered over to the window to look out at the beach. Her stomach churned as it set in that Jeremy now knew there was someone else in her life, or he at least had strong reason to suspect it. He hadn't figured out, though, that he'd seen Michael getting off the plane with her in Jacksonville.

Michael came up behind her and rested his chin on the top of her head. "What are you thinking about? Or do I not want to know?"

"I was deluding myself when I thought no one was going to get hurt, wasn't I?"

"What do you mean?"

"When I came up with the idea for this break from Jeremy, I thought we could lead separate lives for a few months and no one would get hurt."

He wrapped his arms around her shoulders. "You couldn't have known what would happen between us. Who could've predicted all this?"

"I need to call him."

"Yes."

"I'm going to have to tell him you're just a friend." She turned to him. "You're so much more to me. You know that, right?"

"Of course I do." He leaned in to kiss her. "Maybe you could tell him the truth? Would that be so awful, Juliana?"

"Not on the phone. I'll talk to him in three weeks when I'm due to see him."

"You'll tell him about us?"

"I'm not sure yet what I'm going to tell him."

Michael's face fell with disappointment. "That means you still haven't decided."

"I'm not really thinking about it right now. There've been so many other things to think about."

He nodded in agreement.

"I'll be back in a minute." Juliana went upstairs to the bedroom and closed the door. She dialed Jeremy's cell phone, and he answered right away, as if he had been praying she would call.

"Jule?"

"Yes, it's me."

"Oh my God, what's going on? I almost choked on my coffee when I saw the news this morning. Who's that Maguire guy?"

"A friend of mine."

"How do you know him?"

Juliana took a deep breath. "The prosecution hired me to cut the hair of the witness who was poisoned. She and I became friends. Needless to say, I'm terribly upset about what happened to her."

"But you were holding hands with him. You looked like a couple."

"We're friends, Jer. It was a terrible day, and the media was all over us when we went to see her. He was just pulling me through the crowd. You don't have to worry about anything right now. I'll see you in three weeks, and we can talk then, okay?"

"Where have I seen him before? I know him from somewhere."

"I don't know."

"Are you in danger?"

"No."

"Jule?"

"Yeah?"

"Read my letters, will you?"

"I will."

"I love you."

"Bye, Jer."

Juliana went back downstairs a few minutes later to find Michael engaged in a heated exchange with Paige.

"They're *not* going to kill me. No, I'm not coming there." He paused. "She's my roommate. You know that. I don't care what it looks like. I've told you, *if* there's a baby, we'll talk about it after the trial. Don't you think I've got enough to think about right now? Fine. I'll talk to you then." He slapped the phone closed and shut it off. "That's enough for now. How'd it go with Jeremy?"

"A lot like that, actually. But I think he's pacified for now."

"Paige saw the news, too. Her concerns about my safety gave her another opportunity to remind me she's pregnant."

"Did you check on Rachelle?"

He nodded. "They expect to release her in the next day or two."

Juliana sat down next to him on the sofa and leaned her head on his shoulder. "Will you be able to secure a conviction without her testimony?"

He put his arm around her. "We've got her sworn testimony on videotape, and hopefully we can get it admitted. That's going to have to be good enough. The case is strong without her testimony, but I'm less certain of a conviction without her."

"Could you force her to testify?"

"Yes," he said with a sigh, "but I'm not going to."

"Maybe she'll change her mind when she's had a little time to recover."

"I'm not counting on that."

Sensing he didn't want to talk about it anymore, she said, "Are you hungry?" The cops had been to the grocery store for them.

"No. I'm tired, though. Suddenly, I'm really tired."

"Why don't we lie down for a while?"

"Okay."

They walked upstairs together, and Juliana closed the blinds in the big bedroom while he turned down the bed.

She snuggled into his embrace, her head resting on his chest. "Tom must be loaded to own a house like this."

"He was a very successful corporate lawyer before he ran for state's attorney," Michael said.

"Must be nice to have a spare house at the beach. I wish I was in the mood to enjoy being stuck here."

"I know," he yawned.

"Want me to rub your back?"

He raised an eyebrow. "Yeah?"

"Sure. Turn over."

He did as she asked and sighed when she kneaded the tension from his shoulders. "God, you're good at that."

"Remember the other time I gave you a backrub? That was the first night we slept together."

"Platonically, as I recall," he said with a small smile that quickly faded. "That was the night before opening

arguments. I'd give anything to go back to that night."
His eyes moistened and then closed. "I would've called
Rachelle first, and none of this would've happened."

Juliana kissed his cheek and rubbed his back until he
finally drifted into restless sleep.

Chapter 24

THEY FELL INTO A ROUTINE AT THE BEACH. JULIANA cooked for them, they took long walks—with cops trailing close behind—they played board games, and watched movies. On the third day they tuned in to a TV news special about the Benedetti trial.

"There's Tom and his wife, Jane," Michael said when the cameras followed them into the hospital to visit the family of Officer Brown, who was still in a coma.

"They look like Ken and Barbie."

Michael smiled at her description. "They're the perfect political couple. I hear he's going to run for Maryland attorney general next year, and I have no doubt he'll win unless we somehow fail to convict the Benedettis."

"What would that mean for you?"

"He could take me with him to Annapolis, or I could work for the new state's attorney if he or she wanted me. But I've been thinking about hanging up my prosecutor's hat when this trial's over."

Juliana turned to him. "Really?"

"I've had enough. I was sort of reaching that point before this case—and this one's just worn me out. I'm so sick of dealing with the dregs of society. You finish one hideous case, and there's another one right behind it. Just when you think you've seen everything, you confront some other example of how evil mankind can be. Young victims, old victims, kids, babies, I've seen them all." He shook his head. "No one's immune. And no matter how well we do our jobs, the victims are never entirely satisfied because their lives are still in ruins. It's like what Monique said—having the bad guys in jail doesn't always matter to the victims the way you think it will. The person they lost is still dead. They were still raped or assaulted or burglarized. They're always afraid. For the rest of their lives they're afraid."

Mesmerized, Juliana hung on his every word.

All of a sudden he seemed to realize he had said more than he'd meant to. "So it might be time for a change."

"But you're so good at it. I remember when I told my co-worker Carol that I'd met you on the airplane. She's Timmy Sargant's cousin." Juliana referred to one of the slain teenagers. "Carol said you'd been so good to her aunt and uncle. I didn't know you very well yet, but even then I could picture how wonderful you would've been with them."

"That's nice to hear. I try to always remember I work for the people, especially those who've been victimized. I just worry I'll start to become immune to it all, that I won't have any reaction when I see a baby without a head or a rape victim beaten to within an inch of her life."

"I don't think you could ever become immune to those things. That's just not who you are."

"Well, nothing's going to happen right away. I meant it when I told Rachelle's parents that going after the people who attacked her will be my top priority once the trial is over."

A photo of Officer Brown flashed onto the TV screen.

"Remember Scott laughing at my haircut?" Michael asked.

"Yeah. That seems like years ago rather than weeks."

For the first time they also showed the poisoned pizza being delivered on videotape that had finally been released to the media.

Juliana gasped when she saw the deliveryman's face. "Oh God, Michael! That's him!" she sputtered. "The guy who talked to me on the street, the same one I saw in Newport!"

Michael sat up. "Are you sure?"

She nodded. "Positive."

Michael went outside to have a word with the cops. He came back in a few minutes later looking pale.

"What?" Juliana asked. "What did they say?"

"They've identified him as Roberto Escalada. He's a hired gun."

"What does that mean?"

"They *were* planning to kill me," he said haltingly, "but he must've never gotten the chance. He even followed us to Newport."

Juliana's hand flew to her mouth as she broke down.

"Baby, if they catch him…"

The look on his face stopped her heart. "What? Michael…"

"You'll have to pick him out of a lineup. You're the only one who's actually seen him."

"How can that be? He delivered the pizza…"

"He delivered it to Scott. If he doesn't recover—"

"No, *no*," she whispered as it set in that if she was the only one who could identify a killer, she would be in the same situation Rachelle had been in.

Michael put his arms around her and dropped his head onto her shoulder. "I've dragged you into a freaking nightmare."

Shell-shocked, Juliana said, "Maybe there's someone else who saw him. There were other cops at the hotel, weren't there?"

He looked at her with shattered eyes and shook his head. "They were asleep."

"What about people at the hotel?"

"No one remembers seeing him."

"But I didn't see him at the hotel," she argued, pulling free of Michael's embrace to pace the room.

"You can tie him to me and the trial and thus to the Benedettis. The tape puts him at the hotel."

"You were with me in Newport. You saw him, too."

"I didn't see his face."

"Maybe they won't find him."

"Then he gets away with poisoning Rachelle and Scott."

"Oh, Michael," she said, sobbing.

He went to her. "No one will ever hurt you. Not as long as I have a breath left in me."

"I'm scared."

He brushed away the tears on her cheeks. "When I went outside I asked them what they knew about the guy on the tape. I didn't tell them you recognized him."

"Why not?"

"I won't involve you unless I absolutely have to—unless there's no other way. Let's just wait and see what happens."

She nodded and rested against him as they absorbed yet another blow.

❖ ❖ ❖

Michael went into caretaker mode that night. He grilled steaks and made salad for dinner, which he served with a bottle of wine he "borrowed" from Tom's wine cellar. Juliana pushed the food around on her plate, and only when Michael urged her to eat did she make an attempt.

After dinner, he lit a dozen candles in the master bathroom and drew a bubble bath for her.

She was soaking in the big tub when he brought her another glass of wine.

"I could get used to this treatment."

"That would be fine with me." He leaned over to kiss her and then sat down next to the tub.

Extending a soapy hand to him, she laced her fingers through his and gave a tug.

He laughed. "You are *not* pulling me in there."

"Come on."

"Why don't you come out here if you want to play?"

"Yeah?" They hadn't made love since Rachelle was attacked.

He pulled on her hand to encourage her out of the tub.

She stood up, covered with suds.

He scooped her into his arms and carried her to bed.

"Michael! I'm all wet!"

"Perfect," he said with a lecherous grin as he lowered himself down on top of her.

Laughing, she buried her hands in his hair and kissed him. When he came up for air, she brushed the suds off his face. "You're overdressed." Reaching for his now-damp sweater, she pulled it off.

He filled his hands with her breasts and dipped his

head to feast on her. "I must've been a very naughty boy," he sputtered against her breast. "I'm getting my mouth washed out with soap."

"You're the one who wanted to skip the whole towel portion of the bath," she reminded him. Her breath got caught in her throat when he rolled her nipple between his teeth. "*Michael,*" she sighed, pushing him onto his back and undressing him. She kissed her way from his chest to his belly. Wrapping her hand around his erection, she stroked him.

He closed his eyes and released a long deep breath when she took him into her mouth. "Oh, *God,* Juliana," he said with a shudder.

She drove him to the brink with a combination of lips and tongue and teasing teeth. Then she straddled him and took him in.

Rolling her hips back and forth, the sensations were so intense, so overwhelming that she bit her lip to keep from crying out. When he reached for her breasts, a jagged, breathless cry of complete surrender escaped from her parted lips.

"Juliana." His voice choppy and hoarse with emotion, he slid his hands down to her hips and came with a great cry of his own.

She slumped down on top of him.

"Just when I think it can't get any better," he whispered, closing his arms tight around her.

Brushing her lips over his, she said, "It gets better every time."

"If it gets any better, we're apt to spontaneously combust."

She laughed and rested her head on his chest to listen

to the rapid beat of his heart, reveling in the knowledge that only she had the power to do that to him.

Long after Michael fell asleep next to her, Juliana lay awake, afraid to close her eyes. Every time she did, she saw Roberto Escalada's face. If he had tried to kill Rachelle, he could certainly come after her, too. The thought terrified her, and she was unable to control the trembling that shook her body.

"Baby, what's the matter?" Michael asked, stifling a yawn.

"I'm scared."

He pulled her tight against him. "I'm right here. There's nothing to be afraid of."

"He's out there somewhere. He might even be outside right now, and we'd never know it."

"There're cops all over the place."

"Rachelle had cops with her, too."

"Do you know what I realized earlier?"

She turned to look at him. "What?"

He rested the palm of his hand on her face. "That if you hadn't moved in when you did and had the confrontation on the street with Escalada, I never would've asked for police protection. I'd probably be dead by now without you."

Her eyes burned with tears. "I came so close to leaving that day."

Leaning over to kiss her, he said, "I'm so glad you stayed, for many, many reasons, but I hate that I've put you in so much danger."

"There's one thing I still don't understand."

He yawned again. "What's that?"

"Why would they want to kill you? I mean, I know

they see you as the guy who's single-handedly trying to put them in jail, but they have to know someone else would take over the case if they killed you. So why bother?"

"Well, no one else knows the case the way I do, so they'd have a definite advantage with a new prosecutor. They might've also been aiming to bring about a mistrial."

"But why? They're already in jail, so what's in it for them to delay it? Wouldn't it be better for them to get it over with and maybe get off and out of jail sooner?"

"There's almost no way they're going to get off. Even without Rachelle, the case is very strong. They know that."

"I still don't get it."

Michael thought about that for a moment. "Unless…"

"What?"

He sat up. "Unless they're planning something big and needed to buy some time to get their shit together." Getting up, he tugged on his jeans.

"Where are you going?"

"I need to call Tom. I'll be right back."

Chapter 25

MICHAEL'S LATE-NIGHT PHONE CALL TO TOM HOULIHAN set off a full search of the city jail where the Benedettis were being held during the trial. Both their cells were tossed, all the common areas were torn apart, drains were even removed from shower stalls, but nothing suspicious was found. The search succeeded only in further shredding Michael's already frazzled nerves.

He couldn't figure out what the defendants might be up to. Since the rock sailed through the window at his house, the judge had suspended their visitation rights, forbidden the brothers to have any contact with each other in jail, and revoked their phone and mail privileges. If they were planning something else, Michael had no idea how they were managing to do it.

He spent most of the morning on the phone with his office, discussing their trial strategy in light of the week's developments. Thankfully, they had videotaped Rachelle's sworn statement, and Michael planned to introduce it as evidence. The defense would object on the grounds that they couldn't cross-examine videotape, but because he'd videotaped her under oath with a court reporter taking a transcript, he was going to try it.

While Michael was upstairs on the phone, Juliana went through the mail she picked up earlier in the week at her house. She paid the bills from the joint account she shared with Jeremy and sorted out the junk mail until only his two letters sat unopened on her lap.

All morning she had tried not to think about what might be ahead for her if she had to identify Rachelle's attacker. The girl was headed for the witness protection program. Juliana wondered if that's what would happen to her if she had to identify and testify against Escalada. She let her mind wander to the possibility that she could end up living anonymously in some strange place.

The idea wasn't without benefits—no more dealings with her dysfunctional family and a whole new life where no one knew her. Naturally, she wondered who would be with her in this fictional scenario. Did either of the two men in her life love her enough to give up their whole world to keep her safe? If right now, today, she had to pick one of them to accompany her into anonymity, which one would she choose? The answer came to her without a moment's hesitation. Michael. She would choose Michael.

A feeling of peace settled over her as she understood that at some point during the last few weeks, she had made a decision. Jeremy was her past. Michael was her future. He had asked her to marry him, and in the next few weeks, after she ended her relationship with Jeremy for good, she would be able to say yes. *Yes, I'll marry you, Michael.*

She wanted to run upstairs and tell him, but she had things to resolve before she could do that, and so did he. If Paige really was pregnant, he would have to deal with it before much longer. He'd have a child with another woman. They would handle that somehow. After

everything they had already been through together,
there was no doubt in Juliana's mind they would get
through that, too. He didn't love Paige anymore, but he
would love their child, and Juliana would give him her
full support.

Energized by her decision, she felt ready to read Jeremy's
letters and to keep them in proper perspective. She checked
the postmarks to see which one came first and opened it. He
had written it on his company's letterhead.

Dear Jule,

I'm sitting here at work, and I'm supposed
to be figuring out why two of my circuits are
down, but all I can think about is you. I'm
wondering what you're doing right now. It's
Tuesday morning, so I'm picturing you at
the salon making someone beautiful. You've
always been so good at that. Remember when
we were in high school and you gave everyone
haircuts all the time? We'd end up at someone's house after a football game. When I'd go
looking for you, you'd usually be in the bathroom giving one of our friends a trim. That was
even before you'd been to school for it!

I like thinking back to those days, when
we first knew each other and all we thought
about was finding time to be alone together. I
remember looking for you in the stands during
football games. Sometimes thinking about being
with you after the game would be so distracting
I'd forget what I was supposed to be doing
on the field. The only times I really screwed

up playing football were because of you—so there's something you never knew! Even back then, you had such an ability to invade my thoughts and distract me. Ten years later, nothing's changed, babe. Here I am, all grown up with a real job, but I'm at work thinking about the same girl who drove me crazy when I was playing high school football. How many guys can say that?

The other day I was driving home and I heard that Peter Gabriel song we've always loved, "In Your Eyes." He says he's complete when he can see her eyes. It's so true—I never realized just *how* true it was until you weren't here anymore. I keep reminding myself this is temporary, but I worry that maybe it's not, that maybe I hurt you so badly, nothing I do will ever fix it.

I've had far too much time to think over the last month. I think about all the tough stuff we dealt with when your parents were still together. Like the night they had that big fight and the neighbors called the cops. I can still remember the way you sounded when you called and asked me to come get you. I took you home with me, and you were so upset that my mother didn't even care that you slept with me in my room. That was the first night we ever slept in the same bed. My mother has always loved you, Jule. She's been after me for years to marry you. I should've listened to her. If I had I wouldn't be in the mess I'm in now with you. Anyway, I remember waking up with you that next morning and being so thankful you'd called me when you needed me. I've always hated how your family treats you like their own personal Cinderella, but you know I could write a book on that subject!

Well, I'd better get back to work. I just wanted you to know I'm thinking of you and hoping we can find our way through this. Nothing in my world makes sense without you by my side. If you give me another chance, I promise I'll spend the rest of my life making this up to you. I love you,

Jeremy

PS—Are you okay for money? If you need any, you know where it is. There's plenty in the Bank of America account. What's mine is yours.

Juliana wiped away the tears that flowed as she read his heartfelt letter. She was almost reluctant to read the second one, but she opened it because she promised him she would.

Dear Jule,

I had an awful day today. I wish I could call you and tell you about it the way I used to. I can't seem to do anything but wish I was with you, so of course I'm screwing up at work. I'll be lucky if I don't get fired before this separation of ours is over. If they didn't need me so badly to finish this stupid job down here, they

probably would've already fired me. Whatever.
I don't even care anymore. All I care about is
fixing what's happened between us.

I'm finding I have an amazing ability to
torture myself with memories. Do you know
what I can't seem to stop thinking about?
Making love with you. Remember how scared
we were the first time? It was pretty bad, huh?
But we got better at it, didn't we? Sometimes
I think I'll go mad craving your soft skin, or
thinking about the way it feels to be inside you,
and that sound you make way in the back of
your throat… Okay, I've got to stop this before
I seriously go insane. I can't believe I thought
for even one second that I could do that with
someone else… I'm sorry. You're the only one
for me. You always have been, and you always
will be. Don't stop loving me, Jule. I don't think
I'd survive it.

I love you.
J

And just that simply, the decision Juliana had been
so certain of a few minutes earlier was once again back
in play.

An hour later, huddled under a heavy blanket on a
lounge chair on the deck, Juliana revisited all the memories Jeremy's letters resurrected. He had reminded her
that for a very long time, he'd been the only person in
her life who truly loved her.

"Hey," Michael said. "Aren't you freezing?"

Startled out of her thoughts, she said, "What?"

"What's wrong?" he asked, rubbing his hands together vigorously.

"Nothing."

He tilted his head to study her. "Are you sure?"

She nodded. "Everything okay at work?"

"Yeah. The judge wants to see us all on Monday morning, and then he's resuming the trial."

"That's good, right?"

"I'm anxious to be done with it, so, yes, that's good. Can we go in? It's freezing out here."

She took the hand he offered and let him help her up.

"Christ, Juliana, your hand is like ice. How long have you been out here?"

"Not long."

He closed the sliding glass door and hustled her over to the sofa in front of the fireplace. After he threw two more logs on the fire, he sat down next to her and held her close to him. "Tell me what's wrong, baby."

"Did they find Escalada?"

"No, but they found the place in Annapolis where he'd been hiding out. His prints were everywhere, and they found traces of arsenic."

She looked up at him. "Let me guess, he was long gone, right?"

Michael nodded, his mouth set in a frown. "They don't think he's in the area anymore. The FBI has issued a nationwide alert. They'll find him."

"I almost wish they wouldn't," Juliana confessed. "But then I think about him getting away with poisoning Rachelle and Scott…"

"I know." He rubbed her hands between his to warm them. "But hey, we have three more nights here before I have to go back to the city. Can we just put everything else aside and try to enjoy being here together? For just a few days I don't want to think about anything but you." He kissed her. "Can we do that?" He kissed her again. "Can you do that?"

"I'll try," she said, but her heart was burdened by her worries about Escalada and the knowledge that she still had a big decision to make—a decision that was going to hurt one of the men who loved her.

They did their best to put their stack of troubles aside for the time they had left at the beach house, and for the most part they succeeded. On their last day, they cleaned the house, did a load of sheets and towels, and packed while trying not to think about what was ahead in the next few weeks. Just after midnight on Sunday, they were driven back to the lives they put on hold a week ago.

"What are you thinking about?" Michael asked as they crossed the Bay Bridge.

Juliana rested against him in the back of the police car. The cops had closed the panel to the backseat to give them some privacy. "I was remembering when you said this bridge looks like a yard sale bridge."

"Well, look at it."

"I agree with you."

He rubbed his cheek against her hair.

"Michael?"

"Hmm?"

"Can I ask you something?"

"Sure."

"Remember that night when we came back from Florida and you gave me your card and we said good-bye?"

"Of course I do. Why?"

"Well, ever since then I've wondered: if my car had started, would I have ever seen you again?"

"A lot's happened because that car didn't start, hasn't it?"

"Yes."

He tilted her face up so he could see her. "If your car started and you drove away that night, I think I would've suddenly been in desperate need of a haircut. I might've lasted a day, maybe two, but that's about it."

"Really?"

He leaned in to kiss her. "I've told you, Juliana, I already knew then that you were going to matter to me. I never could've imagined how much, but I already knew. What about you? Do you think you ever would've used that card I gave you to get in touch with me?"

"Truth?"

He winced and nodded.

"I don't think so. I would've been afraid to see you again."

"Why afraid?"

"I was such a mess over everything with Jeremy that I probably would've gone into my shell and hid out for three months until it was over."

"You might've been better off. At least you would've been safer in your shell."

"But I wouldn't have known you."

"That might've been better, too."

"No. I wouldn't have missed this time with you for anything. I could never be sorry for loving you."

He brought her hand to his chest. "You still make my heart pound, Juliana."

"There's another reason why I would've been afraid to call you."

"What's that?"

"I thought you were about the sexiest guy I'd ever met."

His face lit up with delight. "Oh, really?"

She traced his bottom lip with her finger. "Uh huh. If I'd had time to think about it, I definitely would've been afraid of you."

"I think," he said, capturing her finger between his teeth, "what you need to be afraid of at this moment is whether or not I'm going to jump you right here in the back of this police car."

She pushed him away. "Stop!"

Michael opened the divider to talk to the cops. "Hey, does this thing have a siren?"

"Sure does."

"Can you use it? I'm suddenly in a big rush to get home."

"Michael!" Juliana said with a nervous giggle as the cops laughed. "He's just kidding."

"The hell I am."

Chapter 26

THE TRIAL RESUMED MONDAY MORNING WITH A MEETING of the attorneys in the judge's chambers.

"Here's how this is going to go," Judge Stein said. "The defense motion for a mistrial is denied—"

"But your honor—" one of the defense attorneys protested.

"You do not want to interrupt me right now. Your clients are attempting to make a mockery of the judicial system I've served for forty years. I'm running low on patience."

"Yes, your honor," the chastened attorney replied.

"Mr. Maguire, you're certain Ms. Griffith is unable to appear in court?"

"She's been very sick. Her parents and doctors are unwilling to permit it."

"In that case, I'm going to allow the prosecution to introduce the videotape of her testimony." To the defense attorneys he said, "Before you object, and you should feel free to do so in open court, I know you can't cross-examine videotape. But it's a sworn statement, so you can take it up with the appellate court. Finally, I want to be sure you're all clear on one critical thing—there is to be no mention from either side about the attack on Ms. Griffith. Not by inference, reference, or any other means. Do I make myself clear?"

"Yes, your honor," the attorneys answered.

"Mr. Maguire, I'm sure there'll be a mighty temptation to give the jury the impression that the defendants had something to do with the reason Ms. Griffith is appearing before us on tape rather than in person. Resist it or you'll not only be looking at a mistrial but a complaint from me to the bar. No matter what you think happened in that Annapolis hotel room, Marco and Steven Benedetti are *not* on trial for the attack on Rachelle Griffith and the police officers. Not yet anyway and not in my courtroom. Keep your eye on the task at hand."

"Yes, your honor," Michael said.

"Very well. We call to order in thirty minutes."

After they filed out of the judge's chambers, Michael asked for a moment alone with Tom Houlihan. They found a deserted conference room, and Michael closed the door.

"Everything all right?" Tom asked.

"No, but before I get into that, thank you for the use of your house. It was a hell of a place to be stuck for a week."

"I figured you'd enjoy it. You've certainly earned the break. What's on your mind, Michael?"

Michael sat down at the conference table, hoping he was about to do the right thing. "Um, Juliana."

"She's a lovely girl."

"Yes," Michael said softly. "She is."

Tom sat down next to Michael. "What's wrong?"

"She can tie Escalada to the trial."

"*What?*" Tom gasped. "*How?*"

"Do you remember the day I finally asked for police protection because someone on the street gave my roommate the creeps?"

Tom's eyes widened. "Escalada?"

Michael nodded. "When she saw the videotape from the hotel on the news, she recognized him. She saw him in Newport, too. He was trailing us, apparently waiting for an opportunity to take me out."

Tom rubbed his face as he processed it all. "Who else knows this?"

"No one."

"Except Escalada. He knows she can tie him to the trial."

The gravity of that statement hung in the air between the two men.

"What do I *do,* Tom?" Michael asked with desperation. "I wanted to bring her to court with me this morning so I didn't have to leave her at home alone."

"Her detail is with her, and everyone's on highest alert. I wish I could tell you not to worry…"

"If anything happens to her, Tom, I swear to God, if anything happens to her…" Michael's voice broke.

Tom put a hand on Michael's shoulder. "She's more than your roommate, isn't she?"

"If I get very lucky, she's going to be my wife."

"Is she the reason you and Paige broke up?"

Michael shook his head. "I know you'll find it hard to believe, but this happened after that was over. The timing could've been better, but timing is secondary when the right one comes along."

Tom studied him for a minute. "Here's what we're going to do. Don't tell anyone about this. No one. We'll only involve her if there's no other option. We'll figure this out after the trial is over. Until then, I want her at home."

Michael shook his head. "She'll never go for that. Her job is too important to her, and she needs the money. But how can I let her go to work and take care of her mother when they've got someone out there watching her? Waiting for an opportunity to *kill* her? How can I do that, Tom?"

"We'll double her detail—and yours. We'll get a home health aide for the mother so Juliana only has to go to work."

"We doubled Rachelle's detail, and look what happened to her."

"We'll do our very best to keep her safe, Michael. I promise."

Michael wanted guarantees his boss couldn't offer. "Okay," he said, wishing he could be with her every minute to ensure her safety himself.

"It's almost over. Stay tough and stay focused."

"Have you ever had a case like this one before?"

"Not in this lifetime."

The jury filed in, and once they were settled, Judge Stein apologized for the lengthy delay in the trial. "We appreciate your patience and your sacrifice," he said. "Mr. Maguire?"

Michael stood up. "Your honor, the prosecution introduces as evidence the video testimony of Rachelle Griffith."

"Objection," a defense attorney said.

"Overruled. Please proceed, Mr. Maguire."

Michael walked over to the TV and VCR to insert the tape. He adjusted the volume and returned to his seat. Watching Rachelle's animated face was like a punch to his gut as he wondered if the attack would permanently snuff out her sparkle. With the judge's warning in mind, he fought to keep his emotions off his face to avoid giving the jury any hint of what happened to her. They were going to have to draw their own conclusions as to why the witness was appearing on tape rather than in person. That, coupled with the timing of the lengthy recess right when the prosecution's star witness was due to testify, was exactly why the defense requested the mistrial.

The tape was made about two months earlier when Michael brought her to a courtroom to prepare her for the real thing. Remembering her begging him to take her to McDonald's on the way back to the hotel, he was so glad he had given in despite his worries about her safety. She had been delighted to share a table with him in the restaurant while the police detail surrounded them at other tables.

Off camera, he could be heard asking the questions that guided her through the telling of her story. As he watched her talk, he could see her affection for him in her eyes and hear it in the tone of her voice. It was something he missed the first time around when he had been engrossed in the asking of questions. Only a man who was blind, deaf, and dumb could have missed the enormous crush she had on him, but sitting in the courtroom fighting to keep his face devoid of emotion, he hurt all the way down to his bones over how totally he'd let her down by failing to adequately protect her.

He glanced at the defense table to find Marco Benedetti's black eyes fixed on him. At just twenty years old, Marco had the eyes of a hardened criminal.

Steven, a year older than his brother, had been charged with murder once before but was acquitted. Michael didn't believe for a minute that he was innocent of the earlier murder. With juvenile rap sheets a mile long, the shootings elevated the brothers' pattern of petty crime from misdemeanors to multiple felonies.

Marco's greasy hair was slicked back, and when his face contorted into a small, evil smile, it took every ounce of control Michael had to remain seated when all he wanted was to smash that smile off his smug fucking face. Michael looked around, hoping someone else had seen Benedetti's smile, but the entire courtroom was riveted to the television.

I promise you, Rachelle. I promise they won't get away with it. A fierce burst of rage coursed through Michael. He was so consumed by it he failed to notice the videotape had ended or that the jurors were deeply moved by it.

"Mr. Maguire?" Judge Stein said.

Michael didn't move.

"Mr. Maguire!"

Slowly, Michael rose to his feet. "Your honor, the prosecution rests."

At home, Juliana sat on Michael's bed folding laundry. He had called and outlined the plan he and Tom worked out. She wasn't at all confident that her mother would accept the help of a home health aide, but she wouldn't have much choice. It was that or nothing since there was no way Juliana could call on Vincent again.

She had been relieved to hear that she would be able

to continue working. Money was always an issue for her, and despite offers of help from both Michael and Jeremy, she didn't feel right taking money from either of them.

Thinking of Michael playing the video of Rachelle if the judge allowed it, Juliana couldn't imagine how hard it would be for him after seeing her so diminished in the hospital. Putting away clothes in his dresser, Juliana found her rent check sitting on top of it and realized he never cashed it. Her heart contracted with overwhelming love for him. He loved her in such an all-consuming way, and he was going to need her to love him just as much tonight after having to sit through that video.

A thump on the roof startled her out of her thoughts. The wind was whipping, and Michael mentioned the night before that he needed to bring the furniture in off the deck for the winter. A second thump convinced Juliana that one of the lounge chairs on the roof deck had blown over. She deactivated the alarm and went out through the sliding door to investigate. Taking the stairs to the roof deck, she stopped short when all the oxygen left her body in one big whoosh.

"Don't you dare scream," Roberto Escalada said in a low, sinister tone. "If you scream, you're dead. You got me?"

Juliana nodded as terror rippled through her and robbed her of the ability to breathe, let alone scream. She couldn't have made a sound just then even to save her own life, which was suddenly in grave danger.

"Turn around and go back down."

Juliana couldn't seem to make her legs move.

"*Now!*"

She turned and on shaking legs went down to the

lower deck and opened the door to Michael's bedroom.

Escalada followed her inside and slid the door closed behind him. "I thought you and lover boy were never going to come home from wherever they had you stashed."

Juliana sat on the edge of the bed and willed herself to keep breathing as she trembled uncontrollably.

He took a look around the room. "So this is where it all happens, huh? I bet you give it up to that mother-fucker Maguire every night, don't you? You look like the kind of girl who likes to get it on." He came over to stand in front of her and leaned down so close she felt his breath on her neck. "Maybe I should have me a taste of what he's been getting."

"No," Juliana whimpered. "Don't touch me."

"Now that's not very friendly, Juliana, and we're old friends, aren't we?" He ran a finger along her neck and jaw. "Is that any way to treat a guest?"

She moved away from him, and he grabbed her arm. "Where do you think you're going?"

"There are cops everywhere," she whispered.

He laughed. "Cops haven't stopped me so far, have they? Believe me, I'd love nothing more than to be halfway across the country by now, but it occurred to me I'd left behind a juicy loose end here in Maryland. You know I can't have you linking me to the trial, Juliana. My clients wouldn't appreciate that."

Juliana began to cry as she struggled against the iron grip he had on her arm.

He smacked her hard across the face. "Shut up! *Shut the fuck up!*"

Falling back on the bed, Juliana saw stars and was

too stunned to cry or even scream as he paced the room. When the haze of fear cleared a bit, she realized the cops wouldn't be checking on her again for close to an hour. If she was going to get out of this, she was going to have to do it on her own.

"I need to go to the bathroom."

He looked her over to see if she was up to something before he gestured for her to go ahead. "Hurry up, and no bullshit. I want to get this over with and get the fuck out of here. Leave the door open."

Her face throbbing from where he'd hit her, Juliana did as she was told. It took all her fortitude to get through the motions of going to the bathroom. She was terrified he would take advantage of her half-dressed state to make good on his threat to rape her, but this was her only chance to save herself.

Slowly, so she wouldn't attract his attention, she reached up to the tiny cabinet above the toilet paper roll. She remembered Michael laughing when he showed her the phone the previous owner installed in this and every bathroom in the house. Relying only on her sense of touch, she lifted the receiver and dialed 911.

Hearing the operator say, "911, please state your emergency," she put the phone down and flushed the toilet. With adrenaline coursing through her, she pulled her pants back up and willed her shaking hands to button them. Only when she had her clothes back in place was she able to breathe again.

"What the fuck are you doing in there?"

"I'm coming." She forced her trembling legs to move and prayed to God the 911 operator had done her job and notified the police.

Escalada grabbed her.

She whimpered at the feel of a cold metal edge resting against her throat.

He ground his erection into her back. "Mmm, mmm, *mmm*, I sure do wish I had time to have me some of you," he growled against her ear. "Your boyfriend's going to come home to a big mess tonight. No more saucy piece of ass for him."

"Freeze!"

Juliana shifted her eyes to find three cops in the doorway with their guns drawn.

Escalada tightened his hold on Juliana. He backed them up to the sliding door and opened it with his free hand.

She felt a burning sensation against her neck and realized he had cut her.

"Let her go, Escalada," one of the cops ordered.

He dragged her outside to the lower deck.

The cops followed them.

Her shirt became wet as a warm, sticky trail of blood accumulated in a pool at her collarbone. The combination of the cold and the fear had Juliana shaking even as she fought to remain still against the knife.

"Let her go!" the cops ordered again.

"Back off or I swear to God, I'll kill her!"

A shot rang out, and Juliana screamed when Escalada slumped over her, knocking her down as the knife fell from his hand and clattered onto the wood deck.

He landed on top of her.

Shrieking, she clawed at him.

The cops moved quickly to free her. One of them

gathered her into his arms and carried her inside while another radioed for paramedics.

"It's okay, Juliana. We got him. You're safe."

She slumped against him and lost consciousness.

Chapter 27

MICHAEL WAS HAVING LUNCH WITH HIS COLLEAGUES AT a deli across the street from the courthouse when Officer John Tanner rushed over to tell him that a 911 call had been made from his house.

He jumped up. "*Juliana,*" he gasped, running with Tanner from the restaurant to a cruiser outside. "What happened? Is she all right?"

"We don't know yet. All I know is there was a call, but the caller didn't say anything. Her detail was going in when I came to get you."

Michael got into the car with John who flipped on the siren to make a path through heavy midday traffic. During the interminable ride, they heard snippets over the police radio that had Michael paralyzed with fear: gunshots reported on Chester Street, a call for paramedics, two victims.

Oh God, please. Please.

John's cell phone rang with a call from a member of Juliana's detail asking if he had Michael. "We're on our way to the scene," John replied. He was told Juliana was being taken to Hopkins.

"How bad is it?" Michael urged John to ask.

"They don't think it's life-threatening."

Michael sagged into the seat, his stomach roiling with nausea. They don't *think* it's life threatening. That meant they didn't know for sure. *Please, God. Please don't let her die.*

They arrived at the hospital at the same time as the ambulance. Michael was out of the car before it stopped. He raced over to the ambulance and for a second time fought the urge to pass out at the sight of a ghostly pale Juliana covered in blood. This time, though, she was unconscious, and the cut on her neck was still bleeding profusely. There was something else all over her that looked an awful lot like brain matter.

"Oh," he whispered. "Oh, God."

John pulled Michael back so the paramedics could get her inside. They hustled her down the hall and into one of the trauma rooms. The nurses stopped Michael outside the door.

"*What the hell happened?*" he screamed when two of the cops from Juliana's detail rushed into the hallway.

"Escalada. We figure he came down from the roof deck. It's close enough to the house next door that he could've jumped."

"But the alarm was on," Michael said. "How did he get in? How did he get to her?"

"The alarm was off."

Michael shook his head. "No way. She wouldn't have shut it off."

"I'm sorry, Mr. Maguire. I don't know what to say. It was off when we went in after the 911 call. Somehow she managed to get to a phone. There's no doubt that saved her life."

Based on what Michael saw a minute ago, he had considerable reason to wonder if her life had in fact been saved. He sat down hard in a chair in the hallway. "Where is he now? Escalada?"

"He's dead. One of our guys got off a shot from the roof next door."

Michael felt a brief moment of relief at that news. At least their other problem had been solved. "Where was Juliana when they shot him?"

The cop looked down at the floor, his face tight with tension.

"*Where was she?*"

"He had her, with a knife to her throat. That's how she got cut."

"Oh my God." Michael put his head down to stop the rush of nausea that struck when he realized how easily the cop could have missed Escalada and hit her instead, or even both of them. Michael kept his head down and prayed like he never had in his life. Even when Tom Houlihan came in and sat next to him, Michael kept his head in his hands and never stopped praying.

"Should you call her family, Michael?" Houlihan asked.

Michael shook his head and ran a trembling hand through his hair. "She wouldn't want them here. You've got to keep her name out of the reports, Tom."

"It's already taken care of."

After what seemed like hours to Michael, a doctor finally emerged from the room where Juliana was being treated. Michael jumped up.

"Are you with her?" the doctor asked.

Without hesitation, Michael said, "She's my fiancée."

"We've got the bleeding stopped, and I've called in a plastic surgeon to suture her."

"She'll be all right?" That was the only thing the doctor failed to say and the only thing Michael needed to hear.

"She lost quite a bit of blood, but she should be fine in a day or two. One millimeter deeper and we'd be telling a different story. She got very lucky."

Tom shook the doctor's hand. "Thank you."

When his legs failed him, Michael sank down to the chair.

Juliana opened her eyes in the dark room and tried to figure out what was pinching her finger. She raised it to discover a medical device clipped to it, and realized she was in the hospital. Attempting to turn her head, she winced when the wound on her neck burned in protest.

Michael's head rested on the hospital bed next to her arm. She raised her hand to run her fingers through his hair.

His head whipped up. "Juliana… Oh God…"

Juliana held out her arms to him, and he crawled right up onto the bed to hold her as deep sobs shook them both.

"Are you all right, baby?" he asked when he could finally speak again. Running his hand over the bruise on her face, he brushed back her hair. "Does anything hurt?"

She tried to shake her head and winced.

"Don't move your head." He kissed her cheek, her lips, and her neck just above the large white bandage that covered the wound. "Thank God you're all right."

"Is he dead?"

"Yeah."

"It's my fault," she said with a fresh burst of tears.

He brushed them away. "How can you say that?"

"I turned off the alarm so I could go see what was thumping on the deck. I thought the lounge chairs had blown over, and I went up to get them. I shouldn't have shut off the alarm."

"So that's why," Michael said with a sigh. "None of us could figure out why it was off. Honey, no one imagined he'd try to get in through the roof. It's not your fault. If anything, we all think you're amazing for figuring out a way to make the 911 call. How did you do that?"

"I told him I had to go to the bathroom when I thought of the phone in the cabinet."

Michael released a ragged deep breath. "I almost took the phone out of there when I first moved in. I thought it was so dumb to have phones in the bathrooms."

"I remembered you telling me that."

He caressed her bruised cheek. "What happened to your face?"

"He hit me when I tried to get away from him. He said he wanted…"

Michael's hand froze. "What?"

She looked away from him, her face burning with embarrassment. "Some of what you've been getting."

"Baby, did he, I mean, *Jesus*…"

"No. He just did a lot of talking about it."

He held her even more tightly. "You must've been so scared."

"I thought I'd never see you again, Michael," she whispered. "I just wanted to see you again."

"I'm so sorry. This is all my fault. I knew it wasn't safe to keep you with me, but I've been so selfish. I'm so crazy in love with you that I was greedy for whatever time I could get with you. It didn't even matter that I'd put your life in danger."

She stroked his face. "We were both greedy for the same things. It's not your fault. You tried to get me to leave a bunch of times. It was my choice to stay. It still is."

"You're not staying after this. No way. I'm putting my foot down."

She smiled. "We'll see."

"I mean it, Juliana. This is it."

"Okay." She would fight that battle later.

Michael managed to fend off the police who wanted a statement from Juliana. He told them she would talk to them in the morning but not before. No fewer than four cops stood guard in the hallway outside the room where Michael slept on the hospital bed with Juliana in his arms.

He woke up in the middle of the night in a cold sweat after dreaming that Juliana had been killed instead of Escalada. At some point, a nurse must have covered him with a blanket. Because he was shaking and breathing hard, he got up so he wouldn't wake Juliana. After he splashed cold water on his face in the bathroom, he sat down in a chair, dropped his head into his palms, and gave in to the need to weep.

When he thought about all the things that could have happened… she might have forgotten about the phone in the bathroom, Escalada might have raped her—maybe even more than once—or cut her throat. The cops could have shot her instead of that animal Escalada. Each scenario was more chilling than the last, and they ran through his mind like a horror movie.

"Hey," she whispered from the bed. "Where'd you go?"

He wiped his face and got up to go to her. "I'm here. I'm right here."

She took his hand to bring him back on the bed. "What is it, Michael? What's wrong?"

"Nothing's wrong as long as you're all right. I love you."

She curved her hand around the back of his neck to draw him down to her. "I love you, too," she said, touching her lips to his. "So much."

He held her as tightly as he dared, his face buried in her fragrant hair.

"Michael?"

"What, hon?"

"I'm worried about work. I won't be able to go in tomorrow, not with my face all banged up… I was already out last week and now this. I'm going to get fired—"

"Shh." He kissed her. "Don't worry. I called the salon. I told them you'd been in a car accident, and they said to take as much time as you need."

She released a sigh of relief. "Thank you for thinking of that," she said, reaching for him.

Thrilled that she felt well enough to even care about work, he fell into the kiss. She was everything, and she was still right here with him. For now, for this moment, she was his and she loved him.

"Is there a lock on that door?"

"I don't know."

She kissed him again. "Why don't you check?"

"You need to get some sleep."

"I've had some sleep." She nibbled on his ear, her hand moving to his chest. "Now I want you."

He groaned as she pushed open his shirt. "Juliana…"

She pressed her lips to his chest. "What?"

"*Sweetheart,*" he hissed. "Come on. You're killing me."

She laughed. "Then stop resisting."

When she reached for his fly, he grabbed her hand. "All right. That's enough. Time to sleep."

"Michael?"

He took a deep breath to slow the frantic beating of his heart. "What, hon?"

"I need…"

Turning on his side to face her, he said, "What do you need? I'll get you anything you want."

"I need to feel like I'm still alive. Is that weird?"

"No," he said, kissing her with a burst of passion that took them both by surprise. "It's not weird. It's normal after what you went through."

"Make me feel like I'm still alive, will you? Will you, please?"

"Right now?" he asked, startled. "Here?"

She bit her lip. "Yes. Right here, right now."

"What about the nurses?"

"They were just in a little while ago."

"I slept through that?"

"Uh huh." Giggling, she added, "They said you were awfully cute all curled up to me in the bed."

He studied her for a long moment before he got up to discover there was no lock on the door. "I don't know about this, Juliana…"

"I'm willing to take my chances," Juliana said with a saucy grin. "What'll they do? Kick me out?"

His heart pounding and imagining the headlines should they be caught, Michael shrugged off his shirt and dropped the suit pants he had put on almost twenty-four hours earlier. "I had no idea you were such a risk taker."

"I'm just full of surprises," she said, pulling the covers over them.

"This is definitely a first," he whispered.

She replied with a hot kiss that robbed him of all rational thought. Her arms went around him, urging him over her.

"Does your neck hurt?" he asked, pushing up her hospital gown to find her naked underneath.

She caressed his back. "No."

Concerned about hurting her, he trembled from the effort to contain overwhelming urges.

"Love me, Michael."

With only the slightest of movements he slid into her. Not wanting to cause her pain, he kept up a slow, easy pace that somehow affected him more than any other time with her ever had. All the anxiety and emotion and love from that long day—not to mention the fear of getting caught—had him on the verge of losing control in a matter of moments. "I'm not going to last long, baby," he whispered through gritted teeth, reaching under her to hold her tight against him.

"You won't have to," she said in a breathy voice that told him she too was teetering on the edge.

He tightened his hold on her to keep her still so her climax wouldn't hurt her.

With a gasp, she clutched him from within, dragging him over the edge with her:

"Did it work?" he asked when he had caught his breath. He could very safely say that making love with her in a hospital bed, after nearly losing her, had been the most erotic experience of his life.

She laughed. "*Oh, yeah.* I'm definitely alive."

He kissed her forehead and then her lips. "Yes, you are. But we're both going to be dead if we get caught like this." He disentangled himself from her and found his clothes. After he got dressed, he said, "There. Now I can breathe again."

Juliana smiled when he lay down next to her again. "Thank you."

"Believe me, it was my pleasure." Kissing her softly, he added in a teasing tone, "I want to be the guy who's there for you in your time of need."

She linked her fingers with his. "You are."

His smile faded. "Except that you're in this bed tonight because of me."

"Don't do that, Michael. You didn't cut me."

"In the morning the cops are going to want your statement." He brought their joined hands to his lips. "Do you think you'll feel up to it?"

"What do I have to tell them?"

"Everything that happened from the time you first heard something on the roof until he was shot."

She looked away from him.

"What?"

"I don't want them to know he said that other stuff about, you know…"

"I think you could leave that part out since he didn't actually do anything."

"He might have if the cops didn't show up when they did. I think that's why he didn't kill me right away. He wanted something else first."

Michael stopped breathing. "Did something else happen, Juliana?"

Her cheeks flushed with color. "He was…"

"Tell me," Michael urged.

"Turned on," she whispered.

"How could you tell?"

"He pushed it against me when he put the knife—"

"Stop." His heart racing with anxiety, Michael hugged her close to him. "That's enough. You don't have to tell the police about that."

"He said he had to come back because he'd left a loose end behind and that he couldn't let me live because his clients wouldn't want anyone left who could link him to the trial."

His blood gone cold, Michael sat up. "He said that? In those exact words?"

"Just about."

"Holy shit. This is a nightmare that refuses to end. You can link him to the Benedettis. They haven't found anything else to tie him to them."

"What does that mean?"

"You're still in danger."

Chapter 28

EARLY THE NEXT MORNING, MICHAEL'S DETAIL TOOK him home to shower and change. He returned in less than an hour with clothes for Juliana to wear home from the hospital. For the moment, his colleague George Samuels was handling the trial. Since they had no real defense, the Benedettis' attorneys were calling a parade of character witnesses to testify on their behalf. According to George, the previous afternoon consisted of glowing praise for the brothers' care of their widowed mother, their work at the YMCA with underprivileged kids, and other bullshit that George didn't think the jury was buying. Michael's absence had been explained as a personal emergency.

Juliana showered and got dressed. The nurses changed the dressing on her cut and showed Michael how to do it at home. The stitches would dissolve, and they hoped the scar would be undetectable. However, the bruise on her face had exploded with color overnight, and she had a black eye. She was weak from the blood loss and the cut hurt like crazy, but otherwise she felt well enough to go home.

"God, I look like hell," she complained to Michael when she came out of the bathroom.

"Not to me."

"You have to say that."

"I don't care how you look as long as you're alive and safe. It's going to be a long time before I care about anything else."

She put her arms around him and rested her head on his chest. "I'm sorry you were so scared."

"Scared doesn't begin to describe it."

"Let's go home."

The detectives were coming by the house in an hour to take her statement. Michael had asked Tom Houlihan to be there, too.

"We need to talk about our living situation," he reminded her as he helped her into the wheelchair the nurses left for them.

"Not now, okay?"

"Not now, but later. Definitely later."

After Juliana gave the detectives her statement—skipping over Escalada's rape threats—Tom showed them out. Juliana rested on the sofa against the mountain of pillows Michael insisted on.

"I think we can work this so the Benedettis won't know that Escalada gave them up," Tom said.

"Until they're tried for the attempted murder-for-hire of the cops and Rachelle," Michael reminded him.

"That'll be a year or more from now. If we can keep a lid on it until discovery, Juliana will be safe from them."

"What happens after discovery?" Juliana asked.

Tom and Michael exchanged glances.

"Protective custody," Tom said. "Followed most likely by witness protection."

Juliana twisted her fingers as she absorbed the news. She'd thought that threat died along with Escalada. Unfortunately, he had told her just enough to keep her ensnared in the case.

Tom sat down next to Juliana. "I know what you're thinking: we failed to keep Rachelle safe, so what's to say the same thing won't happen to you." He took her hand. "I'm not going to feed you a big line of bull because you've seen how bad it can get. I'm just going to promise you that we'll do everything we can to ensure your safety."

"That's all you can do. Thank you, Tom, and thank you for the flowers, too. They're gorgeous."

"Feel better soon." Tom stood up to shake hands with Michael. "Take as much time as you need. George has things covered in court."

Michael thanked him and walked him to the door. When he came back, he sat down next to Juliana. "Can I get you anything?"

"No, I'm good, but you need to get back to work."

"I will, tomorrow probably. We need to talk about what's going to happen now. I think you should go home—to your place. You'd be safer there."

"I'd be alone there."

"You're going to be alone here when I go to work tomorrow."

"But I won't be alone at night. I can ask Mrs. R to come over during the day. She'd love to hang out with me."

Michael sighed with exasperation. "You're working me. I know that look. You think if you look at me that way you can get whatever you want."

She reached for his hand. "What look?"

"That one! You're doing it again! It's not going to work. I want you to go home. I don't want you here anymore."

"Now you're just lying to my bruised and battered face," she said, kissing the palm of his hand.

He rested it against her bruised cheek. "I never knew you were such an operator. Maybe you're more like Paige than I thought."

"Oh!" She punched his chest. "Take that back!"

He chuckled and leaned in to kiss her. "I don't want to."

"I'm not kissing you until you take it back."

"You're going home," he said, nudging at her lips with his tongue.

"Make me." She tormented him by sliding her lips over his without giving him the access he craved.

With a groan of frustration, he gave in. "Fine! Stay. Get yourself killed. See if I care. Now kiss me."

"You forgot something," she said with a victorious smile.

"What?"

"Take back the Paige crack."

He rolled his eyes. "I take it back, I take it back! Now will you kiss me?"

She held him at arm's length. "One more thing."

"*What?*"

"The part where you said you don't want me here and the 'see if I care' comment… I didn't like that, either."

"No?"

"Not so much."

"I'm seeing a whole new side to you that I'm not sure *I* like." In truth he was so relieved by the sassy spark in her gorgeous brown eyes that he would take anything she cared to dish out.

She folded her arms. "Now you've got to take that back."

He laughed. "I take it back. I take it all back," he said, moving her arms and nuzzling the uninjured side of her neck.

"Say something nice so I'll forget all that mean stuff."

He pretended to struggle to think of something.

She pushed him away. "Forget it!"

"No wait, I think I've got it."

Raising a skeptical eyebrow, she said, "This had better be good."

"You're everything to me. You make me happier than I've ever been in my life. Just knowing you'll be here when I get home gets me through anything I have to face during the day. I don't know how I ever lived before I knew you, and the thought of you being in danger because of me…" He shook his head when he couldn't go on.

She held out her arms to him, and he rested against her chest.

"How was that?" he asked a minute later.

"Good," she said in a voice gone hoarse with emotion. "Really, really good."

He tilted his face up to hers and was rewarded with a kiss he would never forget.

Over the next two weeks, word got out among her friends and clients that Juliana was recovering from an accident at home. In an unprecedented display of self-lessness, her sister Donatella coordinated with the salon to organize appointments for hair styling sessions for Juliana's closest friends and longest-standing clients in Michael's living room.

When people asked why she was staying there, Juliana simply said that she and Jeremy were taking a break to figure some things out and that she was renting a room from Michael in the meantime. To her great relief, no one pressed her for more information. While she was self-conscious about being out in public with the colorful bruise on her face, she told her sister and close friends that the bruise and the bandage on her neck were from a car accident.

Juliana enjoyed the parade of friends who came by to check on her and appreciated Dona's efforts to organize "Juliana's Salon," which kept her busy and her mind off her troubles—not to mention it provided some welcome extra income since her clients insisted on paying her.

One day, Dona even brought their mother by for lunch and a haircut. Paullina looked better than Juliana had seen her in years, and she was filled with curiosity about the home health aide who had brought about such a miraculous transformation in her mother.

Since the Benedettis were in isolation in jail and didn't know Escalada was dead or what he told Juliana before his death, Tom and Michael thought it would be safe for her to go back to work—with her detail in tow—when the bruise on her face healed and she felt ready to resume her regular life.

When she wasn't acting as the proprietor of Juliana's Salon, she made good use of the time at home to rearrange almost every room in Michael's house, to make fabulous dinners that he said he dreamed about during the long days in court, and to recover from the trauma of her encounter with Escalada. She also did a lot of thinking about where her life was going as Jeremy's arrival edged closer. He left a message on her cell phone asking her to meet him at their house next Saturday morning.

One more week.

Michael endured endless days in court while the defense
employed one pathetic tactic after another in an effort
to make the jury forget about the powerful evidence
presented by the prosecution. He wished he could bring a
book or a newspaper to read during the ridiculous parade
of witnesses who did nothing to dispel the fact that
Marco and Steven Benedetti, while apparently pillars of
the community, had gunned down three defenseless kids
in a parking lot. Michael didn't even bother to cross-
examine most of the defense witnesses.

Finally, at three o'clock on the Friday before the last
weekend Michael might ever spend with Juliana, the
defense rested without calling the defendants to testify.
Michael thought their attorneys had served them well in
keeping them off the stand. Most of the legal analysts
following the trial had speculated the Benedettis would
not testify on their own behalf, and Michael agreed with
them. But he had been ready if the defense decided to
call them. Judge Stein set closing arguments for nine
o'clock on Monday. The end was in sight.

On the way home, Michael stopped to buy a bottle
of champagne and a dozen yellow roses. He arrived just
after four to find his living room rearranged in a way he
never would have considered. It was perfect. Just like her.
Pulsing music and the smell of something that made him
want to drool led him to the kitchen. He found her dancing
to the beat at the stove and was reminded of their first
week together. He resisted the urge to sneak up on her
since she had been jumpy after her ordeal with Escalada.

"Hey," he yelled over the din.

Her face lit up when she turned to find him there. "You're home early!"

He pulled the champagne and roses from behind his back. "With presents."

"Oh, for me? They're gorgeous! Thank you." She kissed him. "What's the occasion?"

Michael loved that she appreciated even the simplest of gestures. "Let me quote: 'your honor, the defense rests.'"

"Yippee! It's almost over then, right?"

"Closing arguments on Monday, and then it goes to the jury." He pulled off his tie and unbuttoned the top button of his shirt.

"Then tonight we celebrate." She found a vase for the roses and put them on the dining room table.

"Is Juliana's Salon closed for the day?"

"Sure is. We had a banner day with five clients." She tugged a wad of cash out of her back pocket and tried to put it in his. "Rent."

He sidestepped her. "Get real, Juliana. I'm not taking that." Peeking into a pan simmering on the stove, he asked, "What are you making?"

She put the money on the counter, but he knew she'd try again later and looked forward to the wrestling match that would no doubt ensue.

"It's a new shrimp recipe Mrs. R gave me. She cut it out of a magazine, so no guarantees."

"If it tastes as good as it smells, we've got another winner. I was going to take you out tonight to give you a break from all the cooking you've been doing."

She reached up to cover the faded but still visible bruise on her face. "Not yet. Another couple of days maybe. Besides, I love to cook."

"And I love to eat what you cook. I think I've gained ten pounds since you moved in."

Juliana wound her arms around his neck. "Why don't we open that bottle of champagne, light a fire, and hibernate all weekend? It's freezing out anyway."

With his hands on her hips, he drew her close to him and leaned in to kiss her. "I like how you think."

Late on Sunday night, after Michael practiced his closing for Juliana one last time, he snuggled with her in bed. "Thanks for the excellent suggestions. You'd make a good lawyer."

"Nah, I'd never make it through all that school. I don't have the smarts."

"*Are you kidding me?* Someone who's smart enough to find a way to make a 911 call when there's a killer in the same room? Give me a break. You're smarter than most of the people I went to law school with."

"You think so?"

"I know so." He turned on his side to face her. "This was the best weekend I've ever had."

"It was fun, wasn't it?"

"Is it going to be our last weekend together, Juliana?"

She shook her head.

"You've made a decision?"

"I think so," she said softly, reaching up to stroke his hair. "When everything happened with Escalada, when he was holding that knife against my throat, the only thing I could think about was you and finding a way out of it so I could be with you again."

"Juliana..." He rested his forehead against hers where

a tiny white mark was all that remained of the cut from the coffee table glass.

"Jeremy asked me to give him a couple of days, and I'm going to do that. I have to play it out with him and end it the right way. You understand, don't you?"

"I'm trying to. It's just the thought of you…"

"What?"

He ran a hand over the warm, soft skin of her back. "In bed with him…"

She raised herself up on one elbow. "I'm not going to sleep with him."

"You're not?"

"I couldn't. Not after being with you."

Michael closed his eyes and released a jagged deep breath. "God, I wish we'd talked about this sooner. I've been driving myself nuts imagining you with him."

"I'm sorry." She combed her fingers through his hair. "I'm going to hear him out, but that's it."

He arranged her so she was lying on top of him. "I love you. I'll love you for the rest of my life. You and only you."

Juliana kissed the engagement ring nestled in his chest hair. "Soon, Michael. Soon enough, I hope I can say that, too."

"I can wait one more week." He drew her down for a kiss. "By this time next Sunday, we'll be free and clear."

Chapter 29

MICHAEL DELIVERED HIS CLOSING FIRST THING Monday morning. He took the jury through the last day in the lives of Jose Borges, Timothy Sargant, and Mark Domingos. Earlier, he warned the boys' families of what he planned to do so they could prepare themselves.

He reminded the jurors of the argument the boys had with the defendants in the arcade, talked about the testimony of the boys' friends who witnessed the fight, and reiterated the evidence offered by the detectives and ballistics experts.

"You heard the eyewitness's chilling account of the shootings and her description of how ruthlessly the defendants shot first Mark Domingos, then Jose Borges, and finally Timmy Sargant. All of this over an arcade game." He paused for effect like he practiced with Juliana. "Throughout the course of the trial, you've heard the victims' names repeatedly. You already know they liked to play video games and they spent their last moments skateboarding in the parking lot of Jose's apartment complex. What you maybe don't know is they were honor roll students." Michael smiled as he paid tribute to boys he'd never met but had come to know so well over the last year.

"Jose was an outstanding baseball player—a promising pitcher with a fierce curve ball—who loved to torment his little sisters. Timmy made the all-city basketball team in sixth and seventh grade, and he knew everything there was to know about *Star Wars*. Mark was on his way to being an Eagle Scout and played a mean guitar. His hero was Richie Sambora from Bon Jovi."

The parents of the boys wept quietly in the gallery as Michael moved over to lean against the jury box.

"They were good kids who made the fatal mistake of arguing with two men who were capable of murder." He paused to let that thought settle and was satisfied when two of the female jurors dabbed at their eyes. "My job is to leave you with no doubt that Marco and Steven Benedetti murdered Jose Borges, Timothy Sargant, and Mark Domingos. If I've left you with reasonable doubt that it was the Benedettis who pumped one round after another into those defenseless boys, then you'll have no choice but to acquit them. But if I've done my job and you have no doubt—no doubt whatsoever that it was them," he said, turning to point to the defendants who were both looking elsewhere, "then you must convict." Making eye contact with each of the jurors, Michael said, "Jose, Timmy, and Mark are counting on you. Don't let them down."

With an empathetic glance at the boys' families, he returned to his seat next to George Samuels.

"Perfect," George whispered. "Spot-on perfect."

"Let's hope so," Michael replied as the lead defense attorney got up to do her closing. He said a silent thank you to Juliana who suggested the last line—don't let them down. George was right. It was perfect.

Michael found it interesting that the defense attorney didn't refute Rachelle's videotaped testimony in her closing, which told him she too believed her clients probably had something to do with the arsenic attack. No doubt the defense attorneys had a few difficult moments of their own during this trial. She summed up her closing by saying, "They didn't do it. You must acquit."

After she sat down, Judge Stein gave the jury their instructions. Before Michael knew it, the jurors were filing out to begin deliberations. The Borges, Sargant, and Domingos families were effusive in their praise of Michael's closing.

"Thank you, Michael, for bringing them to life again," Mrs. Sargant whispered as she gripped his hand, her face pinched with grief and wet with tears. "Thank you for everything."

"I just hope it was enough." Michael would have felt much more confident if Rachelle had been able to testify in person.

"It's in God's hands now," Mrs. Sargant said.

As Officer John Tanner escorted Michael and George back to their office, Michael tried to remember what life had been like before he was accompanied by police officers everywhere he went.

"That went really well," George said. "I don't think there's anything else we could've done."

"I guess," Michael said, thinking of Rachelle and how desperately he wished he had the whole thing to do over again.

"Your closing was really good, Mr. Maguire," Tanner said, surprising Michael.

The young officer hadn't had much to say since the

rock went through Michael's window on his watch. "Thank you."

When they arrived, Michael went into his office and closed the door. He hated waiting for juries. Usually, it was the most stressful part of any trial. Not this one, though. The whole thing had been stressful. He picked up the phone to call Juliana.

"Hey," he said. "What're you up to?"

"Having lunch between appointments. How'd it go in court?"

"Good, I think."

"Did you use my line?"

"Sure did. I ended with it, just like we practiced."

"I wish I could've been there to watch you."

He wished he'd thought to bring her. "Me, too. Next time, maybe? If there is a next time…"

"I'd love that."

As he was thinking about how much he loved *her,* there was a knock on his door.

"Hang on a sec, hon." With his hand over the phone, he said, "Come in."

"They're back," George said.

"Already? It hasn't even been an hour."

George shrugged. "We've got thirty minutes to get there."

"Tell Tom." Into the phone, Michael said, "I've got to go. The jury's back."

Juliana gasped. "Are you worried it was too fast?"

"That's often good news for us, but you never know."

"Good luck, Michael. I love you."

"Love you, too. Turn on the news in about forty-five minutes."

"I will."

❖ ❖ ❖

The jury filed into the courtroom half an hour later.
Michael was encouraged when several of them glanced
over at him as they were seated. In his experience, it was
when they didn't look at you that you needed to worry.

After they were settled, Judge Stein asked, "Have you
arrived at unanimous verdicts?"

"Yes, your honor," said the foreman, a tall, burly man
who worked on the docks in the port of Baltimore. He
handed the verdict paper to the bailiff who walked it
over to the judge.

Judge Stein read the verdicts, passed the paper
back to the bailiff, and asked the defendants to rise.
"In the matter of the People versus Marco and Steven
Benedetti, murder of Jose Borges in the first degree,
what say you?"

Michael held his breath.

"Guilty," the foreman said.

The gallery erupted.

Judge Stein wrapped his gavel. "Order!" he bellowed.
"There will be order in this courtroom!"

When the only sound was the quiet weeping of
the victims' families, Judge Stein continued. "In the
matter of the People versus Marco and Steven Benedetti, murder of Timothy Sargant in the first degree,
what say you?"

"Guilty," the foreman said to more whimpering from
the gallery.

"In the matter of the People versus Marco and Steven
Benedetti, murder of Mark Domingos in the first degree,
what say you?"

"Guilty," the foreman said.

Michael rested his head on his hands and fought the urge to weep.

Guilty.

Thank you, God.

Pandemonium broke out all around him as the families of the victims rejoiced and the people sitting behind the Benedettis sobbed.

It took Judge Stein several minutes to restore order. He thanked the jury for their sacrifice and hard work. "Sentencing is set for one month from today. We are adjourned."

Michael stood up to accept the congratulations of George Samuels, Tom Houlihan, the paralegals who worked with them, and the overjoyed families of the victims.

He was talking to Mr. and Mrs. Borges when out of the corner of his eye he saw Marco Benedetti lunge for the gun belonging to the sheriff deputy who was attempting to cuff him.

Michael screamed and everything shifted into slow motion.

Before the other deputies could reach him, Marco waved the gun erratically and fired a wild shot.

The people still in the courtroom dove for cover under chairs and tables. Michael, on the other hand, couldn't seem to make his legs move. He watched, transfixed, as Marco grabbed one of the other deputies, held the gun to her head, and screamed for his brother to help him.

Michael glanced over to find Steven locked in an epic struggle with another deputy. Steven prevailed, wrestled the gun from the deputy, and rushed to his brother's side.

Marco flashed a victorious grin at the people who

remained in the courtroom before he shoved aside the woman he'd held hostage and zeroed in on Michael. "Fuck you, Maguire." He aimed the gun at Michael.

Too surprised to even move, Michael locked eyes with Marco, and for a brief, sickening moment he found out what goes through the mind of someone who's about to die.

Marco fired, and another shot rang out from behind Michael, who was suddenly flying through the air. He landed on the floor under John Tanner as one of the other deputies put a bullet between the eyes of Steven Benedetti.

With that final shot, the case of the People vs. Marco and Steven Benedetti came to a bloody and deadly end.

Juliana forced herself to stay busy at home while she waited for the local news to break into programming to announce the verdicts. When she couldn't sit still any longer, she paced back and forth, praying they would be found guilty. While she wanted justice for the families of the three boys, she had her own reasons for wanting to keep the Benedettis in jail. She opened the front door to ask the cops if they'd heard anything.

"Not yet. We'll let you know as soon as we do."

"Thanks."

She went back inside and paced for another ten minutes before the local anchors came on with the news that verdicts had been reached in the Benedetti trial. They went live to their reporter on the scene.

Juliana sat down on the sofa and clasped her hands together in prayer as anxiety and adrenaline coursed through her.

"Just a minute ago, we received word that Marco and Steven Benedetti have been found guilty on all three counts of murder in the first degree. To repeat, the Benedettis are guilty."

Juliana screamed with joy and relief as she bolted to the front door in search of someone to celebrate with. She ran down the stairs and jumped into the arms of one of the two cops guarding her that day. Imagining how Michael must feel at this moment, tears slid down her cheeks. He had done it. He'd gotten them—for the families of the three boys, for Rachelle, and for everyone touched by their reign of terror.

She was still talking to the police officers when their radios began to crackle with the news of shots fired at the courthouse. "What's going on?" she asked in a tiny voice.

The cops listened intently to the back and forth, much of it in code that Juliana didn't understand.

"Please," she begged. "Tell me what happened."

"It sounds like one of the Benedettis grabbed a gun and shot up the courtroom," the younger of the two cops said.

"*Michael,*" Juliana moaned, sinking to the cement stairs. "Oh, Michael."

As the younger cop went to the patrol car to find out more, the other one sat down next to her and took her hand. "We're going to find out what happened just as fast as we can, okay?"

She squeezed his hand and nodded, knowing all the cops who had guarded them in the last few weeks had become fond of her and Michael. They knew exactly what she needed to hear just then.

Her heart raced as she absorbed the very real

possibility that Michael could be dead. Promising anything God wished to ask for in return, she asked Him to protect Michael and bring him home to her.

The waiting became unbearable, and she began to cry. The movie of her brief time with him ran through her mind over and over again. Resting her head on her arms, she was overcome with love and fear unlike anything she'd ever experienced, even when Escalada held a knife to her throat. Her worries for Michael's safety were far greater than any she had ever felt for her own.

Just when Juliana thought she would go mad if she didn't hear something soon, a police car pulled onto the street. The back door opened, and Michael ran for her. Later, she wouldn't recall the exact moment when it registered with her that it was him, and he was safe. All she remembered was running and crying and screaming his name.

Right in the middle of Chester Street, he scooped her off her feet and into his arms.

She rained kisses over his face before she found his lips.

"It's over, baby," he whispered. "It's really over."

"So then John fired from behind me and hit Marco right in the heart," Michael recounted to Juliana. They were curled up together on the sofa after saying a tearful good-bye to the police officers who'd provided protection over the last two months.

"Thank God he was there." Juliana couldn't seem to stop touching Michael—his face, his hair, his chest—as if to confirm he was really safe.

"Yeah, he was unbelievable. He fired while he was in

midair tackling me, and the shot was dead-on accurate. I don't know how Marco missed us both. When I tried to thank John, he said, 'I owed you one, Mr. Maguire.'"

"It must've been so scary."

"It all happened so fast there was no time to be scared, but I'll tell you what, in that one second when Marco fixated on me and I thought I was going to die, a lot of shit ran through my head."

She caressed his face. "Like what?"

"I had just enough time to be really sad that I wouldn't get to spend my life with you. And I thought about my poor parents who've already lost one son. That's why I called them on the way home, before they heard it on the news. My mother was hysterical."

Juliana closed her eyes tight against the burn of tears. "I was so sure you were dead."

He pressed his lips to hers. "All I could think about was getting home to you. I left Tom to deal with the media and got the hell out of there." He checked his watch. "They're having a press conference in a few minutes."

She released him so he could turn on the TV.

They listened to Police Chief Noonan recount the events that occurred in the courtroom. He announced for the first time that the Benedettis had been linked to the attempted murder-for-hire of the eyewitness and the police officers guarding her in the Annapolis hotel room. The chief answered a flurry of questions about the connection between the Benedettis and Escalada without naming Juliana.

"Thank God it's over," she whispered.

"Thank God they're dead, and they can't hurt you or anyone else."

Tom appeared next. "I want to thank everyone on my staff who worked so hard over the last year to secure the convictions of Marco and Steven Benedetti. In particular, the entire city of Baltimore owes a debt of gratitude to lead prosecutor Michael Maguire. Despite repeated threats to his safety and that of his loved ones, Mr. Maguire never wavered in his commitment to see justice served on behalf of the Borges, Domingos, and Sargant families. I think it's safe to say the Benedettis are now facing a higher form of justice than anything we could've meted out here on earth."

"Isn't that the truth?" Michael said. "I hope they rot in hell."

They listened to interviews with several jurors who expressed shock over the events in the courtroom, as well as what they finally learned about the arsenic attack.

"I wondered why she didn't testify in person," the foreman said. "We had our suspicions that something happened to her, but we never could've imagined all of this."

"This means Rachelle's family can go home again, right?" Juliana asked.

"They're on their way as we speak, and I heard today that Scott Brown is on the mend."

"That's great news," she said, overcome with relief to know that Rachelle would get back at least some of what she'd lost on that fateful night and that Officer Brown would recover from his injuries. "I don't ever want to hear the name Benedetti again. Can we never, ever talk about them again?"

"Fine by me." Michael flipped off the television and turned to her. "I have a big idea."

"What's that?"

"Tom told me not to show my face in the office until next Monday, and you don't have to be anywhere until Saturday. What do you say we get out of here for a few days?"

"I'd love to."

Chapter 30

MICHAEL AND JULIANA SPENT THREE BLISSFUL NIGHTS at a resort in the Bahamas. The sunshine and relaxed atmosphere did wonders to restore their battered nerves, but they were subdued as they flew home late on Friday afternoon. Juliana was due to meet Jeremy in the morning, and Michael had decided to go to Jacksonville to finally deal with Paige and her alleged pregnancy.

"I wish we could've stayed there forever," he said after they landed in Baltimore.

"I know. Me, too. But the sooner we take care of things with Jeremy and Paige, the sooner we can get on with our lives."

"I like the sound of that. Where do you want to get married?"

"I don't really care. I've never wanted a big wedding because of all the crap with my family, so whatever you want is fine with me."

"My mother and sisters would never forgive me if they weren't there, so maybe we can do it in Rhode Island?"

"That's fine."

"I love you." He kissed her left hand. "I can't wait to get my ring on that finger where it belongs and put another one right on top of it."

Holding hands, they walked through the airport.

"I'll never be in this airport again that I won't think of you and the night I met you here," Juliana said.

"What a long, strange trip it's been since then, huh?"

She grinned. "The craziest two months of my life, that's for sure."

"For me, the craziest *and* the best."

"Same here."

After they dropped off their luggage at home, they went to Fell's Point for pizza and beer at one of the waterfront restaurants.

"It sure does feel good to be free of the cops, doesn't it?" he asked.

"And free of the fear. The cops were all so terrific, though. We got really lucky."

"They have a tough job. I have a whole new appreciation for them after spending so much time with them."

"I have a whole new appreciation for a lot of things after everything that's happened," she said. "Regular people don't pay much attention to the criminal justice system until we need it, so I never had any idea how much danger people like you and the cops put yourselves in on our behalf. It's impressive and admirable."

"Thank you," he said, touched by her insight. "Luckily, it's not usually this dangerous."

"What are you going to do now that the trial's over and Rachelle's attackers are all dead? I know you'd like to go to Rhode Island to open your practice there."

He laced his fingers through hers. "And I know you have an obligation here to your mother, so we'll be staying put for the time being. I'll probably get a few offers because of the publicity the trial generated. We'll see what happens."

"You'd really put your plans on hold for me?"

"Of course I would. The Rhode Island thing was

always a pipe dream anyway. It'll still be there if someday ever comes."

"My mother could live for years yet," she warned him.

He squeezed her hand. "I hope she does."

When they got home, they unpacked from the Bahamas and repacked for the weekend away from each other.

Juliana zipped her bag closed, sat next to him on the bed, and leaned her head on his shoulder. "I wish we didn't have to do this. I wish we could just run away together and never look back."

He put his arm around her. "It's just a few more days, baby. We can get through a few more days to have forever together, can't we?"

"You've never had a moment's doubt, have you?"

"Not about my feelings for you. How you feel has given me a few worries."

"I'll tell you how I feel: I love you, Michael. I admire you, I respect you, I adore you, I want you."

He sighed with contentment as he kissed her softly at first and then with growing passion when she responded with equal ardor. They rolled across the bed, pulling at clothes without breaking the kiss. His hands were everywhere, uncovering the soft skin he craved. He pushed aside the last of their clothes and entered her.

She gasped and clutched him tight against her.

Their lovemaking was desperate and almost frantic throughout a night neither of them would ever forget.

As the sun came up the next morning, Michael was filled with a sense of foreboding that left him wondering if what she had given him that night was going to have to last a lifetime.

Juliana took her time in the shower, wanting to prolong her departure as long as she could. She heard the bathroom door open.

"Want some company?"

"Sure."

He got in behind her and wrapped his arms around her, resting his chin on the top of her head. "I don't want you to go."

She turned to him, the water sluicing over them. "You have things you need to take care of, too," she reminded him.

Capturing her mouth in a plundering kiss, he lifted her, pressed her against the wall, and made love to her one last time. When it was over, tears mixed in with the water on his face as he struggled to catch his breath. "I'm sorry," he said against her ear. "I didn't come in here for that."

"Don't be sorry." She kept her arms and legs wrapped around him until the water turned cool, and they released each other with great reluctance.

They got dressed in silence, and Juliana dried her hair. She covered what remained of the bruise on her face with makeup before gathering the last of the things she needed from the bathroom and adding them to her bag. Then there was nothing left to do, no reason left to stay.

Michael walked her downstairs and held her coat for her. He gathered her hair from under the collar and let it slide through his fingers.

"What time's your flight?" she asked.

"Noon. I'll be back tomorrow night around seven."

She rested her hands on his chest. "Good luck with all that." With a small, sad smile, she added, "Don't let her hit you."

"I've learned to be ready for it."

She hugged him.

"You'll be back tomorrow night, right?"

"Yes."

He kept his arms around her. "I don't want to let you go."

They held on tight for a long time before Juliana took a step back, gazed at his handsome face, and reached up to kiss him. "I love you."

"I love you, too." He stepped aside so she could open the door. "Don't forget to come back."

"I won't." She leaned in for one last, quick kiss and was startled when he responded with a burst of desperate passion.

"Go," he whispered against her lips, his eyes bright with tears.

Without another word, she went out the door to her car.

Juliana drove around for almost an hour to get her emotions under control before she faced Jeremy. She willed herself not to cry so she wouldn't have to explain red eyes to him. Pulling up in front of the house on Collington Street, she noticed his black Toyota SUV parked outside for the first time in nearly a year.

For several minutes, Juliana was unable to move. Finally, with a last deep breath for courage, she grabbed her bag, got out of the car, climbed the cement stairs, and used her key in the front door. Inside, she dropped her bag on the floor and took off her coat, filled with the odd sense of having landed somewhere she no longer belonged. In just two short months, Michael's house had become home to her.

Jeremy came bounding down the stairs with a big smile on his face. "Oh, babe, I'm so glad you're home!" He flung his arms around her and lifted her off her feet. By the time he put her down, they were both in tears, but for different reasons. "It's so good to see you." He caressed her face as if to convince himself she was really there. "I missed you so much." He brushed his lips over hers but was so caught up in the moment he failed to notice her lack of response.

"Jer, we need to talk," she said, pulling back from him.

He reached out to run his fingers through her hair, and she was stricken by the memory of Michael doing the same thing only an hour ago.

"I know, but I just want to be with you for a while first. Is that okay?"

She hesitated and then nodded.

"Are you hungry?" he asked.

"Sort of."

"Why don't we go get some breakfast?"

Juliana didn't think she could eat, but it was something to do. "Okay."

They put on their coats to walk the short distance to their favorite coffee shop. On the way, Jeremy kept his arm looped around her shoulders. Juliana prayed that Michael wouldn't drive by on his way to the airport and see them together. She was finally able to breathe again after they ducked into the tiny restaurant where they were greeted like returning royalty.

"Hey, you guys!" their waitress friend Carla said with a warm smile. "We were just talking about you the other day! Where've you been?"

"I was working in Florida for the last nine months. I just got back last night." He reached for Juliana's hand. "It sure is good to be home."

"It's great to see you," Carla said. "Can I get you the usual?"

"That works for me. Jule?"

Juliana swallowed the lump that lodged in her throat as she and Jeremy slid back into their old life like nothing had happened. "Just coffee and wheat toast for me, please."

"You're sure, babe?"

She nodded.

"Coming right up."

Jeremy smiled and reached across the table for Juliana's other hand. "I can't believe you're really here with me. I thought today would never get here."

"It's good to see you, too." She hadn't expected to be so glad to see him.

"I'm surprised I can even function after the last two weeks. I worked sixteen, seventeen hours a day to finish everything so I could leave by Wednesday. A couple of nights I slept on the floor at the office because it wasn't worth going home."

"Did you get it all done?"

"My part's done. I might have to go back for a day or two in the next few weeks, but that's it. The rest of them have at least another month, maybe two, before they're done."

"So you didn't have to quit to come home early?"

"Fortunately, it didn't come to that. They even gave me next week off and a bonus for getting the install done early."

"That's good. Congratulations."

"How's everything at the salon?"

"Oh." The question startled her. She hadn't been to the salon in almost three weeks and was due back to work on Tuesday. "Fine. Nothing new."

Carla brought them coffee.

Jeremy added cream and sugar to Juliana's and slid it over to her.

"Thanks," she said, touched by his attentiveness.

"I missed you so much, Jule. Did you miss me?"

"Of course I did."

His face sagged with relief. "I'm glad to hear that. I was so nervous about seeing you today, but the minute you walked in all the nerves went away." He kissed both her hands and then released them when Carla brought their food.

"Just holler if you need anything else."

Jeremy dove into his omelet while Juliana picked at her toast.

"I thought you were hungry," he said.

"Not as much as I thought."

"Are you okay?" he asked, his eyebrows knitting with concern.

Her heart ached when she realized this was going to be much, much harder than she ever could have imagined. "We really need to talk."

"Later. I promise." After they had a second cup of coffee, he paid the check and extended his hand to her.

"Take care, you guys," Carla said. "Come back again soon."

Jeremy held the door for Juliana. "We will," he replied.

At home, he took her coat and hung it next to his in the closet.

Juliana wandered into the kitchen to flip through the mail. Most of it was junk, which she threw away. She wished desperately for something else to do, anything to avoid confronting the needy, hopeful vibe coming from Jeremy. When she couldn't put it off any longer, she went to sit next to him on the sofa.

He put his arm around her and brought her close to him.

Juliana resisted his efforts to kiss her.

"What?"

"Don't."

"Why?"

She pulled free of his embrace and stood up. "I can't do this! I can't just pick up where we left off like nothing's happened!"

He got up and rested his hands on her shoulders. "Let's just take it a step at a time. Can we do that?"

"No, Jer, we can't." She took a deep breath. "I don't know how to say this—"

He held up a hand to stop her. "Don't. Don't say anything right now, please? Just give me today and tonight. You can say anything you want to tomorrow, okay?"

"Okay," she said reluctantly.

After ten years, she could give him one more day.

Chapter 31

MICHAEL MOVED THROUGH THE HOUSE LIKE HE HAD hundred-pound weights attached to his legs. He'd experienced the worst feeling watching Juliana drive away to meet her boyfriend or ex-boyfriend or whatever the hell he was. Michael feared he would regret letting her go, even for just two days.

Before he left for the airport, he called his mother to let her know he was going to Florida for the night.

"Oh, Michael, *why?*" Maureen cried. "I thought you were done with her. Didn't you just go to the Bahamas with Juliana?"

"I *am* done with Paige, and things are great with Juliana." He hoped he wasn't jinxing himself with that statement. "I just have a few loose ends I need to sew up with Paige."

"What kind of loose ends?"

He struggled to find the words.

"Michael?"

"She says she's pregnant."

"*Pregnant?*" Maureen gasped. "Are you *kidding* me?"

"I wish I was."

"Oh, dear God. How could that have happened?"

"The usual way, I suspect."

"I'm surprised at you, Michael. I would've expected you to be more careful."

"I'm *always* careful, but the one time I wasn't…"

"She's trying to trap you." Maureen's voice grew more desperate by the second. "You can't let her do that."

"Mom, listen. I agree with you. I highly doubt there's a baby, which is why I'm going down there today. I want to settle this with her once and for all."

"Do *not* marry her, Michael. No matter what, you can't marry her."

"There's no way I'm going to marry her. Don't worry."

"What does Juliana think of all this? She must be thrilled."

He couldn't even think about where Juliana was right then or what she might be dealing with. "She's supportive. She knows whatever happened with Paige happened before she and I were together. But we both hope Paige is lying."

"And if she isn't?"

"Then I guess I'm going to be a father."

"Oh, Michael," Maureen sighed. "All this on top of everything with the trial."

"I know. As always, her timing is exquisite."

"I'll be thinking of you, honey. Call me when you get home, okay?"

"I will. Love you, Mom."

"Love you, too. You're a good man. Don't let her do anything to make you feel otherwise. Do you hear me?"

He smiled. "Yes, ma'am."

All Michael could think about on the two-hour flight to Jacksonville was the last time he made this trip and met Juliana. The plane landed in the midst of a stormy downpour in northern Florida that mirrored his mood as he rented a car to drive to Amelia Island. He hadn't told Paige he was coming so she wouldn't have time for plots or schemes.

The relentless rain turned what should have been a thirty-minute ride into an hour-long ordeal. Michael parked in the Simpson's driveway and was drenched by the time he got to the front porch. He rang the bell and pounded on the door, but there was no answer. "Goddamn it!" *Now what?* Shivering in the cold rain, he ran down the street to the home of their friends where he knocked on the neighbor's door and almost groaned with relief when it opened.

"Michael?"

"Hi, Mrs. Davis. I'm glad you're home. Do you know where the Simpsons are?"

"Come in. Get out of that rain."

"I'm soaking wet."

"It's fine. Come in."

She went into the powder room and came back with a towel for him.

"Thank you." He wiped the towel over his face and was careful not to move off the mat in the front hall. "Do you know where they are?"

"Honey," she said in a lilting southern accent. "Paige is in the hospital."

"Why?" Michael gasped. "What hospital?"

"I'm not exactly sure why, but she's at Baptist. Do you know where it is?"

He shook his head, so she wrote down the directions. Handing her the towel, he thanked her for the information. As he ran back to his car, his heart pumped with exertion and anxiety.

Michael sped through the rain, squinting to see the

street signs as he followed Mrs. Davis's directions. Arriving at the hospital forty-five minutes later, he noticed that the rain had let up some.

He asked for Paige at the information desk and was directed to the third floor. In the elevator, he read that the third floor housed the obstetrics department. "*Fuck,*" he groaned. "Fuck!" The elevator opened, and he rushed into the hallway, stopping short when he came face-to-face with Admiral Simpson.

"Hello, Michael," the Admiral said coldly.

Michael wiped the rain off his face. "Admiral, where is she?"

The Admiral studied Michael for a long moment before he gestured to a door on the left side of the hallway.

Michael went to the door and took a second to compose himself before he pushed it open.

Asleep in a hospital bed, Paige was so pale her face blended in with the stark white sheets. Even her lips were all but invisible. An IV hung over her with a bag of blood next to it.

Eleanor looked up when Michael came in.

"Mrs. Simpson, what happened? What's wrong?"

"She had a miscarriage, Michael. It was pretty bad. She lost a lot of blood."

"*Oh.*" He fought off a sudden rush of nausea. *I didn't believe her. Oh God, I didn't believe her.* "When?"

"Two days ago."

"Why didn't you call me?"

"She asked us not to."

Michael moved to the side of the bed, overcome by guilt over how badly he had handled this. Tears burning his eyes, he reached for her cold hand. *Oh, Paige, I'm sorry I didn't believe you. I'm so sorry.* Keeping a firm grip on her hand, he stared down at her. He was so intent on Paige he didn't notice when Eleanor slipped out of the room.

What felt like an eternity passed before Paige finally stirred. She blinked him into focus. "Michael?" she whispered, her blue eyes swimming with tears. "I told them not to call you."

"They didn't. I came to see you like I promised I would when the trial was over. Mrs. Davis told me you were here. I'm sorry, Paige. I don't know what to say."

"I'm so sad, Michael. I wanted our baby so badly. I've lost you. I've lost the baby. There's nothing left."

He brushed the hair back from her face. "You can't think like that. You've got your whole life ahead of you."

She shook her head. "I drove you away, and I probably did something to make the baby die, too. You were right when you said I'm a horrible person. This must be my punishment."

"I never said you were a horrible person." He sat on the bed and took her in his arms as she sobbed. "And you didn't do anything to hurt the baby, Paige. You couldn't have."

"I was so awful to you. I was like someone I didn't recognize after you broke up with me. You didn't even believe me about the baby."

"No," he admitted. "I really didn't, and I'm sorry for that."

"I told my parents not to call you because I knew you'd think it was just another ploy, and I wouldn't have blamed you."

"I'm sorry things got so bad between us that you couldn't call me when you needed me."

"I'm the one who's sorry." Sobs shook her fragile body. "Losing you was the worst thing that's ever happened to me—until now. I was such a monster, and I'm so ashamed."

He settled her back against the pillow but continued to hold her hand. "It's all in the past now. Let's just forget about that and focus on getting you better."

"Michael, can I ask you something, and will you tell me the truth?"

"Of course."

"First, I want you to know I've learned a lot about myself in the last two months, and I've realized I need to make some changes. I've let my parents, especially my dad, be too involved in my life, and that needs to stop. I know now it's time to start acting like a grown-up and not like their princess. So here's my question: in light of these discoveries I've made, is there any chance at all that we can put things back together between us?"

"I don't want to hurt you, Paige."

"Just tell me. I need to know."

"I'm sorry but no. Our time together was so special to me, and I'll never forget all the good times we had. But it's over now. It's time for both of us to move on."

Tears spilled down her cheeks. "That's what I figured you'd say. I really blew it with you, and I'm always going to be sorry for that. You were so good to me, better than I deserved."

"I loved you, Paige—very much—and for a very long time."

"I loved you, too."

"Can I ask *you* something?"

"Sure."

"The baby… could they tell if it was a boy or a girl?"

She shook her head. "It was too soon to tell."

"And you're okay? You can have others?"

"I should be able to."

"That's a relief."

"What would we have done if it had lived?" she asked.

"Hopefully, we would've worked something out so he or she would've grown up with two loving parents who were able to put aside their differences to do what was best for their child."

"I think we could've done that."

"Eventually," he said with a small grin.

She smiled. "I'm sorry I was so crazy. I've thought a lot about that last night, the night of the engagement party, the way I acted." Shaking her head, she added, "I can't believe I hit you. I'm sorry, Michael. I was just out of my mind. I can't even explain it. There're so many things I wish I could do over again."

"I'm sorry I insinuated the baby wasn't mine. That was an awful thing to say." He kissed her hand. "And if I've learned anything from the last couple of months it's that being an adult means piling up the regrets."

"I was horrified when I heard about the shooting in the courtroom. Thank God you weren't hurt."

"It was pretty crazy. I'm just glad it's over."

She squeezed his hand. "I appreciate that you came, Michael, but you can go home now."

"I'm not going to just take off and leave you in the hospital."

"It's okay. There's nothing you can do, and we've said everything we needed to say. I want us to end on a good note."

"Paige…"

Her eyes glistened with new tears. "Please, Michael."

"I'll call to check on you," he promised with a kiss to her forehead.

She nodded.

"You're a special girl. You just need to believe in yourself, and you'll find what you're looking for."

"Thank you," she whispered, releasing his hand. "Thank you for everything, Michael. You waited for me to grow up a lot longer than most guys would have."

He leaned in to kiss her cheek. "I loved you, and I won't forget you."

"I love you, too. I probably always will."

"Be well, Paige." He waved one last time from the door. In the waiting room at the end of the hallway, he found Admiral and Mrs. Simpson. "We, um, we had a good talk." His neck stiff with tension, Michael ran a hand through his damp hair. "She asked me to go, but I don't feel right about leaving while she's in here."

"What she needs hasn't been of much concern to you lately, Michael," the Admiral said.

"Be quiet, Joe," Eleanor said to her stunned husband. "Paige behaved terribly, Michael, and I know she's ashamed of herself. I was ashamed of her, too, when I found out just *how* awful she'd been to you. It's no wonder you cut all ties to her. I have no doubt you would've done the right thing by that child, if it had lived. Just the fact that you came here after the trial like you said you would, despite what she put you through, tells me *everything* I need to know about you. But you have no reason to be here anymore. We'll take care of our daughter, and when she's back on her feet, it'll be time for her to take care of herself. In fact, it's long overdue."

Astounded by the longest speech he had ever heard Eleanor Simpson make, Michael had no idea what to say.

She went up on tiptoes to kiss Michael's cheek. "It was a pleasure knowing you, Michael. I wish you all good things in your life."

"Thank you."

"Joe, let's go back in with our daughter." She took her husband's hand to lead him from the room.

Overcome, Michael sat down in the waiting room and dropped his head into his hands to weep for the child he hadn't wanted until he lost it, for the woman he once loved, and for the woman he loved now who was somewhere in the world tonight with the other man she loved.

Chapter 32

JULIANA WOKE UP DISORIENTED IN THE FADING LIGHT OF the late afternoon, and realized she must have dozed off on the sofa while Jeremy was upstairs taking a shower. He had covered her with a blanket and left her to sleep.

She looked around the room, remembering when they bought the furniture on a payment plan they feared they wouldn't be able to afford. That was before Jeremy landed the job he had now, which took care of most of their financial worries.

The stylish entertainment center came from IKEA, and Juliana smiled when she recalled Jeremy complaining that there were no fewer than ten thousand pieces to it when they got it home. But as usual he put it together in no time. His ability to fix anything, build anything, or puzzle through any mechanical problem made him the "go-to" guy in their group of friends. It was only thanks to him that her old car still had any life left in it.

Everything in the room, from the color of the paint to the framed artwork to the curtains, was chosen together. Juliana's friends liked to tease her about living with a guy who cared about things like curtains, but she enjoyed the shared pleasure they took in making his mother's place their own.

It was hard to believe what had happened to them in the last couple of months. After ten almost perfect years together, it all came undone during one disastrous weekend that undermined everything she believed to be true about them. And it had opened the door just wide enough for her to find a new, unexpected love.

She reminded herself that Jeremy claimed he hadn't acted on the freedom he'd thought he wanted so badly. If anything, he'd done nothing but regret asking for it. So if she had never met Michael, would she be lying here pretending to still be asleep while she heard Jeremy moving around upstairs? Or would she be celebrating his return home after the long separation?

She tried to find the words she would need... *Jeremy, it's over between us. I'm sorry, but the time we spent apart has shown me I want other things out of life. We both outgrew this relationship while we were apart over the last nine months, and it's time for us to learn how to live without each other.* Her eyes teared when she imagined his reaction to hearing that. No way would he let her go without a fight, and the idea of an emotional battle exhausted her.

He came downstairs looking handsome in one of her favorite shirts and black dress pants that must have been new. As he made his way to the sofa, he tugged the maroon cashmere sweater she bought him one Christmas over his head and adjusted the collar on his shirt.

"Babe?" He caressed her face. "Are you awake?"

"Yeah. What time is it?"

"Almost five. You really conked out on me."

"Sorry."

"Have you been burning the candle? You know how run down you get when you don't get enough sleep."

She swallowed hard as visions of the erotic night with Michael flashed through her mind. "No, I was just tired."

"I ran you a bubble bath. Why don't you go soak for a while? We have reservations at Chiapparellis at seven," he said, referring to their favorite restaurant in Little Italy.

"We do?"

He held out a hand to help her up. "Uh huh." He kissed her cheek. "Go on up. Take your time."

"Thanks for the bath."

"My pleasure."

She climbed the stairs to the master bedroom. The last time she had been up there was just before she left for the Bahamas with Michael when she came to get some summer clothes. As she pulled her sweater over her head and tossed it on the bed, she wondered how Jeremy would react to the news that she had no plans to sleep with him that night.

Peeling off the rest of her clothes, she walked into the large bathroom and gasped at the vases of pink roses—at least five or six dozen of them. In the tub, rose petals floated on top of steaming bubbles and soft music wafted from the speakers he installed a few years ago. On the edge of the tub, he had left a glass of wine for her.

"*Oh, Jer.*" She stepped into the tub and let the hot water ease the ache in her heart and in muscles still tender from a night spent locked in passion with another man. Sinking down into the tub, she thought back to Dewey Beach when Michael pulled her—suds and all—from the tub and took her to bed. *Where is he now? What happened with Paige?* She was dying to know.

Jeremy came to the door. "Everything okay in here?"

"It's beautiful."

"So are you."

"When did you do all this?"

"You were asleep for a long time. I had some time to kill."

"Thank you."

He walked in to hand her the glass of wine. "I've realized some of the romance had gone out of our relationship before I left for Florida. Now that we're back together, I hope we can remedy that."

"Jer—"

"Enjoy the bath. Call me if you need anything." He bent to kiss her forehead and then left the room.

Groaning, she slipped underwater.

Juliana wore a long black skirt with high-heeled black boots and a sheer ivory silk blouse over an ivory camisole. She got dressed with a heavy heart, dreading what he most likely had planned for tonight and wondering how she would ever say no to him.

Out of habit, she touched perfume to her neck and smoothed on lipstick. "Well, here goes," she whispered to her reflection in the mirror.

Jeremy came to the foot of the stairs when he heard her coming down. "Oh, Jule, look at you." He offered her his hand. "You're so gorgeous. So unbelievably beautiful."

"Thank you," she whispered, moved by the raw look of love and desire on his face.

"Will you kiss me?" His hands on her face, he bent to touch his lips to hers. "Just once?" he whispered, tilting her head to gain better access.

As his tongue caressed hers, Juliana's stomach knotted with nerves.

His kiss quickly became hungry and needy.

"Jeremy," she gasped. "Don't. Please.

"I'm sorry. I can't resist you. I never could."

She reached up to wipe a trace of lipstick off his mouth. "We need to get going, don't we?"

He ran his finger over her cheek. "Yeah. Let's go."

"Mr. Dixon, Ms. Gregorio," the maitre d' at Chiapparellis said. "Welcome. Right this way, please."

Following him through the busy restaurant, Juliana remembered all the occasions they had celebrated here—anniversaries, birthdays, Jeremy's big job. They came here long before they could afford it and continued to come even after they could afford better.

The maitre d' opened a door and gestured them into a cozy private room filled with pink roses and a violinist playing just for them.

"Oh," Juliana said, taking in the romantic setting. Again her stomach lurched with nerves mixed now with fear and regret—tremendous regret that he hadn't done this a very long time ago.

"Jule?" Jeremy startled her out of her thoughts. He gestured for her to have a seat at the table.

Numb, Juliana slid into the chair he held for her.

He poured her a glass of champagne and handed it to her. After he filled a glass for himself, he raised it in toast to her. "I love you, Jule. Thank you for spending tonight with me." He touched his glass to hers and took a long sip.

Juliana saw his glass tremble ever so slightly as he returned it to the table. In that moment she realized he was nervous, and her stomach took another sickening dip.

They were served fried calamari, which Jeremy knew was one of Juliana's favorite foods, and a delicious shrimp Nicola, another of their longtime favorites. Even though she'd had almost nothing to eat all day, Juliana pushed the food around on her plate and had trouble actually swallowing anything. Dessert was a chocolate soufflé that she picked at without her usual enthusiasm for all things chocolate.

"Is everything okay, babe?"

"It's wonderful. Thank you for doing all this. I'm overwhelmed."

He put down his fork and pulled his chair closer to hers.

Oh God. Here it comes. She wanted to whimper. She wanted to beg. *Please don't, Jer. Just don't.*

He took her hand and brought it to his lips. "You know how much I love you, don't you?"

"I think so."

"There's nothing in this world I wouldn't do for you. There's nothing you could want that I wouldn't find a way to get for you. I hope you know that."

The lump in Juliana's throat became so huge she didn't trust herself to speak, so she nodded.

"There's something I want to show you. Will you come with me?"

That wasn't the question she expected. Thrown off balance and more than a little confused, Juliana let him help her up. He thanked the violinist and led her through the jam-packed restaurant, the noise of the Saturday night crowd jarring after the quiet of their private room.

He retrieved their coats from the coatroom and helped Juliana into hers. While they waited outside for the valet to bring his car, he kept his arm around her.

"Are you warm enough?" he asked as they headed south on Interstate 95.

"I'm fine." Baffled by the odd change in direction their evening had taken, she asked, "Where are we going?"

"You'll see," he said with a mysterious smile. "Just relax and enjoy the ride."

The miles rolled by as they left the city behind. After about twenty minutes, Jeremy took the exit for Ellicott City and made a series of turns that seemed quite familiar to him. At last, he turned into a development Juliana recognized.

"Do you remember this place?"

"It's where we came that day for the open house. What are we doing here?"

"Give me a minute, and I'll show you."

They traveled another half mile into the development of sprawling new homes before he pulled into a driveway and turned off the car.

"Where are we, Jer?"

"Come see."

He met her on the sidewalk and took her hand. At the front door, Juliana watched astounded as he inserted a key and pushed the door open. "What's going on? Where did you get a key to this house?"

He flipped on the lights, and she gasped when she saw more pink roses on the massive staircase, in the empty dining room, in the huge family room, on the hearth in

front of the marble fireplace, and on the granite countertop in the kitchen.

"Jeremy." Her hands came together over her racing
heart. "I don't understand."

"The dream house. Isn't that what you called it?"

"Yes, but… Jeremy. What—"

He took her coat, hung it with his over the banister,
and reached for her hand. "Come with me."

Leading her in to sit on the hearth in front of the fireplace, he kneeled down and took her hands. "I've told
you this hundreds of times, maybe even thousands over
the last ten years, but I've never meant it more than I
do right now. I love you, Juliana. I love you more than
anything in this world." He touched his lips to both her
hands and struggled to collect himself.

She found it hard to breathe as she waited to hear
what else he had to say.

"Earlier, I told you there was nothing I wouldn't do
for you. To prove that, I have this for you." He nudged
the door to the fireplace open and withdrew a piece of
paper, which he handed to her.

"What is it?"

"It's the deed to your mother's house. I paid off the mortgage so you won't have to worry about that anymore."

"*What?* Jer, oh my God. You can't stand her. Why
would you do this?"

"Because you're worried all the time that you'll miss
a payment and she'll end up homeless. Now you don't
have to think about it anymore."

Tears pooled in her eyes and spilled down her cheeks.
"You can't do this."

He wiped the tears from her face. "It's already done, babe."

"I can't accept it, Jer. I just can't."

"You have to, or you'll hurt my feelings."

She tried to absorb the enormity of it. "I can't believe you'd do something like this."

"I told you, there's *nothing* I wouldn't do for you. You're my family, Jule. You've been my family and I've been yours for so long that I could more easily live without food or oxygen than I could without you."

He leaned in to kiss her gently. "The other thing I told you before is there's nothing you could want that I wouldn't find a way to get for you, right?"

Wiping her tears, she nodded.

"I never forgot how much you loved these houses or the look you had in your eyes that day—like you'd seen something you knew you'd never have, so you didn't even let yourself hope for it. I promised myself right then and there that if I could ever swing it, we'd live here." He held up the key, which now had a diamond ring hooked around it. "We have the dream house, now we just need the dream. Will you marry me, Jule? Will you make me the luckiest guy in the world and be my wife?"

Sitting in stunned silence trying to absorb it all, Juliana suddenly thought of Michael's proposal.

Don't forget who asked first.

Chapter 33

"JULE?"

"I, uh, I just don't know what to say."

"'Yes' would work for me."

Juliana tugged her hands free from his and stood up. She looked around the huge room and struggled to comprehend the magnitude of his grand gesture. He'd made it all but impossible for her to say no to him. "When did you do all this?"

He turned to sit on the hearth. "I bought the house the weekend I was home when I couldn't find you, and I closed on it yesterday. I was hoping I'd chosen the right one. We looked at quite a few that day, but I thought this was the one you liked best."

"It was." Chilled, she crossed her arms and went to look out the window. There was just enough moonlight to make out the large backyard and the wooded area behind the property. It now seemed so unimaginable that she had expected to just walk away from Jeremy after everything they'd been through together. How could she have ever thought he would step aside when she told him she had outgrown their relationship? Of course that hardly mattered since he had made sure she'd never get the chance to say any such thing. "How can you afford all this? My mother's mortgage? This house?"

"We'll have to sell the place in the city—pretty quickly," he said with a grin. "But I told you, I made a bundle when I was in Florida, and I was working so much that I hardly spent a dime of it. Your mother's mortgage wasn't much really. There was just a year or so left on it, but I knew it would give you peace of mind to have that taken care of."

Juliana turned away from the window to face him. "I just can't get over you doing that."

When he stood up and walked over to her she knew she couldn't stall any longer.

"Are you going to marry me, Jule? Are we going to live here together and fill this big house with kids? Are we going to have what we were always meant to have, from the time we were seventeen?"

She bit her lip and ventured a glance up at him. "What if, in a year or two…"

"What?"

"What if you get itchy feet again?" she asked, using Mrs. R's words.

He took a step back as if she had struck him. "I can't believe you'd ask me that."

"*Why can't you believe it?* What if you do all this to win me back only to discover down the road that you still have wild oats to sow? What if I'm pregnant with our first child, or even our second, and you begin taking me for granted again and start wishing for *anything* but the life you have with me? *What will I do then?*"

A muscle in his cheek twitching with tension, he fixed his eyes on the window behind her. "That's not going to happen. I've learned a big lesson in the last two months, and it's one I'm never, ever going to forget." He shifted his eyes back to her. "All I can do is tell you I love you. I've always loved you, and I always will. I'm asking you to marry me. If you want me to beg, I will. I have absolutely no pride left when it comes to you." His eyes filled, and the helpless despair she saw on his face finally did her in.

She took a deep breath and blocked all thoughts of Michael. "Okay."

Jeremy's face went slack with shock. "Yes?"

It was inevitable. It always had been, and for her to deny that was to deny what he had meant to her for the most important years of her life—the years when no one else had loved her or cared about her or been there for her. He was right. He was her family, and she was his. Taking a deep breath, she said, "Yes."

He let out a whoop and swept her off her feet and into his arms. His tears of joy left damp spots on her face. "You won't be sorry, Jule. I'll spend every day making you happy. I promise I'll never let you down." He reached into his pocket for the ring and slipped it on her finger. "*Oh, no,*" he groaned. "It's too big."

Juliana tried not to think about how perfectly Michael's ring fit her. If she allowed herself to think of him for even one second, she would never make it through this. "That's okay. We can get it sized down. It's a beautiful ring." Smaller diamonds framed a large, square-cut diamond.

His face fell with disappointment. "I took that ruby in your jewelry box to get the size right."

She smiled. "That was my grandmother's. She had much bigger hands than I do."

"Sorry."

Taking it off, she handed it to him. "You'd better hold on to it until we get it sized. I don't want to lose it."

"I wanted it to be perfect."

"It's a beautiful ring, Jer," she said, reaching up to kiss him.

He looked at her with his heart in his eyes. "Do you still love me, Jule? After everything that's happened, do you still love me?"

"Yes."

"Will you tell me? I need to hear it."

"I love you, Jeremy."

"You're really going to marry me?"

"Yes," she whispered as his lips took fierce possession of hers in a hot kiss filled with the promise of things to come.

"Let's go home, to our current home," he said in a voice hoarse with desire and emotion. "I want to make love to my future wife."

"Um, about that, Jer…"

He pulled back to look at her. "What?"

"Two things. First, I don't want a long engagement. I want us to go somewhere and get married. No big deal, okay?"

"I don't want to just sneak off and get married like we've got something to hide. I want to do it up. I know the deal with your family, and we don't have to make it a big production."

"No production, Jer. I mean it. I don't want it."

He thought about that for a moment. "A guy I met in Florida told me he and his wife went to St. John with a couple of friends and got married over a weekend. How about something like that in the next few weeks? We could take Pam and David and my mom and Gary," he said, referring to his stepfather. "Would that work?"

"That'd be great. I could tell my family after the fact that we eloped."

"Okay, so that takes care of one of your two things. What's the other?"

"I won't sleep with you until we're married."

He snorted. "You're kidding me, right?"

"No."

Realizing she was serious, he said, "Why? We've been having sex for ten years, Juliana. I don't get it."

"I feel like we let sex become too important in our relationship. I want us to stay focused on what really matters over the next few weeks. Please?"

"I've been *dreaming* of making love with you for two months already."

"Then a couple more weeks won't kill you."

"I really think it might."

"You can do it."

"You drive a tough bargain, babe, but okay. If it means that much to you, we can wait."

"Thank you."

"Thank *you* for saying yes." He hugged her again. "You've made me the happiest guy in the world."

As Juliana remembered Michael telling her that she made him happier than he had ever been in his life, the numbness wore off and she began to ache.

After Jeremy served Juliana breakfast in bed in the guestroom the next morning, they called his mother and stepfather to share the news of their engagement. His mother cried tears of joy and promised to be there for the big day. They also called Pam and David, who were equally thrilled to be included and agreed to serve as their matron of honor and best man. Jeremy got busy on the Internet, and an hour later he booked their wedding at a resort on St. John.

He came downstairs to find Juliana when he finished. "We got really lucky. They had a cancellation on New Year's weekend just this morning." Embracing her, he sighed with contentment. "Three weeks, babe. I can't believe we'll be married in *three weeks*."

Drawn in by his contagious delight, she smiled up at him.

He slid his hand around her neck and kissed her. After he spent several minutes letting her know just how badly he wanted her, his breathing was heavy and labored. "You're really sure about this no sex thing?"

"Think about how great the wedding night will be."

"I can't. If I think about it, I'll need another cold shower." He had already told her all about the one he took the night before after their hot make-out session at the guest room door.

She laughed. "You're pathetic."

"Babe? Can I ask you something?"

"Sure."

"When we were apart, did you, you know…"

She struggled out of his embrace. "We're not talking about that."

"*I need to know, Jule.* It makes me crazy to think about you with someone else. Tell me I don't need to be worried about that, and I'll never mention it again."

"I'm only going to say this once, and I really want you to listen, okay?"

He nodded.

"I'm *never* going to talk to you about the two months we spent apart. We said we wouldn't do that. I've agreed to marry you. If you're going to badger me about this then we've got a problem."

He studied her for a long time before he answered. "Okay. I'll let it go."

"Good."

Late on Sunday afternoon she told Jeremy she needed to do a few errands and left him unpacking the boxes and suitcases he brought home from Florida.

"Hurry back, babe," he said, kissing her good-bye. "I miss you already."

Juliana went to her mother's house for the first time in three weeks.

"Well, look at what the cat dragged in," Paullina said.

Stunned to see her mother up, dressed, and sitting at the table eating an early dinner, Juliana noticed that both her mother and the house were immaculate. There were even fresh flowers on the table.

"You must be Juliana." A young blonde woman extended her hand. "I'm Allison, the home health aide."

"No, you're Allison, the miracle worker," Juliana said with amazement.

"I told you she was a brat," Paullina said to Allison but without the usual edge to her voice.

Juliana was startled to realize her mother was also sober. She couldn't remember the last time she saw her that way.

"I'm sorry it's been so long since I was here, Ma. You look wonderful."

"Well, Florence Nightingale over there is on my ass day and night," she said, but Juliana noticed the affection in her mother's eyes.

Paullina took a close look at her daughter. "The bruise is just about gone, huh?"

"Yes, finally. Juliana's Salon has shut down. It's back to Panache on Tuesday."

"It'll be good for you to get back to normal."

Normal, Juliana thought, not sure what that was anymore. She sat down at the table. "So, Ma, Jeremy and I got engaged last night."

Paullina seemed stunned as she put down her fork and wiped her mouth. "Did you now? Where's the ring?"

"It was too big, so we're having it sized. It's gorgeous though."

"Congratulations, Juliana. You've certainly waited long enough for that."

"We're going to St. John in three weeks, just Jeremy and me." Juliana told the tiniest of lies to protect her mother's feelings since she had been unprepared to find her sober and rational. "We don't want a big wedding."

"It sounds lovely. I hope you'll be very happy."

Juliana's chest tightened with emotion as she caught a glimpse of the mother she remembered from before life and alcohol took their toll on her. She leaned in to hug her mother. "Thank you. Well, I need to keep moving. I've got a million things to do." She couldn't even think about the unimaginable thing she had to do next.

"Don't be a stranger," Paullina said.

"I won't. Nice to meet you, Allison."

"You, too," the aide called from the living room.

Juliana drove down Eastern Avenue still amazed by what she had just witnessed at her mother's house. Now that Jeremy had paid off the mortgage, Juliana would put her money toward keeping Allison around. That would certainly lift a big weight off her shoulders.

Turning onto Chester Street, her heart began to pound with anxiety and dread. She had come early, so she could get her stuff out of there before Michael got home from Florida. The palms of her hands were damp, and her mouth went dry as she used her key to let herself in. She deactivated the alarm and was assaulted by a flood of memories and emotions and despair—utter despair over what she was about to do to this man who so totally didn't deserve it.

Forcing herself to move fast, she went upstairs to his bedroom to pack her remaining clothes and personal items. She tried not to think about the last passionate night they spent in his bed or making love with him in the shower before she left to meet Jeremy. Was that really only yesterday? Brushing away a tear that escaped despite her iron will to get through this without them, she zipped the last of her bags and carried them downstairs and out to her car.

When there was nothing left to do, she sat on the sofa to wait for him. The room soon grew dark, but Juliana couldn't seem to move, even to turn on a light. She had no idea how much time passed before she heard his key in the door.

"Juliana?" He flipped on a light. "Hey, baby, I was so happy to see your car out there. What're you doing in the dark?" A smile lit up his face as he dropped his overnight bag inside the door and crossed the room to

her. But when he noticed the tears in her eyes, he froze
and his smile faded to an expression of agony that would
remain etched upon her heart forever. "No," he whispered, shaking his head. "No, you're not going back to
him. You can't."

His devastation rendered her helpless against the flood
of tears she had managed to contain until that moment.

"Do you love him the same way you love me?"

"No," she said, wiping her face.

"Then why are you doing this? I don't understand."

"Because I don't love you the same way I love him."

He grimaced in unabashed pain.

Wincing, Juliana stood up to go to him. "That
came out wrong." Frustrated, she buried her hands
in her hair. "Oh, I never should've let this happen
between us!"

He took her by the arm. "Don't insult me by pretending
you had any more power over it than I did."

"Michael," she said softly, "I love you so much. You
know I do, but I've been with him my whole adult life.
He made one mistake, and he regrets it terribly. I just
couldn't bring myself to walk away from him after he
was there for me during all the years when no one else
was. I'm so sorry."

The anger seemed to leave him as fast as it had
come. "I don't want you to be sorry. You had a decision to make, and you've made it. I've always known
this could happen."

"I'll never forget any of it." Tears streamed down her
face. "I'll never forget you. I promise you that."

"I want you to promise me something else—
something much more important."

She brushed at her tears. "What?"

"That when it blows up with him, you'll come find me."

"No, Michael—"

"I'm only asking you for one thing, Juliana. Come find me. I'll either be here or in Newport—you know where—and I'll be waiting for you. I don't care if it's a week, a year, five years, twenty years. Find me."

"But surely you'll be married with a family—"

He shook his head. "Never. It's you or no one. So don't think for one minute I won't still want you or that my pride is too wounded to forgive you. I've already forgiven you. That's how much I love you."

"You can't mean that," Juliana said, choking on a sob. "You'll meet someone else. You'll fall in love again."

With his index finger to her chin, he forced her to look at him. "Have I ever said anything to you that I didn't mean?"

"No," she whispered.

"Do you promise, Juliana? I need to hear you say it."

"Okay, I promise, but I don't want you to wait for me. I want you to find someone else—"

He laid a finger over her lips to stop her. "It's not going to happen."

"I'm so sorry, Michael." She handed him her house key.

He put it in his pocket and reached for her left hand. "He didn't even give you a ring?"

"It was too big."

Michael made a sound that might have been a chuckle if he was amused rather than devastated. "And mine fit perfectly. Ironic, huh?"

Juliana couldn't dispute that point so she didn't try. "What happened with Paige?"

"Turns out she *was* pregnant."

Juliana gasped.

"She lost it. She was in the hospital when I got there."

"Oh, Michael. I'm sorry. Is she all right?"

"She will be."

"Will you be?"

Resting his hands on her face, he ran his thumbs gently along her jaw in a gesture so familiar, so uniquely his, it took her breath away. "You'd better go while I'm still able to let you." He brought her into his arms one last time, as if to prepare himself for all the days he would have to live without her. "Remember what I said, Juliana. Come find me."

"I don't ever want you to think, for even one second, that I don't love you as much as I said I did."

"I know you do." He touched his lips to hers. "That's why I'll be waiting."

Chapter 34

JULIANA WENT BACK TO WORK TWO DAYS AFTER THE emotional scene at Michael's house. Her co-workers were full of questions about her long absence, but she kept the details vague because it was too painful to think about everything that had happened with Michael.

She was so sad about what she had done to him that it took tremendous effort just to get out of bed, let alone function. Their time together had been brief but intense, and she couldn't deny that she left a big part of her heart with him. Despite what he had said, though, she hoped he would eventually find someone else who could give him the happiness he so deserved.

The next three weeks were a whirlwind. Jeremy and Juliana put their rowhouse on the market and sold it four days later, scheduling the closing for the end of January. Pam helped her find the perfect white silk sundress for the beachfront wedding. During their shopping outing, Pam asked what became of Juliana's relationship with the prosecutor.

Cut to the quick by the question and the reminder of Michael, Juliana forced herself to say, "Nothing. Nothing became of it."

Jeremy was thoughtful, attentive, and considerate. He seemed to understand that she needed space to work through some things before the wedding. At the same time, he went out of his way to keep his promise to bring the romance back into their relationship. As their wedding day drew near, Juliana loved him more than ever and felt confident that she had made the right decision to marry him.

On the thirtieth of December, they took an early morning flight with Pam and David to St. Thomas. They caught a ferry for the brief trip across the sound to the remote island of St. John. The four of them were in high spirits as a taxi deposited them at the oceanfront resort. Juliana and Jeremy checked into a two-bedroom suite and then joined Pam and David to explore the lush resort.

They were enjoying elaborate tropical drinks at the bar when Jeremy's mother Barbara and her husband Gary arrived. She whispered, "It's about time, huh?" into Juliana's ear as she hugged her.

Gary shook his stepson's hand and kissed Juliana's cheek. "I sure do hope you kids will be as happy as your mom and I are."

Barbara, a petite blonde who was dwarfed by her husband and son, blushed.

Jeremy ordered drinks for his mother and Gary before they all walked over to check out the pavilion where the wedding would take place at sunset the next day.

"It's beautiful, son," Barbara said, dabbing at her eyes.

"Oh, jeez, Mom!" Jeremy said with a grin. "You're already blubbering! What will you be like tomorrow?"

"Leave me alone. My only child is getting married. I can blubber if I want to."

"That's right, darlin.'" Gary put his arm around his wife. "You just go right ahead and cry if you want to."

Jeremy rolled his eyes at his mother and took Juliana's hand to lead her up the stairs to the pavilion. At the center of the big open area, he put his arm around her and turned her to face the ocean. "What do you think, babe? Will this do the trick?"

"Definitely. It's just right, Jer, isn't it?"

He kissed her left hand where the resized engagement ring now resided. "Everything's just right as long as I have you."

With their guests whistling, he leaned in for a passionate kiss that had Juliana blushing by the time she finally managed to extricate herself.

"Get a room!" David hollered.

"We've got a room," Jeremy replied, adding just for Juliana, "two of them, in fact."

She smiled up at him. "One more night. You're almost there."

"And hanging by a thread," he whispered. They went down the stairs to join the others. "Who's ready for some lunch?"

That afternoon, David announced that he and Gary would be throwing an impromptu bachelor party for Jeremy at the poolside bar while the ladies went to the spa.

"I don't know about that," Juliana said with a wary look at Jeremy.

"What do you mean?" David asked with indignation. "It's a right of passage you can't deny him. Now go get your nails done, and leave the groom to me."

"I don't want you hung over tomorrow," Juliana said to Jeremy.

He leaned down to kiss her. "Don't worry, babe. I'll behave." Into her ear, he whispered, "There's *no way* I'm going to be sick for our wedding night."

Juliana smiled at him, and he kissed her again. "Love you."

"Love you, too."

"Behave, David," Pam warned her husband. "I mean it."

"It's all right, girls." Barbara put her arms around Juliana and Pam. "Gary will keep an eye on them."

With a reluctant last look back at Jeremy, Juliana let Barbara lead her away to the spa where they were pampered for the next three hours. Barbara surprised them by springing for massages on top of the manicure and pedicure.

"Oh my God, this is heavenly," Juliana groaned as the masseuse worked out all her kinks.

"I thought you might enjoy it," Barbara said from the next table. Pam had opted for a private room.

"I'm so glad you and Gary could be here for the wedding," Juliana said.

"We're delighted to be included, honey. I'm sure it's no secret that I've been urging Jeremy to take this step with you for years. He's very lucky to have you, and I think he knows now just *how* lucky he is."

"So you know about what happened? About the time we spent apart?"

"Yes, he told me. I think it says an awful lot about the love you have between you that you were able to find your way back to each other."

"I do love him, Barbara, and I'm going to do everything I can to make this marriage work."

"I have no doubt you'll make it work, honey. None at all."

They met Pam in the lobby of the spa.

"I don't know about you girls, but I'm like a new woman," Juliana said. She rolled her loose shoulders, feeling rested, refreshed, and ready to take the next step in her life with Jeremy.

"What do you say we crash the bachelor party?" Barbara asked with a twinkle in her eye.

"Sign me up," Pam said.

They strolled through fragrant gardens on their way to the pool to find the guys. Approaching the bar, Juliana gasped when she heard Jeremy and David singing at the top of their lungs. A row of overturned shot glasses lined the bar in front of them.

Gary greeted the women with a sheepish shrug. "I tried to stop them, but they're on a roll."

"There she is!" Jeremy hollered. "There's my bride! Come on over here, babe, and give me some love."

Juliana took a step toward him, intending to tell him to pipe down.

He almost knocked her over when he put his arm around her and hauled her to him.

"Jeremy, cut it out. You're embarrassing yourself."

"Do you hear that? She says I'm embarrassing myself!"

Juliana pushed at him in an attempt to break free of his tight embrace.

"You know what's embarrassing?" he asked in a loud voice that had everyone in the poolside bar listening to him. "I'll tell you what's *embarrassing*. My good buddy

Dave here has been telling me *quite* a story about my bride. Something about her hanging *all over* a guy she told me was *just a friend.*"

"David!" Pam gasped. "*You did not!*"

David took a sudden interest in the floor as his wife glared at him.

"*Oh, ho!*" Jeremy bellowed. "What do you know? You saw it, too, did you, Pam? What am I? The last *asshole* on earth to find out what my *bride's* been up to?"

"Jeremy, stop this right now," Barbara hissed.

Everything in the bar came to a halt, and all eyes were on Jeremy and Juliana.

"Come on, son, let's get you out of here," Gary said, reaching for Jeremy's arm.

He shook off his stepfather and tightened his grip on Juliana.

Juliana pushed him as hard as she could, and he stumbled backward into David. She worked the engagement ring off her finger and threw it at him. "We're done. Don't call me, don't write to me, and don't come back to me begging. I'm through with you. I was a fool to think you deserved another chance." She turned to walk away. If she allowed herself to think for even *one second* about what she had given up for him...

"*Did you fuck him?*" Jeremy screamed at her back.

The others gasped.

Juliana stopped short and spun around to face him. "What did you say to me?"

He took a lurching step toward her. "*Did. You. Fuck. Him?* It's a simple yes or no question."

"Jeremy, I'm telling you to stop this immediately," his mother said, wiping tears from her cheeks.

"Not until she answers the question."

Juliana leaned into his face. "You want me to answer the question? Fine, here you go: No, Jer, I didn't fuck him." Gratified by the expression of relief that flashed across his face, she added, "But I *did* make love with him—over and over and over again. And you know what? Not once, in *all* the nights I spent in his arms, did he *ever* make me feel like I wasn't enough for him. Happy now?"

"Jule," he whispered, the magnitude seeming to register all at once.

"Go to hell, Jeremy." She turned and left the bar where not a pin drop could be heard except for the sobs Jeremy dissolved into the moment she walked away from him.

"Juliana!" Pam called from behind her. "Wait." Pam ran to catch up with her. "I'm so sorry. I'm going to *kill* David for this."

"Don't. He did me a favor."

"Will you be all right?"

"I'm going to be just fine." Juliana embraced her friend in a quick hug. "Tell Barbara I'll call her when I can. Go on back there with him. He's going to need his friends when he sobers up and realizes what he's done."

"Are you leaving?"

"As fast as I can."

"Call me?"

Juliana nodded, and with a last squeeze of Pam's hand she ran for the lobby to hail a taxi. There was nothing in her room but clothes she bought for a wedding that wasn't going to happen.

Chapter 35

JULIANA CAUGHT THE DAY'S LAST FLIGHT OFF ST. Thomas. She didn't take a deep breath until the plane took off, when she was certain Jeremy hadn't come after her. If she never saw him again it would be too soon. More than anything, she was mortified that Barbara and Gary had been forced to witness the horrific scene in the bar.

As the plane made its way to Miami, the shock wore off, and Juliana began to shake. Her thin sundress offered scant protection against the air-conditioned cabin, so she asked the stewardess for a blanket and wrapped it around her shoulders. Once the trembling subsided, she wept quietly into the blanket.

What a mess she had made of things, and what a stupid fool she'd been to give him a second chance. She should have ended it with him that day on the beach when he said he wanted to see other women. Instead she'd walked away from the best guy she had ever known for someone who wasn't worth it.

In Miami, she learned she had just missed the last flight to Baltimore, so she booked a flight at six the next morning. Tapping into the wad of cash Jeremy had gotten for their trip, Juliana bought an overpriced sweat suit and sneakers in one of the fancy airport boutiques as well as a toothbrush and hairbrush in the newsstand. With her purchases in hand, she went outside into the warm night to take a taxi to a hotel near the airport.

The room was small and inexpensive, but it was clean. After requesting a four thirty wake-up call, she took a long, hot shower and changed into the sweat suit. She would have ordered some food, but the thought of eating made her sick, so she lay down on the bed and stared up at the ceiling.

The wake-up call turned out to be unnecessary because Juliana never fell asleep during that long night. But she did make some decisions. Before she did anything else, she was going to find out if Mrs. Romanello was right when she said Juliana could stand on her own two feet in any situation. One year was ending and another was beginning, and she would spend this year alone.

For the first time in her life, she would live by herself. She would take the time she needed to recover from everything that had happened in the last few months and to figure out what she wanted next. She couldn't go running back to Michael after what she had done to him. Maybe during this year she would discover that it was over with him, too. Or maybe she would find out that he was what she wanted more than anything. If that was the case and he loved her as much as he said he did, he would still love her in a year.

She got up in the morning satisfied she had a plan to put her life back together, to find some self-respect amid the ruins, and to put her love for Michael to the test of a lifetime.

The skimpy sweat suit was no match for the frigid cold in Baltimore. Shivering her way home in a taxi, she wished for the winter coat she left in Jeremy's car in the long-term parking lot.

At the Collington Street house, she spent the last day of the year, what was supposed to have been her wedding day, packing four years of her life into three suitcases and six of the boxes Jeremy brought home from Florida. She took only the things that mattered most to her, leaving behind all reminders of their ten years together.

By five o'clock she had loaded the last of the boxes into her car. Climbing the front steps one final time, she peeled the key off her ring and left it on the kitchen counter. She took a last look at the room full of memories that only a few days ago had seemed strong enough to build a lifetime on. Then she set the alarm, pushed in the lock, and closed the door to that life forever.

It was only when she got into her car that she realized she had nowhere to go. She laughed so hard she cried as it settled in on her that she had no idea what to do. Remembering that Michael was right around the corner and would want her to come to him, she wavered in her resolve to be on her own.

But only for a moment.

Wiping her tears, she started the car and drove to the only place in the world she had left to go—home to her mother.

The new and improved Paullina welcomed her daughter with open arms and a closed mouth. She never said "I told you so," didn't ask any questions, and, if anything, seemed to appreciate the opportunity to mother her wounded child.

On New Year's Day they read the notice in the *Baltimore Sun* about the wedding in St. John that hadn't happened. Jeremy sent it in before they left, and Juliana had forgotten about it until she saw it in the paper. She hurt when she thought of Michael seeing the article and thinking she had actually gone through with it.

Receiving love from a mother Juliana had long ago given up on was an unexpected gift in the midst of disaster. It was tempting to settle in, put her feet up, and let her mother take care of her for a change. But that went against the promise she made to herself in the Miami hotel room. So within a week, Juliana signed a one-year lease on a furnished studio apartment in Fell's Point. Even with the rent she could still swing the cost of Allison, the home health aide who had brought about such a miraculous change in Paullina.

Juliana moved her meager belongings into her new apartment and spent the first night wide awake, thinking about Michael and wondering if he'd seen the announcement in the paper. By the time the sun came up in the morning, she knew she had to do something about that. Picturing him in his bedroom getting ready for work, she reached for her cell phone and dialed his number from memory.

"Juliana," he said, his voice flat with shock.

She closed her eyes tight against the instant rush of tears.

"Baby, what is it? Are you all right?"

"I didn't marry him," she said softly.

"But the paper… I saw it…"

She winced. "I'm sorry you had to see that. He sent it in before we left, and it was a holiday weekend…"

"What happened?"

"The blowup you predicted occurred about twenty-four hours before the I dos."

"Are you okay?"

"I'm better than I was."

"God, Juliana, you can't imagine what's been going through my mind. The thought of you... in bed with him... It's been making me *insane*."

"I never slept with him after we got back together. I was making him wait for a wedding that never happened."

Michael released a tortured groan. "So where've you *been* for the last week?"

She swallowed hard. "I've made a few decisions."

"What kind of decisions?"

"I signed a one-year lease on an apartment in Fell's Point."

"*Why,* Juliana? You could've come here! You know that!"

"I need some time to figure things out. To decide how I feel..."

"About me?"

She hated the despair she heard in his voice—again. "No," she whispered. "About me. I need to be by myself, Michael. I have some things I need to prove to myself."

"Baby, *please*... Don't do this. I love you. No matter what's happened, that'll never change. You don't have to prove anything to anyone. The biggest mistake you made was being loyal to someone who didn't deserve it. Don't punish yourself—and me—for that."

That he still could be so forgiving astounded her. "I need to do this for me. I know it's hard for you to understand, and I don't expect you to wait for me. I just didn't want you to think I'd married him."

"I appreciate that—more than you'll ever know—but don't tell me not to wait for you. Did you hear *anything* I said to you the last time we were together?"

The lump lodged in her throat made it difficult to speak. "I heard every word," she said softly.

"You promised me, Juliana."

"I haven't forgotten."

"You're really going to do this? You're going to put us both through this?"

"I'm sorry."

Sounding resigned, he said, "Can I call you?"

"It would be better if you didn't."

"Better for whom?" When she didn't answer him, he said, "What happens at the end of the year?"

"I don't know."

"Come find me, Juliana," he said urgently. "You know where to look."

"I'm so sorry for all the pain I've caused you."

"You've caused me more happiness than anything in my life. I'd wait forever for you."

"Bye, Michael." Her heart aching, she ended the call while wondering—and not for the first time—if she was taking too big a risk with the most precious thing anyone had ever given her.

She ate alone, slept alone, shopped alone, watched television alone. It took a while to get used to the quiet, but after a month she had grown accustomed to it. By then she had also managed to set the record straight with just about everyone in her life—she hadn't married Jeremy despite what the paper said. The salon had been abuzz about it for three or four days until someone else's drama took center stage and Juliana's was mercifully forgotten.

In the second month, she decided to try something else she had always wondered if she could do—she signed up for a class at Johns Hopkins University. The introduction to architecture class met twice a week for three hours, and Juliana loved it. Between work, school, and visiting with her mother and Mrs. R, she began to feel human again as February inched toward March.

She received a heartfelt letter from Jeremy's mother in April, apologizing for the horrific way her son had behaved and expressing her undying love and affection for Juliana, who wrote back to say the same things. Barbara had always been lovely to Juliana, and it wasn't her fault that her son had acted like such an ass.

Her class ended in May, and Juliana was delighted to receive an A. She danced around the small apartment when she received her grade in the mail, and it took all her willpower not to pick up the phone to share the news with Michael. She knew he would be so proud of her.

In June, he made news of his own when he resigned from his job. The *Baltimore Sun* ran a front-page article that recapped his role in the Benedetti trial and contained glowing quotes from Tom Houlihan, Judge Stein, and others in the criminal justice system who worked with him during his five-year tenure. Juliana read and re-read the article, looking for any clue to his plans, but he said only that he was moving into the private sector. She cut out the article and the large photo that ran next to it. As she hung the photo on the wall next to her bed, she was startled to realize it was the only picture of him she had.

She took Mrs. Romanello out to dinner at least once a month, and that's how she found out in July that Jeremy had sold the dream house, moved to Florida, and married a girl named Sherrie.

Mrs. R clucked with disapproval as she delivered the news. "I don't know what that boy is thinking, but rushing into marriage with another woman isn't the answer to his problems."

"Maybe it'll work out for them," Juliana said with sincerity. She had nothing to gain by wishing against the success of his marriage—apparently to the girl who called his cell phone all those months ago and set off a chain of events that changed their lives forever.

After she dropped off Mrs. R, Juliana drove down Chester Street for the first time since she last saw Michael. She slowed to a stop outside No. 8 and watched a young couple carry a baby stroller up the stairs. Even though she was sad that he had sold the place where they'd lived together, she was delighted to know he was in Newport seeing to pipe dreams.

In late August, she was strolling through the mall at the Inner Harbor on her lunch break one day when a teddy bear dressed as a bee wearing a tiara caught her eye in a window. She walked into the store to buy the bear, flooded with thoughts of her own Queen Bee. That night she called Monique Griffith to ask if she would mind if Juliana visited Rachelle.

Monique hesitated before she replied. "I'm sorry, Juliana, but we've decided it's best that she not have any reminders of the trial or of that time in her life."

"I understand," Juliana said, even though she was disappointed.

"She's doing so well, and it's not that seeing you would be a setback—"

"I'd be a reminder."

"Yes," Monique said, sounding relieved that Juliana understood.

"I'm thrilled to hear she's doing well. I have something I'd like to send her. Would that be all right?"

"Of course. I'm sure she'll love anything that comes from you." She gave Juliana the address. "Michael called a couple of months ago. I was sorry to hear you two aren't together anymore. I always thought you made such a lovely couple."

"That's funny," Juliana said with a small, sad smile. "Rachelle said the same thing. I miss her. I only knew her for such a short time, but I think about her all the time."

"She's a special kid to go through what she did and come out of it so unaffected. Ever since those monsters were killed in the courtroom, she's like a new person."

"Will you keep me posted on how she's doing?"

"Of course. I have a school picture I could send you if you'd like."

"I'd love that. Thank you."

"Thank *you,* Juliana. Your friendship made an enormous difference to her at a very difficult time in her life."

"Every minute I spent with her was such a joy."

They hung up with promises to keep in touch. Juliana lay awake that night thinking about Rachelle and Michael and the night she cut their hair in the hotel room. How far they all had traveled since then.

Paullina died in her sleep in September. The medical examiner said she'd had a massive heart attack and didn't suffer, but Juliana was devastated to lose her mother just when they had finally begun to form a real bond. It was left to her to call her brothers and sisters with the news. Donatella and Vincent came right away to their mother's house where they waited for Domenic and Serena to arrive from the West Coast. Juliana couldn't remember when she last saw her older siblings, but the minute they came in the door it was like no time had passed.

They got through the wake and funeral where it seemed that Allison, the home health aide, was more distraught than any of Paullina's five children.

"Thank you so much for everything you did to make her last months so comfortable." Juliana hugged the sobbing Allison. "I wasn't kidding when I called you a miracle worker."

"She was a lovely person, and I'll miss her."

After the funeral, the siblings spent two days cleaning out the house, each setting aside things they wanted to keep. On the last night before Domenic and Serena were due to fly home, they sat on the floor of the empty living room and finished the food that had poured in from neighbors and extended family.

"We've been talking, Juliana," Donatella said as Domenic opened a second bottle of wine.

"About what?" Juliana asked.

"We all agree that you should sell the house and keep whatever you can get for it," Vincent said.

"No way. It belongs to all of us."

"You're the one who did the heavy lifting with Ma for all these years," Serena said. "It's only fair you should get back some of the money you put into the mortgage and her other expenses."

"You guys, really," Juliana said, enormously touched by the gesture. "I wouldn't feel right about it."

"It's a done deal," Domenic said. "We've already decided."

"Are you sure?"

"We are," Vincent said. "She would've died a long time ago if you hadn't taken care of her and forced us to help."

Donatella nodded in agreement.

"I hope we can see each other once in a while," Juliana said. "I know we all have our own lives and you guys have families in California, but maybe we can try to get together once or twice a year."

They agreed to try. Over the third bottle of wine, Juliana told her brothers and sisters about everything that had happened to her in the last year. She found it hard to believe that it had already been a year since she met Michael in the airport. Her siblings were stunned to hear how much danger she'd been in during the trial and astounded by the way her relationship with Jeremy ended.

"So," Vincent said with a wry grin, "Mr. Wonderful didn't turn out to be so wonderful after all, huh?"

Juliana smiled. "You don't need to look so pleased, Vin."

He made an attempt to hide his grin. "Sorry."

Juliana laughed and threw a wadded up napkin at him. "No, you're not."

"What I want to know is why you haven't gone after Michael like you promised him you would," Donatella said. "What the hell are you waiting for?"

"I was just about to ask the same thing," Serena said.

"I'm thinking about it," Juliana confessed. "When my self-imposed year is up, we'll see."

"Don't think too long," Domenic advised. "He sounds like a good guy."

"He is," Juliana said softly, missing him more in that moment than any other in the last nine months.

Her mother's house sold in November, and Juliana was staggered to clear just over forty-six thousand dollars after she paid the taxes. She wrote a check to Jeremy for seventeen thousand dollars and sent it to him via his mother with a note that said only, "Thank you for paying off my mother's mortgage. Please accept the enclosed check as reimbursement."

Part of her windfall went toward the early December purchase of her first-ever new car—a silver Honda Accord. She said a sad good-bye to her old Tercel, which had served her well for many years and was one of the last remaining links to her old life. The rest of the money went in the bank, giving Juliana more of a nest egg than she'd ever had in her life.

By then it had been almost six months since she hung Michael's picture on the wall, and she had fallen into the habit of telling him about her day as she lay in bed each night.

"Do you still want me?" she asked the picture one cold night about a week before Christmas. "Am I really supposed to take this huge gamble that you'll still love me?" *Have I ever said anything I didn't mean?* The memory was so powerful he might have been in the room with her rather than hundreds of miles away.

She studied the faded picture for a long time that night. "I think I'm ready to find out if you meant it, Michael. I miss you so much that sometimes I worry I'll go crazy if I don't see you soon. For what it's worth, I like myself a whole lot better than I did a year ago, so I hope you'll forgive me for waiting this long to keep my promise."

The next day, she gave the salon two week's notice. It was time to find out if he'd meant what he said.

Chapter 36

JULIANA LEFT BALTIMORE EARLY ON NEW YEAR'S DAY
with even fewer possessions than she had taken to her
place in Fell's Point. She had found out over the last
year that she could live without a lot of the things she
used to think were essential.

Driving through the pre-dawn mist in her new car,
she thought about how yesterday would have been her
first anniversary with Jeremy. But she wasn't thinking
about him today. No, today she was thinking about
Michael and how proud of herself she was for taking
this last year to get her life in order. Wondering if she
had waited too long to keep her promise, her stomach
fluttered with nerves. Because she had given herself the
time she needed to heal and to grow, she knew that no
matter how this day turned out, she would be okay. She
had proven to herself that not only could she survive on
her own, she could thrive.

The road was deserted, so she gave the new car a
workout and was in Connecticut in just under three
hours. Remembering Michael's horror at the way she had
driven his car gave her the giggles. She didn't believe in
wasting time behind the wheel. That was something he
would just have to get used to if they were going to be
together. *Don't jinx yourself by thinking that way.*

It seemed to take forever to get through Connecticut,
but she finally made it into Rhode Island around noon.

She had used the computer at the salon to get directions to Newport, but once there she'd be relying on memory to find the place she had been to only once—and in the dark.

The view from the Newport Bridge was different in the wintertime than it had been in autumn but no less striking. She took the Newport exit, and as she drove along America's Cup Avenue she remembered Michael comparing Newport to Annapolis. Taking a right onto Lower Thames Street, Juliana's heart began to beat fast with the knowledge that she was within blocks of him—and everything she wanted.

She drove slowly along Lower Thames until, all at once, she recognized his building and pulled into the first available parking space on the street. Without giving herself even a minute to get nervous, she freshened up her lipstick, tucked her purse under the seat, and got out of the car. She locked the car and with her shaking hands tucked firmly into her coat pockets, she set off down the street, stopping only when she reached the sidewalk outside his building. The glass on the right side of the door was still covered with paper, but painted on the left-hand window in gold script were the words, "Michael Maguire, Attorney at Law."

"Good for you, Michael," she whispered, her heart swelling with pride. "You really did it."

With a deep breath for courage, she pushed open the door. Once inside the vestibule, she was surprised to find the lights on in his office even though it was a holiday. She opened the office door, where again his name was painted on the glass. It was exactly as he said it would be—a comfortable waiting area, a reception desk, and his office in the back. Nothing fancy but it suited him. The receptionist looked up and gasped. Michael's sister Mary Frances got up to come around the desk.

"Juliana." She hugged her. "Lord, is it really you?"

"It's me," Juliana said, returning the warm embrace.

"Oh, is my brother going to be happy to see you!"

"Is he?" Juliana's spirits lifted. "Is he really?"

"You have *no* idea. Come in. Let me take your coat."

"Is he here?"

"No, he's downtown at the police station, but I expect him back any minute. We came in for a couple of hours today to deal with a few clients whose New Year's Eve celebrations landed them in jail."

The phone rang, and Mary Frances excused herself to answer it. "Michael Maguire's office. Yes, Mrs. Fitzpatrick, he's still out." She rolled her eyes at Juliana. "I'll give him your messages as soon as he gets back, but he's going to tell you the same thing he told you the last time Fifi got locked up. You have to keep her on a leash."

Juliana giggled at the look on Mary Frances's face as she got rid of Mrs. Fitzpatrick.

"There are great clients and then there are high-maintenance clients."

"Let me guess," Juliana said. "Fifi's owner is high maintenance?"

"The *highest*."

The phone rang several more times in the next few minutes, and Juliana was delighted to realize his practice was busy. "I'm sure he loves having you here with him," Juliana said between calls.

"I share the job with Shannon and Maggie. We work every three days, but with all our trading of days,

Michael complains that he never knows which one of us will be here in the morning. He calls it one of life's little mysteries."

Juliana smiled, knowing how thrilled he must be to have his sisters working with him.

The phone rang again. "Sorry," Mary Frances said. "The world goes mad on New Year's Eve. Why don't you wait in Michael's office? He should be here any second."

"Okay." Juliana wandered into his office, which looked an awful lot like his office in Maryland—organized chaos. A framed photo on the credenza caught her eye, and she went behind his desk to get a closer look. She gasped when she realized it was the photo of them taken by the resort's roving photographer in the Bahamas. They'd been sad about forgetting to pick it up before they left. In the photo they wore big smiles and had their arms around each other, looking for all the world like a couple madly in love.

"It took me two months to track that down."

She spun around. "Michael," she said, dumbstruck by the achingly familiar sound of his voice and the sight of him wearing a shirt and tie and leaning against the doorframe. She feasted her eyes on him. "You let your hair get long again."

"I didn't have anyone to cut it for me."

She returned the photo to the credenza. "I can't believe you have this."

"When it occurred to me that I didn't have a single picture of you, it became my mission in life to track down that one. You ought to try dealing with Bahamians by telephone sometime." His eyes danced with amusement and what appeared to be joy. That he seemed happy to see her was an enormous relief. "It was quite an experience."

Reaching into the back pocket of her jeans, she carefully withdrew the folded newspaper photo. She let it fall open so he could see it. "I've had my own photo to keep me company. I've spent a lot of time talking to him over the last few months. He's a very good listener."

Michael smiled. "And what have you been telling him?"

"That I miss him more than I've ever missed anyone. That I love him, I never stopped loving him, that I was a fool to ever let him go, and I hope he meant it when he said he'd wait for me."

Michael came around the desk to her. "I think I can speak for him when I say he meant it." He lifted her into a fierce embrace. "God, I missed you, baby. You really had to take the full year, huh?"

Juliana chuckled as she clung to him, reveling in the familiar scent and feel of him. "I was so afraid too much time had gone by and you would've forgotten about me."

"I could never, ever forget about you." He brushed his lips over hers. "I kept having these visions of you back together again with Jeremy."

"To borrow a line of yours, I've come to realize I spent ten years killing time with him."

"Until what?" he asked with a smile.

"Until I found you."

He hugged her again. "What about your mother?"

"She died in September."

"Oh, baby. I'm so sorry! I wish I'd known."

She shrugged off the burst of grief. "We were lucky it

didn't happen sooner, but it was still hard. She had been doing a lot better. I'd started to feel almost close to her for the first time."

"I'm glad you had that time with her."

"Me, too."

He took her hand. "I've got things to show you."

"What kind of things?"

"You'll see." In his outer office, he said, "Mary Frances, I'm taking the rest of the day off. Tell the drunks to call another lawyer."

"You got it, counselor."

"Go ahead and call Mom, too. I know you're dying to tell her that Juliana's come home."

A guilty look crossed Mary Frances's pretty face. "I already did."

Michael and Juliana laughed as he hustled her out the door into the vestibule. "Okay, close your eyes." He led her across the hall to the other retail space and flipped on the lights. "You can look now."

Juliana opened her eyes and gasped when she saw mirrors and chairs and sinks and gleaming hard wood floors and a reception desk. He had built her a salon, right across the hall from his office. "Oh, *Michael.*" With her hand over her heart, she looked around in disbelief. "Oh my God."

"Wait, you haven't seen the best part yet." He walked over to the window and pulled off the brown paper that covered it from the inside. Written back-wards in the same gold paint as the sign on his window was "Juliana's Salon."

Tears streamed down her face as she struggled to absorb it all.

He put his arms around her. "If you had any doubt

that I knew you'd eventually find your way back to me, I hope you don't anymore."

"After what I did to you." She shook her head with disbelief. "After what I did, that you could still love me this much astounds me."

"I love you this much and so much more. I have since I first looked over and found you sitting next to me in the airport, and I always will." With his hands on her face and his thumbs skimming her jaw, he finally kissed her the way she had dreamed about during the long year without him.

The kiss went on for what felt like forever until she pulled back to gaze up at him. With her palm resting on his face, she kissed him again. "Thank you, Michael, for all of this and for all the faith you've always had in us. I wasn't worthy of it before, but I think I might be now."

"You were always worthy of it, silly. You could've saved me a lot of sleepless nights if you'd skipped over your whole Zen phase and come home to me sooner." He took her hand again. "Let's go upstairs. There's more I want to show you."

He gave her a tour of all the improvements he had made to the second floor since she was last there, including a new kitchen, remodeled bathrooms, and a fresh coat of paint in every room.

She recognized most of the furniture from his house in Maryland, including his big bed. On the bedside table was another copy of the photo from the Bahamas.

He put his arm around her and kissed her cheek. "You ever think about the last night we spent in that bed?"

Her cheeks burned. "I've never forgotten it."

"I've relived it a few thousand times myself. Maybe we can have a reenactment tonight?"

She snuggled into his embrace and kissed him. "Do we have to wait that long?"

"No." He laughed against her lips. "We definitely do *not* have to wait that long. Come see the third floor. I've done the most work up there."

She followed him up the stairs. "Oh, it looks wonderful!" He had torn out the kitchen and knocked down walls to make four more big bedrooms.

"They'd make for good kid rooms, don't you think?"

"Maybe when they're older." Juliana ran her hand along the smooth wall and then turned to him. "When they're babies, I'll want them downstairs with us."

He blinked back tears and shook his head as if to convince himself this was really happening. "Yeah?"

"Uh huh."

He took her hand and put it over his heart. "Feel that? My heart hasn't pounded like that in more than a year." With his arm around her, he led her over to the window seat and brought her down on his lap the way he had on a long-ago autumn night. "Remember the last time we were right here?"

She rested her head on his shoulder and nodded.

"I wanted to be the first guy to propose, but I've since learned that sometimes being last is *much* better than being first."

Juliana chuckled.

"So what do you say? Will you marry me, Juliana?"

Raising her head to meet his blue eyes, she said, "Yes, I'll marry you, Michael Maguire." She pressed her lips to his. "Yes, yes, *yes!*"

With his fingers buried in her hair, he kissed her

senseless and then tugged the chain out from under his shirt and tie.

Her heart skipped a beat when she saw that the ring was exactly where she had left it. "All this time you've kept it right there," she whispered, amazed.

Unhooking the chain, he freed the ring. "Right where I said it would be until you were ready for it." He slid it onto her finger and left a lingering kiss on her hand. "Now it's right where it belongs."

"And so am I."

Author's Note

WAITING FOR A DELAYED FLIGHT IN BALTIMORE'S BWI airport in the fall of 1999, I overheard a man and woman discussing their long-distance relationships. Both were headed to visit their significant others in Florida for the weekend. When they discovered they were on the same flight home, I imagined them falling in love with each other, and a novel idea was born. I carried the idea with me until I finally wrote Michael and Juliana's story many years later.

Thank you to April and Rich Pardoe for "loaning" me the Baltimore rowhouse I used as Michael's home. Right down to the hanging kitchen cabinets, the roof deck, and the phones in the bathrooms, his home is their former home. April also answered numerous questions about Baltimore and Butchers Hill.

To my husband Dan and our children Emily and Jake, thanks for putting up with my crazy moods—and a dirty house—when I'm writing. Once again, thank you to daily reader Christina Camara, proofreader Lisa Ridder, copy editor Paula DelBonis-Platt, and character naming committee charter member Julie Cupp. My high school classmate, attorney Martin Medeiros, helped with the legal aspects of the trial, and I'm grateful for his assistance. To my agent, Kevan Lyon, thank you for your support and dedication. To Deb Werksman, Danielle Jackson, and everyone at Sourcebooks, I appreciate your hard work on my behalf. To my Casablanca sisters, your friendship has been a source of great joy to me.

I married my husband ten years into his Naval career and spent the next decade in Spain, Maryland, and Florida before we moved back to my home state of Rhode Island in 2002. I was homesick most of the time we were away, but now I'm so grateful for the experiences we had and the friends we met at each stop because they've given me great fodder for my writing. Maryland and Florida, along with my hometown of Newport, RI, feature prominently in this book.

Read on for an excerpt from Marie Force's

Line of
SCRIMMAGE

Now available from Sourcebooks Casablanca

Chapter 1

IF THERE WAS ONE THING SUSANNAH SANDERSON—SOON to be Susannah Merrill—excelled at, it was setting an elegant table. Along with sparkling crystal and gold on silver flatware, there were dainty tapered candles perched in sterling candlesticks. A floral centerpiece in buttery yellows and golds complemented the main attraction: her grandmother's Limoges china. Susannah often said that in a fire she'd grab the photo album from her debutante ball and as much of Grandma Sally's china as she could carry.

Not every dinner party warranted the use of the china with the pale flowers and strip of fourteen-carat gold around the edge. But entertaining her fiancé and his parents certainly qualified as a china-worthy event.

Susannah glanced at Henry, and he smiled with approval as he took a bite of the succulent leg of lamb she had prepared with just a touch of mint.

"This is absolutely delicious, honey," Henrietta Merrill said to her future daughter-in-law.

"You're a lucky man, son," Martin Merrill added. "There's nothing quite like being married to a beautiful woman who can cook."

Henry reached for Susannah's hand, his love for her apparent in his worshiping gaze. "I know, Dad."

When a strand of his salt and pepper hair fell across his forehead, Susannah had to resist the urge to brush it back from his handsome face. Henry wouldn't approve of such an overt display of affection in front of his parents. The paisley bow tie he wore with his starched light blue shirt was a little crooked, but it only made him more adorable to her. He filled her with such an overwhelming sense of safety and tranquility—two things that had been sorely lacking in her life until Henry had returned to it. In just one month she would be his wife, and she'd have that safety and tranquility forever. Susannah couldn't wait.

Almost as if he could read her thoughts, Henry squeezed her hand and then released it to reach for his wine glass.

"Have you found your mother-of-the-groom dress yet, Mrs. Merrill?" Susannah asked. Henry's parents were spending the month before the wedding with their son in Denver.

"Just yesterday at Nordstrom. It's a lovely pale green silk."

Susannah forced herself not to cringe. The color would be horrible with the deep reds she had chosen for the late February wedding. "I'm glad you found something you're happy with."

"Now tell me," Henrietta said with a twinkle in her eye. "What's with this 'Mrs. Merrill' business?"

"Sorry," Susannah said with a small laugh. "Old habits die hard. I've been calling you Mrs. Merrill since Henry and I dated in high school."

"Well, now you're going to be his wife, so I thought we'd agreed to dispense with the formalities, hadn't we?"

"Of course . . . Mother."

Henrietta's portly face lit up with a warm smile.

After Susannah served her famous chocolate mousse, her future in-laws lingered over coffee—decaf so Martin would be able to sleep.

Susannah was startled to hear a chime echo through the house, indicating the front door had opened.

"Were you expecting someone, honey?" Henry asked.

"No." She pushed back her chair but froze halfway up, flinching when she heard first one boot and then another drop onto the marble floor in the foyer. Only one person had ever dropped his boots in her foyer . . . *It couldn't be. Could it? Oh, God, please no . . .* "Excuse me," Susannah stammered to her guests as she rushed from the dining room, through the kitchen, and into the foyer, stopping short at the sight of her ex-husband, Ryan.

"*What are you doing here?*" she asked in an exaggerated whisper.

He was bent in half putting something into the shabby duffel bag that sat at his feet. When he slowly stood up to his full six-foot, four inches, his signature Stetson shaded half his face. One deep dimple appeared when he smiled at her. "Hello, darlin'," he said in the lazy Texas drawl that used to stop her heart. But now, like everything else about him, it left her cold.

"What are you *doing* here?" she asked again.

"I'm home," he said with a casual lift of his broad shoulders. He shrugged off a beat-up calfskin jacket and tossed it at the coat stand.

Susannah wasn't surprised when the coat snagged a hook and draped itself over the antique brass stand. "What do you mean *home?*" she hissed. "This isn't your home."

"See, that's where you're wrong." He made a big show of checking his watch. "For ten more days I own the place."

"This house is *mine*," she whispered. "You need to get your stuff and get out of here. *Right now*." She reached for his coat and yelped when his hand clamped around her wrist.

Bringing his face to within inches of hers, he grinned and asked, "Why are we whispering?"

"Because I have guests." She made a futile attempt to break free of the grip he had on her arm. "And you're not welcome here."

He sniffed at the air like a dog on the scent of a bone. "Do I smell lamb?" He ran his tongue over his bottom lip. "You know I love your lamb. I hope you saved some for me."

Realizing the movement of his tongue on his lip had captured her attention, Susannah tore her eyes away. "I don't know what kind of game you think you're playing, Ryan Sanderson, but you need to pick up your stuff and *get out*," Susannah said in an increasingly more urgent tone as she struggled once again to break free of him.

But instead of letting her go, he brought her left hand up to his face, his brown eyes zeroing in on her engagement ring. "Is that the best old Henry could do? Not exactly the rock you got from me, is it?"

"It doesn't come with any of the headaches I got from you, either. Now, let me go and *get out!*"

"*Let go of her!*" Henry roared from behind Susannah. "This *instant!*"

Ryan snorted. "Or else what?"

Susannah wished the marble floor would open up

and swallow her whole. "Henry, honey, go back to your parents. Everything's fine. Ryan was just leaving."

"The hell I was. I just got home. Is this any way for a wife to greet her husband?" Ryan asked, adding in that exaggerated drawl of his, "Got yourself another man while I was off fighting the wars, did ya, darlin'? You didn't even send a Dear John."

With desperation, Susannah glanced up at Ryan. The half of his face that wasn't hidden by the big hat was set into a stubborn expression that told her he was determined to get his way. This was *not* good. "Henry, please. Go back in with your parents and give me a moment," Susannah pleaded with her fiancé, who shot daggers at her ex-husband—or, well, her soon-to-be ex-husband. "*Please.*"

"Only if he takes his hands off you," Henry said. His ears turned bright red as he clearly struggled to keep his rage in check.

Ryan released Susannah's arm. "Happy now, lover boy?"

"I'll be happy when you get the hell out of here and go back to whatever rock you crawled out from under."

"*Ohh,*" Ryan said with a dramatic shiver. "I'm scared. You're *so* intimidating in that bow tie."

"That's enough, Ryan," Susannah snapped. With a weak smile for Henry, she nodded toward the dining room.

After one last long, cold stare for Ryan, Henry turned and left them.

"He's a real tiger, that one," Ryan said with a growl. "I'll bet he tears it up in bed."

"What do you want, Ryan?"

"In a word? You."

"Well, you can't have me. So this visit—while unexpected—has been nice." She spun on her heel and walked away from him. "You know the way out."

"Not so fast. I'm not going anywhere. This is my house. I bought it and everything in it."

Susannah whipped around to face him. "And you gave it all to me in the divorce!"

"Which, I might remind you, is not final for ten more days. Now, I'm a pretty reasonable guy, and believe it or not, I'm not looking to start trouble for you and lover boy. So let me make this easy for all of us, okay?"

Wary, Susannah nodded. "That would be best."

"We've got ten more days as Mister and Missus, and we're going to spend them together."

Susannah started to protest, but Ryan held up his hand to stop her. "Every minute of every day for the next ten days."

"You're out of your mind! There's no way I'm spending ten *minutes* with you, let alone ten *days*. *No way*."

"You always had such a soft spot for the McMansion." He sent his eyes on a journey through the spacious foyer, the sweeping staircase, and the formal living room. "It took us long enough to hammer out a settlement the first time. A renegotiation would tie things up for months, and in light of your *engagement,* I'm thinking that might be a little inconvenient for you . . . "

"You *wouldn't!*" Susannah fumed, but even as she said it she knew he would. Her stomach knotted with tension as she thought of the wedding and all her plans with Henry.

Ryan crossed the marble foyer to her. His scent, a woodsy mixture that always reminded Susannah of the mountains, was as familiar to her as anything in her life. "Watch me," he said so quietly she might not have heard it if he hadn't been standing so close to her.

Her blue eyes filled with tears. "Why are you doing this?"

He reached out to touch her shoulder-length blond hair. "We made a mistake."

"*How can you say that?*" She slapped his hand away. "Our marriage was a nightmare. The divorce was the best thing we ever did."

He shook his head. "It wasn't a nightmare. Not always. Remember the first few years, Susie?"

"Don't call me that. That's not my name, and you know I hate it."

"You didn't used to hate it. Remember when we made love and I'd call you Susie? Do you ever think about how hot it was between us?"

"No! I never think of you. *Ever.*" She pushed him away, and he gasped. "What? What's wrong with you?"

Struggling to catch his breath, Ryan said, "Nothing." But his lips were white with pain.

Susannah reached up to remove his hat and recoiled when she revealed the side of his face the hat had hidden. "*Oh my God!* What happened to your face?"

"Sack gone bad on Sunday. Shoulder pads to the ribs, helmet to the face. Three busted ribs, but fortunately the mug is just badly bruised. Won't hurt my endorsement deals."

"Well, thank God for that," she said sarcastically.

His face was so black and blue Susannah had to resist the urge to reach up and caress his cheek. She couldn't help but ask, "What about your helmet? How could this have happened?"

"The dude hit me so hard, it didn't do me much good," he said, shaking his head before his grin returned. "We won, though. They didn't knock me out of the game until late in the fourth quarter when we'd already sewn it up."

"Great," she said without an ounce of enthusiasm. If she never heard another word about the Denver Mavericks, it would be too soon.

"The *Super Bowl*, baby," he said with the cocky grin that was all Ryan. "That makes three in five years in case you were counting."

"I wasn't but congratulations. Now, please leave. I mean it, Ryan. This trip down memory lane was interesting, and I'm sorry you're hurt, but there's nothing left for us to talk about."

"I beg to differ." He hooked his arm around her neck and dragged her to him, flinching when she made contact with his injured ribs. Tipping his head, his lips found hers in a kiss that was hot and fast.

Susannah tried to protest, and he took advantage of her open mouth to send his tongue on a plunging, pillaging mission.

When he finally pulled back from her, Susannah could only stare at him.

"How could you forget *that,* darlin'?" he asked softly.

She shoved him and didn't care about the flash of naked pain that crossed his handsome face. Whether it was the hit to his ego or his ribs that caused it, she didn't know and didn't care.

"*Don't touch me!* Do you hear me? I'm *engaged* to another man. You had your chance with me, and you blew it. You come in here like a big conquering hero jock and think that crap is going to work on me. I've heard it all before, Ryan, so you can save it. I've asked you nicely to leave. If you don't go, I'll call the police."

He snickered and combed his fingers through his dirty blond hair. "And what do you think they're going to do to the guy who just brought home *another* Super Bowl trophy?" Reaching into the pocket of his faded, form-fitting Levis, he withdrew his cell phone and held it out to her. "Give them a call. Be my guest."

"*Ugh!*" she growled with frustration, knowing he was right. The cops wouldn't do a damned thing but fawn over him the way everyone always did.

"If you're going to be pig-headed about this, I guess that leaves me no choice." He casually scrolled through the numbers on his cell phone. When he found what he was looking for, he pressed the send button.

"Who are you calling?"

"My divorce attorney. Putting the brakes on things."

She snatched the phone out of his hand and turned it off.

He raised an eyebrow, and his battered face lit up with amusement. "Does that mean we have a deal?"

"And just what am I supposed to tell Henry?"

"I don't give a flying fuck."

"Lovely, Ryan. That's just lovely. You're as rude and crude as ever."

"And you're still hot for me," he said with a smug smile. "*Damn,* that just pisses you off, doesn't it?"

"I know your over-inflated ego will find this hard to believe, but I'm not even lukewarm for you."

"Whatever you say, baby," he said, wincing as he bent to pick up his worn Mavericks duffel bag. He took the Stetson from her, tossed it at the coat rack—where it landed with spot-on perfection—and started up the stairs.

"What do you think you're *doing?*" Susannah asked with mounting desperation.

"Going to bed. Feel free to join me when you ditch lover boy. Oh, and if you're feeling generous, you can bring me some ice for my ribs."

"When pigs fly."

"If that's how long it takes, I can wait. The season's over, and I've got nothing but time."

Helplessly, she watched as he trudged up the stairs and disappeared down the hallway. She stood there for a long time trying to figure out what to do until Henry finally came to find her.

"Did you get rid of him?" he asked.

With a glance at the top of the stairs, she said, "Um, not exactly."

About the Author

Marie Force has worked as a reporter, editor, and writer over the last twenty years, serving most recently as the communications director for a national membership organization. A lifelong romance reader, she lives with her husband, two children, and a seventeen-year-old dog named Consuela in her home state of Rhode Island where she spends as much time as she can at the beach or on her father's boat. She is also the author of *Line of Scrimmage*. Visit Marie online at www.mariesullivanforce.com, on her blog at http://mariesullivanforce.blogspot.com, or on the Casablanca Authors Blog at http://casablancaauthors. blogspot.com. Marie loves to hear from readers! Contact her at mforce@cox.net to say hello or to arrange a visit to your book club.

Line of SCRIMMAGE

BY MARIE FORCE

SHE'S GIVEN UP ON HIM AND MOVED ON...

Susannah finally has peace, calm, a sedate life, and a no-surprises man. Marriage to football superstar Ryan Sanderson was a whirlwind, but Susanna got sick of playing second fiddle to his team. With their divorce just a few weeks away, she's already planning her wedding with her new fiancé.

HE'S FINALLY FIGURED OUT WHAT'S REALLY IMPORTANT TO HIM. IF ONLY IT'S NOT TOO LATE...

Ryan has just ten days to convince his soon-to-be-ex-wife to give him a second chance. His career is at its pinnacle, but in the year of their separation, Ryan's come to realize it doesn't mean anything without Susannah...

978-1-4022-1424-0 • $6.99 U.S. / $8.99 CAN

Romeo, Romeo

BY ROBIN KAYE

Rosalie Ronaldi doesn't have a domestic bone in her body...

All she cares about is her career, so she survives on take-out and dirty martinis, keeps her shoes under the dining room table, her bras on the shower curtain rod, and her clothes on the couch.

Nick Romeo is every woman's fantasy—tall, dark, handsome, rich, really good in bed, AND he loves to cook and clean...

He says he wants an independent woman, but when he meets Rosalie, all he wants to do is take care of her. Before long, he's cleaned up her apartment, stocked her refrigerator, and adopted her dog.

So what's the problem? Just a little matter of mistaken identity, corporate theft, a hidden past in juvenile detention, and one big nosy Italian family too close for comfort...

"Kaye's debut is a delightfully fun, witty romance, making her a writer to watch." —*Booklist*

978-1-4022-1339-7 • $6.99 U.S. / $8.99 CAN

Too Hot to Handle

BY ROBIN KAYE

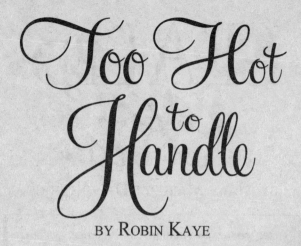

He sure would love to have a woman to take care of…

To Dr. Mike Flynn, there's nothing like housework to help a guy relax, while artist Annabelle Ronaldi doesn't have a domestic bone in her body.

When they meet at her sister's wedding, Mike is sure this is the woman he wants to take care of forever. While Mike sets to work wooing Annabelle, she becomes determined to sniff out the truth of the convoluted family secret that's threatening to turn both their lives upside down.

978-1-4022-1766-1 • $6.99 U.S. / $7.99 CAN

SEALed
with a *Kiss*

BY MARY MARGRET DAUGHTRIDGE

THERE'S ONLY ONE THING HE CAN'T HANDLE, AND ONE WOMAN WHO CAN HELP HIM...

Jax Graham is a rough, tough Navy SEAL, but when it comes to taking care of his four-year-old son after his ex-wife dies, he's completely clueless. Family therapist Pickett Sessoms can help, but only if he'll let her.

When Jax and his little boy get trapped by a hurricane, Picket takes them in against her better judgment. When the situation turns deadly, Pickett discovers what it means to be a SEAL, and Jax discovers that even a hero needs help sometimes.

"A heart-touching story that will keep you smiling and cheering for the characters clear through to the happy ending." —Romantic Times

"A well-written romance...simultaneously tender and sensuous." —Booklist

978-1-4022-1118-8 • $6.99 U.S. / $8.99 CAN

SEALed

with a
Promise

BY MARY MARGRET DAUGHTRIDGE

NAVY SEAL CALEB DELAUDE IS AS DEADLY AS HE IS CHARMING.

Professor Emmie Caddington's quiet intelligence and quirky personality intrigue him. When he discovers that her personal connections can get him close to the man he's vowed to kill, will their budding relationship be nothing more than a means to revenge...or is she the key to his salvation?

Praise for *SEALed with a Kiss*:

"This story delivers in a huge way." —Romantic Times

"A wonderful story that will have readers experiencing a whirlwind of emotions and culminating with an awesome scene that will have your pulse pounding." —Romance Junkies

"What an incredibly powerful book! I laughed and sniffled, was turned on and turned inside out." —Queue My Review

978-1-4022-1763-0 • $6.99 U.S. / $7.99 CAN

Wicked by Any Other Name

BY LINDA WISDOM

> "Do not miss this wickedly entertaining treat."
>
> —Annette Blair,
> *Sex and the Psychic Witch*

STASI ROMANOV USES A LITTLE WITCH MAGIC IN HER LINGERIE shop, running a brisk side business in love charms. A disgruntled customer threatening to sue over a failed spell brings wizard attorney Trevor Barnes to town—and witches and wizards make a volatile combination. The sparks fly, almost everyone's getting singed, and the whole town seems on the verge of a witch hunt.

Can the feisty witch and the gorgeous wizard overcome their objections and settle out of court—and in the bedroom?

978-1-4022-1773-9 • $6.99 U.S. / $7.99 CAN

Destiny of the Wolf

BY TERRY SPEAR

Praise for Terry Spear's *Heart of the Wolf*:

"The chemistry crackles off the page."
—*Publisher's Weekly*

"The characters are well drawn and believable, which makes the contemporary plotline of love and life among the lupus garou seem, well, realistic." —*Romantic Times*

"Full of action, adventure, suspense, and romance... one of the best werewolf stories I've read!" —*Fallen Angel Reviews*

ALL SHE WANTS IS THE TRUTH

Lelandi is determined to discover the truth about her beloved sister's mysterious death. But everyone thinks she's making a bid for her sister's widowed mate...

HE'S A PACK LEADER TORMENTED BY MEMORIES

Darien finds himself bewitched by Lelandi, and when someone attempts to silence her, he realizes that protecting the beautiful stranger may be the only way to protect his pack...and himself...

978-1-4022-1668-8 · $6.99 U.S. / $7.99 CAN

WILD HIGHLAND MAGIC

BY KENDRA LEIGH CASTLE

She's a Scottish Highlands werewolf

Growing up in America, Catrionna MacInnes always tried desperately to control her powers and pretend to be normal…

He's a wizard prince with a devastating secret

The minute Cat lays eyes on Bastian, she knows she's met her destiny. In their first encounter, she unwittingly binds him to her for life, and now they're both targets for the evil enemies out to destroy their very souls.

Praise for Kendra Leigh Castle:

"Fans of straight up romance looking for a little extra something will be bitten." —*Publishers Weekly*

978-1-4022-1856-9 • $7.99 U.S. / $8.99 CAN

ROGUE

BY CHERYL BROOKS

Tychar crawled toward me on his hands and knees like a tiger stalking his prey. "I, for one, am glad you came," he purred. "And I promise you, Kyra, you will never want to leave Darconia."

"Cheryl Brooks knows how to keep the heat on and the reader turning pages!"

—Sydney Croft, author of *Seduced by the Storm*

PRAISE FOR THE CAT STAR CHRONICLES:

"Wow. Just…wow. The romantic chemistry is as close to perfect as you'll find." —*BookFetish.org*

"Will make you purr with delight. Cheryl Brooks has a great talent as a storyteller." —*Cheryl's Book Nook*

978-1-4022-1762-3 • $6.99 U.S. / $7.99 CAN

The WILD SIGHT

BY LOUCINDA MCGARY

"A magical tale of romance and intrigue. I couldn't put it down!" —Pamela Palmer, author of *Dark Deceiver* and *The Dark Gate*

HE WAS CURSED WITH A "GIFT"

Born with the clairvoyance known to the Irish as "The Sight," Donovan O'Shea fled to America to escape his visions. On a return trip to Ireland to see his ailing father, staggering family secrets threaten to turn his world upside down. And then beautiful, sensual Rylie Powell shows up, claiming to be his half-sister...

SHE'S LOOKING FOR THE FAMILY SHE NEVER KNEW...

After her mother's death, Rylie journeys to Ireland to find her mysterious father. She needs the truth—but how can she and Donovan be brother and sister when the chemistry between them is nearly irresistible?

UNCOVERING THE PAST LEADS THEM DANGEROUSLY CLOSE TO MADNESS...

"A richly drawn love story and riveting romantic suspense!" —Karin Tabke, author of *What You Can't See*

978-1-4022-1394-6 • $6.99 U.S. / $8.99 CAN

IN OVER HER HEAD

by Judi Fennell

"Holy mackerel! *In Over Her Head* is a
fantastically fun romantic catch!"

—Michelle Rowen, author of *Bitten & Smitten*

○ ○ ○ ○ ○ **HE LIVES UNDER THE SEA** ○ ○ ○ ○ ○ ○

Reel Tritone is the rebellious royal second son of the ruler
of a vast undersea kingdom. A Merman, born with legs
instead of a tail, he's always been fascinated by humans,
especially one young woman he once saw swimming near
his family's reef...

○ ○ ○ ○ ○ **SHE'S TERRIFIED OF THE OCEAN** ○ ○ ○ ○ ○

Ever since the day she swam out too far and heard voices
in the water, marina owner Erica Peck won't go swimming
for anything—until she's forced into the water by a shady
ex-boyfriend searching for stolen diamonds, and is nearly
eaten by a shark...luckily Reel is nearby to save her, and
discovers she's the woman he's been searching for...

978-1-4022-2001-2 • $6.99 U.S. / $7.99 CAN

A Duke to
Die For

by Amelia Grey

The rakish fifth Duke of Blakewell's unexpected and shockingly lovely new ward has just arrived, claiming to carry a curse that has brought each of her previous guardians to an untimely end...

Praise for Amelia Grey's Regency romances:

"This beguiling romance steals your heart, lifts your spirits and lights up the pages with humor and passion." —Romantic Times

"Each new Amelia Grey tale is a diamond. Ms. Grey...is a master storyteller." —Affaire de Coeur

"Readers will be quickly drawn in by the lively pace, the appealing protagonists, and the sexual chemistry that almost visibly shimmers between." —Library Journal

978-1-4022-1767-8 • $6.99 U.S./$7.99 CAN